NEITHER THIS NOR THAT

ISBN 978-0-557-22302-2

NEITHER THIS NOR THAT

Aliya Husain

This book is dedicated to all who struggle to find their identity…

Acknowledgements

First and foremost, Alhamdulillah.

I would like to thank my parents for inspiring me, my sisters for the stories we created together, and my husband for all of his support and encouragement.

Much gratitude to Naazish YarKhan, my editor, my coach, and my friend.

I am also indebted to Shirin, Nabeela, Shereen, Nadia, and especially - Sarah. Your advice and candor was invaluable. Thank you all.

Mustafa, Muzzamil, and Amina - this is for you. Know that you are not alone in any struggles in life.

Chapter 1

It was a cool fall morning and the leaves were already pallets of orange, brown, and rust. Fall in New Jersey was creeping up on the landscape. Against the crisp autumn breeze, Fatima stood in line in front of Bookbinder Elementary School -along with the rest of her class - anxiously awaiting the sound of the first bell. Once the bell rang, her classmates would be allowed to enter the school and for the first time enter their third grade classroom.

"Hey, Keysha? Helllooo… Keysha… Are you there?" asked Fatima.

Keysha Ryan, Fatima's good friend since kindergarten, was standing in line next to her, but she wasn't talking to Fatima. Keysha was too preoccupied with Tyrone Smith, the stud of the neighborhood, who was now standing right next to her. 'Great,' Fatima thought to herself while rolling her eyes, 'Now who do I talk to?'

Fatima was frustrated that Keysha wasn't paying any attention to her, so she turned away and tried to find any of her other former classmates, but it was to no avail. 'Where are Tawana and Monica?' she thought nervously, as her eyes scanned the group of students. 'This isn't how I wanted to start my first day in upper elementary,' she sadly thought as her shoulders drooped.

Mr. Thomas, the principal, made his way out and garnered everyone's attention.

"Everyone get in line according to your grade level. Once the bell rings, first grade will enter first, and second grade will follow and so on and so forth," he spoke into his megaphone. And right on cue, the bell rang.

Fatima and the long line of excited third graders headed into the school, walking to the classroom to which they were assigned. Fatima looked at the letter her parents had received a few weeks back to confirm that she was to go to room number six. As she approached what she believed was her classroom, Fatima's heart sank. 'Nooooooo…' Fatima's inner voice cried. Waiting outside of the classroom with the number six clearly posted on top of its doorway was Mrs. Nielsen.

"Welcome everyone, welcome to our third grade class!!" she exclaimed with a huge smile on her face.

A tall, slim middle aged woman with thinning black hair, Mrs. Nielson came off as a gentle woman, but her temper was notorious amongst the children. If a student was caught breaking any class rules, Mrs. Nielson was known to grab their chin and the bottom portion of both cheeks with a potent force. A force that was frightening enough to have reportedly made some students wet their pants. There were no adult confirmations of these types of stories that would circulate amongst the children, but for the children it was as if these incidents were true facts written in divine manuscript. Because of these rumors, Fatima had prayed all summer long for Mrs. Brown to be her third grade teacher. *All* of Mrs. Brown's students raved about her. No one wet their pants in her class. But to her great disappointment, it just wasn't meant to be. 'Well, at least Keysha is in my class,' Fatima thought. But then she noticed that Tyrone Smith, who Keysha was *still* ogling at, was walking into her classroom. 'Oh God,' she thought, while rolling her eyes and sinking her head into her two hands. 'This is hopeless,' she despaired.

The classroom was neatly arranged, everything in order and ready to start the new school year. It was clear that no students had been in the classroom, at least not till now. The bulletin boards were bright and colorful. They were also neat and undamaged. Nothing was pulled off or vandalized. 'I'll give those boards one week to stay like that,' Fatima predicted to herself. Even the blackboard was spotless. No eraser marks or dust, it was a blank slate, except for the date- September 3, 1985 written neatly in the top right hand corner.

As everyone sat down on the desk labeled with their name tag, Mrs. Nielson began to address the class.

"I'll start off by checking attendance," declared Mrs. Nielson as she began to call out names.

Fatima had butterflies in her stomach. Every year, it was the same. It seemed like no one could pronounce her name correctly, a fact that would make her more and more aware that she wasn't the all-American girl that she so desperately wanted to be. Her name wasn't the usual Jennifer, Megan, or Emily - she was Faa-the-ma. She was sure that Mrs. Nielson would butcher her name just as every teacher before her had. And sure enough Mrs. Nielson called out "Futteema Hoozin?" and everyone giggled looking at Fatima. Fatima turned red and wanted to shrink under her turtleneck.

"Is that how you pronounce it dear?" Mrs. Nielson asked.

"It's Faa-the-ma Hoo-sayn" Fatima replied, placing great emphasis on the syllables so that Mrs. Nielson would know how to say her name properly.

"That's a different name dear. Where are you from?" asked Mrs. Nielson.

How Fatima hated that question. Actually, she despised it. 'What kind of question was that anyway? I was born in New York and am living in New Jersey. As American as it can get,' she would think to herself. So why did everyone just assume that she just came from a foreign land? Was it her difficult to pronounce name, or was it her tan skin color, or did she just look like she didn't belong? Despite her annoyance with the inquiry, Fatima politely-yet-firmly replied, "I was born in New York, so I guess I am from New York," much to the surprise of Mrs. Nielson.

Mrs. Nielson, realizing that she had upset Fatima, quickly moved on to the next name on her roster. The day had already started out dismally for young Fatima.

When lunchtime came, the class walked in a line to the cafeteria. Fatima nervously held her lunch box close to her thigh and as far away from everyone else as possible. The students were seated at one of many tables, each of which was marked according to its grade level. The cafeteria was actually a multi purpose room that would also serve as an auditorium. During lunch time, the collapsible lunch tables were unfolded and spread out into two neat columns for the length of the room.

Lunch was a nerve wracking time for Fatima. The first dilemma she would face during this half hour was who to sit with. 'Where is Tawana?' Fatima anxiously thought, as she glanced around the cafeteria. Keysha was already seated next to Tyrone, and Fatima wanted no part of that. Tawana had not yet arrived in the cafeteria. 'She's probably in the hot lunch line,' Fatima thought. And since Monica had not shown up to school at all, Fatima reluctantly decided to sit at the far end of the lunch table by herself. 'I hope Tawana finds me after she gets out of the lunch line,' she uneasily thought.

As if that wasn't stressful enough, Fatima cringed at the thought of what smell would reek out of her lunch box once she unlocked it. 'God please don't let it be something ridiculously stinky,' she prayed. She couldn't count how many times fellow classmates had gawked at what would come out of Pandora's lunchbox and how strongly it smelled. Luckily, today it was simply a *shaami* sandwich which was less odorous than many of the *Desi* items that could have been packed in her lunch. Fatima couldn't count how many times her classmates had commented on what stank when she opened her lunch box. Thanks to comments like, "Who cut the cheese in your lunch, Fatima?" and "Oh my God, that smell is going to make me barf!" Fatima was extremely conscious of the slightest odor that would emit from her lunch. She would much rather have bought hot lunch, but that was not an option since any meat that she would consume had to be *halal*, or cut according to Muslim dietary law. In fact purchasing meat at the local supermarkets wasn't even an option for her family. *Halal* meat was only available at a butcher shop in Berlin, NJ, where Fatima's father would go and slaughter the animal himself in accordance to Islamic law. This was the only meat that was consumed by the local Muslim families. Therefore a protein packed lunch had to come from home, which meant that it would be prepared in a *Desi* fashion filled with odoriferous ingredients. She inhaled her lunch and closed her lunch box tight so that any remaining smell from her food would be locked inside before Tawana arrived.

Fatima saw Tawana enter the room and feverishly waved her hand, "Here, Tawana, I am here."

By the time Tawana had joined her at the table, lunch was over and done with for Fatima.

"How could you be done so quickly?" inquired Tawana.

"I am a fast eater," was Fatima's brief answer…

At the end of the day, Fatima packed her book bag, waved good-bye to Tawana, and walked outside the one story brick building along with all of the third graders. She was greeted outside by her mother and younger sister, both sitting in their big blue boat, also known as their Chevy Impala. Her mother was not stepping out as she was late in her third pregnancy, and Fatima's little sister, Ayesha, was a handful at the age of four. Fatima could hear Ayesha shouting, "Fatima *baji* … Fatima *baji!* There she is!" while pointing towards Fatima.

Secretly, Fatima was glad that her mother did not step out. Although she was the personification of Indian beauty, fair skinned with long jet black hair tied in a waist length braid, and dark tear shaped eyes, her mother was never dressed in American garb. Her five foot four frame was always clad in *Desi* attire. Fatima feared that had she stepped out of her car, her classmates might laugh at her mother's *shalwar khameez*. Worse yet, would they poke fun at Fatima for the different type of clothing that adorned her mother? Would this confirm that Fatima was different and abnormal?

Relieved at avoiding this dilemma altogether, she jumped into the car and greeted her mother, "*Assalamu Alaykum,* Mummy."

"*Walaikum salam beta,*" her mother sweetly replied, as she began to drive her home.

Everyday, upon coming home, Fatima would go up to her room and change out of her jeans and shirt into the traditional *shalwar khameez*, the same clothes she was deathly embarrassed to have her mother be seen wearing in front of her American friends. Fatima's mother would put great effort into making these elaborate outfits for her. She was a wonderful seamstress who would spend hours and hours stitching *shalwar khameez* for both Ayesha and Fatima with her yellow Brother sewing machine. And although Fatima loved these clothes dearly and wore them proudly in front of her Indian and Pakistani friends, they were not fit to be worn in front of her American friends. All of this awareness at the ripe old age of nine.

Every day after school, Fatima and Ayesha would play together and eat the fruits that their mother would peel ever so perfectly. Mummy would call out from the kitchen saying, "*Beta*, finish all the fruit and don't waste any of it. You know how many poor people don't have anything to eat? We should be grateful for every morsel that is given to us."

The guilt of hungry children made the girls finish the rest of their fruit. After snack time, Mummy would cover her thick black mane with her turquoise cotton *dupatta,* and sit with Fatima to read at least three pages of The Holy Qur'an. It was a difficult task, but Fatima slowly mastered the art of reading Arabic, a language that she neither spoke nor wrote but had learned to read so that she could recite the holy word in its original form. It was imperative that she, as well as most of her Muslim friends, learned to read this language so that they would be able to recite the Qur'an on a daily basis in their prayers. Although Fatima was not required to pray the five daily prayers properly and punctually at her age, she would stand behind her parents and imitate their actions as the prayers were said. Prayers were not to be neglected as they were one of the basic pillars of their Islamic faith. The importance of observing these prayers was instilled within the girls from the age of four. No matter where they were or how occupied they may have been, once time for the prayers arrived, all of their business was set aside for a period of five to ten minutes in which they would remember the Almighty Creator.

Around five o'clock, the highlight of Fatima's day would come - the arrival of her father. When the pistachio green Dodge, driven by the *Desi* version of Abraham Lincoln, would pull up in front of their home, Fatima's heart would leap with joy and she would run to the front door yelling, "Daaaaaaaaddy!!" and jump into her Daddy's arms. It was quite a leap considering that her father's six foot tall frame was twice her height.

Ayesha would follow suit and they would all gather together as Mummy would begin to serve dinner. The family would sit at the table and eat with their hands, sans utensils, as this was the way *Desis* truly enjoyed the taste of their cuisine.

"*Beta*, are your hands clean?" Mummy would regularly ask, and the girls would always nod affirmatively, even if it weren't always the case.

While eating her *daal*, chicken, and rice, gregarious Fatima would tell her Daddy about all of the day's occurrences in school, all that is but the ones that showed how embarrassed she was of being different.

In one breath she would spill out a paragraph with no pauses or stops where someone could possibly interject.

"You know Daddy today I walked into my class and was so sad Mrs. Nielson was my teacher when I really didn't want her I wanted Mrs. Brown but Mrs. Brown wasn't in room six and I had to go into room six because the letter that was sent to you said room six and I took that letter into school and opened it up again to make sure I was going into the right room and sure enough it was room six but Mrs. Nielson was there and I heard that she yells a lot and grabs kids by their faces real hard maybe she even leaves marks on their faces what if that happens to me what if I get yelled at and she..."

"Fatima ... Fatima..." her father tried to interrupt her run on sentence, but when he failed after numerous attempts, he raised his voice and said with a smile on his face, "Fatima. Please *beta*, slow down. I can't understand one sentence that you've said."

Fatima just dropped her head and said, "Forget it Daddy, just forget it." There was much too much to share and she had to get it all out at once, whether it made sense or not. Slowing down was not an option.

The family sat down for dinner and Fatima remained unusually quiet.

"Now *beta*, what were you saying?" Daddy inquired.

"Nothing Daddy, nothing…" she mumbled.

After dinner and *chai*, Mummy would call Fatima and Ayesha to sit in between her legs on the floor while she sat up on the ottoman.

"Ayesha, get the red box of hair bands," she would say reminding Ayesha to bring the tin that was originally a container of Danish butter cookies, but now held all the girls' hair accessories. Once the girls were sitting, she would bend her back forward slightly and comb her daughters' hair with a perfect part in the middle. Once the hair was parted she would grab a hold of the blue Parachute Coconut oil bottle and sprinkle a few drops on their heads. She would massage that oil into the depths of their hair follicles so that every follicle would be enriched with the nutrients that this oil was so sure to provide.

"Mummy, this stuff smells…" Ayesha complained.

"What do you mean smell?" Mummy replied. "Your hair needs nutrients," she insisted.

The girls did not inherit their mother's dark tresses; instead they had brown hair with many red highlights, like their father. Unfortunately, they also inherited the fineness of his hair. Their locks didn't have the body that most Indian women's hair enjoyed, so their mother tried her best to nourish their hair with the traditional oil treatment. Their mother, like many Indian women, was sure that this oil treatment was the secret to thick beautiful hair.

After the deep head massage was complete, their hair would be tied into two tight braids, one on each side, so that the possibility of entanglement was eliminated.

"Now look how nice and clean you two look, no longer looking like a couple of *junglees*," Mummy would laughingly remark.

The girls would sleep with the long taut braids, and the process would be repeated in the morning before school started.

Elementary school was a fun time for Fatima. She grew accustomed to Mrs. Nielson and eventually managed to like her. She was a respectful child that paid attention in class and completed all her seatwork without any problems. Unlike other students, she did not dread Parent-Teacher conferences. She actually looked forward to these meetings so that she could bask in the glory of all that her teacher would share with her parents. She would remind her father days in advance about the conference, "Daddy, please don't forget *you* have to meet Mrs. Nielson on Thursday. And please Daddy, please *you* go. Mrs. Nielson might not understand what Mummy is saying."

Fatima was very protective of her mother. She worried that people would have a difficult time understanding her mother's English because of her thick Indian accent. She did not want to embarrass her mother by putting her in a position that would ask her to speak, so she always had her father deal with anything that would require talking with people who spoke English.

Fatima was a child that loved learning and was open to all sorts of intellectual challenges. This was especially so when she entered Mrs. Zeppino's fourth grade class. Mrs. Zeppino was a teacher with a vibrant personality. She managed to make Fatima feel right at home in her class.

She showed great pride in her Italian roots and shared stories with her class of her visits to Italy. She even showed them pictures of her extended family. Many of these pictures made Fatima think of her extended family. Like most Indian families Fatima's family was relatively large. Her father was one of nine children, and her mother was one of six. Both parents kept their ties with their siblings tight even though the siblings were dispersed throughout the world. Letters would periodically arrive from uncles and aunts who were residing in Pakistan, India, Kenya, and Saudi Arabia. The occasional overseas phone call to Fatima's grandparents, who lived in Hyderabad, India, was a family event. Everyone would gather by the phone so that they could talk to their relatives back in the Motherland. But the atrocious cost of international calls in those days kept these calls brief. The family wouldn't be able to speak to their heart's content or share all that they were anxious to relate. To overcome this they would congregate around the tape recorder, and record their voices on cassette tapes to send to their loved ones. A sixty-minute tape would easily be filled up with Fatima and Ayesha's voices along with that of their parents', updating the elders on their health, the arrival of their third daughter, Amina, and all the small accomplishments that the children were making. Some family friend who was fortunate enough to be able to visit his/her family in Hyderabad would deliver these tapes to their respective families.

Initially, there was very limited physical interaction with the extended family. With the exception of a few of Fatima's father's cousins, there really was no kin nearby.

Once a year Fatima's *chacha*, Saad, would visit from Saudi Arabia, and bring a wonderful world of first cousins to Fatima's home. This was an event that the children would anxiously anticipate. They were even willing to make the two and a half hour journey to JFK airport at five o' clock in the morning to pick up Saad *chacha*, *chachi*, and their daughters, Sana and Zaina.

Fatima and her sisters would sleep in the back of their family car, their 'booger green and wood paneled' station wagon, on a makeshift bed. It was a comfortable abode for their journey to NYC; it was a trip that the girls would treat as an adventure that would lead to a priceless treasure – their cousins.

The thread of light was on the morning horizon and as the sun rose so did the girls' spirits. The Saudi Airlines flight arrived into JFK at seven o'clock in the morning and Fatima's family was there to greet her cousins with huge smiles on their faces. After warm embraces and excitement beyond what words could express, all of the girls would jump into the back of the wagon and the fun would begin. The chitter chatter of the giddy girls would drown out any conversation the adults were trying to have.

"Girls, you have to settle down..." was the mantra of the mothers, but the girls would have none if it. There were stories to share and giggling to enjoy. There were silly games to play and goofy looks to impart…Settling down wasn't in their plans…

Fatima's earliest glimpse into what life with an extended family would be like was an exposure that she enjoyed immensely. The girls would have control of the house for the next week, and their every wish was granted. They ran around with their arms in the air, flying in and out of each room. They played house in their makeshift tents and pretended to cook and create elaborate meals for their tea parties. Sana was a songwriter incognito and she scripted numerous melodies that the cousins would conjure and sing to entertain each other.

"No, no, not like that…" Sana would correct Ayesha when she sang out of tune.

Dramatic Ayesha would try again, but this time she added some Hollywood flair… "Okay, you want it to sound like this…?"Ayesha would inquire as she swung her hips from side to side and yelped out the tune once again…

Laughter would roar through the room at Ayesha's dramatics. The performances would go on and on and on….

For the girls, this was the epitome of family fun. But alas as all good things must come to an end, so would the weeklong stay of Sana and Zaina. The departure of their cousins was painful for Fatima and her sisters. Teary eyes and moans and groans would envelope their home. They were to be left alone, yet again, with their family returning to their nucleus of the three girls and their parents.

Fatima would often dwell upon memories of Sana and Zaina, as life seemed empty and boring after they had left. How would she ever pass time now that her cousins had gone back to Saudi Arabia?

The best way, and the only way, she knew to overcome her sadness was to throw herself into school. Indeed, the weekdays were all about school. School was never a burden for Fatima; in fact her parents could hardly keep her away. Waking up in the mornings was never an issue nor was eating breakfast. She ate while watching "Transformers" on TV, and once the show ended she knew it was time to go.

"Mummy, let's go let's go!" was Fatima's way of rushing her mother along as she put on Ayesha's coat.

A quick toss of the Flintstones vitamin into her mouth and Fatima was out the door and on her way to Bookbinder Elementary. It would take more than a natural disaster to keep Fatima from school. So it was no surprise that even when chicken pox struck the Husain home, it was no match for Fatima's determination to go to school.

"But I have to go Mummy, I have to! I'll miss everything! The class will watch 'Charlotte's Web' without me and I'll miss all the fun," she argued as she scratched her red arms profusely.

"*Beta*, if you go - you will get sicker and will miss more days than you have to. In fact the school won't even let you in with the pox," her father tried to reason with her.

"We don't have to tell them Daddy, I will wear long sleeves and they'll never be able to tell," Fatima tried to explain, forgetting that her face still sported little red pox marks all over.

"How about we get you a roll of Rainbow Brite stamps to stick in your journal in exchange for you staying home until your chicken pox is all gone?" was her father's offer.

Under protest, Fatima finally relented and accepted her father's proposal. At home, she passed her days watching closely monitored television. Like all conscientious parents, Fatima's parents would have to approve of the programs that were being watched by their girls. Cartoons and PBS shows, like 'the Electric Company' and 'Sesame Street,' were the only programs that were acceptable. Other than that, her parents needed to censor all programs that would promote and glamorize ideals that were contrary to the teachings of Islam. If a show contained any foul language, racy relationships, sexual innuendo, or provocatively dressed men and/or women - it was off limits. Although Mr. and Mrs. Husain knew that the society they were raising their children in was much more liberal than they were, they were doing their best to shelter their daughters from the Hollywood version of American life.

Fatima was already aware that boyfriends were never to be a part of her life. Marriage was the only relationship that was acceptable between a man and a woman. Men and women who dressed in a risqué manner were frowned upon, in fact those who dressed provocatively were often assumed to have weak moral character. And although Fatima's mother did not wear a veil or *hijaab*, at this time, she would always dress in a modest fashion. Similarly, conservatively dressed Fatima never wore tank tops or shorts, nor did her sisters. In fact they lacked the desire to dress in these types of clothes altogether, even if this was what their fellow classmates wore. They knew that modest attire was imperative amongst Muslims and that there was no room for deviation in what parts of their body were to be covered and what was allowed to show. The girls had already adapted the same values that their parents possessed despite the fact that these values strikingly contrasted the ideals of the school children that they spent much of their time with.

On the weekends there would frequently be dinner parties that would include the family's closest friends. These friends were mostly Muslim immigrants from the Indian subcontinent. They all met in Willingboro – a lower middle class town in southern NJ- and became a source of strength and comfort for each other within this new world that they were all working to establish themselves. At these gatherings, the women would be busy cooking for the six or seven families that were the core of this social circle. You could smell the delicious aroma of the *biryani* seeping out of the oven while the chicken was being marinated in the *masala*, or spices, just before it was baked. As uncles would enter the host's home they would declare, "*Wah,* smells just like back home- *zabardast!*"

But there was no such thing as a party with two main courses. There had to be an elaborate menu that needed a variety of dishes, enough to overflow off the table. So in addition to the *biryani* and chicken, there would be a vegetable curry, yogurt chutney, *samosas*, and who knows what more would be added based on the specialties of each aunty that would be the host for that specific weekend. The uncles would regularly compliment the hostess aunty, "*Aray Wah Bhaabi*, the foods is von-der-full. Just like back in India."

And the aunty would most certainly reply, "*Nay bhai sahib*. You are embarrassing me. You must finish the food if you like it so much," while her husband would forcefully refill the gentleman's plates.

Even after shoving large amounts of food down all the guests' throats, doggy bags would be made and food would be sent home with everyone. The local Tupperware businesses thrived off of these gatherings. In fact, every mother had painted her initials in nail polish on her Tupperware. That way there was no mistaking whose boxes were whose.

This social circle of immigrant Muslim *Desi* families was the heart of Fatima's social life. Within this group there were some girls that were close to her age, friends of hers that would remain as such well into her adolescence. There were also many boys in this community, but it wasn't kosher to be close friends with the opposite gender, so although they all played together - it was the girls that were her core crew.

By the time the third daughter, Amina, was a toddler, these gatherings had become a monthly event. All the aunties and uncles, many of whom had three or more children, would bring their families so that when all the guests were present, the host's home was just as rambunctious as a day care facility. Many times Fatima would hear an uncle call out to his wife, "*Aray Begum* watch the kids, they are running around like monkeys."

The wife would then come out of the kitchen, huffing and puffing, in search of her overactive child. Things were especially loud when the most active of the bunch would arrive, the infamous duo, Faseeh and Amaar. These two brothers were renowned for their perpetual energy and their imitations of the action sequences done by Bollywood actor Amitabh Bachchan. Aunties would ask laughingly, "Will they ever settle down?" or sympathize with their mother and say, "We must compliment her *himmat-* they are a handful!"

The younger girls were somewhat nervous around their flying fists and high kicks, all except for Ayesha. Ayesha would occasionally jump into the rumbles and prove to be a formidable foe to the hero wannabes. Ayesha could have easily been the boy of her family, had it not been for her long hair and big beautiful eyes. But Fatima and her friends, Afia, Mona, and Rubi were the exact opposite. These girly girls would be busy playing with their Barbie dolls and pretending to be grown up ladies.

These gatherings would grow much larger when an achievement would be marked, like that of a *Bismillah*, when a child begins to read the Qur'an, or an *Ameen*, when a child has completed reading the entire Qur'an. The core group would be ever present, but the guest list would grow exponentially at these larger events so as to include all of the Muslim *Desi* families within a fifty-mile radius. If you had ever exchanged phone numbers with any fellow *Desi* Muslim, whether at the gas station or in the public library, they had to be invited. Thus the contacts within the *Desi* Muslim community grew and blossomed.

Most of these people were the ones that Fatima and her family would spend the majority of their time with and identify with best, as they were all raising children who were growing up as Muslim ABCDs (American Born Confused *Desis*)

Chapter 2

As the years passed at Bookbinder Elementary, Fatima's friendship with Keysha and Monica dwindled, and only Tawana remained her good friend. Soon she realized that most of her friendships in school would remain simply at school. She didn't go over to her classmates' homes often, the rare exception being when she was invited to a birthday party. Nor did she invite her school friends over much. However, her limited exposure to *non-Desi*s included her neighbors, Lareen and Lavinia. These girls were at least three or four years older than Fatima, but at that age, three or four years seemed like a generation gap. Nevertheless, there were some times when they would all hang out with Fatima and play a few games. But even when it came to these neighbors, Fatima didn't go over their homes much or vice versa; it was simply a matter of congregating in each other's backyards or in the street to play freeze tag or softball.

With her classmates, Fatima lived in a world that was a product of her imagination. She would be able to tell far-fetched stories and no one would question her. This was because her stories were not over the top; they just made her family sound more American than they actually were.

A prime example of this was when her classmates returned from Christmas break. They would all rave about all the Christmas presents they had received and all they fun they had over their Winter break.

Tawana bubbled over with excitement as she told Fatima, "My mom and step-dad got me a Strawberry Shortcake doll, but I liked the Easy Bake Oven that my dad and his girlfriend got me better," to which Fatima, without a moment's hesitation, replied, "I received a Cabbage Patch kid from my parents, and my aunt gave me a 'My Little Pony' named Cotton Candy that has a pretty pink tail."

The reality of the situation was that Fatima's family did not celebrate Christmas, nor did they enjoy any of the celebrations that most of her classmates gloated about. But Fatima couldn't accept that she could not be part of all the enjoyment her peers were relishing in. Thus, she put on a nice show for her friends, and told vivid stories about their Christmas dinner.

"Our whole family came over our house on Christmas Eve and my mom made this really yummy turkey, and we had French fries with it because my sister really likes them…"

According to Fatima's narrations her family also celebrated Thanksgiving and marked Valentine's Day, when in reality her parents didn't know anything about these holidays or the manners in which to celebrate them in an American fashion.

She also told her peers about how her family celebrated the Muslim holidays, and thus the image of a family that was well assimilated into American culture was successfully presented. When in reality, that was not the case at all.

Fatima's parents were working endlessly to instill and retain their religious and cultural identity within their children. The children were taught that Islam was their way of life, and all other identities had to tie into that primary one. And their efforts to retain their culture went beyond simply having an Indian heritage; it went to the degree of honoring the city they came from, Hyderabad. The cuisine was described as incomparable, as was its colloquial form of Urdu; even its history was described as especially unique. The cultural pride that the family had was universal to most families from this region of India and it was a characteristic that none of these immigrants would let go of without a fight. So Fatima felt that she was left with no other option but to make up her own fantasy land that was comprised of both her worlds which she was balancing ever so carefully.

At the end of fourth grade Fatima's family received some fantastic news, her *Khala's* family would be moving to America from India, along with her maternal grandmother, *Nanima*. This was music to the ears of a family that was yearning for close relatives to share their lives with. Questions were being asked left and right, "Mummy does this mean we can have Nanima and Khala over for our birthdays? And can we take them to the pool with us? And do you think they will want to go to the zoo? What if we took them to Mill Creek Park?"

With a big grin on her face, Mummy held Fatima close and calmly replied, "Yes, *beta*. Yes to all your questions."

The mere thought of having cousins near by made the girls hyper.

The arrival of their cousins, Anam and her younger brothers, was a dream come true for Fatima and her sisters. If these cousins were anything like Sana and Zaina, the good times were getting ready to roll.

Even Mummy was a different person with her family now nearby. She was more relaxed and had many helpful hands around to offer assistance with all of her daily tasks, but Fatima was sure that having her Nanima nearby was the real reason for her Mom's apparent spike in happiness. Nanima was finally getting an opportunity to spend time with a set of grandchildren whom she did not have the chance to know before. Unfortunately *Nana* had died before the birth of Ayesha and had only one opportunity to meet Fatima. Fatima's memories of him were very vague, but Nanima would bring him back to life with her vivid stories of how he spent his time with Fatima during that brief period when she first visited India, at the age of three.

"Your Nana would purchase cookies that you liked from Karachi Bakery and keep them hidden in his room until you asked for them," she told Fatima.

"He would walk with you in his arms even though he was a frail man and you, my dear, were a very healthy child."

"Healthy" in *Desi* lingo simply meant fat. Healthy is even pronounced differently by *Desis*, its "hell-dhy". So hell-dhy Fatima was pampered silly for the two months she had been in India when she was three years old. Fatima loved to hear stories about her family, and now that there were finally some relatives close by she would begin to enjoy their company. There would be drawn out dinners and family game nights that all the family members would revel in. There were nights when all would sit together and watch Bollywood movies. In fact, Amitabh Bachchan and Rekha had become unofficial members of their extended family. While watching these movies, they would exchange loud humorous commentary that these movies elicited. It was fun and laughter, in the way only a close-knit family could enjoy.

It was a blessing that Fatima's relatives had arrived in more ways than one. A few months after her Khala's family settled down in their new home, Fatima's father fell ill. He had complained about stomach pain for some time, but had passed this discomfort off as indigestion. However, one of these episodes turned excruciatingly painful. Fatima's father was taken to the hospital without the girls' knowledge. Nanima and Fatima's cousins came to stay over, and the girls were so preoccupied with their guests that they failed to ask where their parents were. After a day passed and their parents were still not home, the girls began to question what was going on.

"Where is Mummy, Khala?" Amina would ask, but Khala would distract her and get her involved in some game or activity.

But the older two girls were relentless.

"Khala, where is Daddy? Why are both Mummy and Daddy not home? Khala what's going on?" they repeatedly asked.

It was only after much prodding that Fatima and Ayesha were told by their Khala that their father was sick and in the hospital.

"*Beta*, your daddy wasn't feeling well because his tummy was hurting. He went to the hospital and they had to keep him there to monitor him carefully. Mummy is with Daddy so he has somebody to talk to. She will come home tomorrow, and Daddy will come home when he feels better, *Inshallah*."

But in fact things weren't that simple. Daddy's ulcer had perforated and he had lost a lot of blood.

Despite the simplified explanation, the girls became extremely worried. They had watched too many over dramatic Bollywood movies, where the parents of the hero or heroine were tragically lost, to accept this simple explanation. Thoughts of these movies lead their over active imaginations to run amuck. Fatima began to grow very uneasy and insisted that her Khala take her to the hospital.

"*Chalo*, Khala, let's go now, *chalo chalo*..." Fatima persisted.

After many tantrums and tirades, Khala decided that Fatima needed to see at least one of her parents.

Fatima was driven over to the hospital without her sisters. The younger girls did not completely understand what was going on and were preoccupied by their cousins with activities that would keep their minds off their parents. Fatima on the other hand was not that naive. She was determined to get to the bottom of this upheaval.

Fatima walked into the hospital with her Khala, but the nurses would not allow the young girl to enter. The ICU, in which Fatima's father was being held, did not permit children to visit its patients. Upon hearing this, Fatima's face turned red and frustration steamed out. She angrily folded her arms across her chest and shouted, "I want to see Daddy! I want to see Mummy, NOW!!"

But her tantrum was to no avail. Instead the nurses let her mother know that Fatima was waiting outside, so that she could meet with her in the waiting room.

Fatima's mother paced out of the ICU towards her daughter, who was still throwing a fit in the waiting room. Upon sight of her mother, Fatima stopped shouting and flew into her arms. She hugged her mother tightly and then bent backwards ever so slightly so that she could look at her mother eye to eye. She ran her fingers over her mother's soft face. Her eyes were red from the lack of sleep and crying, and the dark circles underneath them made her face look haggard. She looked exhausted and worried. Just the sight of her mother troubled Fatima.

"Mummy what's wrong? Is Daddy okay? Is he inside? Why won't they let me see him?"

Fatima's mother managed to force a smile so that her daughter wouldn't get scared. She took Fatima into her lap and began to explain in very basic terms what had happened.

"*Beta*, Daddy is okay, but he needs his rest. His tummy was not feeling well and now the doctors are giving him medicine to feel better-kind of like I give you when you don't feel good."

"But Mummy, I don't have to stay in the hospital when I take medicine, so why does Daddy?"

Mummy replied, "Don't worry, *beta*. Daddy is fine. He will come home soon, *inshallah*."

But Fatima was not convinced. She didn't want to leave her mother, and she really wanted to see her father. Unfortunately, the hospital would make no exceptions to its strict visitor policy. Much to her dismay, she had to accept that she would not be able to see her father.

After a heartfelt half hour with her mother, Fatima's Khala walked her out of the hospital as she reluctantly waved good-bye.

"Mummy I will make *duaa*, for Daddy; I won't forget," she said to her teary eyed mother who had to quickly turn her face away.

Fatima was repeatedly told that her mother would return home tomorrow, but everything stable in life had just been questioned. Would she really come back? Would Daddy come home at all? What would happen if they didn't return? Nothing seemed certain anymore.

After a few days, which seemed more like an eternity to the family, Fatima's father's health began to improve. He was shifted from the ICU and in to the regular ward, where he could at long last have his daughters visit. The girls were thrilled that they would finally be able to see their father. This was the longest that they had ever gone without seeing him, and the thought of another day without seeing him was unbearable. The girls had made beautiful cards and drawings to give to their father, all of which said, 'Get Well Soon Daddy. We love you.' They gathered all their creations and packed them so that they could share them with their father.

At the hospital all three girls ran to the front desk to get a visitors pass.

"Husain is his name. H-U-S-A-I-N," spelled out Fatima.

"And he is tall and thin. He has a beard, but no moustache, just like Abraham Lincoln," added Ayesha, as the receptionist smiled at the girls.

"You guys must be very excited to see your Daddy," she said.

"Oh YES!!" all three cried back in unison.

"Well, he is on the third floor and his room number is 313."

The girls darted towards the elevator even before the lady finished explaining how to get to Daddy's room. Once they arrived on the third floor, the girls ran into room 313 screaming, "Daaaaaaadyyyy!" as they tried to jump on to his bed. Luckily, their mother was there to buffer the attack on Daddy's bed.

"*Beta. . . beta*, easy! Daddy can't handle all of you guys at once. Let him relax," she told her daughters.

But their joy was overwhelming. They were relieved beyond words to see their father. Although their father looked pale and exhausted, the girls refused to acknowledge that he appeared even the slightest bit different.

"Daddy, you don't look sick! So why did you stay here?" asked little Amina.

Daddy smiled at his little one.

"You should have seen me a few days back," he chuckled. But the girls weren't listening. They were simply delighted that their father was finally with them again.

"Daddy, you can't leave us again! I hate not having you at home!" Ayesha declared.

"I don't like being away from you guys either. But I had no choice. I had to stay at the hospital," he tried to explain.

"Never again Daddy, never again. Next time we will take care of you. We will be your doctors!" Fatima enthusiastically stated.

"Let's just pray that there isn't a next time," Mummy quickly interjected.

The girls returned to their home where their Khala was preparing dinner as she had been doing for the past week. Their cousins were all playing in the backyard, and Fatima could once again join in their recreation without a care in the world.

Sadly, these good times with her cousins were about to end. After a year in America, Fatima's Khala's family decided to move back to Hyderabad, leaving behind Fatima's disheartened family. After all that they had gone through, it seemed as if they would not be able to manage without her Khala living close by. Worse yet, Nanima would return to India with Khala's family.

"But why, Khala? Why must you all go?" the girls tearfully asked their aunt.

Khala's somber reply was a stark reminder of reality...

"The job market here isn't what we were hoping it to be. It would be easier for us to go back and resettle in a land we are more familiar with. Hyderabad is a city where we can get jobs and build a stable future."

The loss was nothing short of devastating for Fatima's mother. Quiet reservation was evident in Fatima's mother, as she was not an emotional woman. Her quietude spoke beyond what any words could have. But there was little choice in the matter. Upon their departure, Fatima's family was left in a state that would be best described as depression.

Their weeknights were no longer as fun as they had been for the past year. There was no one to pop in unexpectedly, nor was there anyone they could pop in upon. There were no loud and obnoxiously funny cousins to tell jokes with, nor enjoy Bollywood films with. When the girls were bored, they could not play with their cousins, it was back to just the three of them. The departure of their Khala's family left a gaping hole in their lives. One that they never thought they could fill…

* * * *

After the school year ended, Fatima's parents decided to take a trip to Hyderabad so that they could visit the family that was still residing there, the most important of which were the girls' paternal grandparents. This was the first trip to Hyderabad for the Husains with all three daughters. Despite their nervousness to travel with three children, Fatima's parents took the initiative to fly to India on a twenty hour flight that was filled to the brim with NRIs. All that were aboard the plane were anxious to visit their homeland and the loved ones that they had left behind.

The children were very excited to be reunited with their cousins, and behaved extremely well during the long flight over, in anticipation of great fun and merriment. Once the Air India flight landed at Bombay International Airport and taxied into its gate, the passengers began to disembark. While exiting the aircraft the Husain girls were immediately overcome by the intense heat and stench.

"Mummy, it stinks here. What's that smell?" Ayesha bluntly asked.

"Daddy, why is it so hot? It's toooo hot!" said Amina.

Fatima and her siblings wanted to run back into the plane, but there was no chance of that. Their parents prodded the girls along out of the plane and into the airport.

The family arrived at Bombay International Airport and was daunted by the long lines that were in the customs area. Fatima's parents were nervous about how the girls would react to the heat, the crowds, and lack of organization at the airport. Their concerns were rightly founded and it was a test of patience for all. While waiting for their turn, they were approached at least two times by petty officers trying to solicit bribes while insuring that they could get the family through customs regardless of what they were taking into the country – all for the right price.

"Madam, we will take care of everything, you will have no problem. Only give hundred Rupees, madam. You will leave in no time," they said to mother.

She shook her hand and replied, "*Nay Nay*, We are fine." But the persistent men nagged on.

"*Bhai sahib*," they told her father, "We will get you through, *bhai sahib*, only five hundred rupees. . . Okay okay, you know what - for you three hundred rupees, only three hundred rupees. . . "

The Husains politely declined their persistent and rather bothersome offers. Amina began to cry out of hunger and Ayesha looked as if she would pass out due to the heat. Fatima was irritated by the annoying petty officers and was sick of standing in line. After a horribly long hour in the queue, it was finally their turn to talk to the customs agent. The agent was strict and curt.

"Are you bringing any electric items? Or gold? Any gold?"

Since they were not carrying anything of this nature, Mr. and Mrs. Husain declared a righteous no. Not believing them, the agent ordered a search of all the luggage.

"Open it. Open all of the luggage. *Jaldee*, don't waste my time. *Jaldee karo!*"

This insured at least another hour at the station, during which every piece of luggage was inspected to insure that no electronics or gold were being taken into the country. After a fruitless search the inspector allowed the hot, hungry, irritable, and exhausted family to walk out of the customs area to the lobby.

"*Theek hai*, okay. You can go," he rudely said.

'This couldn't be the wonderful India that my parents are always talking about,' Fatima thought to herself. She could never imagine dealing with these circumstances back home in the US. Strangely she was supposed to be at home in her parents' homeland, but somehow things didn't feel right at all. Fatima felt like a foreigner in a land which was supposed to be hers.

The Husains now had to stay in Bombay overnight since their train to Hyderabad did not depart until tomorrow morning. Unfortunately, a hotel room had not been confirmed before their arrival so they had to settle for a place that one of the airport staff recommended. The trip to the hotel in the auto rickshaw was an adventure in itself.

"Daddy, why doesn't this car have doors?" asked Ayesha.

Her father tried to explain, but his voice was lost in the noises of the busy street. The auto rickshaw raced down a packed unpaved street avoiding street peddlers, cows, goats, children, innumerable pedestrians, and other cars that seemed to be driven by people without any clue as to how to drive. It was a miracle that they made it to the hotel alive and with their luggage still tied to the roof.

On their ride over to the hotel the girls witnessed a whole new world. Never before had they seen palm trees.

"Look trees like in Hawaii Five O," Mummy said to the girls, but Fatima said, "That's the *only* thing that looks like Hawaii around here Mummy."

Tall palms were sporadically dispersed throughout a landscape that they thought was morbid and filthy. There were makeshift huts that filled the streets as far as the eye could see. Straw, concrete, and brick were all components of the outer structure of these shanties. Scantily dressed children were playing in the narrow pathways that would separate one line of huts from the next. And an intense smell radiated from these edifices, an odor that was never experienced before by the Husain girls.

"Mummy, I can't breathe here, I feel sick," Fatima said at least two times, but her mother ignored her knowing that if she paid her too much heed, the drama would escalate.

The girls noticed what seemed to be hamburger patches on the dreadful walls of these homes and inquired to their father, "Daddy, why is their meat all over the walls?"

Their father laughed. He then explained what it actually was.

"You see *beta*, those are not patches of meat. They are patches of cow manure. The manure is spread out on the huts so that it will dry. Poor people then use it as fuel for the fires that they will build to cook their food upon."

Fatima was sad to hear this. Through her young eyes, she was witnessing the crippling effects of poverty that gripped her parents' homeland. For the first time in her short life she was truly grateful for all that she was blessed with back home in the comforts of her suburban neighborhood.

The auto rickshaw stopped in front of a small garbage infested alley that ended in front of a dark structure with a cracked feeble sign that said Hotel Roopam. 'This was not happening,' the girls thought.

"Daddy where are we? I don't see a hotel here," Fatima stated, ignoring the sign that was weakly dangling in plain view. This could not be a hotel - it couldn't even be a roach motel. However, much to their chagrin, this was it. As soon as they pulled up, Indian "bellboys"- who looked more like beggars- ran to the auto rickshaw and pulled off the luggage with great speed and raced it into the hotel so that the family couldn't run away after discovering the reality of their atrocious accommodations. As if that wasn't bad enough, they then hassled the Husains for money even after receiving a tip.

"*Sahib,* that was so much stuff, *sahib.* We carried it all in on our own. It was so heavy *sahib,*" trying to extort more money out of Fatima's father. Fatima's father responded, "I didn't tell you to take our luggage. You came and ran off with it. It was a job that you jumped at the chance to do. I have given you some money and that's enough. Now please leave us alone."

Exhausted and desperate to sleep Mr. and Mrs. Husain decided to stay at this shack just for one night despite the screaming and crying of their three daughters.

"No Daddy please not here! Please Daddy! This is a dump!" wailed Fatima.

"Daddy, this is so nasty! It smells like a barn in here!" whined Ayesha, but it was to no avail.

The girls were led down the dark hallway and up the concrete stairs surrounded by walls with gaping cracks and shattered windows. The girls were still moping and complaining about how horrible this place was, but their parents were too tired to answer them or shut them up. As the door to their room was opened, the girls let out an earsplitting screech.

"Holy Cow! This isn't for real!!" yelled Fatima.

There was a small lizard crawling along the edges of a crack that was in the wall. Fatima and Ayesha were never more upset in their life. How could they be brought into this rotten hotel?

"India sucks! It totally sucks! I wanna go home!!!!" cried Fatima with big tears rolling down her face.

These sentiments were firmly established even before setting foot inside the horrendous bathroom which had a toilet that was essentially a hole in the ground. There were no proper plumbing fixtures, and the water that was a murky brown tint, not to mention all the mildew that infested the walls. 'Never again!' Fatima vowed - never again would she come to India.

After what seemed like the longest night of their lives, the family left Bombay the next morning and boarded the Minar Express to Hyderabad. The train ride was long but it was tolerable. Anything was tolerable after their stay at the Hotel Roopam. The only difficult aspects of the ride were the stops at which loud vendors would shout "*chai, chai garam*" or "Poppins Poppins" into the train windows hoping to find customers to purchase their tea or candy. Initially the girls didn't understand what these people were shouting, as their accents were so strong, but their parents clarified what the shouts were conveying. The other difficulty was another horrid bathroom situation. Fatima needed to use the bathroom so she followed the signs to the narrow lavatory entrance. She struggled to walk through the constricted doorway, and when she finally got through she entered a smelly filthy cabin that had yet another hole in its floor.

'Holy crap,' she thought. Literally, holy crap. Through the hole she could see the railroad tracks being crossed over, but the foulest thing that Fatima had ever seen was what sat around that hole. Remnants of excrement lay all around it with flies buzzing all about. Fatima wanted to vomit. She no longer needed to pee and she returned to her family's cabin.

"I would rather hold my pee for a week than pee in there!" she exclaimed.

"Fine, if that's what you want," her father casually replied.

Fatima had determined that answering the call to nature was torture in India. By now the girls were desperately hoping to find some modern comforts in their grandparents' homes.

Arriving at the Naampalli train station in Hyderabad was a welcome change. Familiar faces greeted them with flower garlands that were placed around their necks. Hugs and kisses were abundant and finally it seemed as if this trip may have some good to it after all.

Fatima and her sisters were meeting their paternal grandparents after ages. Fatima could not recall when she met her *Dada* and *Dadima* last. They were fortunate to have had *Nanima* stay in the US with them, and now they finally had a chance to spend time with their paternal grandparents. As excited as the elders were to meet the grandchildren there were small issues that had to be dealt with immediately.

The first hurdle that was encountered was the issue of proper *adab*. In a society where respect for elders is of paramount importance, mouthy American children were not tolerated. The girls had to immediately cease all conversations in English and switch into full gear with their Urdu. Luckily, the girls were well versed in Urdu, as they spoke it fluently at home with their parents, but their mannerisms were still very American, and these could be interpreted as rude by standards of traditional Indian culture. So despite the fact that they spoke very respectfully to their elders, the girls now needed to modify their manners. The first and most important change was that they could no longer just smile and convey their *salam*; they would now have to lift their right hand to their forehead while bending forward ever so slightly to give a proper salutation to an elder. Any questions they had were to be addressed solely to their parents; that too, only at bedtime. In this manner their parents hoped the girls would not offend anyone, even unintentionally, yet still have their curious inquiries answered.

Additionally, any food that was served to them was to be eaten without any comments and/or questions. No "Eeews" or "What the heck is this?" type of comments were going to be tolerated. This rule held true until their digestive systems fell apart and consuming food no longer was an issue.

Last but not least, no glorifying their lifestyle back home *or* degrading the standard of living in Hyderabad. No doubt that these were two totally different worlds and much adjustment was necessary. But the girls' parents felt it necessary to explain to their daughters that they should act humbly, and never degrade the homes and lifestyles of their extended family.

The Husains unloaded their luggage at Dada and Dadima's home. Lodging at a hotel was out of the question, and staying at Nanima's wasn't the way to go, according to traditional Hyderabadi culture. A son was to remain with his relatives, and a wife married *in* to her husband's family; not vice versa. Therefore the Husains would *obviously* be staying with Fatima's paternal grandparents.

Dada and Dadima lived in a white cement home that was rather attractive. Pretty impressive compared to all the homes that the girls had driven by in both Bombay and Hyderabad. It was a large one story home that had an open floor plan and a huge yard around it. The yard had mango trees, guava trees, neem trees, and a coconut tree that seemed to reach the sky. It was no less than luxurious compared to the Hotel Roopam.

Dadima pointed to the tallest tree in her backyard, "That coconut tree was planted by your father when he was just a boy. And now look at how tall it is. Whoever thought his kids would come to marvel at it."

How true that was. Whoever thought that one of the boys that grew up in this home would move half way across the world and rear his family in a world so different from the one he was raised in.

The girls were lead into the room they would be staying in by way of the large hall where two day beds were situated, separated by the doorway to the dining room. The hall also led to a corridor to which the kitchen and bathroom were adjacent. The first impression of this home was great compared to all that the girls had seen in the past forty eight hours. They were now anxious to see where they would be sleeping, and much to their relief their accommodations were pretty decent.

"Thank God," said Fatima with a relieved countenance.

"I would've died if this place was anything like that nasty place we were in last night," she went on.

"Fatima!" snapped her mother. "Mind your tongue! What did we tell you about behaving humbly? Don't say anything like that again! I want you to show nothing but respect for all that you see here. When you see things that you may find 'unworthy' of you, be grateful for all that you have. And if you don't like it, just stay quiet. Don't belittle it!" The vein in her mother's forehead was throbbing.

Fatima looked down. She had really disappointed her mother and she knew it. But there was nothing more that could be done about that. She had to learn to keep her mouth shut and move on.

The younger girls admired their large and spacious bedroom. It had a large semi circle shaped window almost four feet by three feet in size that overlooked the backyard.

"Daddy, where is the screen to this window?" Ayesha asked her father. He just laughed and said, "*Beta*, in India we make sure our mosquitoes are well fed."

Ayesha failed to find the humor in his statement. Sure enough at night the mosquitoes were feasting on the American blood that must have tasted especially good since they were flocking towards the girls. Fatima and Ayesha couldn't stop scratching and soon they were red all over.

"God this is so crazy," Fatima said.

"Well at least we get to sleep in a mosquito net," Ayesha replied trying to comfort her sister. However, the mosquito nets seemed to have backfired. Both Ayesha and Fatima felt like the net actually trapped the two of them inside with the mosquitoes rather than keep the mosquitoes out.

"This is gonna be a loooooong trip Fatima *baji*," Ayesha said as she dozed off...

Every morning the girls would find Dada sitting on his daybed and reading the *Siasat* newspaper. He would grasp the paper with his left hand, as his right arm was pinned to his chest. A massive stroke years ago had left his right side incapacitated and he taught himself how to function entirely with his left hand. He was a tall bronzed man who was thin and semi bald. What remained of his hair was a salt and pepper gray and he always had a five o'clock shadow. It was obvious that he was once a handsome man whose health was rapidly deteriorating. He walked with a cane that Amina would love to run off with.

"Dada, I have your cane ..." she would teasingly say to him.

Many times she would imagine that the cane was a microphone and would sing songs loudly into it pretending she was a superstar.

"Look *baji* I can sing like Michael Jackson," she would say and then offer a rendition of her favorite song, "Billie Jean."

These antics greatly amused Dada. Watching his granddaughters brought great joy to him, and Fatima caught him many times with tears in his eyes while observing the girls. He would call Fatima and Ayesha to his side daily and teach them how to read small words in Urdu.

"You children must learn how to read and write Urdu. If you do not carry on your mother tongue then who will?" he would always ask the girls.

Although they spoke the language fluently they were unable to read Urdu, and Dada was determined to change that. The girls were already familiar with the Urdu alphabet as it was very similar to the Arabic alphabet in the *Quran*. They just needed to learn how to recognize these letters and the words they formed in Urdu. So they applied these skills by turning to the Cinema page of the *Siasat* where he knew the girls would be able to read the titles of the Bollywood movies based on name recognition.

"*Dekho*, you girls know all these words already, just try to recognize them in written form. It is very easy, I know you can do it," he would say encouragingly.

Being avid fans of Bollywood films was finally paying off for the young girls. To the pleasure of their grandfather the girls quickly picked up on reading a language simply based on how to read the movie directory.

Dadima on the other hand was not much of a reader; she was much more of a talker. A fair stocky lady with henna dyed red hair, she wore a brightly colored *saree* and was constantly giving orders to the servants. Her *kaali poth*, the Indian equivalent of a wedding band, was always around her neck along with a few gaudy gold chains. She would have her *pandaan*, small box, open in front of her and she would crack betel nuts with her nutcracker while chewing on her *paan*. She was very good at relating stories to her granddaughters while sitting on her daybed in the large hall that looked over the huge backyard. Her stories were numerous, enough to fill up a library. Some were historically factual while others were sprinkled with lots of *masala* to make a dull story more fascinating.

Fatima was very interested in hearing about the youth of her father, his brothers and only sister, stories that Dadima was only too happy to relate. Fatima would sit for hours with her grandmother, listening attentively to all the soap opera-ish details that would emerge. Details that she knew couldn't be entirely true but they made the narratives all the more entertaining. Fatima was the only one that would enjoy these stories, as Ayesha, Amina, and Salwa, their cousin, were busy running around in the backyard and even passing through the gate into the neighbor's property.

"*Aray dekho*.......The girls have run into *Bhabi's* yard again," Dadima would shout so that someone would look into the girls' whereabouts.

But it was all good. The younger girls were at the neighbor's place drinking some freshly squeezed lemonade. After all, the house next door was the home of Dadima's brother, which basically meant that all that land belonged to one big family.

Family in this society took on a whole new meaning. The American family unit that Fatima was exposed to consisted of simply parents and children. The Indian family was a grand phenomenon. Extended family was the nuclear family. Parents and sons would share a home along with the spouses and children of their sons. Daughters would generally move out to their husband's homes that were filled with their husband's brothers and their families. Every member of this unit performed integral roles in making sure that such a large household was taken care of properly. Cousins would grow up under the same roof and develop relationships much like that of siblings. Everything was shared by all members of the family and there was no concept of private ownership. In fact the only private space that seemed to exist for a husband and wife was their bedroom, but even that in many cases was shared by their children. All of these circumstances ensured that family squabbles were to occur. Daughter-in-laws were known to have issues with each other as well as with their mother-in-law, and the sons were the ones that were generally walking a tight rope in trying to maintain sanity.

Despite these problems, the entire clan would show intense loyalty to each other and were recognized as one group. The elders played as important a role in the decision making aspects of the lives of the grandchildren as did the parents. All of these ideals presented problems to the small mind of Fatima. This was a family structure that was totally foreign to her. The idea of having ten parents sounded crazy. She couldn't imagine trying to balance so many opinions in one home without causing havoc. Fatima felt grateful that she had only two adults to answer to and was pleased to know that this type of lifestyle could never survive in America.

One aspect of Indian life that the girls were intrigued by was the servants. The majority of the cooking and cleaning was done by the house maidens, a concept that was unheard of back home in their middle class neighborhood. Mummy was the cook, cleaning lady, and nanny all wrapped up in one perfect package. However, in Hyderabad they met Haju and Haleema. Haju and Haleema were a curious pair, a thin septuagenarian and a young, healthy woman. These women were coming from hutments like that the family drove by in Bombay. They would make the daily trip out of their quarters to earn their living. Their husbands would work labor jobs and at times their children would accompany them to the homes in which they were working, as day care facilities were unheard of.

Haju and Haleema were catty women who were busy gossiping while working and extricating information out of the children at every opportunity. Fatima's parents had bought both of them *sarees* as a present from America, and although they accepted these gifts respectfully in front of the elders, they secretly inquired about the *sarees* with Fatima.

"Fatima, come here come here. Listen for a minute," they would call out to her.

Fatima respectfully obliged, but then they inquired, "You know the *sarees* your folks brought for us? Well, are they new or is your mom just passing on *sarees* to us that she has no use for?"

Fatima was rather surprised with the question, but she honestly replied, "No, they are new."

The twosome continued to prod on, "Well, how much do these cost in America?"

Fatima did not know the answer to these questions but she did know, even at the young age of ten, that these were improper enquiries. From that point on she didn't socialize with the servants, not knowing what kind of enquiry would come up next.

The children of the servants on the other hand, were a source of entertainment for Fatima and her sisters. They taught the girls how to play the local game of '*kabaddi*' and were thrilled to share some of the American snacks that mother had packed for her girls in their suitcases. Once the girls offered these children some Coca Cola, but they hesitated in accepting the glasses. They asked, "What is this?"

Fatima replied, "It's cola."

"What is that Fatima *bibi*?" the kids inquired again.

Fatima then realized that these kids had never seen or tasted cola before. But thanks to Fatima and her sisters, these children would soon consume not only Coke, but also Doritos, Oreos, Capri Sun, and Fruit Roll Ups; American novelties that Mummy packed for the girls- novelties that these children would most likely never be exposed to again.

The next two months had both their ups and downs but definitely more downs. The girls were thrilled to see all of their cousins, the ones they already knew, and the ones they were meeting for the first time. They became friends with Yusra and Kulsum, their *phuppu's* daughters, and spent much time learning about the local area from them. Amina was occupied with Salwa, their younger *chacha's* daughter, who became her playmate for the duration of the trip. Sana and Zaina were also visiting from Saudi Arabia, so the family reunion aspect of the trip was great. What was difficult was dealing with all of the other issues.

The heat was intolerable, the water undrinkable, the food indigestable. Anything they consumed would give them diarrhea, indigestion, or nausea. Within a month each of the girls had dropped a significant amount of weight. Their grandparents were trying desperately to order food from the over-priced international markets so that the upscale food would not affect their girls' health. Even their water was boiled meticulously. But despite these efforts, the girls' stomachs proved to be too delicate to the handle the local cuisine. Living off of *chapattis* and *daal,* the girls became accustomed to simple dinners that proved to suit them best.

During the few occasions that Fatima was able to visit her mother's family, Fatima befriended her mother's cousins who were oddly enough, closer to her age than her mother's. The two young girls, Mushu and Naju, became her best friends for the next two months. They would play together, read books together, and even do each other's hair. There were days when Fatima would choose to spend the night at their homes over that of her grandmother's just to keep company with her two new buddies.

Mushu and Naju even took Fatima to their respective schools, while she would quietly observe the manner in which classes in Hyderabad were run. 'So different from Bookbinder,' Fatima would think. All the children were dressed in uniforms and had their hair neatly done. The boys had it parted to the side, each and every one with the same exact hair cut. The girls were all wearing two braids, the only variation being that those with longer hair would have their braids pulled up from their ends to their heads so that each braid formed a perfect loop on both sides. The children were extremely disciplined. There were no side conversations occurring when the teacher was speaking. Fatima couldn't even find one student that was passing a note to his/her friends. Every child was diligently copying notes from the blackboard. The teacher, Mrs. Gopal, was a thin dark woman with large black framed glasses. She wore a red and blue *saree* that seemed loud in this environment. Her bangles matched perfectly and clicked rhythmically as her arm moved up and down while writing on the chalkboard. She too had a braid, except that it hung down to her waist. She did not laugh once or even smile at the children. It was a very business like relationship, and there was a job that had to get done.

There were no individual desks and no pretty bulletin boards with lively posters. Instead the classroom was austere and serious. There was nothing there that a student could be distracted by except the plain white walls and the long blackboard that the teacher would write on. But in today's case the big distraction was Fatima, who proved to be a mini-celebrity as she was "American." This was the irony of ironies for Fatima. In the US she wasn't completely accepted as a normal American; in fact she was usually labeled as Indian, but here in India she was definitely not considered an Indian. She was an American. Neither culture was willing to embrace her even though she identified with both. Confused and uneasy she wanted to go back to her grandmother's place.

A month had passed and Fatima was very upset when her father had to return to the US, since his vacation time had expired. She and her siblings were staying behind with their mother. Amina was only two years old, and she began to miss her father terribly within days of his departure. She had generally been a low maintenance child, always smiling and with a sweet disposition. But even she was troubled by her father leaving, and began to show signs of discontentment. The girls were getting tired of the heat and were frustrated with the lack of modern facilities. Squatting in the outhouses was taking its toll, along with the numerous mosquito bites that covered their bodies.

A fortnight after their father left, Ayesha began to fall seriously ill. She ran a fever for days and slowly stopped eating what little she was consuming to begin with. She was at high risk for dehydration and the medicines available in Hyderabad would not help her temperature subside. Almost lifeless, Ayesha would lie in her mother's arms, head tilted back and eyes bulging out like one who suffers from Graves' disease. Desperate to help her daughter regain her health, their mother gave *sadaqa*, charity, immediately, and chose to utilize alternative medicine due to the failure of the allopathic treatments. She consulted the local homeopathic doctor who prescribed Ayesha with some herbal medications that were supposed to alleviate her suffering. It was a seven day course that was accompanied by specific dietary restrictions. This made the task of completing the course far more problematic as some of the few foods that Ayesha's stomach would tolerate were not to be eaten while taking the homeopathic pills.

With great difficulty the course was completed and slowly Ayesha's health began to improve. Tremendously relieved, the family prepared to wrap up their trip and head home to New Jersey.

Chapter 3

In September 1984, Fatima had left both the summer and India behind to begin the fifth grade. This was the year she was to qualify for a new program that was being developed by the Willingboro school district known as PATS- Program for Academically Talented Students. When the letter arrived informing her parents of her achievement, their pride was endless.

"This is my product," their father would say proudly hugging his daughter, whose height was now just shy of his chest.

This was just the beginning Fatima's parents believed. They had very high hopes for their daughters.

"God has blessed my children with sharp brains. Now they must use them properly," her father said repeatedly.

They had not moved half way across the world to raise "average" children; they were going to raise exceptionally talented and well educated women. This was their dream.

Of course, like most *Desi* families this meant that all of their daughters had go to medical school and become physicians, as this was the pinnacle of achievement amongst *Desis* back home and in America. And this letter would be the starting point of their eldest's road to medical school, or so they hoped.

For one day a week, Fatima was bussed to Hawthorne Elementary, a school about three miles away that housed these gifted classes. Soon enough Ayesha followed suit and also qualified for PATS. Two daughters on their way to medical school....their parents could start smelling their daughters' success.

At Hawthorne, Fatima and Ayesha would meet students from throughout the school district that were "academically talented." Many of them happened to be fellow *Desis*, including some that were children of family acquaintances.

It seemed that all these children had high aspirations. When asked what they wanted to be when they grew up many responses ensued.

"An astronaut," one student replied. Another said, "A pilot." A couple of extremely motivated students even said, "I want to be President."

It was not a surprise that when this question was directed towards the children coming from Indian families, the answers were, "I would like to be a cardiac surgeon," and "I think I should be a neurologist", and one even said, "I want to be the Surgeon General of the United States."

How typical!

Miss Epplen, the Computer teacher for PATS was introducing the children to innovative technology that would change the way the world would function. For the first time, the children were exposed to a Macintosh PC, and were being taught the language of computer programming - BASIC. Up to this point, these children had only seen computer technology expressed through video game systems like Atari and Colecovision. They would spend hours playing Pac-Man, Q-bert and Donkey Kong. But the PC was something totally new and amazing. The kids were in awe of what could be done with this gadget.

But that was not the only course that PATS had to offer. Mrs. Red taught Spanish, Mrs. Knapp taught American History, Ms. Andersen taught Literature, and Mrs. Feinman taught Personal Finance. These five classes initiated the concept of critical thinking within a group of children who were absorbing all this new knowledge like a sponge, and were most anxious to put it all to use.

Expectations rose higher and higher and Fatima's grades were luckily fulfilling these expectations. The same was true with Ayesha and soon enough Amina was in kindergarten. Now only the newest member of the family, Malikah, was at home with their mother.

Fatima enjoyed school immensely but she also looked forward to coming home and having some downtime with her younger sisters, especially Malikah. Malikah was the doll of the family. Everyone oohed and aahed at her every accomplishment, and to Fatima she was the apple of her eye. But that sisterly love wasn't Malikah-specific. Each sister possessed unique and endearing qualities that were essential pieces to the Husain family puzzle. Ayesha, with her entertaining and humorous personality, was the life of the home. When she was around everyone lit up with joy. Ayesha and laughter were synonymous in the Husain home. Amina was the caring and motherly figure of the four daughters. From a tender age she was working besides her mother and making sure that everyone in the home was tended to. She was everyone's second mother. And then there was Fatima. The Husain sisters were very close knit. The girls spent every waking moment with each other and developed a unique bond. They were each other's best friends and playmates. Although they wished that they had some cousins nearby to play with as well, they learned to have fun amongst themselves.

But soon enough they would have more play mates than they'd know what to do with. A flood of immigrant family members was about to arrive in the USA. The applications for residency that their father had submitted on behalf of his brothers and their respective families had been approved. Soon Fatima's *chachas* and their families moved from the Indian subcontinent to Willingboro, New Jersey, right into Fatima's home.

Rizwan *chacha*, her father's older brother, came first with his family from Pakistan. He had two sons and looked forward to the future that America could provide his boys. Fatima's father would express to his brother the potential that this country had for those children who were studious and conscientious in their efforts to succeed.

"All the children have to do is work hard. They will gain much from applying their intelligence at school. I have drilled this into my daughters' and look now."

He then proudly pulled out his daughters' report cards and showed all the O's that they had earned. But Rizwan *chacha* didn't understand what his brother was beaming about. In fact, he looked mortified at the sight of these report cards.

"*Aray bhai*, how is it that your bright daughters have earned zeroes in every subject?"

Fatima's father laughingly responded, "No Rizwan bhai these are not zeroes. They are 'O's, which in America, stand for outstanding."

Relieved the girls' eldest *chacha* leaned back in his chair and smiled.

"Thank God. For one minute I was terrified," he said.

Fatima's youngest *chacha*, Nabeel, also immigrated to the USA. He was a bachelor and lacked the responsibility that the other *chachas* had on their shoulders. He was a relatively quiet, twenty something man who loved to tease his niece, knowing exactly which buttons to push. He knew she was very proud to be American, so he would constantly tell her, "Fatima you are not a true American, you are just a *Desi* living in America."

If there was one thing that Fatima couldn't stand it was the questioning of her Americanness. As if that was not bad enough, he would add fuel to the fire by making silly comparisons between India and the United States.

"You know in India the milk is very rich because it comes from strong buffaloes. Here the milk comes from feeble cows; it is not fit for anyone to drink. My friends would laugh at me back home if they knew I was drinking cow's milk here. That too with no cream on top. Pssh...."

These types of comments would profoundly annoy his niece. Fatima had zero tolerance of anyone putting down her country. This was her homeland and no one was about to disrespect it in her presence.

"Nabeel *chacha* if India is so great than why are almost all the people poor there? And why don't they have normal toilets? And why are the streets so dirty? And why does it smell so bad there?" she would go on and on.

Childish arguments would follow and Fatima was repeatedly left exasperated. This banter continued until one day when she was riding in the backseat of her father's car while Nabeel *chacha* and her father were seated in the front. She lay down in the back, and Nabeel *chacha* mistook her for being asleep. He started telling his elder brother how much he was enjoying his new life here.

"*Bhai* it really is a nice place here. And people here are surprisingly sincere. You can reap what you sow, not like back home where connections are everything, and being a minority would hold one back."

Fatima jumped up shouting.

"Haaaaaaa!!! I knew it!! See you said it too!! America is better than India! I told you!!!!" With a defeated smirk on his face Nabeel *chacha* softly replied, "When did you wake up?"

These *chacha*s and their families were welcome guests in Fatima's home, but space began to run tight in their three bedroom abode. After months of job searching, the *chacha*s and their wives, *chachi*s, found work in the northern NJ town of Somerville, which was about an hour and a half drive away from Willingboro. Thus, they all slowly moved out of her home, and into apartments in Somerville.

A few years after the arrival of her *chacha*s, Fatima's grandparents decided that they could no longer remain alone in Hyderabad. Tapes of Dada and Dadima's voices would arrive saying, "Now it is too much for us to live here alone. All of our children are abroad and we have nothing to look forward to but the visits of our neighbors and tenants. They come for tea and chat with us to keep us company, but then they return to their families. We are old and weak and can no longer bear to be separated from ours."

Thus, they too immigrated to the United States. Upon arrival to the United States, Fatima's grandparents were received warmly. But with their grown children now living in two separate towns, they had to make the difficult decision as to which son they would choose to live with.

"Dadima, you must stay with us!" exclaimed Fatima.

"I want to hear all your stories about what Daddy used to do when he was young and how you used to have a servant for each child and..."

Fatima began to list many reasons for Dada and Dadima to stay at her place. But they had to think their decision out carefully. After much thought, they chose to reside in Somerville where most of their children were, especially out of concern for Nabeel.

"You see, he is young. And he is not yet married so who will attend to him? While I am still alive I can take care of him," explained Dadima. "I would love to stay with you Fatima, but I must first get him married and settled with his own family. Then we will see what happens."

Although Dadima chose to stay in Somerville, Dada decided that he had other plans. Dada chose to rotate between the homes of his sons'. He told his wife, "Manjli, you stay where you wish, but I will spend time with everyone. I do not want to be a burden on any one son. Besides I have a lot of catching up to do with all of my grandchildren."

Thus, weekly visits to Somerville became a staple in Fatima's family's routine. Even if Dada was staying at their place, they would drive up to where Dadima was every weekend. The relatives that these girls had longed for were finally here...

Not too long after the arrival of Dada and Dadima, Fatima's parents made the decision to move out of Willingboro. Fatima's father spoke to his children, "We have to move for a several reasons. First, the commute to work is getting to be too much for me. I don't want to be in the car for as long as I am every day. I would much rather spend that time with you guys. Secondly, Willingboro is just too far from Somerville. Our weekly trip to Dadima's is getting to be more and more difficult. Thirdly, the masjid is also quite far. We really should be closer to the masjid to enjoy its benefits. And finally, you girls are getting older now. I want you to attend better schools and get the most out of your education."

All of these were valid reasons, but Fatima and her sisters did not need any convincing. Daddy was preaching to the converted. They knew that their father needed to reduce his commute to work in Trenton. They knew that the drive to Somerville on the weekends was draining. They also knew that their parents were always eyeing schools in better districts. Equally important was the fact that the masjid was becoming a major part of their lives, and they were aware of the fact that, it too, was not close by.

Fatima's parents had become very active in the community's largest local masjid which was based in Trenton. The trip to the masjid every Sunday for Sunday School in the big blue "refugee van", as they all lovingly called it, was fun for the children, yet exhausting for its driver, Fatima's father.

The van was the property of the masjid and it transported children from South Jersey north to Trenton so that they could attend Sunday school. The poor condition of the van was rather amusing. In the days before car seats and strict seat belt laws, this van was without seats and stripped entirely of carpet upholstery. To accommodate the ten to twelve children that were riding in the Sunday school van, there were folding chairs that were placed in the open space, upon which the older children would sit. The chairs would then slide back and forth with every stop and acceleration that the van would make.

"Man, this is as cool as a Great Adventure roller coaster!" Fatima exclaimed.

"And we didn't even have to pay for a ticket!" laughed Rubi.

The younger children, for whom there weren't enough folding chairs, sat on the metal floor. They would constantly shift their weight from one butt cheek to the other to avoid getting burnt from the heat of the floor. The weekly bus ride may have been fun for its young passengers, but it was getting to be too much for Fatima's father. He really wanted to move closer to the masjid and quit this second job.

The condition of the masjid was much like that of the "refugee van." Unlike other mosques the world over, it was not a grand structure with a beautiful dome and towering minarets. In fact it was quite the opposite. It was an old brick building in downtown Trenton, an area that few braved to visit.

In the heart of a run down neighborhood stood the edifice that was deemed useless by the previous owner and practically given away to the *Imam*, leader of the masjid. It was a building that was renovated to provide a large hall on the first floor, in which one hundred people could stand comfortably for prayer. There was also a sizeable multi-purpose room in the basement, and the rooms upstairs were set aside for the ladies, since prayer was segregated by gender.

Sunday school was held in the rooms on the second floor. The children would attend classes, and socialize afterwards every Sunday morning. Their humble place of worship became a second home to the local community. This was especially true for the Husain girls. This masjid was a place they grew to love dearly and despite its unattractive facade they treated it with the respect that every house of worship deserves. They looked forward to Sundays, and wished that they could spend more time at the masjid. Moving closer to Trenton would make this a lot more feasible.

But relocating was not an easy decision to make. Even though there were many positive aspects to moving, there were also a few negatives. The biggest con was leaving behind the family's social network, which was firmly grounded in Willingboro and South Jersey. Moving out of Willingboro was equivalent to leaving their second family.

"It will not be easy to move out of Willingboro. I can't imagine leaving all of the friends we have made here. These people have been there for us through thick and thin," Fatima's mother complained to her father.

"Yes dear, but look at all the benefits in moving. Think of the great schools our girls will be able to attend. Look at how close we will be to everything else. There will surely be a community like this one by Trenton. We already know quite a few people there. And with the masjid growing the way it is, people will surely move nearby it," Fatima's father consoled his wife.

There was truth to the fact that many Muslim families were making the effort to move closer to the masjid. In fact some of their friends had already begun to branch out of Willingboro and into areas of more promise and better school systems.

"And the Rizwans will be across the street from us. Can you imagine there will be a family right in our neighborhood that our children are already familiar and comfortable with? We don't have anything like that here. What a nice change that will be," Fatima's father told his wife.

There was consolation in the fact that the Rizwans were moving out of Willingboro and into the same neighborhood as the Husains in Morrisville, PA, a town separated only by the Delaware River from Trenton, NJ.

Fatima and Ayesha were good friends with the Rizwan girls and looked forward to moving close to them.

"I can ride my bike with Maariya and we can walk to the park, and we will go to the same school too!" trumpeted Ayesha.

"Mona and I can play Perfection and Operation while you guys are doing all that," Fatima planned.

The girls were thrilled at the fact that they would finally be able to walk down the block and play with their friends, and even enter a neighbor's home. They were more than ready to move to a place that would have more girls their age that they could play with.

The prospect of moving was made even more enticing by the fact that their new home would be new construction. The Husains were able to choose the colors of the walls and carpets, the tiles in their kitchen and bathrooms, even the cabinets and countertops were selected by the girls and their parents. This made the whole process of moving even more enjoyable for the entire family.

Subsequently the family of six prepared to leave what was their very first home to move across the Delaware River.

With the cooperation of family and friends the Husains moved into their new abode. Uncle Syed let them borrow his truck to use as a moving van. Two other uncles helped with the loading and driving of their cargo to Morrisville. And many helpful aunties prepared dinner for the family, and sent it over so that they would eat well after the long move. Friends like these were priceless.

The new place was more spacious than their previous residence. It provided an extra bedroom and the backyard was a lot more private and conducive to play sets and children's activities. Ayesha had big plans for the backyard, "Mummy I'm gonna get a volleyball net so we can have a tournament right here!" she excitedly said to her busy mother.

But Mummy had a lot on her mind. She had to figure out what stuff to put where and how best to organize the new place. She could not do all of this work on her own so she decided to delegate tasks.

"Fatima, Ayesha, Amina come here! There's much to be done. I can't do it all alone. This is America, everyone must help here! We have no servants running after you all!!"

Fatima was half-heartedly listening, as she was too busy admiring their new home, and inhaling the new scents that surrounded her. Due to the new construction, the fresh smell of paint was invigorating. The carpets were the colors that the family had chosen at the design center, and looked even better laid on the floor than on the samples that they had seen. The bathrooms were bright and almond in color, looking a lot larger than what they really were because of the large mirrors that covered one entire wall. Most of the furniture from their old home had been abandoned so their new home was relatively empty. This made the house seem even more spacious, a fact that the girls loved. The excitement of the new home was too much for the girls to concentrate on working.

"We can run around the whole place and not break anything!" Ayesha cried out as she ran from room to room singing and playing at a time when their mother kept calling on them to help unpack their belongings.

"*Beta*, come on! I need you guys here now! Ayesha stop running around! You need to watch Malikah so I can work. Fatima you start putting away the canisters in the pantry. Amina you just keep up the good work!" Mummy shouted.

Amina was always doing the right thing. She was Mummy's right hand, forever earning praise for how wonderful she was. She was even the only one of the four girls that looked like her mother, jet black tresses and all. Fatima and Ayesha constantly teased her about being a "Goody Goody" which eventually became her nick name, and how the older two loved to use it!

The biggest change for the girls in this new house was that Fatima and Ayesha would no longer need to share a bedroom; each now had a room to herself.

"Now you won't kick me in the middle of the night," Fatima said with relief to Ayesha.

"And you won't hog up my side of the bed!" retorted Ayesha.

"That's enough of the arguing girls. Get to work. There are four girls in the house now. It should sparkle," their father called out from the master bedroom.

Fatima and Ayesha stopped their bickering and looked at each other with stunned expressions. They dropped everything and went over to their father.

"What does that mean Daddy? Four girls mean a clean house? Are we all cleaning ladies? Aren't you the one that always said we have brains and need to put them to good use? Is cleaning the best use of them? Isn't that a really old fashioned thing to say Daddy? We aren't back in India you know?"

The girls went on and on until their father got very irritated. He snapped, "I just want you guys to stop fighting and start putting things away! People will drop in to see the house and it's still a big mess. Get to Work!"

"Well, just say that Daddy. Why do you have to say four girls and clean house and all that *Desi* stuff?" Fatima said as her father walked away from the annoyed girls.

"Jeez Louise…." she said as she shook her head and begrudgingly got back to work.

"You'd think we were living in Hyderabad or something…" she mumbled to herself.

Sometimes the *Desi* mentality got to be too much for Fatima. For her, being a girl didn't necessarily mean that she alone had to clean, or be the only one responsible for all the housework. She felt that this was everyone's responsibility, and even if there were a son in the household, he better have pulled his weight too. These were the types of semi-feminist ideals that were beginning to evolve within her. The irony of ironies was that they weren't necessarily coming from her American exposure. In fact, most of the "rights" she began to assert had clear Islamic backing. And no well-read Muslim could argue against them.

"You gotta love our religion," was her favorite closing statement after asserting a right that was given to the Muslim women that many would be unaware of. She would purposely read Islamic books that talked about the rights of Muslim women. Many were texts that were way beyond her understanding at the young age of twelve, but she would try very hard to comprehend whatever little she could make out.

It was her zeal in learning about gender equality in Islam that fueled her desire to talk about Islam to others. People were so ignorant of all the rights she had, and she was most ready to show them off to everyone. But for now, there was work that had to get done, and Fatima had to get herself focused on unpacking.

Ayesha's mind wandered from the chores at hand, too. She was anxious to find neighbors to play with, true to her tom-boyish nature. Ideally she would have liked to form teams so that the kids on the block could play softball or volleyball, but there did not appear to be that many children close by. However, she saw two young boys, about four and five she guessed, across the street playing touch football with their father in their front lawn. She couldn't control her excitement; she tied up her hair in a ponytail and then ran across the street, leaving all the work that had to get done behind.

"Hi, I'm Ayesha and I was just wondering if I could play with you guys?" she asked.

The young father welcomed her, "Sure dear. My name is Ned. And this is Adam, and this is Dustin," pointing towards his sons.

That was the beginning of a long friendship between Ayesha and Ned and his two sons. One that always involved some sport or another. Once they were settled in their new home, Ned and his family became the first friends of the Husain family in their new neighborhood, always playing with all of the kids.

Amina was also an enthusiastic participant in the games that Ayesha would play with Dustin and Adam. She would follow Ayesha over to Ned's every time they got together.

"I wanna play too Ayesha *baji*, I wanna play too!" she would say as she ran behind Ayesha and across the street over to Ned's yard.

But Fatima was not interested in playing outside. She felt like she was too old to play with the younger kids, and that too in sports that would require a lot of pushing and shoving. She would much rather sit at home and read her Laura Ingalls Wilder books or watch 'Namak Halal.'

'Namak Halal' was the only Bollywood movie that her family owned. All the other *Desi* movies that they had watched they had rented from a lady named Madhavi, who lived in Willingboro. Madhavi knew the demand for these movies amongst the NRIs was high, so she put her Gujarati business genes to work, and purchased many tapes and began to rent them out for one dollar per movie per week. Soon, the demand for her movies was so great that one copy of each movie was not sufficient. Pirated Indian movies had become a necessity, and copies floated around in the homes of most of Fatima's family friends.

In this new neighborhood, there weren't that many Indian families, and the search for a Madhavi-type lady was fruitless, hence that one 'Namak Halal' tape became priceless. This was one thing that the family would surely miss about Willingboro.

Besides the new neighborhood, the girls were also anxious to learn about their new school district. The Pennsbury Schools were recognized for academic excellence and were known for their great facilities. And since the girls were so fond of school, Fatima and Ayesha were excited to begin the academic year and taste what the new schools had to offer. Fatima would commence school at Pennwood Middle School while Ayesha and Amina were both enrolled at Eleanor Roosevelt Elementary. Malikah was only a year old and enjoying her time with Mummy at home.

At first sight Pennwood looked massive. Bookbinder was a one story facility that accommodated about five hundred students, while Pennwood was home to double that number of pupils. The school was easily twice the size of Bookbinder if not larger. It was a large two story brick building that had a white clock tower in its center. The grounds of the school were nicely landscaped and the surrounding homes were obviously owned by members of the upper middle class. Within its confines were at least two gardens that were conscientiously nurtured and admired by students and teachers alike.

Inside, Pennwood was just as well maintained. The attractive school had an indoor pool and two large gymnasiums, one for the boys and one for the girls. The auditorium was massive. It must have seated at least six hundred people. It was initially confusing to find where homeroom was within this large building, but Fatima, with the help of some teachers, managed to find her way into the newly built 'B' wing that housed the sixth grade.

In an air conditioned room that had wall to wall carpeting Fatima found her way to a newer desk that had papers with her name upon it. She sat down and silently observed her new surroundings.

Fatima was immediately struck by the fact that she was one of only a handful of students who were not Caucasian. She could not find any student in her homeroom that was Indian or even Asian. Bookbinder was very diverse with an equal division of Whites and Blacks in addition to some Asians and Hispanics. But Pennwood appeared to be nothing like that.

Her new classmates were predominantly well dressed mini-yuppies that were sporting shoes and purses of name brands that Fatima had only heard of before. The eleven to twelve year old girls were already wearing makeup, and were doused in perfumes that you could smell a mile away. Many had their hair permed and their nails manicured.

Not a pair of jeans was in sight that wasn't of the Guess? label nor did anyone carry a backpack that wasn't either Eastpak or Jansport. All of this upper class trendiness was overwhelming for Fatima. It was as if she was experiencing, yet again, some type of culture shock.

While mentally recording all of the aspects of her new environment Fatima began to skim through the stack of papers on her desk. On top was a schedule that listed all the classes that she was taking along with the name of the teacher that would be instructing the class. As she was reading her schedule the loudspeaker turned on. A voice over the speaker asked all the students to rise while the national anthem was played. Fatima dutifully stood up, but some of her peers were too busy carrying on their conversations to stand. Fatima shook her head in disappointment. Mrs. Jonus, from the head of the class, scolded the young women who would not stop talking.

"Disrespect to the national anthem will not be tolerated," she informed the girls.

Fatima heartily agreed; their behavior was unacceptable. 'Maybe these girls are too rich to have to show respect to their country,' Fatima thought.

Once the anthem was over the students pledged their allegiance to the flag and sat down at their desks. Yet again the thought of an attendance check worried Fatima. The threat seemed to be even more severe here as there seemed to be no ethnic names that the teachers would have been exposed to. When Mrs. Jonus called out the names on her roster, Fatima prepared for the worst. Once it was her name's turn Mrs. Jonus very politely turned to Fatima, the only person in the class that would obviously have a different name, and asked

"Dear, could you please say your name so that I don't mispronounce it?"

Fatima was caught off guard with this question. No one had ever done this before, but to her relief she simply stated her name and the teacher moved on. No weird looks and no giggling came from the students; actually no one seemed to have even cared. Fatima was all of a sudden pleased with the way her day was starting.

The week went on and Fatima began to familiarize herself with her classes and teachers. She had met a girl named Aliza, who was in most of her classes and with whom she began to talk frequently. Aliza was also new to the district and this was a nice bond to have shared in a school where most of the friendships were being carried on amongst peers from elementary school.

Lunch had become a less stressful event as Fatima was now packing her own lunches with items like PBJ sandwiches and chips, food that was a lot less odorous than the *Desi* lunches that her mother had dutifully packed in the years past. Soon enough she had made enough acquaintances to occupy a table. Aliza, Carmen, Tara, and Fatima would all sit together and enjoy their lunch.

Curiously enough, even without any of her classmates saying anything Fatima became very conscious of what she was wearing. In a school packed with Calvin Kleins and Z. Cavariccis, her wardrobe seemed below par. Her parents had always shopped at large department stores such as Sears and K-Mart, but amongst these students those were retailers fit for paupers. The clothes conscious girls would readily discuss their shopping habits and mention all the trendy *and* pricey stores from which they would purchase their overpriced clothes and accessories.

Fatima knew that her family could not afford to spend ninety dollars on a single pair of pants nor seventy dollars on a designer purse for her to wear to school. But in an effort to better assimilate into her new environment Fatima discovered the beauty of TJ Maxx. All the fashionable labels at half the price. But even these prices were pushing it for Fatima's family. They were a humble unit that would always wear home sewn clothes and items that came off of a sale rack. Now Fatima felt uneasy doing either. This was a change that began to frustrate her parents.

Fatima's father scolded his daughter, "When I was your age I owned two shirts and two pairs of slacks. And there were times when I would have to share those with my brothers."

He maintained that he carefully washed and ironed those clothes and kept them in perfect condition for years just so his parents would never feel the need to purchase new clothes for their son.

"I would never want to add any burdens upon my parents," he said.

"Whatever I had I was happy with and I knew what we were able to afford."

"Yes Daddy, I know. You not only look like Lincoln, but you act like him as well," Fatima sarcastically interrupted.

Fatima's father was not pleased with his daughter's rudeness.

"You children have no idea how difficult it is to earn a few bucks. You just go out and spend like there is a money tree growing in our backyard. You don't have any idea how hard your father works. You should thank God for all his blessings and just wear what you have. In fact why don't you first keep the things you have well. Why are there clothes on the floor in your room?"

And the subject then changed to keeping her bedroom clean. Unfortunately, all of this admonition fell on deaf ears.

Demands for brand names escalated and lectures from her parents about humbleness increased.

"Half of the clothes that your schoolmates wear are not suitable for Muslim girls," was an overused statement in the Husain household to get across the point that Fatima would never be able to dress like her peers, even if she could afford it.

Fatima's mother occasionally felt for Fatima and her pathetic need to fit in. On those rare occasions, she secretly took her girls to TJ Maxx and indulged them with one item each. A hidden gesture of love and understanding that was invaluable in Fatima's eyes. This was enough for her to thrive on.

Soon Fatima realized that despite her reformed wardrobe, she was still not fitting into the puzzle of Pennwood as well as she would have liked. It was a strange desire for her to develop as she never worked so hard to fit in at Bookbinder, simply accepting that the friends that she had in her parents' social circle were her true friends, and her classmates were merely acquaintances. But during middle school this all changed. Insecurity heightened and the differences between her family and her peers seemed profound.

Fatima found herself running out of her bedroom into the kitchen to grab a quick bite and bolting into the car early in the mornings just so she would avoid contaminating her clothes with the smell of the fried onions and curries that were already beginning to cook on their kitchen stove.

"I gotta run Mom, I am late and I need to get out before I stink. *Khuda hafiz!*" Fatima would say to her mother.

Once she was in the car, she would sift through her purse and locate a small vial of perfume that was forever there, ready to be splashed upon her clothes so that any trace of the scent of *Desi* cuisine was effectively masked. Although she may have looked Indian - a point of contention to some as her height, hair color, and complexion didn't fit the mold of the average *Desi*-Fatima didn't want to smell like an Indian or even dress like one, at least not in school. She tried desperately to dress cool, carry trendy accessories, and wear nice perfumes. Her pants were always rolled up about a half inch above her ankle as this was the latest fad. Fatima's father found this particular trend extremely irritating. He didn't understand why the kids were rolling up their pants, and in an attempt to mock Fatima he would walk around their home with his slacks rolled up.

"Look, am I as cool as Fatima?" he would sarcastically ask his other daughters.

Fatima would humor him, thinking that her immigrant father would never understand the dynamics of the American social scene, as if she had a clue.

Interestingly, the Social Sciences were discussed in great detail at Pennwood. The introduction to international cultures in these classes was the first exposure of its kind to many of the students there. The MG (Mentally Gifted) Program, for which Fatima had qualified, was exceptional in its effort to teach about the understanding, tolerance, and appreciation of foreign cultures. Mr. Snifer, a teacher whom she had heard was a friend of all intellectuals, made his classes an open venue to discuss and vent about anything. His was a class that all of the students loved attending. Their opinions were welcome, and finally here was a teacher who was willing to talk with them and not down to them.

A few students whose families were recent immigrants were tapped by Mr. Snifer to enlighten the majority on what riches these foreign societies and cultures had to offer to the "melting pot" or "salad bowl" of the US. Diya, one of the few obviously Indian students that Fatima had spotted in the hallways was asked about India. Sadly, she showed great hesitation in responding to her teacher's questions.

"Umm... ...Well....Ummm.... I am not sure that I am the best person to answer that Mr. Snifer. I really don't know much about the people over there. I don't even remember the last time I saw India, my parents are the ones that visit but even they haven't gone in 10 years. Our lives are too busy here to go to there."

It was apparent that her cultural baggage was not something that Diya wanted to discuss. This made Fatima feel even more isolated. She had felt that even though Diya and she had not become friends, they still had a connection because they were both from the same background, growing up in a world that was nothing like that of their parents'. However, Diya's visible reluctance to discuss India made it very clear that it was her parents that were Indian, not her.

On the other hand, Joe Shinto, a first generation immigrant from Korea, was asked to tell his peers about his native country and did so with great enthusiasm. Joe brought in Korean handicrafts, clothes, and even elementary textbooks, and offered all the information he possibly could about the country he had left behind. Fatima wished that the few other Indians that were in the school would have shared the same passion for their heritage as Joe did for his.

Religions were also discussed, and for the first time Islam was brought up in a classroom setting outside of Sunday school for Fatima. The teachers were thrilled to have a real live Muslim in their midst that was willing to share whatever she could about her religion.

"Fatima, could you please share what you know about your faith with us?" was a common request, to which Fatima happily obliged.

Being the only Muslim in her school, Fatima was delighted to convey her thoughts and opinions on what the school texts had to say about her faith. All that most of the students knew about Islam was linked to the Ayotollah Khomeini, who Fatima knew little about as she was Sunni; or the fact that Muslim men were allowed to have four wives, not one of whom Fatima had ever met or even heard of. Or that most Muslim women they saw in the media were draped from head to toe in black *chadors*, a type of covering that Fatima came across with in Hyderabad. Beyond that there was little that anybody knew about her religion.

Fatima took this as an opportunity to discuss not only the fundamentals of her creed, but also the rights of women in Islam.

"Did you know Islam grants women the sole right to their money and total access to her husband's money, while clearly denying the man access to his wife's money? In other words, what's my Mom's is my Mom's and what's Daddy's is hers too," she stated to a captivated audience.

Generally, the exposure that most of these students had to Islam would remain limited to their real live Muslim classmate, but there were a few well read students, like straight arrow Peter Stroffers, who would put together interesting details, such as the fact that Fatima shared the same last name as the King Hussain of Jordan. Peter was a bright student who Fatima took a liking to because of his respectful nature. He was a polite young man who was intelligent and very friendly. Although she could not be a good friend to him, he was a kind boy whom she enjoyed talking to. Fatima explained to Peter, "Husain in the Muslim world is a very common name, kind of like Johnson or Smith is here."

Peter nodded and listened to Fatima's explanation about her last name without any further enquiry; but this was before her name took on a whole new burden in the years to follow.

With the ability to openly discuss religion came some independence from the fictional stories that she had told as a young girl about her family commemorating all the holidays that her classmates observed. She no longer needed to pretend that her family celebrated occasions other than their own, and she became confident in voicing her religious beliefs on many subjects.

"It's funny. I think back to when I was in elementary school, and how I used to pretend to celebrate all holidays just so I could feel like I was a part of the American culture. Now I realize that even if I don't observe Christmas or Easter, I am still part of this culture. And that doesn't diminish my American identity," Fatima told her peers.

"Didn't your classmates realize that Muslims don't celebrate Christmas?" a classmate asked of her.

"No, they didn't. Do you think that most Americans even know what Muslims believe? All they know about Muslims is the stereotypical nonsense they see on TV. I don't think that most people know much about Muslims, let alone first and second graders," Fatima replied.

Fatima was well aware that the media continuously portrayed a negative image of Islam and Muslims to the common folk. She knew that the majority of Americans were not being exposed to what the bulk of the Muslim world believed or how they lived their lives. This was her opportunity to change that in the lives of the few people that she would come into contact with.

She took this responsibility very seriously, and did her best to help her peers and teachers see Islam and Muslims under a new light. Fatima's dialogues, as well as her own actions, introduced a new window to view Islam and Muslims with.

Ironically, the difference in faiths that existed between Fatima and her peers didn't bother her at all. In fact Fatima thought that if she would make her beliefs clear to her fellow classmates, some of the ideological variations that existed between them would be addressed and clarified. After all, Muslims had much in common with the other two monotheistic faiths, Christianity and Judaism, than most would acknowledge.

Clearly Fatima was not a scholar in her faith, and she had much to learn. Her over-sheltered lifestyle became very apparent when her friends would discuss topics like sex, where prudish Fatima would confidently declare that it (sex) was against her religion. Her more mature classmates knew that this was an absurd statement and asked her, "Well how did you get here then?" Her response was blunt and simple; "In the same way Jesus was born," she would say, to the horror of her Catholic peers. But that was truly what she believed. No one would ever talk about *the* subject with her. No one even discussed what puberty was. If it weren't for her fifth grade health class Fatima wouldn't even have known what a period was. But that's the way conservative Muslim *Desi* families functioned. One would learn what they needed to learn when they absolutely had to, either through a book or maybe a friend, but never through their parents.

While boyfriends and girlfriends roamed the halls of Pennwood hand in hand Fatima knew she was never to carry on in that manner. It had been made very clear to her by her family and Muslim ideals that her mate would be a permanent one, like that of all 'good' Muslim men and women. Her religion had made it very clear that relationships out of wedlock were unholy and defiant to the will of God.

"The bottom line is that these relationships are frivolous," explained her parents. They would result in "a disturbed youth" and "certain heartbreak." It was not the "stuff that good Muslims would waste their time on" as her parents put it. Thus when school dances were becoming important events in the lives of middle school students, Fatima had to make it very clear that she would not participate in events of this nature.

"I can't go to the dances because a lot off stuff happens there that I just can't do, and at this point I don't care to do," she would explain to her friends.

This did not mean that she wasn't curious as to what actually took place at these gatherings; but she figured now that she was older and the tight TV restrictions were slowly being lifted, she could watch any TV show that featured teenagers. These shows would fill her in on what dances were all about, and if she wasn't satisfied with the television shows she could always rent movies like "Ferris Bueller's Day Off" that would definitely expose her to what she was missing out on. In Fatima's limited understanding, the best part was that she would not have to deal with all the issues that would come with going to or being at a dance. She didn't have to deal with boys and girls slobbering all over themselves in an attempt to imitate what they saw on TV. That was just pure nastiness in her eyes. And in the end they all left each other anyway. 'Who wanted to be a part of that?' she thought. But not everyone understood how she felt.

"Man you can't do anything, what a sad life," Joan, the notorious school bully, talked down to Fatima.

"No Joan, it's not that bad," Fatima tried to interject.

"Yeah right, you can't party, you can't have a boyfriend, you can't do jack- that's really pathetic. I am so glad not to be you," she said to a miffed Fatima. Joan had a knack at hurting people.

Fatima was unsure of how to react. She knew that part of what Joan said was true, but she really believed that none of those things were priorities in her life. She didn't care to go to the dances; she didn't want to party like the other kids, sneaking off and drinking from their parents' bars. It was just not her scene.

"You know Joan I have more fulfilling things to do with myself than get drunk or desperately seek a boyfriend. I don't need that stuff to make my life complete," she harshly replied.

"Try getting a boyfriend and you will see what you're missing out on," Joan replied with a brazen smile.

"If getting laid after the dance is what you're talking about – I would rather not get screwed. Do you have any idea what could happen if he has a VD? Or if you got pregnant? Are you ready to take on that responsibility?" she smugly replied and stormed off without waiting for Joan's response.

Fatima had let Joan have it, and she felt really good about it. The irony was that Fatima didn't know much about getting laid or pregnant; she just knew that these things were related to having boyfriends. She also heard that having a boyfriend can lead to getting a VD, but how that exactly occurred was something she had no idea about. But all Fatima wanted was to put Joan in her place. She wasn't going to be bullied into doubting herself or her beliefs. Restrictions or no restrictions, she had defined herself based on her faith and a sense of practicality that was well beyond her years. And she was proud of it.

The dances were not the only thing that Fatima avoided. She did not take the sex education classes that Pennwood health teachers were teaching once a week during gym period. Fatima's parents did not feel it necessary for their twelve year old daughter to know all about human sexuality at an age when they strongly believed that she would have no use of this knowledge. This knowledge would come in due time when it would be applicable to her personal life, but in middle school it was, in their opinion, absurd. So while all the children were in sex ed Fatima would sit in study hall. Hence her knowledge about sex remained that of a ten year old for many years to come. In fact in her prudish mind, Muslims didn't have sex. The word itself was taboo, let alone the act, whatever that actually entailed. It was just a subject that wasn't discussed and the word wasn't even used for its other meaning. 'Gender' was the preferred word to utilize.

The gym uniform presented a dilemma for Fatima as well. The orange t-shirt could slide but the black shorts were not Islamically acceptable. Fatima had to secure permission from her gym teachers to wear sweat pants on top of her gym shorts, resulting in numerous comments and questions being asked by her classmates.

"You must be hot," Carmen condescendingly remarked to Fatima as she passed by her while running the mile.

"No, I am fine," responded a pink faced Fatima.

"I don't know how you could not want to wear shorts."

"It seems to bother you more than me, Carmen", replied an annoyed Fatima while shaking her head and shrugging her shoulders.

Everybody was hot when they were running the mile so what's the big deal with her sweatpants? Fatima was not bothered by the extra layer of clothing on her legs; she wore slacks or jeans most of the time anyway. It wasn't as if she was abstaining from gym, she simply modified the gym uniform to suit her beliefs. She had become very accustomed to doing this throughout her life.

Swimming was also a gym requirement, and that too was a concern that needed to be addressed. Wearing simply the swimsuit was out of the question, so this too had to be modified with long sleeve spandex shirts and leggings that had to be worn under the black one piece suit.

The aspect of swimming that most disturbed Fatima was how freely the girls would undress in front of one another. She would change in and out of her swimsuit in the toilet stall, while all the other girls would have no problem getting naked in front of each other. This was totally contradictory to all the Islamic values of modesty that Fatima had been taught since childhood.

"Jeez Fatima, why do you have to hide in the stall? It's not like we are all checking you out," Joan called out in a condescending tone. But Fatima would much rather deal with those types of comments than undress publicly.

"I just don't feel comfortable changing out there," she replied.

This was just another accommodation that she had made to balance the two worlds she was growing up in.

On top of all those restrictions, her overprotective parents did not allow Fatima to participate in any after school sports unsure of what environment these settings may provide.

"All those girls out there half dressed running around in front of men. It's shameless," her mother would say.

And her father thought that sports were for boys not girls, so he didn't think it was necessary for her to pursue any type of athletic activity. His advice was, "Just focus on your studies. That is what you are in school for." Although she had the desire to join a few intra mural activities, it was never enough of a thirst to actually argue with her parents over. She realized that she was totally uncoordinated and unable to get an A in gym, let alone excel at any sport. At best she received an A- , since her effort was sincere. The lack of any of these physical activities did take a toll on her. She was not as fit as her classmates were, and the Presidential Physical Fitness Test was probably the only test in her life that she near failed. She was always amongst the last that was chosen to be on any sports teams and even though this bothered her, Fatima knew that she wasn't a good sportswoman so why would anyone choose her first to play on their teams? In fact, she would make herself feel better by thinking that at least she wasn't the very last one chosen.

Since there was no emphasis placed on being a successful athlete (and no physical talent to even make that possible) Fatima had no desire to be good at any sport. She just had to do well academically, and her parents would be pleased. So she focused her attention on academically challenging tasks. That was why the only after school activity that her parents allowed to her to participate in was the Olympics of the Mind (OM), as that was an educational venture that stimulated intellectual growth.

But even these types of activities had to be thoroughly explained and clarified to her family.

"Daddy, this is something that only smart kids do, it's not a place where druggies show up," Fatima explained.

It had to be made clear that there would be no drugs, alcohol, or promiscuous behavior taking place in the school within the realms of such activities. The OM team was, in the crudest terms, a group of nerds, which as most people know, generally lag far behind in making any advances in the forbidden fields.

Fatima and her sisters realized that their activities after school hours would never be school based, and they accepted that fact. Their parents were mortified of losing their daughter's religious and cultural identities to what they viewed as the dissolute values of America that they witnessed on racy TV shows. They had to do whatever they could to raise righteous daughters in an environment that seemed to foster sex, drugs, and alcohol. This is why the girls' pastimes were encouraged to be focused around their home, family, and their masjid.

Chapter 4

As Fatima's father began to take on more responsibility at the masjid, her family became very involved in its events, most importantly Sunday school.

"Let's go! Its 9:45! Classes start in fifteen minutes," Fatima's father would shout every Sunday morning.

The girls would race down the stairs, jump into their car and be off to the masjid. The "refugee van" was no longer in service, but Fatima's father was still driving his daughters to Sunday school.

The first class the girls had was taught by Syed Uncle. He taught Islamic history from the time of the Prophet Adam to the time of the last prophet, Muhammad.

"I would like you all to tell me who some of the greatest messengers of God were." Syed uncle said as soon as everyone settled down.

"Abraham!" shouted Rubi.

"Yes, very good. But let's raise our hands please. Mona, your turn," Syed Uncle said pointing towards the young girl.

"Moses," Mona replied.

"Good. Now you Irfan."

"Noah," Irfan responded.

"Good. Any more?" Uncle asked.

"Ishmaeel!" Afia exclaimed.

"Yes! and…?"

"Jesus," Fatima answered.

"Definitely. Do you see how many of these great Prophets were sent to mankind? We didn't even mention Isaac, Solomon, David, John the Baptist...the list goes on and on. Now I want you to tell me what they all have in common?" Syed Uncle continued.

"We believe they were all Muslim," Fatima replied.

"Exactly! Muslim simply means one who submits to the will of God and all of these great Prophets did just that. They carried out God's message to mankind. They were sent for all of us and are a part of world history. In fact they are part of *our* history!" Uncle taught the class.

Fatima loved his class. The more she learned the more she wanted to know. Every bit of information that she absorbed, was not only for her benefit, but a part of her was anxious to share this knowledge with her peers at school. Somebody had to let them know what Muslims were really like.

The second class was a bit more difficult but it was an imperative course of study. The students would sit with a *Hafiz*, one who memorized the entire Qur'an, and learn the art of *Tajweed* - the skill of proper Quranic recitation.

The proper manner of pronunciation glorified and brought out the beauty of the Qur'an and was a must for these children to understand. These classes nurtured the Islamic spirit within the hearts of these children and helped them develop into "good Muslims".

It never stopped to amaze her how different her Islamic lessons were from what they were perceived to be by her peers at Pennwood. What Fatima wanted to express to her peers at Pennwood was that not one of her Sunday school classes discussed "fundamentalist" ideology or ideas that would parallel the so called "sword of Islam". In fact Fatima never understood what this "sword" was. The classes she took were more like the CCD classes that her Christian peers would take or the Jewish studies courses that her Jewish classmates would go to.

After *Tajweed* class ended, the *adhaan* could be heard over the loudspeaker.

"Okay, it's time for *Dhuhr* prayer. I want you to wrap up what you were reading and prepare surah 101 for next week," the teacher said as he began to put away his texts.

"But I am not sure about all the rules of surah 100 yet. Should I still on move on to the next chapter?" Rubi inquired.

"Try to do both."

"Both? Are you serious?" Rubi replied with an attitude.

"*Yes*, I am. You know young lady that is not how we respond to our elders. That kind of slang is not appreciated and will not be tolerated."

Rubi turned pink.

"I didn't mean it to come out that way Uncle. I was just surprised at your response."

"If you can organize your day such that you can devote even ten minutes to this class you will do fine."

"*Inshallah*, I will try my best."

"I know you will," he replied as he picked up his books and left the classroom.

Rubi left the class with red cheeks and a warm forehead. She was clearly embarrassed by the teacher's scolding.

"I can't believe I showed him attitude," she said as she shook her head disapprovingly. "It just slipped out," she told Fatima while they were both performing their ablution in preparation for *Dhuhr*.

"I was shocked you said it the way you did too. You know, with respect being so important to the elders," Fatima answered as she washed her arms while sitting on the stools that were placed in the ablution area.

Rubi joined Fatima on an adjacent bench and began to take off her socks so that she too could properly perform the rites of the ablution.

"I know I have to work on it. My parents are always telling me how Muslims need to address everyone respectfully, and how people were in awe of the sweet language and proper etiquette shown by our ancestors."

"Just last week we were reading that the majority of people who converted to Islam did so based on their interaction with Muslims during trade. It wasn't this 'so called sword of Islam' that converted people to the religion was the Muslim attitude and lifestyle," Mona interjected.

Turning back to look at her Rubi responded, "Can you imagine telling that to the world today?"

"They would laugh at us," Fatima replied.

"Their laughing doesn't make that untrue. We know our history. We know that violence wasn't the only answer. We need to share that reality with everyone. Why should we allow everyone to continue believing that Muslims are violent people?" Mona retorted.

"That is soooo true Mona," Rubi acknowledged. "How many of us have any desire to harm anyone? Nor do we approve of all the violence that's carried out in Islam's name."

"Exactly! That is what we need to let everybody know," Mona advised.

"And the best way to do that is through our actions, at the risk of sounding cliché," Fatima replied.

"Okay, now I definitely know that my attitude has to stop here," Rubi remarked while drying her feet.

"That holds true for all of us, Rubi. Whether we like it or not, we represent Islam. It's a responsibility that has been placed on our shoulders by our society," Mona added.

"Does that mean I can't tell off my snotty classmates anymore?" Fatima jokingly inquired.

"Well… let's not go that far……" Mona lightheartedly replied. "Some of those Pennwood girls need to hear it from someone."

"Amen to that!" Fatima loudly responded, as the girls all laughed and left for the prayer hall. "But only some, everyone isn't a Joan you know…"

Unlike the image of Muslims that most Westerners had of practicing Muslims, these girls were simply American youth growing up in immigrant families while carrying on their religious traditions. They were being taught to respect their families, their ideologies, and the laws of the land they were now citizens of. Ideas that no sane person would find disturbing or dangerous.

The Husain girls were also encouraged to read about other religions and participate in comparative religious studies. Their father knew that they lived in a country that was predominantly Christian, and that there was also a sizable Jewish population in their locality. He felt strongly that his daughters must be aware of what was going on in the world around them, and he felt that the best way to learn that was by educating themselves about the people they were dealing with on a daily basis. Therefore the girls would watch inter faith dialogues that would enrich them with a level of theological knowledge that surpassed most of their peers at school.

All of these studies would prove to strengthen their faith, even in a country where it seemed that the news broadcasts, papers, as well as Hollywood effectively defamed Islam.

As much as Fatima wanted to be accepted by her schoolmates, the one difference that she was proud of was her faith. This was the only aspect in which she had no desire to assimilate. She knew she was Muslim and she knew she was American; both were integral parts of her unique identity. The same realization held true for most of the children her age that were part of this community.

Friendships that blossomed from Sunday school turned out to be life long because the closeness amongst these children was fostered by their parents. Their community was small and tight, and they would have it no other way.

The Husains' social circle in the vicinity of Trenton was expanding, as some of their friendships from Willingboro were beginning to slip away. Many families had now left the Willingboro area in favor of living close to the masjid, and were seen regularly at the masjid activities. These families continued to meet at their monthly dinners, which were now taking place in all of their new homes.

But the families left behind were surely missed.

"Mummy, why don't the girls from Willingboro come to our parties now? I am really missing them."

"*Beta*, it's not easy for them to drive so far on the two days that their parents have off. They all have their responsibilities too. It's a bit much for them to keep coming here."

"But that stinks. We hardly see them anymore. The only people we see are the ones who moved around here along with us," Ayesha replied.

"Unfortunately that's probably the way it will be from now on," her father said as he picked Amina up and sat her in his lap. He turned his head towards all the girls, "You girls have to make new friends that you can play with around here. This doesn't mean that your old friends will no longer be your friends. It's just that you will have to become better acquainted with kids your age from this area too, because that's who you will be seeing more often now."

The girls knew that this was a sad reality, but it could not be changed. They loved their new home and new neighborhood, and having to make new friends was part of the package too, they guessed.

The local Muslim community was rapidly expanding due to the proximity of the masjid. This was in large part due to the *Jumma* prayers, which are equivalent to the Sunday Service for most Christians. *Jumma* prayers take place on Friday afternoon, and because of the convenient location of the masjid, many Muslims would gather there to participate in the prayers.

The religious activities that the masjid offered were soon followed by social activities. The masjid was especially busy in the month of *Ramadan*, the holy month in which Muslims fast from dawn to dusk. Since the Islamic calendar is a lunar calendar, *Ramadan* was not a predetermined month in relation to the Gregorian calendar. Every year the month of *Ramadan* would occur in a different time frame than the year before, and the Muslim world would begin abstaining from food and drink during the light hours.

It had become a tradition for all the members of the masjid to congregate at the time of sunset on the weekends so that they could all break their fasts together with an elaborate *iftaar*.

A feast was served at every gathering that was held in the masjid in this holy month. The aunties would form groups, each of which would take turns cooking for the entire community each Saturday night.

On the first Saturday of this *Ramadan*, Fatima's mother was responsible for cooking *alu khorma*, meat and potato curry, and *kheer*, rice pudding, for the one hundred anticipated guests.

"Fatima and Ayesha, please start peeling the potatoes. I need to cut and toss them in the *khorma*," their mother requested.

"Mummy, what if more than one hundred people show up, will we have enough food?" Ayesha inquired as she skinned the potatoes in the sink with the hand peeler.

"*Beta*, why do you ask such questions? Can't you see that I am stressed enough about the quantity of the food," her mother anxiously replied while wiping her brow. She was vigorously stirring the huge pot of curry on the stove making sure that it would not burn against the bottom of the pan. Steam from the pot wafted over their mother's face. With her hair all strewn and apron tied tight, their mother looked like an overstressed Indian *bawarchi*. But not that mother minded the work! This venture was something that everyone *chose* to do as a community service. It was regarded as a task that merited great reward and was well worth the labor, especially in this holy month.

While Fatima, Ayesha, and their mother worked in the kitchen, their father was busy at the masjid. He was planning out the logistics of this evening's dinner along with the other uncles that were tonight's hosts. Everything would have to be efficiently organized so that dinner could be immediately followed by the masjid's *Ramadan* activities. The most important event of which were the special prayers delegated to this holy month, the *Taraweeh*.

Taraweeh prayers were long, and required a lot of concentration. Each night's prayer service for *Taraweeh* alone could exceed one hour. The goal was to recite the entire Qur'an in these prayers during this holy month. Despite its length, the local Muslims were anxious to participate and focus on God for that period of time. They would even invite *Huffaz*, people who have memorized the entire Qur'an, to the masjid so that they could lead the prayers in the most beautiful *Qiraat*, recitation. In addition to making the *Taraweeh* prayers, much of the Muslim community would spend this month in acts of charity, community service, and reflection upon their mortality and the impending Afterlife.

After the busy month of *Ramadan* ended, Fatima had to prepare for her final exams. She gathered her notes and reviewed them casually over the last week of school. Without much stress or effort, Fatima passed her exams with flying colors. Overjoyed she shared the news with her parents.

"Daddy you won't believe what I got on my finals?! You are going to be so thrilled!" she gasped as she handed her report card to her father.

Her father grinned happily upon sight of the report card.

"I expect no less from *my* daughter."

"As if only her paternal genes contributed to her intellect," her mother sarcastically interjected into the conversation.

"You have a part in this too. *Some* part…" he said while laughing at his own humor.

"I should have expected this. Everything good comes from your family's genes, doesn't it?" Mummy responded dryly.

"Don't bust your brain honey," her father laughingly responded. "The girls are what they are because of you."

"Good to know that you realize that," she replied in an annoyed tone.

In an attempt to change the subject Fatima's father told Fatima that he had some good news for her.

"You know your mother and I have wanted to go to *Hajj* for a while now. We have thought long and hard about this trip. We initially thought that we would go on our own, but we decided against that because you all are old enough now to come and enjoy the experience with us. Of course, it will not be easy, but we are one family and we must work together to accomplish the goal. So *inshallah* we will be going on the *Hajj* next month. Pray that God accepts our intention and accepts our *Hajj*," Daddy said to the girls. The girls started jumping and shouting in glee.

"I can't believe it!" Fatima screamed.

"This is going to be sooooo coooooool!!" Ayesha shouted while jumping up and down her hands flying in the air.

Chapter 5

The Husain girls had learned about the *Hajj* in Sunday school and from their Islamic text books. They knew that the *Hajj* was a journey to Mecca, that every Muslim was obligated to make once in their lifetime, health and finances permitting. It would be a five day experience in which many rites and rituals would be performed. It was not going to be an easy task, but the girls were ready to take it on. They were unable to fathom that they were actually going to visit the holiest of cities and be the guests of God. They could not contain their excitement and with great anticipation they began to pack for this holy pilgrimage.

"I think we need to keep sun screen because we will all get sunburn there," Ayesha remarked.

"No silly, we will not. We will have on our *hijaabs* and have everything else covered, so where can we get sun burn?" Fatima replied.

"Well Daddy should keep it then," Ayesha said as she tossed her bottle of Coppertone in his suitcase.

"You should worry more about packing comfortable clothes. It's going to be super hot and we have to stay in tents without any a/c," Fatima told Ayesha.

That was Fatima's biggest fear. How would they deal with the heat? They had thought India's heat was bad, and India wasn't even a desert country. Who knew what the desert heat would be like? It was something they had only heard of, yet couldn't imagine. Fatima comforted herself by thinking, 'Somehow we will manage. Every other *Hajji* does and so will we.' After all, their minds would be on other things when they were in the holy cities of Mecca and Madinah.

It was a nine-hour flight to Saudi Arabia, and the heat of the desert blazed into the plane once the exit door was ajar. Luckily there was no stench that overwhelmed the family like what they experienced in India, but the blistering sun blinded them as they walked down the portable stairs.

Under the scorching intensity of the desert sun, the Husains arrived at the massive *Hajj* terminal at Jeddah International Airport. Jeddah was the gateway city into Saudi Arabia, situated off of the Red Sea. Located about an hour and a half away from the holy city of Mecca, it was the first stop for the two million pilgrims who were expected to converge upon Mecca for the annual pilgrimage.

As far as her eyes could see Fatima saw an ocean of pilgrims. White, Black, Red, Yellow, and Brown, the pilgrims came in all colors and sizes. The American delegation of five hundred pilgrims seemed minute compared to the thousands upon thousands that were there from all across the globe.

"Wow, this is unbelievable. Who knew that there were so many different types of Muslims?" Ayesha said.

"I thought I had a clue, but this is just amazing!" replied Fatima.

"Do you think most of them can speak Arabic?" Ayesha asked her sister.

"I doubt they can, but I bet you anything they can read and recite it," Fatima responded.

"Duh," Ayesha rolled her eyes.

Fatima chose to ignore her. There was too much going on around her to keep her from being bothered by her little sister. She scanned the multitude and took in all that was unfolding in this new world.

The male pilgrims were all dressed in two sheets of white cloth called the *ihraam*, and the women covered in their *jilbabs* concealing everything but their face and hands. Everyone was marching into the airport while chanting the *talbiyah* which states, "Here I am Lord at your Service..." Overwhelmed at this site Fatima felt a shiver down her spine.

Once the formalities of customs and immigration were complete the pilgrims began to board buses that were waiting outside the *Hajj* terminal, anxious to get the pilgrims to Mecca. The Husains made their way to a long bus with small flags of the US and Canada posted in the upper right hand corner of the windshield. They allowed a worker to load their luggage upon the roof, but the girls watched their bags like hawks. They had learned their lesson with the baggage handlers in India and weren't about to be conned twice.

Meanwhile, their father stepped into the vehicle, and with his broken Arabic he tried to speak with the driver. After a couple of failed attempts, he simply showed his family's American passports and the driver welcomed them on to the bus with open arms, *"Akhi Amreeki."* (my American brother)

They boarded the air conditioned transport and once it was full, the pilgrims again began to chant the *talbiyah*. Little Malikah was the youngest pilgrim on that bus, yet even she would recite with enthusiasm, attempting to repeat what all the others were cantillating.

Once they left the city of Jeddah, enormous quantities of sand swallowed the landscape. Fatima, Ayesha, and Amina looked out their windows in awe at the barren, desolate desert. There was no greenery in sight, the only colors that seemed to exist in the Arabian landscape were brown and black, brown being the desert sand and black being the mountains that were dispersed throughout the arid region. Just as anticipated, they saw tall humped camels strutting in the breezy sand.

"Mummy! Look! Camels! Like the ones in our house," shouted an excited Amina, referring to some decoration pieces that sat in their living room back in Morrisville.

The camels were much like those that they had seen in books about the Middle East. They had even seen a few at the Philadelphia Zoo, but to see a camel in its actual habitat was fascinating.

In the vast desert they also spotted some tents where the nomadic Bedouins would take rest until they moved on to their next destination. Excited at experiencing a world totally alien to theirs, the girls couldn't stop chatting with each other about how cool it was to be in the land of the Last Prophet.

"How do you think they traveled back then? It's just too hot to ride on a camel! And imagine that too for days so they could get from city to city! Do you think the Prophet rode through this valley? Do you think he would recognize this place if he saw it now?"

They couldn't believe that they were driving through the places where all the Islamic history that they had learned so much about took place some fourteen hundred years ago.

As the bus approached the border of Mecca, the girls finished munching on the travel sized goodies that their mother had packed in her travel bag. Fatima quietly pulled out the book she was reading, The Guide to *Hajj* published by the Saudi Ministry of Information. In this small paperback, every step of the *Hajj* was outlined along with the proper prayer(s) to make at each stage. She had read this book multiple times in preparation for the *Hajj* but she figured there was no harm in reading it once more. As the bus full of pilgrims began to slow down Ayesha shook Fatima's arm and said, "Look! Look outside!" as she pointed to a traffic jam like no other that the girls had ever witnessed. A swarm of busses was waiting in a line that seemed to extend endlessly, in order to enter the city. There were security checkpoints and booths situated around the border of Mecca; gates through which every vehicle would have to pass. Upon sight of the jam that flooded the gates, Fatima moaned in disappointment, "Aaaaaaw" as she slumped down her shoulders. Their mother put down her Qur'an, and opened her travel bag once again. She passed around two pouches of Capri-sun for the girls to drink while they waited for the bus to reach the entry booths. As the bus stood motionless for quite some time Amina anxiously began to ask, "Are we there yet?"

Passports were collected from all the passengers and the bus driver presented them to the attendant after the hour long wait. The attendant sifted through the documents while standing in his booth, and the bus was allowed to proceed into Mecca. It took another two hours to travel a distance of six miles as the streets were jam-packed.

By this time, the girls were extremely impatient and anxious to get out of the bus. Even the passionate adults, who were so enthusiastically chanting the *talbiyah* for the longest time, had fallen silent, quietly reading their Qur'ans to themselves. They had been sitting for the past three and a half hours in the bus, on a ride that most had anticipated would last only a third of that time.

"I bet you we could get there a lot faster if we just walked," Fatima griped to her mother.

"Okay *beta*, then what about our luggage? Do we just leave it on board while we walk in a totally foreign city in search of our hotel, not knowing how to ask for directions because we can't speak the language? Think before you speak Fatima and just please try to stay calm. You are the oldest here. You need to set the best example so that your little sisters learn from you. If you act like this then how will they behave?" her exasperated mother replied.

Fatima knew all that her mother had said was true, since she had heard this lecture about one hundred times before, but the traffic jam had proven to be too much for her. The streets of this city were not built to accommodate the millions that were converging upon it, and the patience of all would be tested severely over the next five days.

By the time the Husains arrived at their relatively comfortable hotel, it was night. With the desert sun sleeping, activity seemed to have picked up and the city was bustling with excitement. The Husains unloaded their luggage and checked into their hotel room.

"Okay let's not unpack immediately. Just wash your faces and relax for a little bit," Mummy told the girls.

The family then rested for an hour and began to perform their ablution or *wudu*, in preparation for their first visit to the *Kaaba*, the house of God. The Kaaba was a large cube shaped structure draped in black velvet that stands in the center of the Masjid al Haram in Mecca. For Muslims it symbolizes the house of God and is given the respect of no other masjid in the world.

The Masjid al Haram, was less than a block away, yet the mass of pedestrians was so tremendously large that it took the family thirty minutes to arrive at its gates. But the sight of the dazzlingly lit edifice captivated its guests, such that the length of time it took to reach its gates seemed minimal.

The masjid was like the bright pearly moon against the black sky. It was a beacon of light that called out to all the pilgrims who were entranced by the beauty and enormity of it. Once the Husains reached the towering minarets they looked up, heads leaning all the way back, to capture the majesty of the soaring gate that was the entrance to the holiest of masjids.

Everyone took off their shoes and placed them in the shoe racks that were situated around every entrance, knowing full well that they may not see their flip flops again. But that was just fine. They would have to leave wearing someone else's flip flops, just like someone would most likely walk off with theirs.

As they made their way through the colossal masjid to the open courtyard where the Kaaba stood, Fatima began to notice the people that were all around her. Many were in prostration for minutes at a time while others were weeping profusely as their hands were raised in supplication. The emotions of nearly all the pilgrims were uncontrollable. Most were simply overwhelmed by their fear of and love for their Lord as they entered and laid eyes upon His Home.

Fatima too had been nervous. She was nervous to enter what was symbolic of the home of her Creator. It would be as if He was standing in front of her, a notion that she was taught was true whenever she stood in prayer. But to be in His symbolic home struck a different type of chord. She couldn't express in words what she was feeling, but it was a mix of emotions that ranged from love, fear, nervousness, and humility.

And there it was. A simple yet wondrous structure. One that millions of people the world over faced and prostrated towards everyday. In the center of the brilliantly luminous courtyard, stood the Kaaba. An onyx cube enveloped in an ocean of white marble. Like the sun being the center of our galaxy, the Kaaba stood as the center of the world for the pilgrims that had converged upon it.

Upon first sight of the Kaaba, Fatima could not stop her tears from flowing. She had never cried like this before. There was always pain or anger involved with this act, but at that moment there was neither of those feelings. She was only thirteen but her love for her Creator was deep, as was the case with almost everyone who was in that masjid. Never before had Fatima seen her father weep, but upon sight of his tears she felt redeemed. She was not the only one that felt such an intense reaction at being there.

Her mother's hands were raised high in invocation while her eyes were fixated upon the Kaaba. Her younger sisters were also staring at the black cube in the center of this masjid and it seemed as if every body and every thing revolved around it, even the sun, the moon, and all of the stars above.

Once they all got over the initial awe, the family held hands and as one unit they began to walk across the cool ivory colored marble floor. They performed the seven circuits around the Kaaba that were required of those who were beginning the rituals of the *Hajj*.

The *adhan* for *Isha*, the night prayer, was called such that everyone in the city was able to hear. Droves of people began to rush into the streets heading in the direction of the house of God. Having completed the circumambulation of the Kaaba and the required walk between the mountains of Safa and Marwa, the Husains found a rare, empty spot in the prayer area and quickly occupied it.

"Here, we can be seated right here until prayers begin. Everybody together, hold hands, and don't lose sight of one another," Daddy told his daughters. They sat together, eyes still wandering, absorbing the majesty of their surroundings.

The Imam arrived in the courtyard and took his place. In unison everyone stood up, and commenced their prayers. These were prayers that were so deep and powerful that Fatima could feel the beat of her pounding heart hasten. It seemed as if this was the best prayer she had made all her life.

The family left the Masjid and headed back to the hotel after their evening prayers. They left most of their belongings in a holding quarter, and picked up the few bags that they would take with them on their next stop in the five day ritual, called Minna. Minna was essentially a campground that Fatima and all the pilgrims would make their home for the next few days. This large area was covered with white tents that would serve as make-shift homes for over two million pilgrims. It was in this campground that the family would spend their days in prayers and remembrance of God.

While staying in the tents of Minna, Fatima's family met people from all over the world. They met Muslims from Indonesia, the Philippines, Africa, Turkey, and the Indian subcontinent. Warm

"Assalamu Alaykums" were exchanged amongst all the pilgrims as they smiled at one another. Almost everyone who was there seemed to be in a peaceful state of mind, drowning in contentment.

Fatima knew that Muslims would be coming from all around the world to perform the *Hajj*, so she expected to meet a diverse group of people, even though the diversity was far beyond what she could have anticipated. But the other pilgrims were very surprised to hear that the Husains were Muslims from America. One pilgrim from Sudan, Amiri, asked ,"Where did you say you were from? America? Really? America? There are Muslims there?"

He, like most of the other pilgrims, did not know that there were Muslims that lived in America. They were surprised to see brown people who looked very Indian practicing Islam in the US. After making acquaintance with the family, most of the pilgrims reacted in a kind manner and expressed their pleasure at the fact that the message of the Last Prophet had reached North America.

"Alhamdulillah, the message has reached even the land of Reagan. Truly God will guide who He chooses," stated Mehmet, a Turkish pilgrim, to Fatima's father.

After the first day, the pilgrims had to move on towards the plains of Arafat, the hill upon which the Prophet Muhammad delivered his last sermon. The vast valley was nothing but sand had not the pilgrims converged upon it. The area of Arafat did not have as many tents as Minna had, and many pilgrims stood under the searing sun as they prayed.

The weather that was experienced on this day was indescribable. Fatima's family was not capable of withstanding the scorching heat. The children could not handle the scalding temperatures, so they searched for a tent that had even the smallest amount of room in which they could hide and claim sanctuary from the blazing sun.

After what seemed like an eternity, they found a tent that could accommodate only three out of the six Husains. Desperate to comfort his family, Fatima's father took off the top sheet of his ihraam, and laid it over the taut ropes that held up the tent. He then told his family to take refuge underneath the shade of his ihraam. All six of them managed to shield themselves from the blistering sun for the rest of that day, and prayed to their heart's content. The prayers made on this day were said to be surely accepted.

The stay at Arafat was followed by a visit to Muzdalifah, the grounds at which they picked the pebbles with which they would symbolically stone Satan. After that they would return to Minna, and then head toward Jamraad, where they would symbolically stone Satan. The entire ritual lasted five days and by the time it had been completed the Husains were exhausted.

Despite their exhaustion, their enthusiasm had not dwindled one bit. There was a unique aura in that holy city, one that would drive them to worship and make the most of what little time they had to spend there. Their last visit to the Kaaba was heart wrenchingly difficult. They could not leave without experiencing a sense of great loss. All of them kept turning back for that one last glance of the Kaaba, with eyes swollen and tears flowing, even as they were walking away. It was as if they were leaving behind a loved one, without knowing if they would ever see them again. It was the most difficult departure from any place that Fatima had experienced.

Upon their return to the United States, the family and friends of the Husains were anxious to have them over so that they could share all of their experiences of the holy pilgrimage. But it was not the same Husain family that they knew before who were coming to their homes now.

Fatima's parents had been moved to great depths by their *Hajj*. They began to reevaluate their lives and made religion a greater priority. Fatima's mother decided to adopt the *hijaab* and began to wear it wherever she would go. She threw out all of her short sleeved clothing and dressed even more modestly than before. Inspired by their mother, the girls also decided to start wearing the *hijaab*. However, there was one place where the girls were not ready to wear their *hijaab*, and that was at school. Although they sported a scarf everywhere else they went, the girls did not commence wearing the *hijaab* in their most unstable surrounding.

Chapter 6

A few weeks after their return from the *Hajj*, Fatima's Dada decided to come stay with her family.

"I want to hear from you all how your trip went. I want to hear every detail," he would implore of the girls.

"And we have to practice your Urdu girls, I am sure that you did not keep up while you were in Saudi. So we have a lot to make up for. If you all don't carry on the mother tongue, who will? So let's not neglect that, okay?" Dada said, yet again.

The girls weren't thrilled about the Urdu lessons but they were happy that Dada was staying with them. Amina was growing into a cooperative little girl, Mummy's little helper and Dada's little assistant. She was already ready to assist Dada with any tasks that he needed help with and she was attached to their mother in the kitchen.

"There goes goody-goody again.." Ayesha would snicker to Fatima. "I think she is beyond goody –goody. She is just Mom's favorite," Fatima replied. But mother overheard the not-so-quiet exchange.

"She is a very big help, that's why she may appear to be the favorite to you both. But it's her actions that merit my love…" Mummy preached to the older two daughters.

Fatima rolled her eyes and Ayesha simply giggled. They knew they weren't ever going to be *that* good. Amina was officially the goody two shoes of their family. She was the one that all the elders adored, especially Dada.

As summer progressed, Dada enjoyed his grand-daughters' company in the mornings and spent the remainder of the day reading Urdu newspapers that his son would bring to him.

On a sunny August morning Fatima came down as usual, and went into the kitchen to get breakfast. Her younger sisters were still in bed so she expected to walk into a quiet kitchen. However, Fatima's father was calling out to his father but was not receiving a response. Once and then again he called out.

"Papa?"

There was still no response. Worried, he dashed into Dada's room. Fatima and her mother quickly followed after seeing Daddy run. They found Dada motionless. He was lying on his pillow with his neck tilted up and his mouth open. His dentures were gone and he looked as if he was in a lot of pain. Fatima then turned her focus from her Dada to her father who was kneeling on the floor and crying while grabbing onto his father's feet.

Dada was not responding but his breathing was loud and hoarse. Fatima thought that maybe he had inadvertently swallowed his dentures and was choking on them. Maybe that could explain his loud, strenuous breathing, but that just didn't make much sense.

"What's happened here? Why is Papa not responding? Did you find him like this?"

Mummy aggressively interrogated her father, but he had trouble speaking. Fatima's father was muted in shock.

After Mummy's consistent prodding, he finally answered, "Papa has had another stroke, I know he has, this is what happened the first time he had one."

Daddy's his head fell down as he wept, still holding on to his father's feet. Fatima's mother called the ambulance, and they rushed Dada to the hospital.

It was true, just as Fatima's father had said, Dada had suffered another stroke. But this one was massive. His entire body was paralyzed and there was hardly any sign of life left within him. The doctors said he was alive because of the pacemaker that he received a few months back, but they did not expect him to last more than another week.

All of the uncles from Somerville had arrived, as did Dadima. The family called the other uncles who lived abroad and shared the news. The eldest uncle from Pakistan could not come because he had no immigration status, and entering the US would be near impossible. Saad *chacha*, on the other hand, said he would do his best to arrive from Saudi Arabia to be at his father's bedside ASAP.

With the concerned family congregating at the hospital there was no time for anyone to take notice of the children. The adults were busy comforting each other and especially Dadima.

All of the day's events had left Fatima very disturbed. It was unbearable for Fatima to see a loved one in such a helpless position. She couldn't get over how he had just sat with her family last night on their new living room sofa and had complimented on how comfortable it was.

"I like this sofa. It is very nice. I can really enjoy drinking my tea on it."

Dada had also made plans to start using another text to help with her Urdu reading and she was not looking forward to that at all. She had become tired of all the stress on Urdu when there really seemed to be no use for that language in America. But all of a sudden she was ready to employ that new text. Any excuse she could use she was ready to utilize just to get some more time with Dada. But the realization hit her like a ton of bricks; she was about to lose her only grandfather and there was nothing that anybody could do to change the situation.

Saad *chacha* arrived a week later and Dada's condition had not changed. The doctors had now given another prognosis, one that was scarier than the first. They said that Dada could live like this indefinitely. This was a scary scenario for the family. They could not believe that the patriarch of their family had been diagnosed with such grim prospects. But decisions had to be made and the family had to act. No matter how difficult it would be, the sons would fulfill their responsibility towards their father and keep him in one of their homes. Amongst Indian children the sense of responsibility towards one's parents is instilled from a very young age. Additionally, the Islamic doctrine demands that respect be given to parents at all times especially when they become old and feeble. Therefore as Muslims and Indians, these sons were indoctrinated since childhood with the belief that the responsibility of the parents in their old age falls upon their children. As their father raised them, they would now care for their father. They would do it with their own hands.

Fatima's father and uncles decided that they would not send Dada to a nursing home. Dadima wanted Dada to stay in Somerville where she lived with the three sons who shared a two flat house. Hence, Dada was moved to Somerville. The sons and their wives would share the task of taking care of him. Saad *chacha* made the decision to leave his job in Saudi Arabia and move to the US to help tend to his father. Being the dutiful sons that they were, Fatima's uncles would care for their ill father as he had always cared for them.

When she returned to school Fatima was visibly shaken by all that had transpired. Mrs. Stancherd, her MG teacher from last year who was also her MG teacher this year, was the first one who noticed her anxiety.

"Fatima, you look upset. I can see it in the way you are carrying yourself, and it's even affecting your work. Is there anything that you would like to share with me?" she asked.

Fatima had established a rapport with Mrs. Stancherd and had no issues with telling her what was going on in her life. She told Mrs. Stancherd about her grandfather's illness and the family's distress during this situation.

Mrs. Stancherd lent her ears and time to a student who desperately needed to vent her stress. She offered her condolences, but she also encouraged Fatima to write about what she was feeling.

"I always find that when I write about my pain it alleviates the stress I may be feeling. I think that this may help you as well."

Fatima took her advice seriously and writing became a stress reliever like no other. Fatima found her feelings pouring out through her pen on to the paper. Fatima felt as if a burden had been lifted off her shoulders all thanks to Mrs. Stancherd.

Under the guidance of this teacher Fatima began to develop a passion for writing, and continued to write well beyond her years in middle school. What a difference this small piece of advice made in her life.

About three months after Dada fell ill; Fatima was seven weeks into the eighth grade. Fatima had settled down into a comfortable routine. Her alarm went off at 6:15 am and she would be the first daughter awake, which meant she had the bathroom first as well. This was a big deal in a house of five women. After she brushed her teeth, took her shower, and tied up her hair, she would exit the bathroom to find Ayesha waiting to run inside. And as Ayesha would be using the bathroom, Amina would be waking up and walking to the bathroom door, rubbing her eyes. After putting on her clothes, adding accessories, and patting on a little bit of eyeliner -all *Desis* NEED eyeliner- and a touch of lip gloss, Fatima would pack up her backpack and head downstairs. Her stay in the family room was still short since her mother could be in the adjacent kitchen already cooking. Her pants were no longer rolled up, as that fad was long gone, but she had begun to wear make up and outrageously large earrings that really annoyed her parents. Her father was adamant that she put on the *hijaab* when she went to school, but Fatima was not ready.

"Daddy, could you please stop telling me to wear the *hijaab*? I'll wear it to school when I'm ready. Right now I just can't do it."

Fatima had worked so hard to make the few friends that she now had in school. She felt that wearing the *hijaab* may jeopardize these friendships. She had no idea how her friends would react to the *hijaab* and she feared that she'd become a total outcast if she wore it.

She wore it everywhere else without any issues, but doing it at school was a whole different ballgame. If only there was one person that would be willing to wear it with her she may have the strength to do it. But she was all alone, and very insecure.

One of the most pleasant surprises that Fatima encountered in eighth grade occurred in Mr. Hoy's American History class. In this class she was assigned a seat next to an obviously Indian girl named Mary Matthews. Upon hearing her name, Fatima was sure that this Indian girl must have had some identity issues since she lacked an Indian sounding name. Fatima just assumed that she was one of those Indians that had anglicized their name so that they would sound more "normal." She had met an Andy who was really Ahmed, a Matt who was really a Mateen, and she knew of at least three Mohammeds that were called "Mo." So this wouldn't have been the first time she would be meeting a *Desi* with a name that throws one off.

It turned out that Mary was this girl's Christian name, and that her family actually referred to her as "Aneesha," much to Fatima's relief. Mary was the first Indian girl at Pennwood that Fatima met that who had no issues with discussing her Indian heritage. She would readily discuss her family's roots in Kerala, India and openly identify herself with Indian culture. Fatima felt that finally she had someone that she could relate to on a different level at this otherwise homogenous school.

Fatima started conversations with Mary simply to foster a relationship with a schoolmate with an Indian background. Although they didn't share the exact same cultural/religious baggage, there was a lot more that they had to offer each other than anyone else did. And since both girls were in many of the same classes they began to help each other with their homework and relied on each other for assistance if one was absent or missed any assignments. Their friendship grew and was one of the first that actually made it past the school acquaintance stage.

Soon enough they had introduced their families to each other and like the typical *Desis* that they were, dinner parties followed. It turned out that Mary's parents were engineers, just like Fatima's father, and they all worked for the same corporation that Fatima's father did, proving the theory that it really is a small world.

Mary was unlike most American girls that Fatima knew not just because she had an Indian background, but also because she was a committed Christian. She not only had the Christian faith in her heart, but she also practiced its moral and ethical doctrine with devotion. In fact it seemed that even though the two girls believed in two separate dogmas, the manner in which they practiced their faiths was very much alike as were their values. They not only had the same morals, but they also had similar academic goals and ideals for achieving success. Despite all that, they were still typical American girls in most respects. They loved to watch Tom Cruise movies, they would hang out at the mall with their friends, and they were addicted to Thursday night NBC TV.

However, there was one part of their lives that would not be carried out in an all-American fashion, and that was marriage. Both girls knew that they would most likely be married in a pseudo-arranged fashion and this was a topic of great interest with their school friends and even amongst each other. They tried to explain to their peers that they would always have the final say and would never be forced into an arranged marriage.

"Think of it this way. It is more like setting up a date. If it goes well then fantastic, the two people can take it further. The twist here is that the families would be involved in the decision making process," Fatima would say.

"Our families always look out for our best interests. We trust them. So they'll help us find the right person, who will hopefully make us happier in the long run," Mary added.

This wasn't a big deal for the girls, who were close to their parents, but their classmates had a very hard time fathoming that parents can have such an input into choosing one's lifetime partner. Even the ever objective Peter, was rather shocked.

"You mean you can't marry for love?"

"Well Peter, if we found someone we really wanted to marry I'm sure our parents wouldn't stop us. But if we allow them to look for us and help us in this process, it takes down a lot of hurdles we would have to otherwise face."

This was always a popular discussion amongst the students in Mr. Hoy's class, as he loved to stimulate dialogue between the students, whether or not it was relevant to American History.

Mr. Hoy's class, in fact, served as a forum for many subjects. Fatima had always been an outspoken child and she never hesitated in expressing her opinions regardless of whether they were politically correct or not. So when hot topics were brought up, she always added her two cents. It was during this year that Salman Rushdie's Satanic Verses was published and the Muslim world was in an uproar.

As with many current events that were discussed in Mr. Hoy's class, the Rushdie affair was also brought up. The class discussion revolved around whether it was acceptable to have a death warrant on the head of Rushdie for writing a book. Fatima, being the only Muslim in her class, was asked her opinion. She responded in a way that showed some inner conflict.

"I do believe in freedom of speech, but I also understand why the anger of the Muslims had escalated to such heights with the statements that Salman Rushdie had made about the Prophet and his family."

She tried to explain to her classmates that the love that Muslims have for the Prophet Muhammad is deeper than what they feel for their own kin.

"The allegiance that Muslims show him is unparalleled, and when anyone insults him it's worse than offending one's mother or child. That's why the kind of reaction that this book is evoking in the Muslim world isn't surprising to me. In fact I wonder sometimes what I would do if Salman Rushdie crossed my path."

She knew that she would definitely not consider killing him, but she would have to restrain herself from smacking him. If she was driven to thoughts of smacking this guy, then surely those people in the world that have no regard for freedom of speech but an intense loyalty to the Prophet Muhammad would consider much more. Most of her classmates could not understand how she and many Muslims felt such a loyalty to someone they didn't even know, but there were a handful that could relate.

"I think you feel for him like I do for Jesus. I wouldn't let anyone disrespect him in my presence, even though he is not my friend or family. In fact he may not be either of those two but my love for him exceeds that of what I feel for many of my friends and family members," said Sharon, a Catholic student whose family was more religious than most.

"Exactly Sharon. That is exactly what I mean. That's how most Muslims feel about Prophet Muhammad. So even though you may not want to kill the person who is disgracing him, you are still really pissed off at him," Fatima replied.

"It's almost as if your entire faith is being attacked by insulting this individual."

Faith is what kept the Husain family strong as they watched Dada fall into a vegetative state. As his weight fell under one hundred pounds, he was fed through a nasal gastric tube. He was unable to perform any normal functions except pass excrement and urine. As he suffered silently, the family would do their best to care for him by bathing him, shaving him, and moving him around to avoid bedsores. They would even talk to him, just in case he could comprehend what they had to say. But there was no response; he never spoke after the stroke occurred.

Over the course of the next year, his six foot tall stature shriveled up into a fetal position. Everyone watched sadly and helplessly as the strong man that they once knew slowly lost all signs of life. After a long ordeal, Dada slipped away quietly in the early hours of a November morning.

As Dada breathed his last Dadima held his hand. She whispered to him, "Your suffering is now over," as she wept.

This was an emotion felt by the entire family. While alive, Dada was with them but in obvious pain. Everyone knew that this was a horrible way to live, and they prayed that it never occur to anyone they know. After Dada's death, for the first time in her life, Fatima saw her Dadima take off her *kaali poth* and put it in her dresser. Never again did Fatima see that *kaali poth*.

The family gathered together and consoled Dadima as well as each other. It had been a terrible ordeal for all of them. No child should see their beloved parent suffer in such a horrible way or vice versa. But these sons had done an incredible job taking care of their father in a no-win situation. They had served him to the best of their ability, and in accordance with Muslim ideology the reward for serving one's parents is immense.

After Dada died, the family immediately gathered and read the Qur'an and prayed for mercy on his soul. For the past year Fatima's family had slowly prepared itself for the inevitable, but when it actually happened, it was hard to believe that it was finally over. Fatima would never see her Dada again. He would no longer be in that room at her uncle's house that came to take on the title of "Dada's room." All the medical equipment that was in their homes would no longer need to be turned on or off, nor would the family members need to adjust his bed so that he could lay in a different position for at least a few hours. There would be no more nurses coming to check in on him. And there would be no more medications to administer. Everything came to a screeching halt. And all of a sudden Dada's sons had a lot more free time on their hands. Free time that they would trade in a heartbeat for a few more minutes with their father. But Dada's time had come.

At the funeral the entire extended family showed up along with all of the friends that the family had made over the past fifteen years in the United States. Even regular masjid-goers made an effort to attend. In Muslim tradition, a funeral is not a private service. It is a public event that all Muslims are highly encouraged to attend, whether they knew the deceased or not. Hence, Muslims in the local community would make an effort to come and mourn the loss of the departed, console the family, and remember their own mortality.

The funeral prayer was brief as is the case with most Muslim funerals. The *salatul janazah*, as it is called, is a simple prayer that is made by the congregation for the deceased. It takes about five minutes and then it is all over. After the prayer ended, Fatima's uncles walked over to their father's casket and performed their last service for their father. They carried Dada to the hearse, which would drive him to his final resting place. Fatima and her entire family watched solemnly as Dada was carried away and out of their lives; but his memories would last forever in their hearts.

Chapter 7

It took months to accept the loss of her grandfather and school became the best remedy to get over it. Before Fatima knew it, eighth grade was wrapping up. With high school just around the corner she had a lot on her mind. After three years at this school, it was time to say good bye. Fatima was not sure how to leave a place that she had grown so attached to. She would really miss Pennwood. It was a great school, and some wonderful friendships had been built under its roof. And yet there was much to anticipate.

"It's not that I am not looking forward to high school," she confided to Mary. "It's just that this place is really special to me. I experienced a whole new world when I came here. And now that I feel comfortable with everything about this school I have to leave. It's a little weird. I don't know Mary, maybe I am just nervous to leave and start all over again at a new place."

But Mary comforted her in her usual practical manner, "It will be fine Fatima. Everyone does it and so will we." Fatima wasn't so sure though.

The first issue that she was sure to face was the combining of the classes from both middle schools. There were two middle schools in the district, Pennwood and William Penn, both of which would send their eighth grade graduates to Pennsbury. This meant that chances were very high that she would not be with any of her friends in her classes. Once again she would have to familiarize herself with many new students. But what was more worrisome than her getting to know the other students, was how they would react to her. She was always conscious of being somewhat different despite being American at heart. How would this new crop of students react to an American Muslim girl who lived her life so differently than they lived theirs? She was not looking forward to explaining, once again, how to pronounce her name, why she couldn't participate in after school events, and how she was just like everybody, but not totally like them.

Summer vacation was a welcome break and Fatima put her fears on the backburner for a bit. This summer the Husains did not have any travel plans, just lots of rest and relaxation for the girls. They would sleep in late and play games with each other or watch TV. The girls found creative outlets to focus their energies on. Experimenting with their father's camcorder, they filmed themselves lip synching to Bollywood songs or imitating older aunties in improvised skits. Ayesha was usually the star with Amina as her sidekick, while Fatima directed. But a new star was definitely emerging. Little Malika was becoming quite a performer. She was quick to choreograph dances and drama was her cup of tea. Fatima loved to dress her up and Malika reveled in the attention. The sisters could clearly run and manage their own acting company. And they became very good at creating their own 'video masterpieces.' But beyond the home movies, summer for the Husain girls was pretty much like everyone else's summer - long and somewhat boring at times. However, that particular summer was a little different. Something special was going to happen for the first time in their lives, something that they really wanted to do, but knew that *Desis* just didn't do. Somehow they got lucky. Somehow, their stars were perfectly aligned....The Husains were going to go camping.

Well, it wasn't only the Husains that were going camping. It was a Masjid sponsored event, and local Muslim families had signed up to go.

"I can't believe we are actually going through with this! Whoever thought that our parents could pull this off!" an excited Fatima told Rubi.

"And that too with so many families participating. I thought we would be lucky to get five families to agree! But we have more like twenty or twenty that plan on attending! It's going to be way cool," Rubi responded just as enthusiastically.

Most of the children did not care that their parents would be with them. They were simply thrilled that they could go camping. The adults were just as excited about taking part in this very "American" activity, much to the surprise of the youth.

The campsite was Tohickon State Park in eastern Pennsylvania. The group of close to thirty families from all across southern New Jersey and southeastern Pennsylvania drove over to the park armed with tents, sleeping bags, lanterns, grills, and mosquito repellant not to mention the teapots to make *chai* in, the igloo coolers filled to the brim with *shaami kababs*, puff pastry *samosas*, *chapattis*, tomato curry, and *kheema*. And who could forget the *lotas*, water pitchers, to keep in the bathrooms.

"Mom are you sure you don't want to pack the fridge itself, it might make taking all of this easier?" asked Fatima.

"You always complain when I pack food and take it with us. But you are all very eager to eat it when you get hungry," Mummy replied.

This was true. Despite all the moaning and groaning while packing, when hunger would strike there would be a chorus of, "Mummy where are the Pringles that you packed?" or "Mom did you keep any more Kool Aid?" This was sure to be one grand picnic in the park.

Activities had been planned for this outdoor adventure that included hiking, water rafting, and even the ever popular Indian game of cricket. This was of course meant for the adults who wished to take a stroll down memory lane, back to their 'glory days.' The youth had no interest in these 'FOB' games. For them, it was football for the boys and softball for the girls.

As the parents grilled chicken and burgers for lunch, the children set up the picnic tables. It was a collaborative effort and both the young and the adults were excited to be venturing into this unchartered territory of "American" life. However, it could not be all fun and games. There had to be some intellectual stimulation and religious knowledge that the children would be exposed to.

To this end, a 'Jeopardy' type game had been designed with the subjects being taken from aspects of Islam, ranging from Prophetic history to Islamic law. The young adults had developed this game to challenge the younger teenagers that were at the camp. The teenagers in turn had devised a scavenger hunt to occupy the even younger children. In this manner everyone took care of each other and made sure that there were enough activities for all of the participants.

The teams were almost always boys vs. girls as separation of sexes was key to most Muslim gatherings. This allowed friendships to blossom between the girls without vying for the boys' attention being any part of it, and since there were many new faces, they had plenty of teammates to acquaint themselves with.

One girl who Fatima took an immediate liking to was Asma. Asma lived in South Jersey about twenty minutes from Fatima's old place in Willingboro. They clicked instantaneously and began to share their life stories as they laughed out loud about how parallel their lives were.

Both girls' families were originally from Hyderabad, a similarity that immediately bonded the two. They began to talk in their parents colloquial style of Urdu, and told each other many stories about how "Hyderabadi" their parents were, almost as if it was a badge of honor.

Asma had much to share with Fatima on how to cope with high school, since she had just completed her freshman year. She too was a Muslim ABCD, so the frame of reference for both girls was very much alike. Fatima could talk about being the only Muslim at her school and Asma knew exactly how that felt because she was going through that same situation. Fatima kept asking, "How is it that we lived so close to each other but have never met before? How could this oversight have occurred? Especially amongst a group of Hyderabadi Muslims? We all are in each others faces all the time!"

Asma just laughed and replied, "Well maybe I didn't want to meet any more Hyderabadis. We already know fifty percent of the ones that emigrated from there. And after this camp it will be sixty percent!"

The two girls were making the most of what they had at that moment during the memorable camp.

The campers awoke every morning just before sunrise to make the *Fajr*, dawn, prayers in congregation. There was no need of an alarm as the *adhaan* was called loud enough to wake even the fish in the brooks. After performing the *wudu* in near darkness, the campers would head over to the campfire and stand together in prayer. Once prayer was over the majority of the children would go back in to their tents and crawl into their sleeping bags to doze off until breakfast time. Many adults however would sit around the campfire sipping their freshly brewed tea and discussing various subjects.

"I don't know about Zia ul Haque. I am sure his plane crash was staged. It can not be such a coincidence. There must be some long arms pulling the strings to have had him removed," Uncle Mirza said.

"Oh *Bhai*, what do you think? That Pakistan will fall apart? It will become even better now with Bhutto in power."

"You ok? You must still be half asleep; she is a puppet to the west."

The conversation went back and forth about politics of a land that was half a world away yet was so close to the hearts of the immigrant uncles. There would be no end to these silly discussions, just raised voices and heated tempers. They would have to be calmed by their wives who would bring out the hot tea that was freshly made on the grill. But this was typical. Everyone was a self-proclaimed expert in politics and needed to voice their opinions. Many of these experts were conspiracy theorists to the core. Everything that happened was at the hands of some agency or some puppeteer that was manipulating the whole world. These were ideas that Fatima and her generation would have a hard time relating to. In fact most of these concepts were completely ignored by the second generation, deemed as complete hearsay, and worthless in their value. But to the uncles, there was no better way to pass a warm summer evening than indulging in such discourse.

As the summer drew to a close Fatima was anxious about high school. She was both excited and stressed about commencing what she had heard were supposed to be the best years of her education. But there would be new hurdles to cross along this journey at Pennsbury High. Her insecurities were still many and there weren't many people that would understand what she was feeling. She tried to explain certain problems to her parents but their reply was brief and simple, "*Beta* you go to school to learn, not to socialize."

But this was not how she felt.

"I know that I am going to learn but I can't be a mute. I have to talk and meet with people and deal with them. I have to cope with their comments and dumb questions. It took forever to meet some people that I could finally relate to. Now they all might be in totally different classes than mine," Fatima said as she knit her brows.

The international politics of that time were also beginning to play a tremendous role in typecasting the common Muslim as a terrorist. Night after night reports of Palestinian Intifada uprisings were broadcast painting a nasty picture of terrorist activities. Bent over his chair and glued to the TV, Fatima's father would witness coverage up the uprisings and lash out at the screen, "Muslim terrorists! Muslim terrorists! These idiots always throw Muslim into the sentence. You never hear Catholic terrorist or Hindu terrorists. A terrorist is just a terrorist! Why must they say Muslim and make the world hate us!" his face red with anger, he would jump off his seat while shouting at the TV.

"Daddy, don't you think people realize that by now?"

"No *beta*, I'm sure they do not. Otherwise they would have objected to this association of the word Muslim with terrorists a long time ago. Struggles that are not motivated by Islam shouldn't be tied to its teachings or followers. Like the Irish – English conflict. Do we ever hear Catholic terrorist bombs Protestant filled shopping center? NO. It's Irish nationalist bombs British mall or something to that effect. Do you see what I am saying? We as Muslims always get labeled as murderers. So many of these people fight for their nation, not their faith. It's ludicrous I tell you!"

As the Muslims were being dragged through the mud, Fatima was afraid that this negative attitude would be brought into the classroom. Fatima imagined the news affecting her peers' opinions, misleading them into forming negative opinions about her and other Muslims. Another fear to add to the many apprehensions that were building inside of her.

Another issue that was making her nervous, although it wasn't at such a grand scale, was that now every grade she earned would be calculated into her class rank. There was very little room for error at this point. She knew what was expected from her and she knew that class rank would be the gauge for how well she was performing. The fact that her class was of eight hundred plus students was of no concern to her parents. They just needed to hear that she was in the top ten. Academic success was everything to her parents as well as most of their friends. Most of the immigrant parents equated their own personal success with the academic success that their child attained. If your child excelled academically, you did something right and were good parents, if not – what the hell did you do wrong?

This was also true of the families that Mary's family would socialize with. The two girls shared the same environment and values when it came to success. The only problem was that Mary, like a fine *Desi* child, was set on medicine as her career. Fatima on the other hand, had lost almost all interest in science and was much more inclined towards the social sciences.

Fatima dreaded telling her family that she did not want to pursue medicine. Her father and mother would surely tell her that she was wasting her "God-given" talent on a useless field. Yet more than what they would say, Fatima dreaded the letdown that they would feel. She knew that upsetting her parents was inevitable, and through life there would be several occasions where it could happen. But she never wanted them to be disappointed with her.

Unfortunately, she knew that her aversion towards the sciences and medicine was a harsh reality that her folks would come to know about sooner or later. However, she chose to remain silent about this issue for as long as possible, in the off chance that she would develop some enthusiasm in biology, physics, or chemistry. Even though the chance of this happening was almost as good as her resorting to use that bucket and stool that forever sat in their bathroom tub.

Chapter 8

The breeze blew the falling leaves in the air. Their colors were beginning to change with the seasons. Fatima peered out at the scene before her. 'The first day of school had quickly crept up,' she mused. She was nervous. She had always been tense on the first day of school, but this year was different. She was far more nervous than she had ever been before.

After her usual morning routine, Fatima made her way out of her home to face her first adjustment to high school- riding the school bus. Pennwood had not been too far from home, so Fatima's parents dropped her off every morning. But Pennsbury High was farther away, and her parents couldn't drive her as they used to before.

The school bus stopped two blocks away from Fatima's home, at the entrance of her subdivision. Fatima felt fortunate for the distance as it allowed her ample time to air out her clothes in case any food smells had contaminated her attire. The odor of the *Desi* kitchen was still a hurdle to overcome, and Fatima had to do whatever she could to keep from smelling of curry. But this was not her only concern regarding attire. Much to her parent's chagrin, Fatima still had not agreed to wear the *hijaab* to school. Fatima had spent much of the summer battling her parents in an effort to get out of wearing the *hijaab* to Pennsbury High. She was nervous enough being a freshman; she couldn't imagine the stress that would come with wearing *hijaab* as well. She knew that a day would come when she would wear it to school, but she needed to grow more secure with herself, and increase her trust in her friendships. For now, she was not at that point.

Fatima waited at the bus stop with two other students, both of whom she did not know. She hadn't seen them around the neighborhood. Maybe that was because the older kids had never played with the younger kids, or more likely because Fatima rarely played outside. She had been too entranced by the TV to actually partake in any physical activity. She quietly eyed them and guessed that they must be at least two years older than her since she didn't remember them from her years at Pennwood. They shared an awkward silence without feeling the need to have a conversation. Each looked in different directions awaiting the arrival of the school bus.

As the bus approached and the door opened, Fatima waited for the others to board, even though one of them was a guy. So much for chivalry. Once the others were in, she took a deep breath and walked up the steps glancing quickly down the length of the noisy bus. She could not see anyone that she knew, so she walked toward the first empty seat and nervously sat down. She placed her backpack in her lap and began looking around for familiar faces. There were a few kids in the back that she knew of, but they were the druggies that she would have nothing to do with. There were others who were blasting their walkmans so loud that she could hear Guns N Roses singing, as clearly as the people wearing the headphones, but even they were not students who she associated with much. Most of the students were faces from years past at Pennwood, more mature and pubescent. Realizing she wasn't comfortable enough to talk to anyone on this bus, Fatima pulled out her notebook and began to write a letter to her camp buddy Asma.

"Dear Asma,
I can't believe that I am on my way to high school. That too in a bus filled with freaks. I can tell that this bus riding isn't going to work out...."

Once the bus docked at Pennsbury, Fatima looked around as swarms of students poured out of the buses at the dock. She barely recognized any faces. She continued to nervously walk into the school when she felt a tug on her backpack;

"Hello stranger," smiled Mary. Fatima let out a huge sigh of relief.

"Thank God you are here. I was flipping out about where to go and who I would know. It's so nice to see a familiar face!"

"I know what you mean. Where's your homeroom?" asked Mary

"You think I have a clue? I have to figure out how to get through this maze myself."

"Ditto. Well we gotta hurry, home room starts in five minutes."

The girls rushed in and followed the signs on the walls to find their homerooms. They were separated early on in their search so each went about on their own. Fatima reached her homeroom where she recognized a good number of students. Feeling relieved she found her schedule on a desk right behind a friendly familiar face, Leona

Hurschwitz. Fatima sat behind Leona in homeroom since sixth grade since they were always alphabetically seated.

"Nice to see you Leona. How was your summer?"

"It was great; I can't believe that it's over already."

"Tell me about it."

"This building is really depressing; there are hardly any windows in it," Leona looked around.

Fatima also scanned the room, and then the hallways. There was hardly any sunlight in the school.

"My brother told me that the architect who designed the school thought that windows would distract the students from learning."

"What? So they decided to dump us all in a cellar?" Fatima asked. Clearly annoyed at what she thought was illogical rationale.

"Guess so."

How strange Fatima thought, 'Windows distracting?' She never thought that the windows at Pennwood were distracting. In fact they were what let the beauty of the landscaping into the school. They made the otherwise dull school, kinda 'pretty.' Pennsbury was nothing like Pennwood...

Well from the amount of work we will have I am sure there won't be any time to enjoy the sunlight," Fatima told Leona.

"Why do you say that? It's what we make of things right? We've always had to work; so why are things gonna get so difficult now? And since when have *you* been sweating your grades? Are you afraid you might get a B or something?" Leona sarcastically replied, but with a smile. Fatima knew Leona was right. She really had to stop with the pessimistic attitude. Things could not be that bad.

The day progressed and Fatima went to her classes with a less negative attitude than what she walked into school with. She was surprisingly pleased to see familiar faces in many of her classes. MG class was pretty much identical to what her class at Pennwood had been, with the addition of a handful of William Penn alumni. Mary was in her class and sat next to her, along with James and Vanessa, the only two African American students that were in any of her classes.

"Do you guys realize that we are the only non-Whites here, and somehow we managed to sit next to each other? Isn't that birds of a feather flocking together?" James laughed.

"Yeah or as the other students are probably thinking, the colored section," Fatima responded with a wink.

They all laughed out loud.

"Let's just say we are the minority corner," Vanessa said.

"Yes that's exactly who we are!" Mary agreed.

They joked together and would continue to refer to themselves as the "minority corner" throughout the year. A comfort level developed amongst the four. They carried on inside jokes and were always giggling about something or another that most of the other students just would not understand. Whether it was hair straightening secrets, or their interest in 'In Living Color', the foursome enjoyed each others company throughout the year. This was all Fatima needed to begin looking at high school in a brighter light. 'This was going to be a great class,' Fatima thought.

The last class of the day was Physical Science; a class that Fatima was hoping would help change her mind about pursuing the sciences. Unfortunately, upon entering the classroom, Fatima realized that there was no one she cared to sit with so she just grabbed a seat anywhere. What she didn't realize was that Joan and her best buddy, Melissa, were seated right behind her, busy inflating each other's egos and raving about how expensive their purses and perfumes were. 'Ugh.' Fatima thought. 'If I have to listen to these two snobs for the rest of the year I'm gonna die!'

As the bell began to ring Tara came strolling into the class.

'Thank God,' Fatima said to herself. She signaled to Tara to sit by her, and Tara kindly obliged.

"Tara, you are a sight for sore eyes!"

"Yeah get a load of this class," she looked around. "The best of the worst huh?"

"I guess so," Fatima laughed.

"Just look at the teacher, he looks like he is a twenty year old jock," said Tara.

"Yeah he also looks cocky, which to me means that he'll be a tough grader."

"Damn Fatima! You're probably right."

The girls grumpily quieted down as Mr. Shanahan, who was also the soccer coach, began to address the class. After five minutes of talking, he confirmed what Fatima and Tara's feared- he was an over enthusiastic jock. Despite that, she tried to go easy on him and thought that she really needed to stop being so judgmental, especially in a class that she desperately hoped to fall in love with. Almost as if he could read her mind Mr. Shanahan said, "Class I will make you love Physical Science. This is a subject that will explain how everything in this world works from the gravitational forces that keep the Earth revolving to the amount of energy I exert when I am breaking records on the track."

Once he began to toot his own horn Fatima was turned off. Fatima made up her mind right then.

"Man this guy is gonna be an ass, Fatima."

"Tara, you took the words right out of my mouth," Fatima said as they both rolled their eyes.

After Physical Science Fatima rushed to her locker and packed up the books that needed to go home. She walked to the bus dock and searched for her bus. Once she found it, she boarded and began to search for a seat. She couldn't find an empty seat towards the front so she had to move towards the back. 'God this sucks,' she thought. But she kept on walking. As she made her way through, a boy obnoxiously shouted, "Why don't you sit back here dot-head?"

He cackled at his idiotic comment.

Fatima shot him a dirty look and sat down in the first open seat, next to some girl she didn't know. Her blood temperature was now sky high and she could feel her ears burning. Despite the surge of anger, she didn't respond to. There was no point. She wasn't going to teach him anything and quite frankly she was too afraid to start something. Her pretty okay school day just ended with a big bust.

Once the bus reached Fatima's stop she darted out. She felt insulted and humiliated. 'Stupid jerk' she thought to herself. 'Who was that loser anyway to make such an ignorant comment? I am not Hindu, I am Muslim. All people who look Indian aren't Hindu. How stupid could he be?' she mumbled under her breath as she walked home. She walked in and her mother knew by the look on her face that something was wrong.

"*Beta*, what happened, your friends aren't in your classes?"

"No Mom. Some jerk just called me a dot-head. I am not going on that bus again. You guys are going to have to drop and pick me up."

"Look *beta* if someone says something stupid you just ignore it. Why upset yourself over something that isn't even true. You only hurt yourself by getting so worked up. And what's the big deal anyway, it seems like everybody thinks all Indians are Hindu. So what. Now eat the snacks I have for you here and please clean up afterwards."

Mom was right, yet again. Fatima knew that the boy wasn't too bright, so why give his comment any value. On the whole, she had expected the worst and her day had not been that horrible. She sat down and ate the *churwa*, a kind of finger food hot mix, which her mother had just made. She then walked over to the family room and drank a cold glass of Halo Farm fruit punch, her favorite drink. She turned on "Oprah", and a few minutes into the show her fatigue got the best of her and she began to doze off.

Fatima waited for the bus the next morning. She dreaded the ride, but she knew she had to do it. She had to face the fact that kids would say stupid things. And she needed to learn to deal with them wisely. She thought to herself that kids like that were everywhere, so why should she stop going out just to avoid being called names? How many times had kids made rude comments to her at the mall or in a grocery store? There were too many instances to count. She couldn't stop living life because of a few prickly thorns in her side. She had to get over this.

Once the bus arrived, she got on, but this time she did not look around. She simply walked on and took the first available seat and didn't bother to look at anyone. It seemed that the early hour kept the rowdy kids in the back quiet as they listened to their loud music. The ride to school was pleasantly uneventful. Relieved she walked into school regaining an ounce of the pound of confidence she lost the past day.

As weeks passed Fatima began to enjoy her classes more than she had anticipated. Her teachers won her over, and adjusting to the new students wasn't that bad. They didn't react as adversely to her as she had anticipated; in fact they were quite friendly. However, Physical Science could not change her loss of interest in the sciences. She did not find any of the experiments interesting nor did they inspire her in the manner that the social sciences did. She loved to read her history texts, not just to fulfill school requirements but simply to enjoy. She felt that all history was intertwined together as if it was a novel written by a most amazing playwright. Whether it was American history or Islamic history, the story of mankind intrigued Fatima. Science simply wasn't as fascinating to her. Fatima shared her thought with Mary.

"Have you told your parents yet?" Mary knew that this couldn't be good news.

"Ummm not yet."

"Well break it to them slowly. Don't just throw it on them," Mary advised.

"I know Mary. It's just that I don't understand why it's such a big deal. The world does not function solely on the shoulders of doctors. There are so many other great careers. Why must we just dive into medicine or engineering? I don't get it."

"I understand what you are saying Fatima, but you have to realize that you are dealing with the FOB mentality. They think that if you aren't a doctor or engineer you couldn't be bright or that your parents didn't guide you well."

"Yeah, but I think that's ridiculous."

"Well it's ABCD life."

"I know," Fatima replied with a frown on her face. American born *Desis* were really confused, and this was proof of it. She knew Mary was right, but she was hoping to find some other way out of this situation so she called Asma to seek a second opinion.

"Well Fatima you could end this all right now?"

"How?"

"Get married to a doctor. At least that way there is one doctor in the family," Asma laughed.

"Haha real funny. In case you've forgotten I am only thirteen. I have got years and years to go."

"Umm hmm that's what we all say. But when a proposal from a doctor comes the parents are on it like a pack of wolves, even if we are ten," Fatima began to laugh out loud - again.

"Asma, you crack me up," said Fatima, cracking a smile.

"Are you denying it?" she asked, still laughing.

"No I am not. I know you're kinda right. It's just that the whole thought of marriage seems so ridiculous right now."

"To you, but not to your parents. They are thinking long term. Get her engaged fast, that way she won't want to have a boyfriend. Then get her married right out of high school, so she can't goof around at college and she can focus on her medical studies. That's what all our parents think. Get with the program Fatima."

Asma had a point. Fatima began to think that there was truth in Asma's words. Marriage was well known to be semi arranged. Proposals never went directly from a boy to a girl; they went through the parents or through some third party that would play matchmaker. It was very Victorian, straight out of 'Pride and Prejudice.' So even if there was a proposal the girl probably wouldn't find out unless the "potential spouse" had passed the initial stages of parental approval. And all Indian parents loved doctors or medical students. They were the golden geese. To snag one was like winning the lottery, or at least the parents' generation thought so.

"I still think that they would rather me become a doctor Asma."

"There's no doubt about that Fatima. But I am just telling you what the next best thing is, since you are so sure that you don't want to pursue medicine."

"Yeah but let's wait and see if Biology appeals to me next year. That class will be the deciding factor."

"No it won't. This is still high school. You have to decide about med school in college. You have a lot of time. Don't be so adamantly against the sciences, at least not yet. If you become that way you'll be taking the route I just told you about"

"Thanks for the reality check Asma."

"No problem H.B." (short for Hyderabadi *bhen*)

Despite her realization that she need not feel so pressured about deciding on her career right then, Fatima was still nervous. She was trying to focus on her studies and perform well in all of her classes. The whole family knew she was a good student so they would always inquire about school and how it was going.

During one of the weekly family trips to Somerville, Fatima was asked by her Dadima.

"Why must you take Spanish? It is not our language. You should first learn your own tongue. Instead you study the language of the Poor-too-ree-kan. I don't understand."

Fatima tried to explain, "You see Dadima, we have to learn how to speak Spanish because we need to interact with Latinos, who are the largest minority in the US. To succeed in various fields you need to be able to communicate properly…."

"But what is the point Fatima? No matter how hard you study, and how well you perform, a woman will always be a woman. You will be at home with your kids and stuck in the kitchen," Dadima interjected.

Fatima was horrified. "Dadima it's not like that here. Women can do…"

"Yes yes I know what you are thinking. But your *gora* mentality will not work with our people. A good Muslim woman will be a good housewife"

"No Dadima that is sooo not true. That was the case in the India you grew up in where all the good *Desi* women were housewives, but it is not that way anymore. I am an American Muslim. So let's not confuse the two."

"What? *Amreekan Shamreekan. Baray ayay angrayz.* Don't you know what these *goray* bastards did to our people, and here you say proudly say you are like them? *Tauba!*"

"That was the British Dadima, I said I am American."

"*Khwabon* mein. (in your dreams) What is the difference? *Goo ka bhai pad, pad ka bhai goo.* (Feces is the brother of flatulence and flatulence is the brother of feces.) Why can't you be a good *Desi* girl?"

"Because it's more important for me to be a good Muslim girl," Fatima snapped back.

"What is the difference? Good Muslim girl, good *Desi*, it's all the same…" Dadima went on.

"I beg to differ. Our culture and our religion are two totally different spheres. We must learn to separate them."

"What kind of thinking are these *goras* putting in your head? Separating Muslim and *Desi*? Who ever heard of that? Silly girl," Dadima responded in frustration.

But Fatima knew there was a big difference between the two. Culture and religion were two very different parts of her life, but they were the two that were most often misrepresented as the other. That too by her own people.

As she grew older Fatima became very aware of the fact that she needed to identify clearly what were *Desi* cultural expectations and what was within the bounds of her religion. She knew that dressing modestly was an Islamic belief, but the Indian *shalwar khameez* being considered as the only form of modest dress was a cultural ideal. In fact, Fatima believed she could dress modestly by wearing long ankle length shirts. But this mortified her grandmother and other elders in the family. Skirt to Muslim *Desis* meant mini skirt and that was it. Fatima would try to justify her dress to Dadima, "But can't you see how loose and covering it is? It is perfect attire for Muslims."

"No dear it is not. Naked legs under the free flowing skirt, how shameless."

"What do you mean? Nothing is showing - Everything is covered?"

"It is not covered when your legs are naked underneath."

Fatima looked puzzled.

"What? Everyone is naked underneath some form of clothing. And the skirt is a form of clothing too."

"Yes, clothing for these *Amreekan* girls who like to be naked all the time."

Fatima just threw up her hands and hopelessly walked away.

"It's just not worth arguing about," she told Ayesha as she left all the adults.

"Yeah I know that. I don't know why you bother trying to explain. They won't change. So don't try to win them over with your American clothing. They all think that if it's American it just can't be Muslim. But anything *Desi*, now *that's* really considered to be Muslim."

"If that's the case then why did the family move here? They should have just stayed back home with all the 'good Muslims'. I wonder if they even knew any full fledged practicing Muslims there."

"Well they might not even know the difference. You know, between what's Islamic and what's cultural. But it's not just them. It's that way with most Muslim *Desis*. They can't tell what's Islamic and what's cultural anymore. And if they had stayed back in Hyderabad they would most likely be jobless because they weren't part of the majority."

"Exactly. That is why this country is so amazing. Equal opportunity for everyone. How can they not love that? How can they sit there denouncing this place saying 'American this American that' when they are here living good lives?"

"Fatima, you really think they will listen? Don't waste your breath," advised Ayesha.

"I guess so," Fatima replied, feeling very annoyed.

Much of the family didn't understand the American lifestyle, especially Dadima. Now that Fatima was in high school she was set on getting Fatima married. She would inquire about any bachelor that walked in front of her.

"How old is he? What does he do? Where is he from?" Question after question followed by numerous calls to Fatima's father on how she had found the perfect boy for Fatima. Fatima was thoroughly irritated. At fourteen, she didn't care about marriage. She kept trying to explain to Dadima that she was not ready.

"Dadima this is so silly."

"What silly silly? I was married at thirteen and had my first son at fourteen. Don't you know?"

"Exactly Dadima," Fatima replied forcibly stopping herself from going on any further.

"I know what it is like to be young. There is a hunger inside you..."

"Eeeeeew Dadima we are NOT having this discussion. Please stop now."

"You better not act like you don't know what I mean. I know these Americans have put more than that in your heads."

"No Dadima they have not. Why are you always on their case? You know I am American and I am not into all that stuff."

"Oh yes I forgot. You are royal *gora* blood since you were born here," Dadima sarcastically replied.

"What?" asked a confused and thoroughly annoyed Fatima. "That's not what I meant Dadima, and you know that. I am American by nationality. Don't take it to mean something else."

"These girls nowadays...Shhhh. In my time if my elders said jump, we would ask how high."

Fatima thought to herself, 'It's not your time nor are we in your country. So all that stuff just doesn't apply.' But there was no point in taking it any further. No point at all.

"Dadima is looking out for you," her father explained. "She just wants the best for you and she really believes that getting you married is in your best interest. She doesn't realize how different life is here. She is stuck back in her era. Just listen to her out of respect. You know that nothing can be done without your approval; so what's the big deal?"

"It's just that all that marriage stuff is so annoying. Especially forcing the *Desi* crap on me and saying 'this is Islamic and that's what good Muslims do' when it totally is not. It's just some retarded *Desi* custom that's trying to being passed off as Islamic. I can't stand that."

"Well that's why you should learn as much as possible about both our culture and faith. Then you can easily differentiate the two and focus on the faith. That will always be top priority."

"Yes Daddy I know that."

"Just take it easy now. School is what your mind should be on. Not all this garbage. You must set the example for your sisters."

"I know. I think I've heard that about one thousand times already. I need to get good grades for myself first, then I can set an example, like you would like. I gotta go do my homework now," Fatima said as she went up to her room.

She picked up her backpack and jumped on her bed so that she could lie on her stomach. She took out her math homework and began to work out her equations. As her homework increased in difficulty she began to think less about all the family melodrama and concentrated more on her work.

Chapter 9

By the time mid terms hit, Fatima was engrossed in school work. She had taken a full load of courses, all honors, so that her class rank would not suffer. Little did she realize how much would be required of her to maintain the grades she had been earning prior to this year.

Geometry was a killer and so was the teacher. Mr. Potomac was a balding stout man who the students were -in the simplest terms - afraid of. He rarely addressed his students by their first names; instead he addressed them formally as Miss Husain or Mr. Smith. There did not seem to be any room for informality in his class. The discipline he demanded was notorious, so even when students were confused, fear suppressed their desire to question any further. Fatima realized that her grades were suffering in the class because of this. She asked for extra help along with a few other students who were just as lost. Mr. Potomac agreed, but now she had to convince her parents that the difficulty of this class required her to stay after school. Fatima pleaded her case to her parents.

"Look at this," she said as she handed her parents her last test. "Can you believe that grade?"

Fatima's parents appeared confused after looking at her test. Although they were unsure of how they could possibly let Fatima stay after school, her parents did know that this was not a good sign. The "C" she earned was not like her usual performance. In their eyes, a "C" was unacceptable, almost equal to an "F", and it would be a crime to earn a "C" grade for the marking period.

Fatima knew that she could not do that, and that all necessary measures had to be taken to bring her current 82% average up.

"If I can't stay and get help with Geometry, my grades will plummet and my class rank will fall. Please understand that I need to stay, it's not a choice at this point," Fatima told her parents.

Once she informed her folks about all these issues they agreed that extra help after school was necessary, especially if Fatima's grades would be hanging in the balance.

"If it means that you can avoid earning a 'C' for the marking period then you best do it. Just make sure that no other funny business is going on," her Dad replied

"Daddy, believe me there is no funny business with Mr. Potomac around. And you have to trust me. You know that I am not like that."

"*Beta* we do trust you, we just don't trust the other students around you," Mummy said.

"Mummy, don't worry about anyone else. I know how to fend for myself. I've been doing it all along. People know what I will and will not do. That's why they don't even ask me to do half the crap they do. They know I won't have any part of it."

"Good *beta*, I am glad to hear that. We just worry for you. We don't want anything to happen to you."

"Yes I know that, but you have to let me get help when I need it. And if it means staying after school, then just trust me to do the right thing."

"Okay Okay, discussion over. You go see Mr. Potomac" her father stated.

Fatima began to periodically stay after school to get Geometry help, and this allowed her to see a more friendly side of Mr. Potomac. He was actually a funny guy who answered her questions very clearly. He just didn't do it while he was teaching as this would disturb his rhythm. Now familiar with the nicer side of Mr. Potomac, Fatima decided she would take this route whenever her Math grades dipped. It worked to her advantage and her average jumped to an 89.5% at the end of the marking period. Seeing all her effort after school, Mr. Potomac said, "Miss Husain, I don't normally do this but I will round up to the A. Your efforts leave me no choice but to do that."

Fatima thought the she could actually detect a trace of a smile as he told her the good news. She was overjoyed.

"You see Mummy, Daddy my *efforts* earned this. If I hadn't stayed after school I probably would have wound up with a C, but now it's an A. I can't believe I got an A in Mr. Potomac's class!!" exclaimed an overexcited Fatima.

"Well, at least it was worth letting her stay after school," her father said to her mother.

"Yes, but let's not make that a habit," her mother replied.

Unfortunately, the same success did not hold true with Physical Science. Despite all her efforts in that class, her mid term average was a solid "B". A "B" just would not cut it for Fatima, so she was very upset. Mr. Shanahan had never been able to explain things clearly to her and she was never comfortable with him as a person. She felt like she was inferior in his class simply because she wasn't an athlete. If one weren't into sports one just could not understand half his explanations of scientific theories as his examples were all sports based.

"Tara I can't get this at all. Is it just me or is everyone confused?" she asked her lab partner.

"It's his jock mentality. He makes it so that the athletes understand what he is talking about. Those of us who aren't into sports can't get that. And then he isn't a great advisor either, even after school help is rather difficult to follow. I think you should ask one of your friends to help you, like I am doing. Especially if they are from the other teacher's class. Maybe he explains concepts better than Mr. Shanahan," Tara suggested.

Fatima took Tara's advice and did just that. Peter was in the other Physical Science class and was most helpful. During lunch hour he would tutor Fatima and do his best to explain concepts in different styles and contexts, ones that Fatima would better understand. Peter's sessions really made a difference and Fatima knew it. The funny thing was that seeking help from Peter would undoubtedly have been forbidden by the family, since he was a boy. Fatima imagined that her mother would surely say, "You can't get any help from a girl? Can't Mary help you? Why must you go to a boy?"

But Fatima realized that avoiding boys was an impossible task. The world she functioned in outside of her family network was not segregated by gender, so she had to learn how to respectfully interact with the opposite sex without anything developing beyond a friendship. There was no question in her mind that a "relationship" with a boy was forbidden, but she felt that interacting with a boy, especially in this context, was not a crime. Peter was a great guy, a helpful tutor, a respectful classmate, and to Fatima- that was all he would ever be. She knew that if she was to develop feelings for him, or any boy for that matter, she must learn to control those sentiments. The feelings were completely natural, but controlling them was what defined her. Practicing self restraint was an essential part of her character. Fatima knew she could handle that. If she could give up eating from dawn till dusk in Ramadan, she could surely control her hormones, at least until she was ready to commit to a more meaningful relationship. That relationship, as defined by her faith and culture, would be marriage. And that was long off. But despite Fatima being confident that she could practice self control and restraint, she was sure that her family would not approve at all. Thus, she never brought up her tutoring sessions.

On the home front things hadn't changed much. Almost every time she visited her extended family, Dadima would pull out a picture of a random guy along with his bio-data, a detailed listing of the bachelor's family history and accomplishments, and show it to Fatima.

"Look he is an engineer and is good looking, tall and fair. His family is from Hyderabad too, and he is looking to move here from Dubai. He will make a good match."

"Dadimaaaaa....don't you have anything else in your purse?"

"Yeah, I have some chocolate? You want some?"

"Yes, please."

Dadima pulled out a stale Hershey's kiss saturated with the scent of her perfume and handed it to Fatima. Unknowingly, Fatima peeled off the wrapper and popped it in her mouth. Overcome by the dryness of the chocolate and the feeling of gulping down Dadima's perfume, Fatima felt sick. She quietly bent over and spit it out in the trash can while Dadima shuffled through her purse.

"Look... here is another boy. He is darker, but with boys skin color doesn't matter. Women should be fairer. And when you look better than your husband he will appreciate you more."

Fatima knew that this guy must be butt ugly for Dadima to give that type of introduction. With no interest whatsoever, she looked at the picture that was handed to her and said, "Dadima, I don't think he is my type."

"Type? What is your 'type'? We know what is good for you! In Hyderabad girls don't say a peep; here you are talking about 'type'. What has this world come to?"

Here we go again Fatima thought. She left the room quietly while Dadima rambled on about the need to get married at fifteen, and how marriage was the answer to all the world's problems. Dazed she decided to join her *chachi*s.

"Did Mamma start up again?" asked her younger *chachi* with a smirk on her face.

"You know it," Fatima replied as she plopped down on the sofa.

When she went home Fatima called Mary and whined about all this marriage business.

"I can't imagine anyone trying to get a fifteen year old married," Mary said after hearing Fatima's story.

"Tell me about it Mary. I am dying here. I have all this stuff to do for school. I feel like my brain is about to explode .So when I'm with my family it should be down time not 'add more stress to my life time'."

"Well, first of all your family is in *your* home. And if *they* aren't giving you a hard time, there is no reason to take all of this so seriously. Older people tend to babble on for no reason, you know that. Just let your grandmother say whatever she wants. Respectfully listen, and then just do what you have to do."

"I don't know man. Does your grandmother do this?"

"No way. My parents would shoot me if marriage came up before all my schooling was over."

"You see that's the way I would like it to be. I don't get it. You aren't going to have boyfriends, and neither am I. So we are not going to be screwing around. That is written in stone. So let's get the stuff that needs to get done first, and then worry about husbands."

"I know, but maybe it's a Muslim thing," Mary suggested.

"NO, it is NOT a Muslim thing. It's a Hyderabadi thing," Fatima curtly responded.

"Okay, okay. I'm sorry I didn't mean to offend you."

"It's not you Mary, I am just irritated with all this, that's all. I'll talk to you later okay?"

"Bye."

Fatima was now thoroughly annoyed. There was no doubt that she now had to consult someone who understood both her religion and culture. Someone who would give her some perspective and would know exactly what she was talking about - that someone was her H.B., Asma.

"Asma, why am I so worked up about this? How come it's bothering me so much?" Fatima inquired over the phone.

"You see it's the whole cultural baggage thing. You have this culture that demands so much of you. Marriage for example, an issue that a fifteen year old in America would never think of, but back home this topic starts when girls get their periods. And your grandmother is stuck back in Hyderabad, in a generation even before our parents. What else can you expect from her?"

"I know, I know. But what bothers me is that she is drilling it into my parents' heads. They're sure to follow suit. I know them. Now they're okay but soon it will be 'What's so wrong with getting engaged?' What will I say then?"

"I see your point, but I think you're really overreacting. No one is going to be able to force you into anything. You're in America, babe. That can't happen here."

"Thank God for that!" Fatima replied.

"Just take a chill pill and think about the top priority in your life-school. The better you do, the more time you may be able to buy in order to delay the whole marriage business."

"Asma, you are a God-send. Thanks so much."

"That's why I am your H.B., right?" Asma laughed.

"You got that right!" a relieved Fatima replied.

Back at school, her freshman year was wrapping up and finals were just around the corner. Anxiety began to set in and Fatima was frustrated with all of the work that had to get done. Mary would work with her in preparation for the History and English finals while Peter continued to assist with the Physical Science. Geometry was getting better, now that she regularly saw Mr. Potomac after school, and slowly the loose ends were being tied up. As finals came around, Fatima studied hard and performed well on all her exams. She earned and "A" in every class except Physical Science, in which she brought home a "B", much to the dismay of her parents.

"What is this *beta*? The sciences are the key to your future, how can a "B" get you anywhere?" her father asked.

"You know I don't think that science is my forte. I worked so hard to get an 'A,' but I still wound up with a 'B.' That tells me that I am just not cut out for science."

"Did you get help in this subject?" her father inquired.

"I tried to Dad, but I couldn't understand anything - even with tutoring." Fatima intentionally answered vaguely. No need to mention Peter...

"You keep working hard, and watch - your science grade will be an 'A' next year," her father replied.

"Even if that does happen... I... don't think... I don't think I want to go into medicine."

Fatima bit her lip. She knew she was diving into shallow water, but before she could stop herself that sentence had just rolled off her tongue.

"What? You can't let one 'B' stop you from being a doctor. Don't waste your brains by giving up that dream," her mother said.

"Actually Mummy, that dream ended a while back."

"Oh God. What has happened to this girl? It's your mother's talk of marriage. She has given up her dreams so that she can get married early," Fatima's mother told her father.

"No Mummy that's not true! I blow off all that marriage baloney that Dadima talks about!"

"It's not baloney. For girls who don't want to pursue medicine that *is* the best route. Mamma knew that marriage was best for you," her disappointed father stated.

"What?!? Dad you must be kidding. This has nothing to do with marriage and I am not giving up school. I love school, I just don't care for science. Is that soooo bad?"

"Then what else could you study? What other decent jobs are out there for?" asked her mother.

"Mummy, there are one thousand fields to choose from. I don't have to decide right now. All I know is that science is hard for me and quite frankly I have no interest in it."

"Your lack of interest in it is what lead you to make this decision. Not your brains. You can be a doctor any day. But you have decided that it is not *interesting* enough for you," her father said.

"I did not decide. I'm just not naturally inclined towards it."

"What are you inclined towards then? Some useless subject that will have you earning nothing?" her father quipped.

"Jeez. Can we please stop the drama here? I'm not saying I am dropping out of high school here. I just don't think I want to do medicine. There are successful careers out there that do not involve medicine you know. I would love to explore those possibilities."

"Like what?"

"For example you both know I love religious studies, I could study about religion. I also like politics and would look forward to pursuing a career in teaching politics. Educating people that Muslims aren't all terrorists and that they face the same problems all other people do is an important job. Don't we have to promote tolerance and understanding?"

As Fatima continued her parents fell silent and began to cool down. Listening to her case, they realized that she may have a point. The reasons that Fatima expressed for pursuing the fields of social science were credible, although difficult to accept, as would be the case for most Muslim or *Desi* parents. After a painfully long pause Fatima's father spoke, "I think you know us well enough to realize that we'll support you in whatever you choose to do with your life. We were just hoping that you would choose a field that garnered respect and would allow you to stand on your own two feet. We want you to be valued in the community, and do good service for our people. We know you have the ability to achieve success in whatever you put your mind to, it just would've been nice to see you apply yourself in a field where there will always be a job and demand is high."

"Daddy, what makes you think that medicine will always fit that bill?"

"It's just something that has always held true."

"What if I could do something along the lines of reaching out to others and educating them about our faith and really impacting their feelings about Islam and Muslims?"

"If you really think you can have some positive effect, then I'd have to commend you and support you."

Her father looked like he had suffered a major defeat. Even as he offered Fatima his support, he appeared to be giving a concession speech.

"Thanks Daddy. I knew you would eventually understand."

"*Beta*, for our children we'll do anything. Even if it's not what we originally thought was in their best interests. We just pray that God guides you to the paths that suit you all best," her mother added.

"Thanks Mummy, I really needed to hear that from you."

Fatima knew full well that this topic was not over, but it was a tremendous relief to have it come out in the open. She was finally honest with her parents, and let them know what she was thinking. She was sure that they had not completely accepted the reality of the situation, even though they appeared to understand. The subject would definitely be addressed again, but for now it was a burden she was free of.

Although high school was out for the summer, Sunday school was still in session. Now that she was no longer a student, Fatima volunteered as a teacher. She had the opportunity to teach a beginner class, Fundamental Arabic, which taught four and five year olds to recognize the Arabic alphabet. Fatima's task was to make sure that the letters were understood in the light of *Quranic* Arabic so that recitation of the Qur'an could be facilitated. Arabic and Urdu share the same letter system, and since many of the students' parents had an Urdu background, they taught their children these letters at home with the Urdu pronunciation of each letter. However, in order to read Arabic correctly, these letters had to be re-taught in the Arabic format.

Fatima shared this responsibility with other teenagers from her community whom she had gotten to know over the past few years. One of whom was Afia, a pleasant girl, with whom Fatima passed many Sunday afternoons. Afia was about five years older than Fatima but the age difference was never obvious between the two, as Fatima had always been mature for her age.

They would also spend time together outside of Sunday school, doing the normal girly things like hanging out at the mall, and going to the movies, except that many times they were accompanied by adults. The supervision wasn't just due to parental paranoia; it was there because of the many instances of harassment that the girls had faced because of their *hijaab*.

The last time they went to the mall alone, while paying for a sweater that Afia was purchasing, a store clerk had given them attitude, and both girls clearly heard the woman saying, "Crazy foreigners," under her breath. The girls were appalled and turned to each other in shock. As the transaction was completed Afia whispered to Fatima, "Did she say what I think she just said?"

"You mean the crazy foreigners comment?" Fatima asked.

"Yes, that's exactly what I mean. What the heck was that about?" an upset Afia wondered.

Had they wanted they could have reported her to the store manager, but they chose to ignore her.

"It's not going to do anything Afia. She won't change. She is obviously ignorant," Fatima said as they left the department store.

"That's not the point. I can't imagine how these people can be so rude to our face, like we don't understand them or something," Afia replied.

"Maybe that is it. They think our English is so horrible that we can't decipher what it is that they are saying," Fatima suggested.

"It's sad man. Born here and bred here. But if we choose to cover our hair we become foreigners. What's that all about?" Afia asked.

"Who knows? These same people respect the nuns for wearing their habits, but our scarves are degraded. I never got that. But let's step back for a second and think... who was it that made this comment? How much do you think she knows about Muslims? She probably hasn't been exposed to Muslims or anyone different than herself," Fatima questioned.

"I know, I know. But her comment was uncalled for. I am just annoyed," Afia stated as she shook her head disapprovingly.

Situations like these were not uncommon and their parents feared that worse incidents could follow. Therefore, they felt that their presence would somehow ward off these ridiculous occurrences. This was obviously not the case.

Despite her negative experiences, Afia really was proud of her identity and wore her *hijaab* all the time. She was the first Muslim girl Fatima knew that had the guts to wear it at school. She was an inspiration to all the other girls in their community and was a glistening hope for all the parents.

"You see how Afia is wearing the *hijaab*. She doesn't care about what others say, she is only concerned with what pleases God. This is how you all should be," Fatima's father advised his daughter while sipping his tea.

"Daddy, I know what she's doing is great. But maybe she handles peer pressure better than I do," shrugged Fatima as she sat down with a glass of milk next to her father.

"*Beta*, I'm not sure why you can't handle this 'peer pressure'. How can you let your classmates keep you from doing what's right?"

"They're not stopping me from wearing it to school. I am just afraid of how they will react."

"You haven't even given them a chance. They may react nicely, you don't know until you try it. You wear it everywhere else and you deal with everyone's reactions outside of school in a dignified manner. Why can't you try to do that at school? Maybe the kids won't even notice and you could wear the *hijaab* without any problem..." her mother interposed as she joined her husband for their evening tea.

"Mummy they *will* notice. How many times have I been followed by security at the mall? How many rude comments have been passed by people about being a terrorist? I don't know if I can deal with that type of atmosphere at school."

"You have already learned to tolerate this ignorance outside of school. You've learned that people will always say some thing or another. Even without wearing the *hijaab* some *gadha*, called you a dot-head. But that didn't break you. You shouldn't let anyone stop you from doing what you believe is right."

"I'll think about it," Fatima replied. "I really want to, I think you know that. I just have to prepare myself to do it. I wish there was at least one person that would wear it to school with me, then I wouldn't feel so paranoid."

"Your wish may come true," her father smiled. "You know Fareha's family is moving close to the high school. She will most likely be joining Pennsbury next year. I know that she wears the *hijaab* as well, so if she continues to wear it in school you will have someone to lean on when you start."

"Really? I didn't know that they were moving here. If she was wearing the *hijaab* along with me, it would make a world of a difference," said Fatima.

"And soon enough Mona will start high school, and she wants to wear *hijaab* to the high school as well. So with all three of you there it really should make your life easier," Mummy added.

"I hope so."

"I'll try to start next year if Fareha is there with me," Fatima resolved.

Chapter 10

Over the summer, Fareha's family moved from North Jersey into a suburb close to Pennsbury High School. Fareha's mother, Shaheen, was one of Fatima's mother's good friends, and their move was a welcome change for the Husain girls. Fareha related well to Fatima and her sisters because of their common heritage and similar personalities. The girls would all hang out and discuss everything under the sun. From their lack of interest in sewing, which happened to be both of their mothers' favorite pastimes, to their interest in Bollywood movies, they would spend hours gabbing away. Of course, the change in Fareha's school also came up in their conversations. Fatima took this opportunity to ask Fareha about her *hijaab*.

"Do you plan on wearing it to school?"

"Of course. Don't you?" Fareha questioned Fatima.

"I haven't decided yet. I would like to, but I'm nervous about it."

"Well, I am wearing it," Fareha replied without any hesitation.

Fareha had made it clear that she could care less what the consequences were. She was going to wear her *hijaab*. However, Fatima still remained apprehensive. She thought that the friends that she had made would abandon her as soon as her *hijaab* was put on. Fareha told her otherwise.

"If they are your real friends, they will accept it as a part of you. They know who *you* are, so why does it matter what you wear."

"Fareha, you have no clue what most of the students are like here. They don't wear anything that's not designer wear and they are very judgmental."

"And *those* are the type of people you want to be friends with Fatima?"

"No, it's not that. I just feel that I would like to maintain the friendships that I have made."

"Which of your friends do you doubt?"

"Well I know Mary wouldn't desert me, she is great. Neither will Tara, she is really open-minded and intelligent. As far as the others go, I just don't know."

"Then you need to sift out who your true friends are. It sounds like you already have two good friends. You have to see if the others are really your friends or if they are just tagging along."

"I guess so...." replied an unsure Fatima. She was confused and nervous. She wanted to wear the *hijaab* at school because she truly felt that it was the right thing to do, but at what cost? She pondered over this dilemma over and over again.

"I need to talk it over some more and then come to a decision," she told Fareha.

She decided to consult both Asma and Afia.

"I can't imagine your friends blatantly deserting you just because of the *hijaab*," Asma stated.

"You were already different because you never partied with them, nor did you socially hang out with them, and that *Desi* skin tone of yours isn't exactly status quo either. So what is wearing the *hijaab* on top of all that?"

"I don't know why it's such a big step for me to sport it at school. Wearing it every where else was an easy decision, and I dealt with all the consequences of wearing it without flinching, but when it comes to sporting it at school, I am *really* nervous," Fatima responded.

"Fatima, speaking from experience, it's no different than wearing it at the mall. You will get a few comments and some weird looks, but the people who will do that to you would've done it for any number of reasons. So if you really want to wear it at school, go for it. You're strong willed, you'll be fine," Afia stated.

Both of these girls convinced her that she had the will power to wear the *hijaab* to school and that it would not be as disastrous as Fatima had originally foreseen.

Fatima knew that all of her classmates were very well aware that she was a practicing Muslim. Thus, she began to realize that Asma and Afia were right. Why would it be such a shock to them to see her with a scarf? Most knew that this was a requirement for Muslim women. In fact, they probably wondered why Fatima didn't wear the *hijaab*.

Fatima finally decided it was time. She would start wearing the *hijaab* to school come fall of her sophomore year. She had made, what in her eyes was, a monumental decision. Wearing the *hijaab* would clearly identify her as a Muslim before anything else.

She now had to mentally prepare herself to carry out this brave step. She would no longer come off simply as a *Desi*, she would now represent her Islamic faith, a fact that she actually enjoyed. She was Muslim, proud of it, and anxious to talk about it, but *now* she would look it too. It was time for Fatima to walk the walk of a Muslim, when it came to proper Islamic dress, and not just talk the talk.

Although she had made up her mind to wear the *hijaab* to school, Fatima did not announce this to her family. She was afraid that if she was not able to go through with it, her parents would be very disappointed. The frustration they felt in her choosing a career other than medicine was more than enough for them to handle at this time.

Ayesha had also committed to wearing the *hijaab* to school and was joined by her friend, Maariya. They too, were ready to face all the baggage that accompanied wearing the *hijaab*. But these girls were secure and intrepid, unaffected by what their peers thought of them. For all her confidence, which sometimes veered towards cockiness at home, Fatima could be the exact opposite at school. She was insecure and unsure of herself. But she realized her decision was the right one, and that she would do her best to carry it out.

By fall, the girls' resolve was strong, and they were all ready to attend school with their *hijaab*s pinned on. This was a part of who they were, take it or leave it - just in time for the school year to begin...

At 6:15 am the alarm went off, but there really was no need for it. Fatima lay in her bed wide awake picturing all the possible scenarios that she may face when she returned to school wearing her *hijaab*. She did not sleep well and was edgy. After turning her alarm off, she jumped out of bed and went on with her usual school morning routine. After she got dressed and was set to go, Fatima pinned her black *hijaab* around her hair. She had chosen a black scarf specifically so that it would not stand out as much as a colored one would have. Black was similar to her hair color and from a distance it may appear to be the top of one's head, whereas a white scarf would stick out like a sore thumb. Anything that would diminish her difference in appearance was good.

Once her *hijaab* was on, Fatima anxiously walked out of her bedroom, throwing her Eastpack over shoulder. Her father and mother saw her come down the stairs, and their faces broke out in the largest smiles that Fatima had seen in quite sometime.

"Okay, let's not make a big deal out of this Mom and Dad. I need to run to the bus stop. *Khuda Hafiz*," she said as she waved good bye and walked out the door.

Fatima knew her parents were pleased and she was sure that they would have had some encouraging words for her, but she was just too nervous to talk to anyone. She just wanted to get to school and get her first day over with.

Her first major test would come at the bus stop. The students all exchanged the normal "Hi's" and "Hello's", but said nothing to Fatima about her head covering. They didn't stare at her or do anything to make her feel uneasy; her insecurity was doing that all on its own. She kept wondering what it was that the other kids were thinking and how she would respond to a myriad of questions that she had imagined they would pose to her. Yet nothing was said after the initial greeting. The silence grew terribly awkward for her.

By the time the bus arrived, Fatima was a wreck. Her body temperature was rising and her hands felt clammy. But more than anything she was worried senseless about what the other riders would say when she embarked on the bus.

Once the bus arrived Fatima boarded and did not make eye contact with anyone. She quickly sat in the very first row of seats, and kept her eyes fixated on the ground. Her ears were on high alert; she was waiting for one of the punks to make some stupid comment, but again, nothing was said. 'Maybe I sat down quickly enough so that no one noticed me walk aboard', she thought to herself. 'Or maybe everyone is still half asleep and won't bother saying anything. Or they may be waiting for the best time to say something horrid.' As she tapped her feet nervously, the bus ride seemed to take forever.

Finally, the bus stopped at the high school and Fatima hastily exited the bus, rushing towards her homeroom. Once again, she avoided making any eye contact with any of her peers. Every body appeared to be a blur at the pace she was moving. She was sure that she had passed by some friendly faces; however, she was too tense to even look up and say "Hello." She was trying her best to avoid running into anyone she knew, even though she knew that was impossible.

She finally found her homeroom and quickly located her desk. By this time she was sweating. She was more nervous than she could have imagined. Discreetly checking her under her arms, she was relieved that her antiperspirant was working. She had applied an extra layer that morning knowing full well that the claims that the deodorant's commercials had made would be tested today! 'Thank God it worked!' she thought, very relieved.

Once she sat down she looked at her schedule and handouts, picking them up off her desk and moving them closer to her face. She wanted to appear absorbed in reading her papers so that she would not have to make any friendly conversation.

While Fatima acted like an engrossed student, Leona walked into the room and to her desk, which was yet again, directly in front of Fatima's.

"Hey Fatima. What's up?" Leona asked.

"Not much Leona," an uptight Fatima replied.

"So you started wearing your scarf...."

Fatima put down her papers and hesitantly answered, "Uhhh...Yeh....uhh.. I did."

"Cool. Hey, are we going to have the same English class, I see Mrs. Cosby's name on your schedule," Leona pointed out as she looked at Fatima's schedule.

"I'm not sure, let me look," Fatima said as she compared both of their schedules. "Yeah I guess we are," Fatima responded with a smile.

"And look we have Algebra 2 together as well, with Mr. Potomac! Again! I can't believe we have him again!"

"Really? I'm actually happy about that. He was actually a very nice person once you got to know him."

"I guess," Leona answered.

Fatima was pleasantly surprised as to how quickly the transition from a question about her *hijaab* to a normal conversation was accomplished. Leona had made it very easy. But Fatima justified this amicable response by thinking that this was Leona, a classmate who had always been sweet and easy to have a discussion with. She wasn't like the majority of Fatima's peers at Pennsbury.

The bell rang and most of the desks were now occupied. Fatima was watching her classmates' reactions to her out of the corner of her eye, while she was carrying on her conversation with Leona. No one seemed to make any obvious gestures or comments that could be interpreted as offensive, but that didn't stop Fatima from being on guard. Everyone stood up as the national anthem played and pledged their allegiance to the flag. After they sat down, Fatima continued to immerse herself in her schedule so that she could avoid conversing with anyone who could possibly insult her.

Once homeroom was adjourned Fatima left the room and walked towards her first class, Biology. Two hallways into her walk, she began to notice familiar faces doing double takes. It seemed as if her peers needed to look twice to recognize that it was actually Fatima- in her *hijaab*. Fatima had not heard any of them say anything, but she definitely noticed the way they were looking at her. She hastened her pace, still averting eye contact. She walked into Mr. Godwin's Biology Lab and took a seat near the back. She sat at an empty table twiddling her thumbs, and waited anxiously to see who would sit next to her. It would be an amazing blessing if Tara were to walk in like she did last year in Mr. Shanahan's class. But the chances of that happening again were very slim. She waited and waited, still trying to look occupied, until finally she had someone join her. She looked up to behold a face that she was not familiar with.

"Hi, I am Stacy. Is anyone sitting here?" the girl asked in a Southern belle accent.

"No, you can sit here. I am Fatima. Are you new here?"

"Yes, my family just moved here from South Carolina."

"I didn't recognize you so I figured you were new. How do you like it here?"

"It's different. It's a lot busier here than back home. And this school is really monstrous."

"Well, have you made any friends since you got here?"

"No. People aren't that friendly in this neck of the woods...."

Fatima laughed.

"I guess you're right. But they aren't that bad either. You just need to get to know them." Fatima was surprised at what was coming out of her mouth.

"I hope that's true. Where I come from the neighbors would have all visited a new family with some apple pie or bread pudding and made small talk with my momma. But people here don't even wave hello to each other. It's so cold."

"Don't worry, you'll get used to all of it. In no time you will fit right in," Fatima comforted her.

"I don't know. I just feel really different here," Stacy said to an amazed Fatima. 'This girl feels different?' Fatima thought to herself. 'Doesn't she see my golden skin and black scarf?'

"Don't worry you will blend in soon enough," again Fatima was surprised at what was rolling off her tongue.

"I sure hope so," she replied in her charming manner.

Fatima was amazed that this girl had not asked where she was from or any silly question that Fatima had expected to be asked. Instead she was worried about how different *she* was. How strange.

Mr. Godwin welcomed the class to his lab and began to conduct his introduction. The girls took notes and placed his handouts in their folders. Fatima kept noticing other students looking at her strangely. But she did not budge; she looked straight ahead and refused to acknowledge their reactions to her. She kept saying to herself, "At least they aren't saying anything," attempting to see the glass as half full.

The day went on and the looks persisted, but still no comments were made. Her friends from previous years greeted her and acknowledged her scarf by looking straight at it, but said nothing of it. As strange as it was Fatima wished that they would come right out and ask about it rather than look at it curiously. But maybe this was their way of being respectful about it and not offending her. Whatever the case may have been, only Leona had asked about her *hijaab*.

Fatima was sure that Mr. Potomac would ask about her *hijaab* especially since he knew Fatima so well from the previous year, but even he remained respectfully quiet. He simply called her name out during attendance, looked at her, and nodded in acknowledgment. That was it. Fatima was rather surprised that he had said nothing but she was relieved as well. This type of silent acknowledgment wasn't bad after all.

At the end of the day Fatima packed up some of her books while she stood by her locker. While she stood there deciding which books needed to go home and which could be left at school, she felt a pat on her back. She turned around to discover Fareha, also *hijaab* clad, standing behind her.

"Salaam Fatima. I see you are wearing it," she said with a big smile as her eyes and eyebrows signaled towards Fatima's scarf.

"Yeah, I know. But I can't tell you how uneasy I was all day."

"But the day is over; your first bridge has been crossed. Congratulations."

"Thanks, but I'm still nervous about tomorrow."

"As nervous as you were about today?"

"Noooo definitely not that nervous. But still nervous. You know what I mean?"

"Yeah I do, but you'll be fine."

"*Inshallah.*"

"I gotta catch the bus, see you tomorrow, *Khuda hafiz*"

"*Khuda Hafiz*," Fatima replied.

On her bus ride home Fatima analyzed the day's events. She wanted to gauge the kind of response to expect the following day. The initial response had been tolerable but what would happen once she began to socialize with her classmates? She was an expert at making a mountain out of a molehill, and she was doing exactly that, all in her head. Once off the bus, Fatima walked home slowly. She expected that questions would be asked about how her day went.

Fatima was clearly unsettled about the propaganda of the whole *hijaab* issue, but she knew it would have to be dealt with. She unlocked the door. Without saying a word, she took her shoes off and ran straight upstairs into her bedroom. She changed out of her school clothes and into her shalwar khameez, just as she had done since she was five. After washing her face she came down and her mother finally saw her.

"When did you come home?"

"Five minutes ago Mummy."

"How was your first day?"

"Not too bad, I can't complain."

"Did you run into Fareha?"

"Yeah I did. It was nice to see her there."

"Well there are some cut fruits in the fridge, help yourself."

"Thanks Mummy."

And that was it. Somehow Fatima's mother knew that Fatima wasn't ready to talk about the *hijaab* at school, thus she said nothing of it. Her mother was very in tune with her daughter's moods and temperament and knew how to deal with them. While Fatima was quietly eating her fruit, Ayesha came home bubbly and excited. Unlike Fatima, she was excited to share her day's events with the family.

"Mummy, Maariya and I are in two classes together and we actually get to sit next to each other. It's so cool having two *muhajabas* in the same class!" exclaimed an excited Ayesha.

"Did anybody say anything to you two?" Fatima asked

"No, I don't think so. Even if they had I wouldn't have cared. What do they know? It's not like I want to be their best friend or something. I have Maariya for that."

"That's good to know Ayesha. We are proud of *all* of you for following our faith's principles. God will reward you for following his orders especially when it's difficult for you to do so."

Fatima knew that a large part of that statement was for her benefit even though it was made to Ayesha. Her mother had comforted her in the best way possible, in a discreet manner, and with that simple sentence she made Fatima feel warm inside.

Fatima went up to her room and performed the afternoon prayers. She thanked God for making her first day a tolerable one and prayed for help to be able to carry on wearing the *hijaab*.

After her prayers were done, she began to cut brown paper bags and customize each such that they were a perfect fit for all the texts that required book covers. From her room, she heard the front door open. She could make out her father's voice as he gave his *salam* to her mother and sisters.

After her books were covered, she went downstairs and found her father sitting in the family room with her mother. Both parents were beaming. Fatima could tell just by their manner and by the way they looked at her that they were very pleased with her decision.

"So *beta*, how did your day go?" her father inquired.

"Well Dad it was not that bad."

"Anybody bother you?" he asked.

"Actually, no. Thank God."

"Good to hear. Are any of your friends in your classes?"

"I think so, but I really tried to avoid everyone today, so I am not sure who is in which class with me," Fatima responded.

"That can't go on too long dear."

"I know. It will just take me a few days," she acknowledged.

"After that you will be fine."

"I hope so."

The next few days were pretty much the same. Her friends were cordial to her and even though they questioned her about her *hijaab*, their interest was genuine. Best of all, they did not change the way they behaved with her. Mary was surprised that Fatima actually wore it, but she was also proud that her friend went through with something that had scared her so much. Tara, the eccentric friend, appreciated everyone for who they really were, so the *hijaab* was no issue for her. For Tara this change was just a part of Fatima coming to terms with who she really was within.

"More power to you Fatima," she encouraged.

The only people who Fatima had seen snickering at her were two girls, Joan and Kelly, who were the epitome of snobs. These two laughed and made fun of everyone; this was not a new pastime for them. Their mocking annoyed Fatima, but it didn't do much beyond that. These were the type of people that Fatima had anticipated would make rude remarks, and were doing just as she had expected, but even they could not say anything to her face.

After a week in school, Fatima slowly let her guard down, and was beginning to feel at ease. She started to interact with her peers and actually had normal conversations with them as she did in her years up till now. She also realized that many of her friends had the same classes as she did. Mary and Leona were in her Algebra 2 class with Mr. Potomac, and Tara was in her Spanish class with Senora Humburg. All three of them were in her MG English class which was taught by the delightful Mrs. Cosby.

Fatima had taken an immediate liking to Mrs. Cosby. She was a frail, middle aged blonde with an amiable disposition. She was passionate about what she taught and that passion infected her students. Fatima was excited to read the texts that were assigned, and even more anxious to discuss them in her class. Her interest in Shakespeare flourished, and it was Mrs. Cosby's doings alone that created her enthusiasm for the subject.

Biology was the only class where Fatima still felt uneasy, but seeing Stacy's insecurity actually helped her feel much better about herself. Stacy was still adjusting to her new environment and turned out to be quite timid. Fatima tried her best to make her feel welcome at the school and to propose activities that would encourage Stacy to get out and meet people.

"Hey why don't you try out for the softball team since you said you used to play it back in South Carolina?"

"No, Fatima, I don't think I will. The girls here seem to be really competitive, and when I play, it's for fun."

"Well *you* can still play for fun. Let them be the competitors."

"No. I wouldn't be comfortable with that."

"Well then why don't you go to Homecoming? You might meet people there that have common interests."

"Do *you* go to Homecoming or the dance that follows?"

"No, Stacy I can't go to the dance." Fatima went on to explain the religious reasons that did not allow her to participate in the dance.

"That's really interesting. I never met a Muslim before you. I just saw them on TV. It's cool to actually meet one."

Fatima laughed.

"That is good to hear. Such a nice change from all the negative stereotyping we face."

"Kinda like all of southerners being Confederate red necks, huh?"

"Yeah kind of like that," Fatima said with a smile.

"But I may just take you up on that advice and go to the game. It never hurts to show some school spirit," Stacy stated.

"Do it. I hope you get a chance to meet some people that you would feel comfortable with."

"I sure hope so too," she responded with a smile. "Do you have your Bio notes from yesterday? I think I am missing part of them."

"Let me check," Fatima replied as class was about to commence.

Mr. Godwin, their Biology teacher, was a laid back teacher who tried to make his class feel at ease, a stark contrast to the fast paced and high strung Mr. Shanahan. This was a blessing for Fatima. Fatima could not have handled another year of a teacher like Mr. Shanahan. She was relieved that this year science wouldn't be a turnoff just because of the teacher. If the subject still did not appeal to her, it would be solely because of the subject matter, and not the teacher who taught it. In fact, she was still hoping that she could develop an interest in Biology just in the off chance that she may want to pursue it further in college. Fatima felt that Mr. Godwin's personality increased the likelihood of that happening. And she hoped this may be the start of something surprisingly pleasant.

As Mr. Godwin wrapped up his class the students began to put away their notebooks in their backpacks. Fatima realized that she had not had given Stacy yesterday's notes.

"Stacy, why don't you come with me to my locker? I am almost positive that the notes are in there."

"Sure," Stacy responded.

The bell rang and the girls walked to Fatima's locker. As Fatima was talking to Stacy and exchanging her books, a student walked behind her and suddenly shouted, "Towel head!"

Before she could turn around and see who had the guts to make such a remark, the student had flown off. Stacy's jaw dropped and she stood in silence, staring at Fatima. Everyone else around Fatima stopped what they were doing and looked at her in anticipation of some sort of reaction. But she remained calm and went back to getting her texts without so much as flinching.

"Just ignore him," Stacy advised.

"That's exactly what I am doing," Fatima responded.

But she could not ignore what just had happened. Fatima was angry. She felt her heart pounding and her blood was boiling. She was insulted, and she wanted to see the coward that made such a statement. But he did not have the guts to stick around. And even if he had, what could Fatima have done besides yell back at him. Nothing. She could do nothing. 'What a JERK,' she thought to herself. 'What a total moron.' She felt humiliated in front of everyone and fought off tears.

"Stacy I need to go to the bathroom. I will see you later," she said abruptly walking away.

Stacy nodded. She knew Fatima was hurt, her wrinkled eyebrows, half frown, and pink eyes said it all.

Fatima walked into the bathroom and closed the door to her stall. Her tears flowed liked a river. The past two weeks of adjustment were marred by this slur. She felt belittled and ashamed. She didn't want to leave the bathroom nor did she want to see any of her classmates. Her strong personality crumbled at that moment and she struggled to regain her composure.

Minutes passed and the bell had rung. She knew she was already late for class. But she was still upset. Her head was still hidden in her hands. As angry as she was, she knew she that she couldn't succumb to this nonsense. 'I will not let this bring me down,' she began to repeat to herself. After a few minutes of wiping away her tears she stepped out and washed her face with cold water. With her swollen eyes, she straightened out her *hijaab*, and stood upright. She intentionally pulled her shoulders back and walked with her neck stretched out so that her head was held high.

'I will not feel little,' she thought to herself as she left for her next class.

Despite her valiant efforts, she could not think straight for the rest of the day. She became aloof with her friends and sat quietly in all of her classes. Mary noticed her remoteness and asked, "Are you okay Fatima?"

"Yeah, I am okay," she responded with a blank stare.

"You don't look okay."

"No I am fine," she reiterated. Fatima didn't want to talk. Not even to her good friends. This was just something that she felt that she would have to deal with on her own.

Fatima functioned on auto pilot. All she could think about was how insulted she felt.

For Fatima this incident proved to be the straw that broke the camel's back. She had faced bigoted remarks for quite some time now and was able to cope with them, knowing that the person dishing it out would not be seen or heard from again. But in school she knew it wasn't the same. Whoever insulted her would be around all the time.

What she feared most was that this person may have inadvertently opened the door for others to act as obnoxiously towards her as he had. This was the very fear that she had which had made her put off wearing the *hijaab* to school. But now that she had made the decision to wear it, there was no turning back. It all came down to how she would react to and handle this situation.

She realized that her hurt was too much and that she needed to vent. She knew that she did this best through her writing. She stopped taking notes. Instead she would write off her pain by composing a letter to Asma.

She began to pen her thoughts:

Dear Asma,

I can't begin to explain what I feel right now, but I know that I need to talk (or in this case -write) to someone. You have always been a good adviser to me so I felt it best to write to you.

As you know, wearing the hijaab isn't always easy. I have been teased numerous times by total strangers and been given the dirtiest looks imaginable. I must admit that these actions would bother me, but somehow I would manage to get over them. That was until today.

This morning while I was at my locker with a friend, some creep walked behind me and yelled out "Towel head". 'Towel-head,' those words keep ringing in my head and I don't know why I can't make them stop. It's not like I haven't been offended before, but this incident hurt me like no other. I am trying to figure out why and I just don't know. Maybe it's because this happened in school, a place where I had never been insulted in this manner before. Or maybe it was because I was just growing comfortable with wearing the hijaab in this environment when this was thrown at me like a ton of bricks. I can't pinpoint to you the reason as to why I am so angry and hurt, but I am both of those things and the pain is so intense.

I don't feel like saying a word to anyone. I feel like if I say anything maybe they will say something like that creep did. I wish I had seen who that jerk was. Not that I would fight him, but I would love to know who the coward was that would say such a thing behind my back and run away. Aaagggggbhh, it's useless. There's nothing to gain in knowing who he was I guess. The damage has been done. I am so sad. Really sad. Any advice for your friend?

Sincerely,

Fatima

The school day ended and Fatima was still abnormally reserved. She got on her bus and sat quietly, staring out the window, trying to figure out who among the swarm of students walking to their buses could have been the one to hurt her this way?

The bus drove her home and even after the ride, Fatima was still aloof. She walked into her house and dropped all of her school stuff right by the door. She stepped into the washroom and took off her *hijaab*, and hung it on top of the towel rack. As she washed her face with cold water she looked at herself in the mirror. She saw her puffy red eyes, circles underneath them, and an all around unhealthy look. Shocked by the sight, she thought, 'What the hell is wrong with me? Why do I look like this? Why am I letting that jerk get to me in this way?'

She finished rinsing off her cleanser and dried her face. 'I am not going to fall apart over some stupid comment,' she decided. 'I just won't do it any more.' She built up her courage and decided that the face she saw in the mirror just now was not one she wanted to see again. Her tough as nails personality would have to re-emerge and she was not going to be a sissy about an issue such as this.

She greeted her mother with her salaam as she walked out of the bathroom.

"*Beta*, are you okay?" her mother asked noticing her pretentious look.

"Yeah Mummy I'm fine," Fatima firmly replied, and in her heart she knew she really was going to be just fine.

She would not let it be any other way.

Chapter 11

The next morning Fatima left for school somewhat nervous, but very much eager to deal with any crap that may come her way. The anticipated "storm" had hit and was now over. She actually felt somewhat relieved that the worst was over and she now knew exactly how it felt. Moreover she now trusted herself were anything to happen again. She felt strong and prepared. 'This is something I can handle. Until it happens again I will not think about it. It's over and done with. My life is moving on,' she thought to herself as she rode the bus to school.

Once at school the day unfolded in the most routine fashion. Fatima was off to homeroom and then Biology.

"Hey are you okay?" Stacy hesitantly inquired while working on their lab assignment.

"Yeah I am fine. Shit happens," Fatima replied. "Could you grab the Petri dish?" she asked.

Stacy was a little surprised by her response and decided not to pursue any more questioning.

"Good to know Fatima. I am glad to see that your head is on firm shoulders," she stated as she pulled out the samples on the Petri dishes that they had to examine.

"It has to be Stacy. I am an American Muslim. It can't be any other way if I want to live my life to its fullest."

"Man every time I talk to you I wish others could see that Muslims can be so normal," Stacy replied.

"Normal and Muslim are two words that you will NOT hear in the same sentence," Fatima laughed while adjusting the magnification of their microscope.

"Especially now with all that's going on in the Persian Gulf."

"I was going to ask you about that. That guy from Iraq – he has the same last name as you!" Stacy pointed out, inquisitive yet surprised.

"I know…." Fatima replied, rolling her eyes and shaking her head.

"Husain is such a common last name amongst Muslims. But if this guy turns out to be a trouble maker I will never hear the end of it," she jokingly predicted.

Little did Fatima realize what was in store for her.

Social Studies this year would prove to be very interesting. As Saddam Hussein began to invade Kuwait and American intervention seemed inevitable, the topic of war was discussed in great detail. The shared last name of the Iraqi dictator and Fatima was brought up numerous times and it eventually became a common joke that Fatima became immune towards.

"Does it bother you that all of a sudden, everyone has a comment about your name?" Mary asked Fatima after one such discussion had ended.

"I was used to everyone butchering my name and saying it all weird. But now everyone knows exactly how to pronounce my last name thanks to Saddam Hussein," she said laughingly. "Seriously though, I know that everyone at school knows that I am nothing like Saddam Hussein or any of the people that he is associated with. I also know that everyone is aware that I am a lot like everybody else *here*. So if I know that all the jokes about this whole situation are in good spirit, then why shouldn't I laugh with all the rest of the class?"

Fatima's positive attitude made the jokes about her last name (Husain) through the months of the Desert Shield/ Storm much easier for her to take, at least within the walls of Pennsbury High. Teachers appreciated Fatima's nonchalant attitude and were quick to make light of the potentially sticky situation. Mr. Lars, her Social Studies teacher, would teasingly say, "Let's not upset Fatima. We don't want her to pull any strings…"

In fact, he wasn't the only teacher that joked with Fatima. Even stern Mr. Potomac would occasionally ask Fatima, "So how is your Uncle Saddam?"

At first Fatima would respond with a quiet smile, but after a couple of times of being asked the same questions she joked, "He isn't doing too hot now that he is getting his butt kicked," garnering a few laughs from the class.

She learned to use humor and respond to these questions with a grin rather than a grimace. It wasn't worth arguing about or getting offended over. She knew that if she reacted adversely it would prove to be fuel for a fire that many obnoxious students would feed off of. Instead she chose to lay low and laugh with everyone so that it would never become a heated issue.

Unfortunately the scenario was not the same outside school. Horrid images of Iraqi soldiers and leaders calling for holy war plagued the TV and the image of Muslims was being trashed yet again. Fatima's family was getting harassing phone calls, and even saying their last name was proving to be very difficult. Any time they were asked what their name was they knew to expect the unexpected.

Even running simple errands had become nerve racking. The stares and not-so-quiet comments were becoming increasingly difficult to tolerate. The changing world became a hugely popular subject of discussion amongst both the local Muslim adults and children.

"I don't know why people act the way they do sometimes. When will they realize that we are normal Americans?" Fatima commented to Fareha at a dinner party.

"You know what I do? If I see somebody staring at me, I stare right back. And after they get flustered I act super nice by starting a conversation 'Hi, how are you? What's your name?'"

"I don't believe you!" Fatima replied.

"Believe her I have seen her do it," Ayesha added.

"Like the time we were at Great Adventure, waiting in line to go on the Log Flume. Fareha just started talking to this woman who was staring at her! It was hilarious!"

"What did the woman do?" Fatima inquired with intrigue.

"She was first surprised. It looked like she couldn't believe that I was actually speaking English. She probably thought I could only speak a foreign language. Anyway, she just said 'I'm fine' and turned around. She didn't stare at me after that," Fareha said with a tilt of her head and raise of her eyebrow.

Fatima laughed uncontrollably.

"Man you've got guts!"

"It's not guts Fatima; it's a need to stop the nonsense."

"Yeah but not everyone can do that. You're brave."

"You could do the exact same thing. You just have to make up your mind to not be belittled."

"I know what you mean. The whole *hijaab* thing at school made me realize that *I* had to change *my* attitude so that no one else would get to me. If I had more confidence in myself then all would be fine," Fatima added.

"Bingo," Fareha agreed. "Unless you're afraid for your life, just be normal, if not a little more assertive."

"It's funny, I am usually such a loud mouth and very aggressive, at least I think I am, but with stuff like this I try to avoid any confrontation and stay quiet."

"It's not confrontation, it's education that we need to get across!" Ayesha added.

"Haha funny!" Fatima snickered at her younger sister. "Since when did you become Miss Smarty Pants?"

"Since my older sister became a wuss. Come on Fatima. You have got to act like you do at home even when you are at school!"

"What does that mean?"

"You know exactly what that means."

"No, I don't."

"Well let me spell it out. You're a loud and bossy person at home who isn't afraid to speak her mind. So just be yourself at school and no one will screw with you."

"I know."

"If you know - just do it."

"Okay okay. I get your drift," Fatima acknowledged.

In the next room a very similar conversation was taking place amongst the adults. It seemed as if everyone was venting their frustration with the international political scene that was now hitting too close to home.

"You know we look like idiots. One Muslim fighting another Muslim, and then calling in the West to help defeat our own people. What has this world come to?" Uncle Mirza was zealously stating.

"But you see Mirza, the Kuwaitis and Iraqis are identifying themselves with their national identities, not their religious ones. So if their country is attacked, they will do whatever is necessary to protect themselves," another uncle responded.

"They are all fools. Money hungry sheikhs who have no army of their own. Too busy spending their wealth on junk. I feel so sad to see this day," another uncle interjected.

"The bottom-line is that we all look like warmongers. Wherever you look Muslims at war, Muslim terrorists, everything bad is equated with Muslims. Why don't they ever talk about other subjects in the news?"

"It's not a need to change the subjects it's a need to change the labeling! They always add Muslim to any negative term. That's where the problem lies."

"Whatever the case may be, our children will suffer here because of this. They are already being made fun of at school. They try desperately to fit in and it doesn't work. I am afraid that they may abandon their religious identity if this kind of stereotyping persists. Our hard work and efforts may be flushed down the toilet if the insanity doesn't stop."

"Don't get overdramatic *yaar*. The kids are not stupid. They know where to draw the line."

"You think so? You are a fool if you think that. The need to fit in supercedes all that they know to be right. If it isn't 'cool' to be Muslim then believe me they will lose their Muslim identity in a heartbeat."

"If we have raised our children properly, they will know what is truly right and what is wrong. You raise them the best you can and then pray that God guides them. Eventually you have to trust in God and hope for the best."

"Array *bhai*, so much easier said than done."

"That is always the case."

"All I know is that Desert Storm is a tangled web being woven. Who knows what will come of it?"

"What ever it may be, we must have faith that God will do what is best for all."

"With that, let's head for dinner!" the host exclaimed. He grabbed the opportunity to end the discussion, and lead his guests to the appetizing and overflowing buffet.

"Let's enjoy the food while it is hot!"

While political discussions reigned amongst the men, the kitchen was void of any such tension. The food was being heated by all the aunties, each outdoing the other in their efforts to help the host. They all chatted about the delicious aroma of the mutton and what the recipe was to achieve such an intoxicating scent. The lives of these women were centered around the kitchen and their families, much like that of the American housewives of the 1950's. These modern Doris Days, clad in *sarees* and bangles, were much too occupied with cooking feasts and raising their children, to take an interest in the wars that were being waged around the world. The only time they had to deal with the ramifications of the conflict was at the grocery stores or department stores, places where they occasionally encountered hostility.

At their local Pathmark, while waiting in line and unloading her shopping cart, Fatima's mother heard a customer behind her curse, "Damn Moslem." Being the non-confrontational person that she was, Fatima's mother completely ignored the rude remark.

Sadly, so did everyone else around her. Not one person, not the cashier nor the other shoppers around her, even blinked at the rudeness of the obnoxious customer. Once home Fatima's mother related what had happened to her daughters as they put away the groceries.

"What!! And you didn't say anything Mummy?" an angry Fatima yelled as she placed boxes of pasta in the pantry.

"No *beta*, what can I say. I can not respond to such people and no one will defend me either. I will be on my own."

"It doesn't matter Mummy!" Ayesha replied. "You can't just quietly take that!"

"You girls leave your mother alone. She is not like you American girls who think they can take on the world." Their father had walked in upon the conversation.

"Daddy, she can't be insulted like that, it's not acceptable!" Fatima heatedly responded.

"Fatima, there was a time in this country, not so long back, when the Japanese were rounded up and thrown in concentration camps, and they couldn't say anything. If they fought back they had hell to pay. So many of them just kept quiet. There was no other choice in the matter. All we have to deal with is some name calling," he retorted.

"Daddy, you can't compare this to the Japanese issue. That was a whole different ball game. In fact if anything was learned from all that nonsense, it was that stereotyping is not okay. You shouldn't have to be degraded for what you believe!"

"Not everything is perfect in America. The ideals that this country was built upon do not represent the attitudes of all Americans. So the best thing to do in this type of situation is to remain passive."

"I am not saying start a movement or something Daddy. I am just saying if someone is acting like a retard, we should be able to confront them. After all isn't that why you left India? To get away from prejudice? So why should we put up with it here?"

"Have you fought back Fatima? When that lady at the mall called you a crazy foreigner what did you do?" Father cornered a dumbfounded Fatima. He continued, "And what happens if that rude person is a mental patient who pulls out a gun on you? Huh? Then what? Is it worth it? You don't know who you are dealing with when it comes to these people. Silence is golden. You will learn the value of this as your life goes on."

"I can't imagine having to put up with this crap much longer," Ayesha replied, annoyed.

"Why are you girls acting like it's a new issue, or even a big one? This has been going on for years. Think about it, how many times have you been insulted in public? You think we don't know how many times you have had to deal with rude comments and dirty looks? Of course we do. But do you fight back with ignorant people? No! I know you girls have never shouted back or put up a fight, so why do you push your mother to do so?" Their father was equally irritated by now.

The conversation flew back and forth between Fatima, Ayesha, and their father. Their mother listened quietly while shelving all the groceries. Young Amina approached her mother in the midst of the heated discussion. She softly commented, "Mummy, the woman shouldn't have been mean like that," as she tried to get her mother's attention.

Seeing that this conversation was bothering even the younger members of the family, Fatima's mother decided to put an end to the discussion.

"*Beta*, it is okay. I am not that upset, so why are you guys so mad? It's over. It's like what you guys say – shit happens? Isn't that it? Well, it goes to show that it truly does happen. So let's not talk about it anymore," Mummy said. "Right now go do your ablutions and prepare for *Maghrib*. It's already time to pray."

"Yeah yeah," Fatima mumbled under her breath and rolled her eyes. Grumpy and disheartened by this situation, the girls stomped out of the family room. Their parents were left sitting on the couch.

"I don't know how to tell these girls that everything isn't black and white. We have to be patient and tolerate some of this garbage," their father told his wife.

"But you need to express this at a proper time and in a proper manner. You can't try to get this point across when the girls are so emotional. All they could see was that their mother was insulted. They didn't see anything beyond that, so of course they will react emotionally. Just let it be right now, and don't bring this up again tonight. We will address this at a better time," Mummy stood up.

"I have to pray. *Maghrib* time flies by."

Although Desert Storm was over in a very short time, it left a profound stain upon the American Muslim identity. That in addition to all the "terrorist" activities that were falsely carried out in the name of Islam throughout the world made the words 'Muslim' and 'terrorist' synonyms.

Name calling persisted and "Moslem" became an insult much like a curse word. What was even worse was that for Fatima's family, their last name, Husain, became a constant target of ridicule and prejudice.

But things were very different when people personally knew and interacted with American Muslims. This was where the saying, 'Actions speak louder than words' proved to be true. Fatima's parents had been such friendly and caring people that when the issue of Muslims being terrorists was brought up, their neighbors knew better than to fall into the trap of stereotyping Muslims. In fact they came to the Husains' aid in a most caring manner. Mike and Liz, their next door neighbors began to ask, "If you feel unsafe please let us know. We will do what we can to help you feel more secure."

Kevin and Minnie, also next door neighbors, were supportive as well.

"Guys, if there is anything we can do - just give us a ring."

"Your kind words are more than enough," Fatima's father replied.

These wonderful sentiments increased the respect that they all had for another. More importantly, they really helped the Husains feel safer at a time when things seemed dubious.

Chapter 12

Once Kuwait was liberated and Desert Storm wrapped up the anti-Muslim propaganda began to dwindle. A sense of normalcy began to return to most American Muslim families. Fatima was thoroughly relieved that the Persian Gulf was no longer the focus of every discussion both in and out of school. She could finally get back to the regular struggles of a 'normal' sixteen year old, PSAT scores, final exams, and college prep classes! And of course there were the weekly visits to Dadima's, who never failed to present the 'bachelor of the week,' irritating Fatima to no end.

Well intentioned Dadima, not to mention all the other relatives, would take great interest in every eligible bachelor, and present a solid case on behalf of the young lad, almost as if they were presenting his case to a judge in a trial setting. Dadima was sure that any stress, even school related, that Fatima would be enduring would be resolved with the all magical cure-for-all-ailments – a husband.

"You girls don't realize that good proposals only come at a young age. When you pass that age the proposals will stop. After all, no one wants to marry an old maid. They boys' families think 'why settle for a twenty five year old when there are seventeen year olds available?'" Dadima would say to her annoyed granddaughter.

"Umm Dadima, we know this is not happening, so let's not waste time on this subject."

"At this rate it will never happen," she snapped back.

"You are sitting like a burden on my son's back."

"What?!" Fatima replied, utterly shocked.

"What do you think? Four daughters!! My poor boy. What did he deserve to get four daughters? Can you imagine the stress he is under?"

Fatima could feel her face flush with anger.

"Dadima you really need to step out of the Dark Ages. In fact I would rather have daughters than sons."

"Don't say such nonsense. Always utter good talk. Not rubbish like that. God spare everyone from having too many girls."

Disgusted and pissed off, Fatima stormed out of Dadima's bedroom.

"Daddy, can we go home now?" she asked, obviously annoyed.

"What happened? Why do you seem so upset?" her father asked

"Because *I* am a huge burden on you, according to your mother."

"That's just Dadima talking. Why are you taking her so seriously?"

"Maybe because no one stops her from saying stuff like that?"

"Come on, who do you think can stop Dadima?"

"Whatever. Can we go now?"

Dadima waddled out of her room into the living room just as Fatima was quickly putting on her shoes.

"What's going on here? Where are you going?" she asked Fatima.

"I have to go Dadima. Lots of studying to do," Fatima snarled.

"You see the girls here? The way the talk to their elders? That American tone they learn in school. This is why they should be controlled well at an early age. Get her married and she will settle down real fast."

"Mamma, why do you say such stuff? These girls are not a problem for me; they are my pride and joy," Fatima's father calmly replied.

"Yeah, yeah… stop the dramatic dialogues. We all know what daughters are," as her arm flew in the air ready to slap anyone in her way.

"Okay *beta*, I am ready to go, are you?" Fatima's father hastily got out of his chair and signaled to his daughter.

"*Khuda hafiz* Mamma," he politely said to his mother.

"*Khuda hafiz*," Fatima mumbled as she darted out.

After buckling her seat belt, Fatima turned to her father, "Every time we come here Daddy something happens. Every time. It never fails."

"Then why do you go in her room and sit there alone with her? If you would sit outside with all of us, that kind of stuff wouldn't happen so often," her father commented.

"I know. I'm such an idiot. It's like I am setting myself up for a fall every weekend."

"Better yet, you can stay at home with your mother; you don't have to come with me every weekend."

"I should seriously do that. It's not like I don't have enough work with finals around the corner."

"There you go. Just stay home and study. That's definitely more important than listening to all this nonsense."

"Tell me about it," Fatima said emphatically.

Once home Fatima hit the books and focused on her finals. At school she joined study groups and stayed after school to get extra help in Algebra 2. Mary, Peter, and Tara were also working with her to ensure that they all did well and earned the grades that they needed. Each of them had high aspirations and good grades were their first key to moving up. Once exams were over, the future juniors were off on their own individual paths until fall.

This summer Fatima was finally able to work. She was looking forward to getting a job and finally earning some spending money.

"I think I am gonna hit the mall and fill out applications there. That's gotta be the easiest place to get a job," she told her mother.

"Go ahead *beta*. But remember I need the car after 4 pm so make sure you let them know that you need to work in the day."

"That should be fine Mummy."

Fatima dressed to the nines as she prepared herself to be dropped off at the mall. A neat pair of black slacks and a pale pink blouse made her look very professional. And the black scarf with pink paisleys, brought out the color of her blouse. Even her broche complemented the entire ensemble. She put together a sharp look and walked out confidently, sure that she would come home with some interviews under her belt.

Once she was there, she made her way through numerous stores with help wanted signs, and filled out at least twenty applications.

"Just fill out the front and the back of this sheet, and I will pass it on to the manager," was what she heard most often.

Fatima had known that a job wouldn't be handed to her on the spot. But she could not stop herself from hoping that she would return home employed. After two hours of filling out application after application Fatima went to the pay phone and called her mother.

"Mummy, I think I have gone through every store here, could you pick me up now?"

"I will be there in fifteen minutes. Meet me by the Macy's entrance," her mother responded.

By the time Fatima reached home, there were two messages on the answering machine asking Fatima to come in for interviews. Excited and anxious, Fatima called the people back immediately and scheduled two interviews for the very next day.

Fatima was determined to make a good impression. Her sage and creme scarf suited her sage blouse and beige slacks perfectly. She even made an effort to find a matching purse. Ready to take on the career world, she enthusiastically left for the first interview, at a large well known department store, one that had been recommended by Tara, a part time employee there.

As she waited in the badly lit lobby, Fatima was getting a tad bit nervous. Her hands were getting moist and she fidgeted, shifting her weight from leg to leg. She looked around nervously at the dreary furnishings and noticed all the cracks in the ceiling. She even spotted areas of the burgundy office carpet that seemed to have been ripped out of its seams.

After ten minutes she was called inside. As she walked in the human relations office, she could see the smile on the face of the interviewer change into an intrigued smirk.

"Hi, I am Mary Ellen," the lady said very slowly as she shook Fatima's hand.

"I am Fatima, Nice to meet you", Fatima answered confidently.

"Oh you speak English well," Mary Ellen replied with a hint of surprise in her voice.

"Why wouldn't I be able to speak English?" Fatima replied with great pride.

"Umm. I don't know…" Mary Ellen replied in a patronizing tone.

Immediately Fatima started to feel uneasy. 'What's going on here?' she thought to herself.

"So you are in high school?"

"Yes, I will be a junior at Pennsbury in the fall."

"I guess that means you want to stop work once school starts…?"

"Not necessarily. If some sort of schedule can be worked out around school, I am open to working on weeknights and weekends."

"I see. Well, it was great meeting you. I will let you know if we will need you. I have your number," Mary Ellen stood up and extended her hand.

Fatima was a little surprised at the brevity of the interview, but she got up and shook Mary Ellen's hand.

As she walked out of the office she wondered to herself, 'what had just happened?' She thought, 'why did the look on Mary Ellen's face change as soon as I walked in the office? And then to talk to me like I couldn't speak English…'

Fatima began to wonder if her *hijaab* had anything to do with what just went down. As possible as that was, she did not want to focus on that as the sole reason for the weirdness of the interview. 'Maybe she is having an off day, or maybe she wanted someone with retail experience,' she tried telling herself.

As she walked across the mall to her second interview Fatima continued to ponder over what she could do differently at the next interview that would prevent this one from ending as quickly and as oddly as the previous one just had.

She walked into the store and let the girls at the register know that she had an interview. One of the employees then led her down a dark hallway into the disheveled back office. The door opened and once again Fatima was received by a surprised looking manager.

"Hi….. I am Laura….. Have a seat," she directed Fatima. Fatima sat down with a smile.

"So you're looking for a job I see."

"Yes. Now that summer is here I'd like to do something with my spare time."

"That's good. Do you have any experience working at a shop like ours?"

"Well, I just turned sixteen, so this would be my first job. But I am a fast learner and I am eager to please."

"That's good to know," Laura replied as she repeatedly glanced at Fatima's *hijaab*.

Fatima noticed how she was not making much eye contact, and that her attention seemed to be focused on what was on top of her head rather than what was inside it.

"You know I should let you know that we do have a dress code here. And we don't allow hats to be worn by our employees."

"Okay. That should not be a problem since I don't wear hats."

"Umm… I don't think your head gear would be appropriate either."

"Excuse me?" Fatima replied. She was taken aback by the bluntness of the statement.

"This is a scarf," she pointed to her head and tried to respond as graciously as possible. "And I have to wear it for religious reasons."

"I understand completely," Laura acknowledged, vigorously bobbing her head up and down.

"You have to do what you have to do. But unfortunately, I don't think our company's policies will allow that."

"Okay..." Fatima replied in a quiet yet disgusted tone.

"It was a pleasure meeting you," Laura said as she extended her hand towards Fatima.

Fatima feebly shook Laura's hand and did not reply. She simply nodded her head and turned around and walked out.

Fatima was in shock. She never thought that in *her* America, of all places, would anyone object to hiring someone based on religious attire. Fatima had always idealized America as a utopia of sorts where everyone would have equal opportunities regardless of their color or creed, despite all of what had transpired in the past few years. The blow that she felt after these interviews was indescribable.

Fatima had a lump in her throat. All that she had felt was true about religious freedom seemed to come crashing down upon her. 'How could this be happening? This is not supposed to happen!' she kept telling herself. She walked despairingly to the phone booths and called her mother.

"Mummy, I am done with the interviews. Can you come now?" she somberly asked.

Upon hearing her daughter's sad voice Fatima's mother knew that something had gone wrong.

"Okay *beta*, I am leaving right now."

Fatima got into her mother's car, shoulders slumped and eyes fixated on the floor. Sensing her daughter's sadness Fatima's mother cautiously approached the subject.

"You know someone called to schedule an interview while you were here. I told them you would call back after you got home."

"There is no point, Mummy. Nobody is going to hire a *muhajjaba*."

"Why do you say that? Did something happen at the interviews?"

"It was crazy Mummy. They were so obnoxious. I never thought people would behave the way these people did, all because I was wearing a scarf."

"What exactly happened?"

"Well the first lady thought I couldn't speak English, and even when I spoke it, she cut the interview short. I don't know exactly why but she did. Then the second interview was even worse. The lady there told me my 'headgear' would not be okay with their dress code."

"Your *head gear*?"

"Yes, my *head gear*."

"*Pagal* people," her mother responded.

"You're telling me. Here I am thinking that this is going to be a piece of cake, and it turns out that no one wants to hire me just because of the way I dress. But I am sure these same fools would hire a grunged out slob. It pisses me off."

"Well you do have one more interview that you need to schedule. Maybe that will work out."

"Mummy, I don't know if I even want to try after today."

"That's not a good attitude. There will be someone out there that is sensible enough to look at who you are and what you offer to their company."

"I really hope so. I can't tell you how upset I am. I never thought that this stuff happens in the real world."

"Then let today serve as a lesson for you. Half of what we learn in life is through our experiences, and what you experienced today is a lesson that you shouldn't forget."

"A sad lesson in reality."

"Whatever it may be. You be true to who you are, and soon enough something better will come your way."

"I hope so," Fatima muttered.

"Just don't tell Dadima. This will be one more reason to get you married in her books."

Fatima broke out laughing. "Mummy…..."

"What are mothers for?" her mother winked at Fatima.

Fatima went home and scheduled her next interview. She was positive that she would not get this job either and was still in a slump. She picked up the phone and called Fareha to tell her what had happened.

"Fatima, you should interview at the place I work. It's a telemarketing place so they don't care what you look like as long as you speak well."

"I hate being hung up on Fareha, I don't know if I can deal with that all the time."

"Well, if you want some extra cash, you do what you have to do."

"I guess so. Where is this place?"

"It's right next to the mall – PCG, Peoples Communication Group. Go in towards the front desk and get an application."

"Are they hiring?"

"They are always hiring."

"Okay, I'll go."

"Don't be so down about your interviews. Something better will come around."

"I guess."

"I gotta go now, time for *Asr* prayer. *Khuda Hafiz.*"

"*Khuda Hafiz,*" said Fatima as she hung up.

Telemarketing wasn't exactly what Fatima would choose to do over her summer vacation, but it was better than no job at all. She proposed this idea to her father.

"After my horrible interviews today, Fareha told me about PCG. It's a telemarketing place that…"

"That's great! That would be the best place to work for you"

"Huh?"

"Think about it. You are behind the scenes, not attracting any unnecessary attention, and it's a much more professional environment than the mall."

"Okay…"

"What does Fareha think of the place?"

"She's okay with it."

"I'd much rather see you at PCG. It gives me a stronger sense of security."

"How?"

"Well, the mall attracts weirdoes from all over. If they were to give you a hard time, I'd be really nervous about letting you go there. In the telemarketing world it's more of an office-like setting. There is some sense of professionalism there."

"I guess."

"I'll take you there tonight after dinner. We can pick up an application for you."

"Okay."

Fatima began to realize that her father made sense. She would have to deal with less crap about her *hijaab* if she was in an office setting. Additionally, Fareha was already working there, which meant that the managers there had some experience with a *muhajjaba*. That alone could make it a lot easier for Fatima to get hired. Her experience with interviewing, so far, had not gone well, and she was still paranoid about going to interview anywhere else. But if she wanted some extra cash, it had to be done.

After picking up the application from PCG, Fatima immediately filled it out and left it with the secretary. Soon enough a call followed and an interview was scheduled. Fatima decided to postpone the interview that she had scheduled earlier on at the store in the mall so that she could first interview at PCG.

She presented herself in the same manner as she did previously and sat in the PCG lobby, unsure of what to expect. As she waited she observed that the facility was spacious, clean and office-like, similar to what her father had predicted. In fact it was a stark contrast to the small, shabby back offices in the mall. The lobby was bright and surrounded by windows. The décor was modern yet friendly. The seat that Fatima was sitting on was ultra plush, and gave great back support, something she noticed right away. It was nothing like the hard metal chairs that she had sat uncomfortably upon at the other two interviews. Overall, the office radiated a comfortable feel. A tall, friendly faced brunette opened a door, and made her way into the lobby. She greeted Fatima warmly.

"Hi, I'm Carol. Nice to meet you. Please follow me", she shook Fatima's hand, and graciously escorted Fatima into her office. Fatima watched Carol keenly; awaiting some sort of weird response like that she had previously experienced. But there were no funny looks or strange reactions. In fact, Carol seemed genuinely nice.

"So what brings you to PCG dear?"

"I'm looking for a summer job and one of my friends told me about this place."

"Really? May I ask who?"

"Fareha. She works here."

"Oh yes! I know her. I didn't realize that you two knew each other. That's great to hear. Well, you know what our job entails…" she stated as she began to explain how an employee was trained in selling life insurance policies over the phone.

"So if you're interested, you can start as early as next Monday. It pays $5.50 an hour and we have a half hour break for every six hours that you put in. After eight hours, it is an hour break. Right now, we need people in the day shift and the night shift."

"Really?"

"Yes. You look a little surprised….."

"Actually, I am. I didn't expect things to happen so fast."

"Well, you can go home and think about it. But I'd like an answer by tomorrow."

"Okay. That shouldn't be a problem."

She handed Fatima her business card.

"Please call me with your response. It was a pleasure meeting you."

"Same here," Fatima enthusiastically replied. "Can I use your phone? I just need to let my mom know that she can pick me up now."

"Sure dear, go ahead."

Fatima's mother arrived and Fatima jumped into the car with all her pearly whites gleaming.

"I guess it went well?" her mother smiled.

"Yes Mummy, thank God. It went great. The lady said I could start on Monday!"

"Fantastic!"

Fatima finally had a job. She was giddy with excitement and was looking forward to diving into this new world. After sharing the news with her family, Fatima called Fareha.

"Guess what? You have a new co-worker!"

"Awesome! How did the interview go?"

"A thousand times better than what I had expected."

"Great! When do you start?"

"Next Monday. I have to set my hours after I call Carol and tell her that I am ready to take the position."

"This will be a blast."

"I hope so."

Fatima glowed with exuberance over dinner.

"Jeez if Dadima were here she would think you're getting married or something," Ayesha joked eyeing her older sister.

"Oh God, could you imagine!"

"I don't think I want to."

"Yesterday I thought this job thing was hopeless. I can't believe how quickly things turned around."

"So does this mean I will be getting a really nice birthday gift this year?"

"Maybe," Fatima responded with a shrug of her shoulders.

Telemarketing wasn't the most entertaining job but it was something that seemed to be a rite of passage for all teenagers. As she spoke to more and more of her friends about her new job, it seemed that everyone had at one time or another been a telemarketer. They knew exactly what it felt like to be hung up on several times a day and occasionally get cussed at for no reason at all. The one thing that Fatima had to learn was that it was nothing personal. Being hung up on was a given and it was part of the job.

Fatima had met some friendly people at PCG, most of who were much older than her. Having Fareha there made the entire experience a fun one. The summer flew by and Fatima had saved up about four hundred dollars by the end of August. That to her, was big bucks. This meant that come junior year, she was going to be able to afford a pair of designer jeans and maybe even a cool backpack. In her mind, she had it made.

As she prepared to splurge her small savings, Fatima's Khala from India called to say that her cousin, Anam, had just gotten engaged. The wedding was scheduled for October and she insisted that Fatima's family attend.

"The wedding will only be complete if you all come. Bring the children and let them experience our colorful weddings," her Khala exclaimed to her sister.

"Apa, it is much too expensive to bring everyone. I will try my best to come but I can not promise that the entire family will fly over."

"At least bring Fatima. Who knows in the midst of this wedding, another marriage may be set."

"Yes, that's possible," Fatima's mother responded much to Fatima's chagrin, who was on the other phone waiting for her turn to talk to her cousin. She immediately hung up the phone and ran downstairs to where her mother was finishing up her call.

"Mummy, what did you just say?"

"Nothing, why?"

"I heard Mummy! You are turning into Dadima!"

"Look Fatima, there is no harm in considering proposals. That does NOT mean you will be getting married anytime soon, it just means we can keep our options open."

"At sixteen?!"

"You will be seventeen very soon."

"Okay, at seventeen?? Are you serious?"

"Look *beta*, I am saying it again. It's a matter of keeping our options open. Anyway you know the best girls and boys get taken early on."

"Holy cow! I can't believe you are actually saying this."

"Fatima, I see it like this. The girls your age already have boyfriends and are doing things that only married couples should be doing. So why not get you engaged if the right proposal comes along? That way you don't get tempted into sin."

"Okay......this is news to me."

"No it's not. You know many girls your age who are engaged and will be married by twenty. I want to know what the big deal is. What is wrong with *starting* to consider some guys? You can't tell me that you aren't the slightest bit interested in boys..."

"Mummy ..."

"Am I right or wrong?"

"Mummy, liking guys doesn't mean you want to marry them. It just means you like them. You could like a dog, but you don't want to marry it."

Completely ignoring the dog remark Fatima's mother proceeded, "What if that *liking* develops into something more, then what? God knows whom that could occur with. If you are engaged it will limit the chances of that happening randomly. Instead you will have feelings for the person that you will actually have some future with."

"Mummy, this is way too weird to discuss with you. I really feel like I am talking to Dadima."

"Oh stop the Dadima business. You knew that this was bound to happen so why are you in denial?"

"Mummy, I know that all this happens. I know it was something that would be discussed, but not to some guy in India!"

"Why not?"

"A FOB Mummy! I would die. *He* would die!"

"What's this FOB nonsense? A good boy is a good boy regardless where he is from."

"Mummy, there would be a major culture clash."

"Haven't Maseeha and Asiya done it? They seem to be happy. And look at Afia, she just got engaged to a recent Indian immigrant."

"Mummy, I am not them."

"Well, whatever the case there is no harm in considering good proposals."

"Whatever," Fatima grumbled stalking off. 'What was this all about?' she thought to herself. She was thrilled at the prospect of going to India but having to deal with green card hungry suitors was not exactly what she had in mind. She picked up the phone and called Asma.

"*Assalamu alaykum* Asma. What's up?"

"Just doing chores. You?"

"Well my Khala wants me to come to India so I can find a nice husband."

"What?!"

"Okay that is a *little* exaggerated. Let me rephrase – my cousin is getting married in India. My Khala wants us to come, us meaning my mom and me. She wants us to attend the wedding and possibly find a good match for me at the same time. Kill two *girls*, I mean two birds, with one stone…."

"You serious?"

"What do you think?"

"Well, I would go along with it just to get a trip to India. Get to enjoy the vacation and wedding, and just act like you will consider the bachelors."

"I guess, but that's not going to be easy."

"Who cares? Go on the trip and have fun. And maybe just maybe you may have the opportunity to meet Mr. Right…"

"I seriously doubt it…"

"Just do it for the trip man."

"You're right; I'll milk it for what it's worth."

When the subject of going to India for the wedding was brought up, Fatima's mother pitched a trip for herself and Fatima to her husband.

"It would be brief, two weeks at most. Fatima can arrange for the time off if she lets her teachers know about the trip as soon as school starts. And who knows, as Apa said, maybe something can be worked out while we are there for her?"

"If you really want to go, then go ahead. Just ask Fatima if she wants to go."

"I will, but I am pretty sure that she will want to come. She has always kept in touch with Anam and has a strong bond with her. I doubt that she would want to miss her wedding."

"I will call the travel agent tomorrow and get some airfare quotes," her husband said.

As plans for the trip rapidly finalized Fatima had to make sure that her teachers in school would accommodate her ten day absence. After all, this was her junior year; the most important by many standards and the pressure to do well was still sky high. The initial nervousness prior to the start of the school year was short lived this time around as the planning for India, dominated Fatima's thoughts. She began junior year with high spirits and immediately told all of her teachers about her trip to India. Most were surprised that she would be leaving just as the school year started, but they still obliged and gave her class assignments and homework, so that she would not fall terribly behind. Once her assignments were in her hand Fatima mapped out her strategy on how to keep up with school work while she was in India.

The plan was to make the most of the twenty hour plane ride to India and to spend the majority of that time reading and doing her class work and homework. She had always gotten bored on the long flights to Hyderabad and Saudi Arabia previously. But this time around she actually had a lot to do. If she were to work through both flights to and from Hyderabad, she would have put in nearly thirty five to forty hours on her assignments. Not to mention the fact that she would open up her books at least once or twice while she was in Hyderabad just to keep most of the stuff fresh in her head. So even though she would miss the second and third week of school, Fatima was confident that she would not fall behind.

Once she decided how to handle the schoolwork, Fatima couldn't stop imagining how things would be in India after a near ten year absence. Would it still look as it did when she visited last or would there have been technological advancements? Would the streets still be overcrowded and impossible to drive through or would there be paved roads upon which there were two lanes which would divide the direction of traffic? All of these thoughts were making her more and more anxious to see what would come in the days to follow.

Meanwhile, Ayesha had a whole different take on the fact that she was not going on this trip.

"Mom is just taking you to market you," she told her sister.

"What?"

"She is just hoping that you find some nice Hyderabadi doctor and that you get fixed up ASAP. That's why you are going and you know it."

"You keep telling yourself that to feel better Ayesha."

"You know it's true."

"So maybe it is. So what. At least I am going," Fatima replied smugly.

Annoyed by the comment, Ayesha left the room.

Fatima knew there was truth in what Ayesha said, but she was taking Asma's advice and going along for the ride. This was an opportunity that couldn't be passed up, and it was one that she really looked forward to. She had always seen pictures of Indian weddings and wondered how it was that these elaborate events were carried out. In Bollywood films every wedding was portrayed as a musical extravaganza with a new love story starting or with one evolving in to something greater. The drama of it all seemed almost magical. Now, finally! She was going to experience the festive and colorful production first hand.

Chapter 13

Fatima had planned out what she wanted to wear to each of the three ceremonies that would lead up to the wedding. The wedding would also be followed by the *walima*, or reception. That meant that there would be a total of five large scale parties that tied in directly to one marriage. *Desis* sure knew how to throw a wedding.

Although she tried to pack appropriate outfits for each ceremony Fatima knew that she was arriving five days before the big day, which may be enough time to pick up an outfit or two in Hyderabad.

Besides her clothes, she neatly packed all her text books, notebooks, toiletries, and every type of medication she could get her hands on. Her memories of India from her childhood were vivid- horrible vomits, endless diarrhea, and red bumps all over her body, courtesy of the friendly local mosquitoes. She stacked up on Pepto Bismol, Tums, Kaopectate, Tylenol, Off! Mosquito repellant, calamine lotion, and any other meds that were sitting around in the medicine cabinet.

Fatima's mother also prepared for the long journey to celebrate such an auspicious occasion. It was the first wedding of the younger generation in her family, so she couldn't help but be excited at the prospect. The wedding would also serve as a family reunion for Fatima's mother. After nearly fifteen years, all of her brothers and sisters would be gathered together in their childhood home. Just the thought of this gave her goose bumps.

As Fatima and her mother packed, the younger girls were extremely gracious in helping them prepare for their journey. Although they knew that they would miss their mother while she was in India, the look of joy that overcame her at the mention of the trip let them know that she really needed to go see her family.

Amina was a mature eleven year old who could hold the fort down on her own, and she took all of her responsibilities around the house very seriously. *'Goody-goody'* was still mother's right hand. Even little Malikah was a baby no more. At seven she was becoming an independent young girl. She was the free spirit of the family and loved to play outside with the youngest Rizwan girl, Sidhra, who was her best friend. As the girls matured each became mother's helper and truly epitomized what it meant to be a tight-knit family.

"AyeshaAminaMalikah come here," Mummy called out.

As all three gathered in the family room mother began to set the rules of the house while she was to be away.

"Ayeshama you will be responsible for making sure your younger sisters are properly dressed and their hair is done in the mornings. Before you leave make sure that you have them dressed and ready to go. Put their lunch boxes in their backpacks and make sure that all the appliances are turned off. And of course you will have to make sure that everyone will not miss any prayers. Amina *beta*, you will make lunches. You help me do it every night so I know that you will be able to do this without a problem. Once everyone's lunch is packed put it in the fridge so nothing goes bad. Make sure that Daddy restocks the milk gallons so you guys have enough. Malikah your job is to obey and respect your older sisters. They know what's best for you."

"Aaaaw Mom that's not fair!!! Why are they the bosses?" Malikah whined.

"Daddy is the boss. They will just supervise when he is not home."

"That's so not cool Mummy…"

"Life isn't cool Malikah. Deal with it," Amina scolded.

Mummy went on to explain how to defrost all the curries she had cooked and frozen for when she would be gone.

"Let me make one thing clear. NO ONE is to try to cook anything. I don't want you girls hurting yourselves since I will not be there to supervise. As far as your dad goes, he needs as much supervision in the kitchen as you guys do, so please limit your stay in the kitchen to defrosting the food and cleaning your dishes."

"Okay Mummy, don't worry so much. We aren't little kids anymore, we will be fine," Ayesha reminded her mother.

"I know you will be," Mummy replied as she put her hand on Ayesha's head. "God will make sure that you all are okay while I am gone."

At the airport, as Fatima and her mother headed towards the Air India gate they turned back and waved good bye and exchanged salaams with their family. As excited as they both were to go to India, there were also nervous about leaving the girls behind. Fatima's father had reassured them that everything would be fine, but still...

"As much as I trust your father, I just feel nervous."

"Mummy you deserve a break too. When was the last time you got some time off from your full time job?"

"*Beta*, a mother's job has no vacations. Even if I am physically not caring for you, mentally I am always concerned about you guys. There is a reason they say that paradise lies under the feet of your mother."

"I know that Mummy, but just try to relax a little. This is supposed to be a fun trip."

"*Inshallah* it will be."

The long flight to India proved to be tiring, just as Fatima had recalled from childhood. But her homework and assignments kept her occupied. By the time they reached Bombay half of her work was done, much to her relief. Once the doors of the aircraft were opened to allow for passenger disembarkment Fatima experienced deja-vouz. The strong stench that she vividly remembered nearly knocked her out.

Still reeling under the assault of the pungent haze she walked down the portable stairs and quickly onto the airport tarmac. She rushed to get out of the overwhelming humidity, and enter a hopefully air-conditioned airport. To her great disappointment, it was not so. Although less humid, the airport was still very warm. Ceiling fans didn't help. In fact it seemed that they would force one to inhale the over-recycled air that was blowing into their faces.

"God this brings back so many horrible memories Mummy,"

Fatima said as she walked into the airport.

"We haven't been here for five minutes and you have started to complain."

"No Mummy I don't want to whine, but ugggggh! And get a load of the custom lines." She pointed towards the customs area.

"Things haven't changed much in the past ten years?"

"We are not here to enjoy the airports. You are ten years older than you were the last time we were here but you are acting like you are still a child. Stop the moaning and help me with all this luggage."

As the women were trying to unload their baggage, porters were anxiously waiting to assist them. Many were standing by ready to carry the passengers' luggage from the baggage claim area to the customs hall. Untrusting of any of these porters, Fatima guarded the luggage she pulled off the conveyer belts ferociously.

"No, no, I don't need your help. Leave it be," she barked at the aggressive porters.

"*Memsahib*, we will make it easier for you, let us help," they would reply in a most insistent manner.

"Only one can help us," Fatima's mother responded. "Only one. The rest can leave," she told the line of anxious porters. As their bags were pushed into the customs hall, Fatima's mother had all her documents in hand.

"Fatima, now you have to be patient. Please let me do and say as I need to. Just remain quiet while I do all the talking," Mummy advised.

Fatima nodded in approval. Customs was not as chaotic as it had seemed from the baggage claim area, and it surely was not as long of a process as it was the last time they visited. Within an hour they were cleared to proceed; Fatima was pleasantly surprised. After the anticipated headache of customs was cleared, the relieved pair hired a taxi to take them to Santa Cruz airport. This domestic airport was where they would catch a flight to Hyderabad.

On their ride over Fatima recalled all that she had seen from her last trip, and sadly not much had changed. She was most grateful that there would be no hotel at which they had to stay, nor would there be a dreadful train ride to Hyderabad. Luckily their domestic fight was set to depart in three hours and things looked relatively optimistic.

After de-boarding their Indian Airlines flight in Hyderabad, Fatima and her mother gathered their belongings and made their way to the lobby. They looked all around to see who had come to pick them up. After a few minutes of searching they located Fatima's uncle and her cousin, Musa. Relieved at finally finding some familiar faces, they handed off their luggage to the jovial men. Fatima's mother couldn't stop smiling now that she was with her brother and nephew, both of whom seemed equally excited to see her and Fatima. Finally, they breathed a sigh of relief. They were almost home.

Driving through the streets of Hyderabad at night was a fun experience. Brightly lit and still very crowded, the car ride was as adventurous as it was ten years go. Cows and goats were still wandering in the middle of the street as were the locals. It almost seemed as if the cars were the ones that didn't belong on the road.

"Musa, how do you guys drive in these conditions?" Fatima asked of her cousin.

"Oh it is great fun. This is the excitement of driving. It's a real adventure. And think of it this way, if you can drive here, you can drive anywhere," he laughed

"No doubt about that," Fatima responded with a smirk.

As the car approached Nanima's house, Fatima noticed the brightly lit exterior. Thousands of colorful lights draped the outer walls of the home in anticipation of her cousin's wedding. As Fatima stepped out of the car she could hear all the singing that was going on inside the home. Even the *dhol*, a hand drum, was being beaten ferociously. The laughter and giggles of women greeted Fatima, as she and her mother made their way through the gate and into the yard of her grandmother's home.

Upon first sight of these guests the whole house stood up in sheer joy. All the women raced down to the courtyard where Fatima and her mother were entering. Greeted with hugs and kisses from relatives of near and far, there was a sense of overwhelming delight. Mushu, Naju, aunts, and uncles some of whom Fatima recognized and some of whom she didn't, swarmed around the two women.

"*Aray ama, dekho.* How tall she has gotten. I can't believe this is the same little girl we saw long back."

"Look Fatima looks just like her mother now!"

"What are you talking about? She is the exact copy of her father!"

"How fair you have become dear, you must be applying lots of vicco turmeric, to your face."

One hundred comments were passed as the excited group of women hugged and stared down Fatima and her mother.

When Nanima finally made her way out to the courtyard, she grabbed a hold of her daughter's face and cried tears of joy.

"How I longed to see you," she cried, as her tears of joy flowed uncontrollably. Fatima's mother bent down and touched her mother's feet, the ultimate sign of respect in Indian culture. She rose up and hugged her mother tightly. Soon enough Fatima's mother was crying too. They embraced for a good five minutes before they let go of one another. Nanima brought Fatima's head down to eye level and kissed her forehead.

"May God shower you with every happiness and bless you with good *qismat*," she prayed.

After everyone settled down, they made their way over to the open hall where the elders were seated. They had been sewing the finishing touches on all the clothes that Anam would be taking with her to her groom's house. Others were frying, *gullgullas*, or dumplings, in a large pot for all to snack upon, or singing merry songs, *dholak*, to celebrate the impending marriage.

The atmosphere was festive, and the chatty women were bubbling. Anam, who was still in her room, had not yet come out. The bride was supposed to be modest and reserved, almost as if she was blind to all the festivities. But Fatima was anxious to meet her cousin.

"Where is Anam?"

"She is in her room. She can't come out here."

"What? Why not?"

"You have much to learn about our customs here. You can go in and see her if you like," an older aunt advised.

Fatima rushed into Anam's bedroom and shouted, "*Assalamu alaykum!*"

Anam jumped out of her chair and shrieked in delight. The two cousins hugged excitedly.

"I can't believe you are getting married!" Fatima told her cousin.

"Neither can I! " Anam replied.

"So what's he like tell me! I want to know everything about him!"

"Let's see. He comes from a very good family and he is supposed to be very intelligent. His practice in Jeddah is booming and everyone had heard good feedback about him. So I guess he is fine!" Anam related blushingly.

"Did you talk to him? What is he like?"

"Oh I don't know. I didn't talk to him. Papa spoke with him and says he is a fine young man with very good manners. So if Papa says he is well mannered, he must be."

Fatima was shocked. She wondered to herself how it was possible to go through with a marriage when one hadn't spoken to his/her prospective spouse at all, but she knew that she could not say a word about that at this time.

"Well, are you happy?" Fatima asked.

"Yes, thank God, I am happy. I trust my parents' judgment wholeheartedly. I know they will always want the best for me."

That was enough to satisfy Fatima. Fatima thought to herself, 'If Anam is happy why should anyone care?' It may not be the way she would want to get married, but if it suits Anam, then that was fine and dandy.

As midnight struck, the festivities were still in full swing and no one seemed to be affected by the late hour. However, Fatima and her mother were exhausted. Their trip was a long one and it had taken its toll upon them. They unpacked their luggage and prepared to hit the sack. Fatima sprayed the mosquito repellant all over herself before she climbed under the mosquito netting, and into bed. As soon as her head hit the pillow, she fell asleep.

The next morning she awoke to the aroma of freshly made *parathas* and *kheema*. Just the scent was delicious, enough to force her out of bed and into the bathroom. Fatima walked out of the bedroom and across the courtyard into the bathroom. She could see the servants preparing breakfast in the kitchen and setting up the table in the dining hall as she strolled along, struggling to keep her eyes open. After she brushed her teeth Fatima opened the bathroom door and was about to step out, when two feet in front of her sat a monkey. Petrified, she couldn't move. 'Holy shit' she thought to herself. Paralyzed with fright she stood and stared at the monkey, who stared right back. In fact it seemed that the monkey was growing aggressive, and Fatima debated whether or not she could get back in the bathroom and close the door fast enough to avoid an attack. As she stood motionless she mumbled, "Mummy...", and then a little louder, "Mummy...", and finally she yelled out loud, "Mummyyyyyyy!!!!!!!"

At the sound of her voice, everyone came running out. They saw the monkey eyeing Fatima. Musa found a long stick and darted outside attempting to chase the monkey away. Upon sight of the young man with the long rod, the monkey jumped up on to the trees in the courtyard, catapulted up on to the roof, and ran away. Fatima was upset.

"What was that? Where did he come from? Are there any more here?" she shouted.

"Relax, those monkeys come and go. They won't bother you if you don't bother them," Musa informed Fatima.

"You mean they move around freely? They aren't in a zoo?"

Yusuf, her younger cousin laughed.

"No, they are free to wander around as they please. This is India, we share our space with the animals."

"That's really scary. I don't know if I could handle another encounter like that."

"Don't worry, he won't come back. The dogs return today. They monkeys are too afraid of Robert and Soni to come when they are around."

"Dogs?! What dogs?" asked a fearful Fatima. Fatima had feared dogs for as long as she could remember. If she saw a dog a mile away, she would turn the other way.

"Nanima's dogs. They are the police dogs that are here for her protection," Musa informed her.

"So there are attack dogs that live here!?!?"

"They won't bother you Fatima. They will see that you are no threat to Nanima and they will ignore you. They know who is a threat and who isn't. They are trained."

"Where did Nanima get police dogs?"

"From her brother, you know he was police commissioner ten years back. So he still has many connections. He had these two dogs sent to Nanima's place."

"I don't know if I can handle this. Dogs scare the crap out of me."

"Well you better carry a pooper scooper with you then," Yusuf said as he laughed at Fatima.

"That's not funny Yusuf."

"Well that's the way it is here. So you have to deal," he stated.

"Great..." moped Fatima.

The family ate a heavy breakfast in the dining hall, while the aunts and uncles reminisced about old childhood memories. It was a wonderful sight.

Fatima had never seen her mother so animated and jovial. She was laughing loudly and joking endlessly. This was a side of her that Fatima and her sisters hardly saw. Fatima stared at that sight and smiled to herself. How nice it was to see her mother so free and relaxed.

The *parathas* were being brought out fresh off the stove by the servants while everyone was pigging out. Fatima thought to herself, 'When would we ever get to eat while being served on hand and foot - this is the life.' India wasn't *that* bad.

As breakfast wrapped up, the elders sat sipping their tea, while Fatima hung out with Anam, Mushu, and Naju. They sat talking about where the bride would go to get waxed, and where she would go to her facial. They informed Fatima that appointments had been made and that they would all go to Begums beauty salon tomorrow morning to have all the services done. Fatima was surprised to hear that girls in India waxed. In fact she was astounded to know that there were salons in Hyderabad. How far India had come in the past ten years...

Today the elders had made specific plans. Fatima was going to go shopping with her mother to purchase a sari for her to wear to the wedding.

After a taxi was called to the gate of the house, Fatima, her mother, her aunt, and her uncle crowded themselves into the back seat and made their way into the market. The stores in Hyderabad were extremely different than the large clean stores in the US. There was no parking lot to park in. The taxi would drop you off on the street, upon which hundreds of stores lined the curb. Children who worked at the stores would call you into every store, at times grabbing your arms and pulling you inside a shop whether or not you wanted to enter.

Fatima and her mother stood out as NRIs, at least to all the locals. How the shopkeepers could tell was a mystery to everyone, but they just knew that these were not locals. Although Fatima and her mother dressed in the native garb and spoke Urdu fluently, somehow everyone knew that they didn't belong. Fatima guessed that maybe it was the way she walked and carried herself, in the confident style that women in America did, or maybe it was her Urdu that may have had a hint of an American accent. Whatever it was, they were definitely from out of town.

This meant that they were courted to no end. Shopkeepers knew full well that foreign visitors would be willing to spend heavily as foreign currency converted into many thousands of rupees.

Fatima and her mother were swarmed by these anxious vendors. Luckily Fatima's aunt knew how to ward off the over aggressive shopkeepers and directed the duo into the bridal shop.

In the bridal shop Fatima found mannequins draped in a rainbow of color unlike anything she had ever seen. 'What a far cry from the traditional white wedding gown that American brides sported!' she thought to herself. In fact the dresses seemed rather 'loud' in taste, but that is what the traditional Indian bride wore, a gaudy bright outfit that would make her look stunning even if much like a Christmas tree. At the shop the store employees brought out all of their latest stock to flaunt to their foreign guests. The owner even had one of his male employees wrap himself in a *saree*, just so that the Fatima and her mother would get the full effect of the beautiful piece. But Fatima couldn't stop laughing. 'A guy draped in a *saree*,' she thought. 'What employee back home would ever agree to do that?' She continued to laugh while sipping her Thumbs Up, courtesy of the owner. Finally, Fatima's mother purchased a *saree* for herself and a *lengha*, for Fatima. After their shopping was complete it was back to Nanima's place.

In the evening was the first ceremony of the wedding, the *manjay*. Everyone would dress in yellow, and more or less bathe the bride in turmeric paste. This was a ceremony celebrated by the bride's family, but even that number amounted to one hundred guests. As everyone arrived, Fatima watched the elder ladies prepare the turmeric paste.

"Mushu, why will they put that stuff all over the bride's face?" she asked her cousin.

"It helps bring out the fairness within the bride."

"Aaaaah," Fatima finally understood. As silly as it sounds, being fair was equated with being beautiful. Fatima knew very well that the standard equation for measuring beauty in Indian culture was – "the fairer you are the more attractive you are." Hence, every measure was taken to appear fairer by most *Desi* women, even if it meant a smelly yellow turmeric paste all over their bodies.

The bride was sitting quietly in her bedroom until she was escorted out by older aunts. She was asked to sit on a small decorative stool in the middle of the room. She was to look down and appear as modest as possible. She also had to refrain from any laughter or display of emotion.

"So Anam can't watch anything that's going on?" an inquisitive Fatima asked.

"No Fatima. She is a dignified bride. Brides don't watch what's going on around them. They simply sit quietly and keep their eyes closed."

"Oh man Mushu. I don't know if I could do that. It's your wedding! Don't you want to know what's going on at your own wedding?"

"Don't be silly Fatima. That is in America, maybe. But here the bride doesn't do all that. The parents arrange everything."

"Man I don't know about that. I trust my parents, but I do want a say in my wedding."

"What will become of you Fatima?" Mushu joked as she slapped Fatima's back. "You have a lot of American blood within you." Mushu said as she shook her head and laughed.

"A lot of? That's all I have!" Fatima replied with a cackle.

Mushu smiled back and replied, "Fatima, your blood maybe American, but your heart is Hyderabadi," she winked.

Fatima had never thought of it that way. An interesting dynamic to say the least.

Fatima and Mushu joined Naju and Parveen, their female cousins in playing the *dhol*, and singing traditonal wedding songs, *dholak ke geet*. These were an imperative component of a Hyderabadi wedding and added an element of fun and flavor to the ceremony-laden event.

While the younger girls sang merry songs celebrating the bride and her family members, the older women lined up in front of Anam. They began to rub the turmeric paste on her face and arms. They then placed garlands of flowers around her neck. So many garlands were placed upon her that she looked like was a big flower bush. It was hard to make out that a girl was under there unless you caught sight of the bright yellow skin that was trapped under the hundreds of flowers. Fatima found it hard to believe that Anam could breathe under the mountain of flora.

After all the garlands had been put around Anam, it was a difficult task to get her to stand. With the help of her parents she stood up and posed for pictures.

"You can hardly see her. It's her parents and a big flower blob in the middle," Fatima remarked to Naju.

"That's the beauty of it. A flower laden bride stands with the people who gave birth to her, raised her, and now will send her off to the home of her beloved.....How romantic," Naju gushed.

"You think?" a confused Fatima questioned.

"Of course. This is a magical time for the bride...."

"But she can't see anything," interrupted Fatima with a lift of her eyebrows.

"It doesn't matter; her heart senses all that is going on around her."

"I sure hope some part of her gets to enjoy at least part of this fiesta."

"Fiesta?"

"Yes, fiesta. It is Spanish for party."

"You know Spanish?" asked a surprised Naju.

"A little. I took three years in school so far."

"Strange..."

"Why strange?"

"I thought they would teach you proper English in America. But they are teaching you Spanish...." she commented, confused.

"No No. They primarily teach us English. But we are also required to take another language besides English."

"But you Americans speak English horribly. Your grammar is awful."

"What?!" swung back an insulted Fatima. "That's absolutely not true."

"Yes it is."

"I suppose people here speak proper English?"

"At least grammatically we do. After all, our schools are based on the British system."

"Oh I see. You learn English from the British but apply that indecipherable *Desi* accent on purpose to confuse the rest of the world," Fatima cynically responded.

"Don't take it personally *yaar*. I didn't mean to upset you. I just said what we hear around here."

"That's okay Naju. I just said what we say about Indian accents back in America."

Naju could tell that she had upset Fatima, and she felt badly about it. She had no malicious intent; she had spoken openly with a cousin she held dear. Maybe it was just that Naju wished to see Fatima more as a *Desi*, like herself, than an American. Whereas Fatima made it very clear that her cultural identity was more American than *Desi*.

Both Mushu and Naju tried to resolve things quickly. They brought up the most recent Bollywood films, and made plans to go see a film with Fatima, knowing full-well that Fatima was a big Bollywood fan. They also discussed the outfits that they were all planning on wearing to the wedding and reception, paying extra attention to Fatima and what she was wearing. All this to let Fatima know that she was loved and respected by her family no matter where she came from or what she though her identity was. To Mushu and Naju, Fatima was family first; a feeling that was entirely mutual. Eventually everyone managed to get their mind's off of the brief exchange and on to happier things.

The next ceremony called the *sanchak-mehndi*, a larger scale event, was where both the bride and groom's family would visit the others' homes. Fatima was very excited about finally meeting the groom and his family.

"So what is it that exactly happens tonight?" she asked Anam while the two girls sat in her room.

"Well Amir's family will first come here and they will bring all my wedding clothes and jewelry."

"Huh?" Fatima jerked back in surprise.

"What huh?" Anam replied nonchalantly.

"You don't know what you are wearing yet?" asked a shocked Fatima.

"Nooo, they will bring whatever *they* would like me to wear."

"Wait wait...you are telling me that you did not choose your wedding dress?'

"No."

"Not even the style or color or something?!?!"

"Nothing."

"Jesus Christ..." Fatima spat out as she slapped her palm on her forehead.

"What's this Jesus Christ stuff? This is the way our tradition is. I value and respect that. What did you expect, an America style wedding?" Anam jokingly asked Fatima.

"No I didn't expect that, but I thought you would have some input in some part of you wedding!" replied Fatima in an animated fashion.

"Fatima, Relax. It's not a big deal. This is they way we do things around here. You just haven't experienced this before and that is why you are so surprised. Actually, what have you seen in terms of *Desi* wedding? There are Hyderabadi families in America that plan weddings, so what do they do?"

"They do some things that everyone is doing here, like the singing and the gifts being exchanged. But the girls there are at least asked what they would like to wear, just out of common courtesy. In fact some choose everything, so I thought you would at least have some say in all this. But most importantly the girls there meet the guy and talk to him, and make sure he is something that they are actually interested in. It is our right as Muslim women, you know....."

"It's not a big deal. Our culture gives all that respect to our elders. You guys don't have that in America. Just think - Amir will wear whatever our family gives him to wear on the wedding day..."

"Did you choose that?" Fatima asked with great interest.

"No...." Anam sheepishly responded.

"Okayyyyyyyyy" said Fatima as she rolled her eyes.

"But in our culture..."

"Culture, culture, culture!" Fatima shouted as she grabbed her throbbing head. "How can you blindly accept the culture when our religion gives you so many rights?"

"Look Fatima, I am not being forced into this, so this is not religiously wrong by any means. I have appointed my father as my legal representative, and I trust and respect his decision. So stop shaking the boat as you all say."

"I am sorry Anam, I do not want to shake your faith in anyone or all this." She motioned towards all their decorated surroundings.

"I am very happy that you are content with this situation and that the entire family is so pleased with your fiancée. It's just very hard for someone that has grown up in America to be exposed to all this. It's like culture shock or something..."

"I know it's hard for you, but don't look down on it. That's the mistake that most *Desi* kids growing up in America make. They look down upon their own heritage. That is wrong. Appreciate the diversity and learn from it. It will make you a better person."

"I know you are right," Fatima acknowledged. "And I appreciate your putting up with my craziness

"Isn't that what family is for?" Anam said as she hugged her younger cousin. "I am so happy that you could make it."

"So am I." Fatima responded.

A shout came from the courtyard, "Get the bride ready the henna artists are here!"

The henna artists had arrived to decorate the bride's arms and feet in the most intricate of designs. It would take them hours to complete their masterpiece, and each bride had to patiently endure being painted upon with her arms and feet stretched out in four different directions. It was a must for a bride to have henna dyed hands and feet for if she did not beautify herself with the red tattooing, she would appear nothing less than naked. After the four hour ordeal, Anam was now ready to get dressed for all the guests that were expected to arrive in a couple of hours.

As the groom's family arrived each of Anam's female cousins had a responsibility assigned to them in respect to the guests. Naju would hand each guest a rose, Mushu would apply scented sandalwood paste to each guest's hand, Fatima would hand each guest a silver tin filled with edible goodies, and Parveen seated all of the guests in the living room.

After everyone had been seated, Anam was brought out by her cousins. She was wearing a yellow *khara-dupatta*, a traditional Hyderabadi bride's dress, and had the edges of the long scarf draped over her head. She took baby steps to the decorated stool that sat, yet again in the center of the room. Not once did she look up nor did she make eye contact with anything but the floor. After she was seated on the stool the girls all left her side so that the groom's family could admire their beautiful new addition.

The eldest married woman of the groom's family presented Anam with all of her clothes, about ten beautiful outfits total, and her bridal jewelry. She fed the bride some sweets and kissed her forehead. All of this while Anam was still staring blankly at the floor.

"I give her credit man. I would be dying to see what they brought!" Fatima whispered into Parveen's ear.

"She has to wait until the whole party is over to even take a peep at all this stuff!" Parveen softly chortled.

"Let's go guys," Mushu signaled to the girls, "We have to change our outfits to go to the groom's house now. Hurry!"

"It's okay Mushu, the women are still eating their *samosas* and drinking their 'Limca.' They don't look like they are in a rush."

"Fatima it will take forever for us to change and get the groom's gifts in the cars. We need to move!" she pushed Fatima into the room with all of Fatima's stuff.

"Okay Okay don't get physical now," Fatima joked.

The girls quickly changed outfits because a different party *obviously* merited a change in attire. They then had all the gifts for the groom, including his wedding outfit, reception suit, and many other goodies, placed in the cars that they were taking to his house.

As the groom's family began to leave the party, Anams' family prepared to depart for his home. Naju and Fatima were totally ready to go, while Mushu and Parveen were putting on the finishing touches of their makeup. It was now the older ladies that had to get ready.

"Okay guys, here is the plan," Mushu spoke as the girls all huddled.

"We are going to let Fatima be the future sister in law who demands all the money."

"We demand money?" Fatima asked

"Of course. We DEMAND it from our future brother in law. We should start at a ridiculously extravagant number, and then negotiate to a number that is acceptable," Naju informed Fatima.

"I say 10,000 rupees," Parveen suggested.

"What?" And he will actually give us this much money?" asked a baffled Fatima.

"Sure, he has to. It's tradition Fatima!" Mushu enlightened a clueless Fatima.

"Now *that* is a cool tradition," Fatima answered.

As the girls concocted a scheme to milk the most money out of the groom, the older ladies were finally ready.

"*Chalo* girls, *chalo*. It's already 11:30pm! We were supposed to be there by 11:15pm," All the women rushed outside and into the motorcade of cars.

The cars arrived at the grooms' house and the ladies of the bride's family made a grand entrance. Each of the younger girls carried candle-lit *thalis*, trays, which contained sweets and edible goodies for the groom and his family. As they all walked in single file they were seated in a brightly decorated hall where there was a decorated stool placed in the center, much like the one back at Nanima's place.

Anam's family was served tutti-frutti flavored ice cream in shiny steel bowls, and were all given a small party favor that held nuts and sweets. As they all snacked, they took in the future home of their cousin, and chatted away about the layout of the groom's home.

Soon after, the groom was escorted in by his close family members. He sat down upon the stool and all the girls from his family (including his extended family) gathered around him while the older ladies sat behind them. Fatima maneuvered to get a good seat where she would be able to take a good look at her future brother in law, and be able to broker the 10,000 rupee deal.

After giving the groom all his gifts, it was tradition for one girl to grab a hold of the groom's finger and not let go until he accepted the monetary demands of the bride's sisters and cousins. Mushu, Naju, Fatima, and Parveen all grabbed on to the groom's right hand as they negotiated the terms of the exchange.

"I will not pay you girls more than one rupee," insisted Amir, the groom.

"Than we will not let go of your hand," the girls simultaneously shouted back. The pulled his hand with great strength and almost had him slip off the stool.

The bantering went back and forth for ten minutes, when Naju finally said, "Look Amir let's not waste any more time. We all need our sleep, especially you. So pony up and hand it over."

"I am fine, I am on night call a lot so I can do without sleep," Amir replied.

Friendly arguing shifted back and forth until it was finally agreed that the groom would pay the girls 5000 rupees. Happily the girls let go of his hand and clapped in merriment. At 1:30 am the ceremony was officially over and Anam's family made their way back to Nanima's place.

So much drama already, and the wedding day had yet to come. Fatima was amazed by all that had taken place. So many events, such late nights, and unending laughter was what a *Desi* wedding now meant to her, and Fatima was in awe of all of it.

The wedding day was actually a lot more relaxed than what Fatima anticipated, at least for Anam and her cousins. They all had a relaxing late breakfast and marveled at the beautiful outfits and jewelry that the bride was given. Her henna looked amazing and the girls were gaga over how beautiful it turned out. They relaxed and chatted for hours, until it was finally time to start dressing the bride. Anam went to take a shower and all the other girls started to prepare for the evening.

Once everyone was dressed and the radiantly red-attired bride was ready to go, the family began to leave for the wedding hall. There they sat the bride down on a beautifully decorated stage. It was as if she was the Christmas tree in the center of Rockefeller Center. Brightly dressed, jewelry laden, and glittering down to her eyelids, the bride could not be missed for miles.

The remaining details of the party were all handled by the adults, and now it was simply time for the girls to enjoy the auspicious occasion. The *Qazi* performed the *nikkah*, or Islamic marriage ceremony, and the two were now legally married. After the ceremony was completed, the bride was greeted by all of her guests one after another as they hugged her and gave her their blessings. All were there, all except the mother of the bride.

In the back corner of the hall, Fatima's Khala stood weeping profusely. Fatima's mother was doing her best to console her sister, but this was an extremely emotional moment, much like weddings all across the world.

In Indian tradition it was poignant beyond words. The bride was now officially leaving her family and joining that of her husband's. Her parents had forfeited all their rights upon her, as they handed her over to her new family. While all the hustle and bustle of the wedding was going on; this was the scene that caught Fatima's attention. Fatima watched silently as her Khala cried and cried. She thought to herself,' How difficult would it be to say that this is no longer my child, she is first your wife and your daughter in law and your this and your that. The child that you gave birth to and raised was now being given away, like some gift. How sad. How terribly sad.'

As she stared blankly at the two women in the corner, Mushu tapped her from behind.

"They are serving dinner now; let's go and grab a bite to it."

"Let's go," Fatima said as they walked into the dining hall.

After dinner was over, the bride and groom were ready to leave. The groom's family escorted the bride off the stage and had her join her husband as they walked towards their cars. The climax of emotional moving events was to follow. This part of the wedding Fatima was prepared for, or so she thought. Every Bollywood movie played up the departure of the bride as the most tragic event, where the parents of the bride were left in deep sadness, and the bride left her family with tears of sorrow. And this wedding was no different.

There was not a dry eye in the room when Anam's father gave her hand to Amir, and she hugged her father good bye as she now left his family for good. Fatima's uncle graciously hugged his daughter and calmly moved away even though his tears were flowing. When Anam approached her mother, everything became unbearable. The anguish on the face of Fatima's Khala was agonizing to watch. As a mother, she was unable to conceal her emotions as well as her husband had, and she held on to her daughter for dear life. Fatima watched motionless and teary eyed. As did every other person in that room. How could one not be affected in such a way at what was equivalent to the loss of a child? How could one not sympathize with the mother that bore her child and fed her and loved her and nurtured her and made her into the woman she was today, all to hand her off to a son in law that would now be her daughter's closest kin? It was an excruciating scene.

Anam and her mother, both bawling like little children, were slowly pulled apart, and the mother had to be taken once again into the back corner, to be comforted by her sister, and brother, and sons. But even then it was an unbearable sight. In the *Desi* world, this was the harsh reality of having a daughter. And Fatima hated it. Fatima never wanted this to happen to her parents', and wished from the depths of her heart that such a scene would never play out in her own family.

After all the guests departed, the bride's family made their way back home. Sadness gripped everyone. The celebration was over, and the wedding seemed to have ended on a somber note for the bride's family.

The next morning was very quiet and relaxed. Everyone woke up late and lazily ate their breakfast. Anam's parents were especially quiet and everyone else dilly dallied into the late afternoon. The *walima*, wedding reception, was in the evening and the family was set to leave for the party at seven pm.

At half past seven Anam's family made their entrance into the banquet hall. The girls excitedly rushed over to the beaming bride and were anxious to hear how her first day in her new family went. They huddled around the shy bride and tried to carry on their normal style of conversation. But even that was going to be difficult. As more and more guests arrived, they all wished to greet the bride. The girls had to find seats in the main hall and hold off their questions until later.

Fatima's mother approached all of them and asked Fatima to come with her. Fatima easily obliged figuring that she had to be introduced to yet another family member that she was clueless about. But this time Fatima's mother escorted her over to an empty area in the hall and began to whisper.

"Directly twenty feet behind you is a young gentleman whose mother has taken an interest in you. She had managed to have her son take a look at you at the wedding last night and it seems that he too is interested...."

'Oh NO' Fatima thought to herself as she rolled her eyes. She had totally forgotten that this type of stuff ALWAYS happens at *Desi* weddings. She was so focused on her cousin's wedding that she failed to notice all the older ladies who were pointing her out and inquiring about her. And all of a sudden BAM it was in her face.

"Mummy do we really have to do this?"

"Do what?"

"You know this whole matchmaking stuff with guys from here. Do you really think that I could actually live with these FOBs?"

"You think too highly of yourself Fatima," snapped her mother. "I can't believe that my daughter is talking this way."

"No Mummy, I don't mean it like that. Our mentalities are so different. Guys from here have different expectations from a marriage than I would. They would have to deal with total culture shock if they were to come over there and I don't know if I could handle that," Fatima hesitantly answered.

"Your father and I moved there and we adjusted just fine. You knew that we would be considering suitable proposals for you here so now why are you acting this way?"

"I am sorry Mummy I didn't think that you were serious."

"Not serious? I have five ladies on my case for the past two days asking about you. I had not told you so that you would behave naturally and enjoy the festivities. Now what do I tell them? Huh?" she scolded. In an arrogant tone she held up her nose and said, "Now I must say my daughter will not entertain anyone who is not raised in the US. I will sound like a snobby *firangi*..."

"Mummy! Stop please. This is so ridiculous. Why can't we just enjoy *this* wedding?"

"I am enjoying it. But now I have to think of my own daughter."

"Mummy, Mushu seems to be calling me. I will be right back," Fatima darted away with no intention of coming back.

As upset as Fatima's mother was over Fatima's lack of interest in finding a suitable mate here, she had to accept that it wasn't going to happen.

Fatima approached her cousins and rejoined their conversation.

"So what was that all about?" Mushu inquired

"Mummy wants me to look at that boy over there," pointed Fatima.

"And…!?" They all giggled.

"And what?"

"What do you think of him?" they sang in unison.

Fatima knew that she could not tell these girls what she had just told her mother, so she simply said, "He isn't tall enough."

"Oh come on Fatima. Where are you going to find a Hyderabadi guy who is taller than six feet?"

"*Inshallah* I will," Fatima laughed.

"Anyway," Fatima looked around. "Is dinner served?"

"Yes it is. We were waiting for you to get started."

"Great. Let's go then. I am starving….."

As dinner wrapped up, so did all the festivities of Anam's wedding. The five day affair was finally over, and the time had come for Fatima and her mother to return to America. They began to pack up their bags and put away all the gifts that they had bought for everyone back home, and all the stuff that Fatima had bought for herself with her share of the money that Amir bhai had given to the girls.

Fatima had kept the handbag filled with her school books close by. It had not been opened once since she arrived, so it was now time to study hard and make up for lost time. That was what was going to keep her from feeling the heartache of leaving all these relatives behind. As everything was nearly complete for departure, Anam and her husband arrived, along with the rest of the family, to say their goodbyes to Fatima and her mother. Everyone was hugging and kissing the two women, not knowing when the opportunity to meet once more would arise. Yet again there was not a dry eye in the house. It had been a great experience for everyone, one filled with memories to last a lifetime. But the journey was now over, and Fatima and her mother needed to get to the airport. As they painfully pulled away from the bosom of their loved ones, Fatima and her mother got into their taxi. They looked back and waved goodbye to a courtyard filled with family, all sad faced and tear laden. As they wiped away their own tears, the two women turned around and gazed forward, knowing that this was it. Their amazing trip was over, as were any hopes of furthering the proposals that Fatima's mother had received for her daughter in Hyderabad. And now they were on their way home.

Chapter 14

As they left the US Customs facility at JFK International Airport, Fatima bobbed her head up and down until she spotted her younger sisters through the doors. They had stepped onto the railing in an effort to catch sight of Fatima and their mother. Finally when the two women made it past the crowd of people and out to the main lobby, the younger girls waved enthusiastically and jumped off the guardrail. They leapt with excitement upon their mother. It was obvious from their faces that they were ecstatic to have her back.

"Mummy!!!!" they all sang in unison as they smothered her with hugs and kisses.

Fatima seeing her sisters excitement over their mother, walked towards her father. She hugged him first. After her sisters were done greeting their mother, Fatima hugged them.

"Mummy we missed you this much," Malikah said as she stretched her hands as far apart as she could reach.

"Daddy tried to cook for us, but he couldn't even fry an egg," Amina informed her amused mother.

"And Daddy used the spoons that we are not supposed to."

"And Daddy put too much soap in the laundry machine so the soap came out all over the floor."

"And Daddy scrubbed the pots with Ajax even though we told him that you said never to do that."

"And Daddy made us drink milk without any Ovaltine and it tasted so bad, but he made us drink it," Malikah continued complaining.

Mummy simply laughed in amusement as she embraced her little ones, while Daddy shook his head as all the complaints were filed.

"All I did for these girls, and they don't see anything. I get no respect," he said a la Rodney Dangerfield, with a smirk on his face.

He was obviously the most delighted to have his wife home. He did not have to say what he felt. They all knew it just by the glow of his face. This was typical of their parents; their looks were their displays of affection. There was no hugging or smooching between them, never in public nor in front of the children, their love was simply understood. Their eyes said it all.

Back at home Fatima scrambled to organize all of her class work in time for school. She had thought of skipping school tomorrow, but after reviewing all of her assignments, and the work that she had completed, she felt that she needed to get back into the swing of things ASAP.

Despite the fact that she tossed and turned all night, Fatima got out of bed at 6:15 am and started to get ready for school. She prayed *fajr*, the morning prayer, and grabbed a quick bite. She then ran to the bus stop and got on the bus. As she gazed outside, Fatima felt a rush of nervousness come over her as she thought about her classes. She was hoping desperately that she had not fallen too far behind, and that her grades would not suffer as a consequence of her trip. After all, this was her junior year. Colleges would look at her grades from this year with great scrutiny - she needed to do well.

As classes started, Fatima felt almost as if she had never gone half way across the world. Overwhelmed with keeping up with the current assignments, she dove full force into her class work. The only reminders of her trip were the 'welcome back' greetings she received from all of her friends and teachers. It was surprising how quickly everything seemed to be falling in place, back to her normal routine. But by the time lunch hit, Fatima felt exhausted. It was midnight Hyderabad time, and after twenty four hours of no sleep she struggled to keep her head up.

"Fatima you don't look so hot," Mary informed her.

"Mary, I think I am going to pass out," she said as she plopped her head down.

"Why didn't you sleep in today?"

"I thought I would at first, but I was too stressed about all this schoolwork," she said as she slammed her hand on all her paperwork.

"So I guess you're not going to tell me how it was?"

Fatima turned her head towards Mary, and without picking it up off the table, she wearily replied, "In short, it was awesome. I loved it this time around."

"You loved Hyderabad?"

"I loved the people of Hyderabad. They made the trip amazing."

"How was the wedding?"

"Great, but I don't have the energy to tell you all the details now, maybe tomorrow."

"By the looks of it, you won't be here tomorrow," said Mary as she stared at the bags under Fatima's eyes.

"No way man, I can't afford to lose one more day. As it is I am feeling lost and confused. I will go home and conk out. By tomorrow I hope to be back on my normal schedule."

"Good luck."

"Thanks, I need it," responded a dazed Fatima.

As soon as Fatima got home, she prayed her afternoon prayer and then jumped into bed. She slept and she slept. A nap turned into a much longer state of sleep. In fact she didn't wake up until 4:30 am the following morning. When her eyes fell upon the alarm clock, she jumped out of bed. She looked outside her window and was shocked to see the darkness. 'Well at least I am up early enough to do my homework' she thought.

She washed and went downstairs. No one was up; it was just her, getting herself a bowl of Fruity Pebbles to start the day off. She put her books on the table and started reading while she ate. By 5:15 am her reading was complete, and she needed to take a quick prayer break. After the *fajr*, morning prayer, it was on to her homework. By the time her father and mother came down she had finished her assignments and was ready to head off to school.

"What happened *beta*? You were sleeping like a log yesterday," her father asked in a most concerned manner.

"I was wiped out Daddy."

"We tried to wake you up two times to eat dinner but you were snoring like you couldn't imagine," Mummy said as she took meat out of the freezer.

"Really? I had no idea. All I know is that I thought I would take short nap, but then I woke up at 4:30 am. That was weird. But hey, I slept well, and I got my work done, so it turned out okay," Fatima said in a positive tone.

"Good. But you better head out to the bus stop."

"Yeah I am ready to go. *Khuda hafiz*," Fatima said as she waved good bye with one hand and grabbed her backpack with the other.

Back at school, classes were in full swing, and while all the other students had familiarized themselves with their routine and schedule, Fatima was still struggling to adapt. Her work was completed and she had caught up with her assignments, but she felt that she still had adjusting to do.

Starting the day off with Analysis was a killer, especially since Fatima wasn't a morning person. Generally, it would take her until the second or third period to get her mind working in full gear, but with Analysis her brain was being jumpstarted early in the morning. Almost as if to keep the momentum going she had Chemistry immediately after, and then things relaxed a little with Spanish. After lunch, she had the classes that she looked forward to most, her social science courses, International Studies and European History. Both were taught by one teacher whom Fatima had heard every Tom, Dick, and Harry rave about, Mrs. Sandra Sheehan. Fatima was interested to find out if she lived up to all the hype, especially since she was the head of the Social Sciences Department at Pennsbury High.

Mrs. Sheehan was a unique woman, and that was obvious from the first time Fatima met her. Her classroom was unlike any Fatima had seen before, crowded with artifacts from all over the world, and brightly colored to keep one's eyes wide open at all times. Her eccentricities were evident from the many pieces of art that also decorated the class and attracted the attention of every student. Her personality radiated life and enthusiasm for the subjects she taught, and it was clear that she wanted to see that same passion exude from her students.

Fatima's first impression of her was that of a Southern belle lost in the liberal North, but her understanding of Mrs. Sheehan was far from over. There was clearly much more to discover about this fascinating lady. Interestingly enough, Mrs. Sheehan also seemed to be intrigued by Fatima, and her outspoken and opinionated style. She appeared to have taken a liking to Fatima and began to ask Fatima many questions about her heritage, religion, and family. Soon enough the two developed a rapport, and Mrs. Sheehan became not only an excellent teacher to Fatima, but also a good friend.

"Mummy you wouldn't believe how cool she is," Fatima told her mother. "She asks me all the time about what Islam says about this and that. And how to differentiate cultural stuff from religious stuff. It's really awesome that she takes such an interest."

"And I am sure you have a mouthful to share with her," Mummy jokingly added.

"You bet. How many teachers are like this? Actually asking a student about their beliefs and background? Most of them just want us to think that they have all the answers to everything and that we are there to simply learn from them. Here Mrs. Sheehan actually wants all of us to learn from each other. Now *that* is cool."

"She sounds great."

"She is."

"Well then learn from her. Like you said, there are not that many people like that around."

Fatima was now even more excited than before about the second half of her school day. Her classes in the morning seemed to drag on endlessly while her afternoon classes flew by, thanks to Mrs. Sheehan. Not only did Mrs. Sheehan inspire Fatima in her classes, she also taught Fatima the value of dialogue. She saw how much understanding was brought out amongst her students when there was an open forum where everyone could speak their minds and learn to relate to the diversity that existed amongst the students. She sponsored a club after school that promoted such discourse, called the World Affairs Club (WAC).

"I think that the WAC is something you should be a part of. We would learn so much from you about Islam and India. And I am sure that you would enjoy hearing from our other students about their cultures and their religions. It's really a fun club that teaches you a lot. I think it would be right up your alley," Mrs. Sheehan stated.

"I would love to Mrs. Sheehan, but I am not sure if my parents would be okay with me staying after for an activity like this. They are really old school about stuff like that."

"Well, I can call them and let them know how beneficial I think your presence at the club would be for all of us and vice versa."

Surprised Fatima asked, "Really?"

"Sure why not?" Mrs. Sheehan responded matter-of-factly.

"That would be great," excitedly responded Fatima.

And Mrs. Sheehan did just that. She called Fatima's parents and let them know what the WAC was all about and how it would be a wonderful learning experience for Fatima. Pleased to have a teacher requesting the presence of their daughter in such a setting, Fatima's parents agreed to let her join the club and stay after school two days a week.

Now with school work and participating in the WAC, Fatima had a tight schedule and barely any time to socialize. In fact she avoided going to Somerville, afraid of what, or who, Dadima had waiting to pop out of her purse this week. Despite her precaution, family meetings were inevitable.

"I don't know what to do with you Fatima. You are getting to be an old hag," Dadima scolded her granddaughter.

"Yeah yeah Dadima. What's new?" Fatima replied indifferently, as she read the newspaper.

"What will you do with all this schooling huh? You will still wind up in the kitchen barefoot and pregnant."

Fatima just rolled her eyes and did not dignify the statement with a response. She thought if she simply kept quiet and did not respond to anything Dadima said, maybe Dadima would forget that she was there, or just give up on trying to carry on a conversation with her.

Fatima loved her Dadima dearly. She truly did. That is why she put with this type of talk. She wouldn't take it from anyone else. But the reality was that now it was not just Dadima that dabbled in this type of talk. The whole family was beginning to wonder how to seriously introduce the subject of marriage to Fatima.

Now that she was seventeen, Fatima's extended family believed that it was time to start seriously considering eligible proposals. Even Fatima's parents felt that it was not a bad idea to have her engaged. They did not want to get her married for at least another two or three years, but getting her engaged became an appealing option, especially since she had made it clear that she wasn't planning on pursuing a career in medicine.

Fatima knew that this marriage business was a dark shadow looming over her shoulder, but she didn't know when it would come out and expose itself. As the whisperings went on, it became obvious that the shadow was preparing to come out of the darkness.

"Look Fatima. You have seen how many friends of yours have already been engaged, so it's not like its something foreign to you," her father said.

"Daddy, I also know friends at school who have had been having 'relations' since they were thirteen, and some have had abortions too," Fatima crossed her arms and replied disdainfully.

"Exactly, now which is the better option?"

"But those aren't the only two types of people I know."

"Fatima, why must you be so difficult!" her father swung his arms up in frustration. "Can't you see we want to protect you from what is out there? We don't want you to fall into something you will regret later on in life."

"I know that Daddy, but this is not the only option," Fatima shook her head with attitude.

"Okay then, what is a better option?"

"Let me be. I have never betrayed your trust. I fear God and respect His law; do you think I would intentionally break it?"

"Not deliberately, but you are human. Girls at your age can be very easily manipulated into situations that will hurt you in this life and the

Hereafter. Why do you think so many parents are getting their young daughters engaged? They are worried like we now are. It's a crazy world out there. And as I have always told you, we trust you wholeheartedly, but we *don't* trust everyone else out there."

"So what exactly do you want me to do?" Fatima asked with her head resting upon her fingers.

"We are not saying get married, we are simply saying let's actually consider the guys that come along. That's all. If you don't like the guy, then fine - it's over. But at least give him a chance."

"Okay Daddy, go ahead. Knock yourself out." Fatima stood up and walked away in frustration.

There was no way to win this argument and Fatima knew it.

The next weekend was her friend Afia's wedding. At twenty one, Afia was the perfect age for marriage, or so all the aunties said. This was not going to help her situation. Considering that her entire family was attending the event, this would just add fuel to the fire. 'All this stress, one month before the SATs,' Fatima thought. 'Could things get any more frustrating?'

As the wedding closed in on them, the gazillion ceremonies of the wedding began. They were not carried out on the same scale as they were back in Hyderabad, but they were lots of fun. The girls would all get together and have a blast singing and joking with the bride to be, while all the aunties would marvel at the gifts to be given to the groom and his family. As much as Fatima was enjoying the event, there was a side of her that was nervous and on guard. *Desi* weddings were a haven for matchmakers and Fatima was very aware of that. Anytime an aunty greeted her too nicely, she became suspicious of the motivation behind the extra wide smile and elongated *salaam*. Fingers that were pointed in her directions also made her antsy, as these were all the signs she had missed in India. She was not about to miss them now. Especially since she had given the okay to her parents, even though it may have been reluctantly so, to look into promising prospects.

Sure enough on the ride home, Mummy was talking about a lady who had approached her in regards to Fatima. Even though her parents were in the front seat and the girls were in the back, Fatima wanted to make sure that she could hear very word of their conversation. She turned down the volume of her walkman and moved the headphones discreetly off her ears. A little tug of her *hijaab* behind her ears and she was set to go. Her sisters on the other hand were busy listening to their walkmans and could have cared less about what the adults were carrying on about.

"The family is originally from Hyderabad and the boy is an engineer. He studied at University of Pennsylvania, or maybe it was Pennsylvania State University. I don't remember exactly...They both sound the same... Anyway he graduated with honors. Now he is working for a large firm right in King of Prussia..."

'Oh God,' Fatima rolled her eyes. 'This is not good news.'

"What else did the mother say?" her father asked with great interest.

"She took our number and said she will call."

'Holy crap' Fatima's head plummeted into the palms of her hands. 'I am screwed' she thought. She could listen no more. She placed her headphones back on her ears and turned on her walkman. She chose to not hear anything more her folks had to say about this bachelor; ignorance was bliss.

The next day was Afia's wedding day, and everyone was excited. Hers was the first wedding of the community, and everybody was looking forward to the big event. Fatima was especially happy for her dear friend. She was anxious to see her friend as a happy bride, and even more anxious to see Afia as her first '*married*' friend.

All the girls and women were dolled up in the brightest and flashiest of *Desi* couture - much like what the women in India were wearing. In fact the wedding here had many similarities to Anam's wedding in Hyderabad. The ceremonies that were carried out were pretty much the same; the pomp and circumstance of the weddings was on par, and the buffet was equally as extensive. Additionally, the aunties here were scoping out girls that would make attractive daughter in laws, just like they did in Hyderabad. But the one thing that Fatima noticed that this wedding lacked was the flowers. There was no intoxicating scent of fresh flowers at this wedding, at least not to the degree that there was in Hyderabad. Here and there were some beautiful floral centerpieces, but that was about it. As Fatima sat at her table and gazed at them, her mother came up and tapped her shoulder.

Standing next to her mother, was a short stout lady whose stomach was hanging out of her petticoat like a kangaroo's pouch. Her orange and green neon sari required sunglasses to be looked upon and her red Sally Jessy Raphael glasses made her face look too small for her frame.

"*Beta*, I want you to meet Qudsia Aunty. She lives in King of Prussia..."

'Shit!' Fatima thought. She didn't hear one word that came out of her mother's mouth after that. 'I can't believe this...I can't believe this.' She kept repeating to herself. After blanking out for a few seconds, Fatima came back to her senses.

Fatima's mother nudged her back and signaled for her to stand up. Fatima reluctantly stood up. At 5'8" Fatima was a tall girl, but for some reason standing next to this particular aunty she felt like she was the Sears Tower.

She gathered her composure and said "*Assalamu alaykum*," in the most decent manner possible.

"*Walaikum salaam beta*. Very nice to meet you. How old are you?" the aunty asked while obviously stretching her neck to look up at Fatima.

'Lady if you don't know that you shouldn't even be here talking to me,' Fatima thought.

"Seventeen," she respectfully replied.

"And what are you studying?"

'Does this woman know anything about me?' Fatima continued to think.

"I am a junior in high school."

An awkward silence followed. Fatima looked down and twiddled her thumbs, and the lady looked at her with a weird smile. Unsure of what would follow Fatima decided to put an end to this embarrassing situation.

"It was very nice meeting you Aunty," she lowered her gaze and sat back down at what would have been eye level with this lady. It was God's grace that at that very moment Fatima's friends joined her at her table.

All the girls were raving about the bride and the groom and the wedding arrangements. Fatima jumped full force into the conversation in the hopes of forgetting the orange and green lady that stood three feet away. The aunty was finally escorted away by Fatima's mother.

When they were out of sight Fatima stuck her head into the middle of the round table and quietly asked all of her friends, "Who is Qudsia Aunty?" tilting her head in the direction that the aunty was walking away.

"She was the woman that was standing behind you a minute ago," Rubi said.

"Duh! I know that. But who exactly is she?"

"I don't know who she is but her son's a stud..."another friend giggled.

"Really?" Fatima sat back in her chair. "You know him?"

"No, I just see him at these types of functions."

"Do you know anything about him?" Fatima pressed on.

"Why the third degree Fatima?" Rubi asked.

"Nothing...." Fatima bit her lip.

"Don't nothing us! What's going on?" the girls impatiently inquired.

"Really it's nothing..."

"Just spill the beans..."

"Well, that lady...you know Qudsia Aunty...well, she was talking to my mom..."

"You mean she was asking your mom about you?!" Asma cut her off in excitement.

"I guess…" Fatima felt herself turning pink.

"Shut the hell up!" Asma pounded her hand on the table

"Okay….."

"Have you seen the guy?" Rubi asked anxiously.

"No, I have no idea who he is."

"I will show you who he is if I can spot him," Rubi volunteered.

"Okay…"

"Holy crap Fatima, who knows the next wedding could be yours…"Asma predicted.

"Umm, I think you need to take a chill pill. Nothing has happened. His mom just asked a few questions that's all…"

"Did they ask for your phone number?" Rubi asked.

"I think so…" Fatima responded unsurely.

"Well that's it. They are going to come to your house and you will have to serve them tea…"

"Umm we are not in India, and you know men and women are always separated in our house anyway."

"Not when there is guy coming to look at you."

"Looking at *me*? Ummm I need to look at him too."

"Yeah yeah whatever you say," Asma laughed.

"And don't kid yourself. You will *not* be separated the whole evening."

"Hellooo guys. Where is all this coming from? The lady talked with my mom for two minutes and you guys have this crazy scenario dreamt up."

"It's not dreamt up. We just know what to expect." Asma informed Fatima.

"How is that Asma? Besides clichéd *Desi* movies – how would you know?"

"Believe me, I know."

"How would you know?" Fatima knit her brows. "Wait a second… are you saying that you've been through this already?"

"Actually…"

"Oh my God! I can't believe you didn't tell me!!" Fatima shouted.

"Relax Fatima, it just happened yesterday." "And you didn't tell me!" Fatima pushed Asma's shoulder.

"Get over it Fatima," Rubi cut off Fatima before turning to Asma.

"So what happened? Don't leave out any details." She scooted in so she wouldn't miss a word.

"Nothing really. This guy came over with his family. They had dinner at our place and that was it."

"That was it??!? You didn't talk to him?" Fatima shook her head in disbelief.

"No. I just saw him when he was getting dinner."

"And...How was he?" Rubi pushed on.

"I haven't talked to him so I have no clue."

"Okay, but how did he look?" asked Rubi.

"He was fine."

"Fine? That's a weak answer. More details please….." Fatima insisted.

"He was fine, Fatima! I don't know how he really is until I talk to him. His personality will make him either better looking or worse …" Asma laughed.

"This is unreal..." Fatima was baffled. "I can't believe this stuff is happening to us?"

"What do you mean *this* stuff?" Rubi asked.

"You know this whole matchmaking stuff? I knew it would happen one day or another, but already!?!" Fatima's eyes popped out.

"Well this is prime time according to the old ladies," Asma winked.

"I guess so…" Fatima shrugged her shoulders. "Who would have thought that it would start at seventeen……?"

"Anyone from Pakistan could have told you that it would start now," exclaimed Farhana, a recent Pakistani immigrant cousin of Afia's, who joined the table.

"Farhana, in Pakistan that may be okay, but here?"

"Oh please Fatima, Who are all these people around you? Indians and Pakistanis! Whether they came here long ago or recently, they are all *Desi* at heart! Aren't they?"

Fatima knew Farhana had a point. "Man Farhana, you just rained on my parade!"

"The truth always stings doesn't it...?" Farhana laughed mischievously.

Chapter 15

SAT prep was in full swing and the big test was only weeks away. Fatima diligently completed all of the practice exams that were given to her at school, and read the numerous SAT prep books that her father had bought. She ignored all mentions of matchmakers and proposals choosing to focus upon the big exam.

Once it was done Fatima could breathe again. She couldn't have absorbed an ounce more of testing strategy or review. Just to get the testing out of her system, she was ready to throw away every #2 pencil that she owned.

"So what did you think?" Fatima asked Mary.

"No comment. It's over and done with."

"I think that I am going to have to re-evaluate my college choices," Fatima laughed.

"I am sure you did fine."

"Whatever. I just can't believe it's finally over. What a relief," Fatima sighed.

"Not for me, I have my ACTs coming up," lamented Mary.

"Aaaaah the pleasure of not pursuing medicine...." Fatima stretched her arms out above her head.

"Don't jinx yourself dear. Your parents haven't given up the quest."

"Maybe not. But I have!"

"Anyway...Did you talk to them about colleges?"

"They would have a cow if I moved away, so my choices are pretty limited."

"So you will stick to applying to the U Penn or Princeton then..." Mary questioned.

"I will apply there, but I would not go there even if I got in."

"What? Are you serious?"

"Come on, Mary. Think about it. I would be drowning in student loans by the time I finished. And my liberal arts degree isn't going to help pay those loans off ..."

"All the more reason to do medicine..." Mary punched her in the gut.

"Ha-ha. Thanks but no thanks. You on the other hand...That is the way you should go."

"Naaah, I am going to try to do an accelerated program or something that locks me into med school."

"So you're determined to commit suicide?" Fatima pulled her leg.

"Ha-ha," Mary wrinkled her nose.

Fatima knew that her parents wanted her to follow in Mary's footsteps on the road to medical college. However, by this time she was sure that medicine was not her calling. She knew that she had let her parents down, but Fatima knew that she couldn't work in a field for which she had no passion. But that did not stop her from feeling badly about not fulfilling her parents' dream. She just hoped that they could get over it so that she could move on without feeling so guilty.

Fatima began to request applications and catalogs from local universities, tapping into all of the higher institutions of the Philadelphia, NJ, and NYC areas. Soon school catalogues spilled out of her mailbox every day. Each was better organized and more attractive than the previous. These catalogues were so impressively put together that they even made dinky junior colleges look very appealing.

Fatima was in awe of all her options. But the reality of her situation was that there were some tacit factors that governed where she would attend college. The first was that she would not be dorming at any university. It wouldn't matter if the dean of Harvard University came knocking on her door, living on any campus was not an option. Fatima's parents were determined to do their best to continue to protect her from what they believed was an unhealthy environment.

The second factor to consider was the tuition of the school. Fatima knew that the tuition of private schools was considerably higher than the state universities. Keeping that in mind, her choices slimmed down to two – Penn State, or Rutgers University. Although attending Rutgers would require her to pay out of state tuition, the fact that its main campus was considerably closer to home than Penn State's main campus made Rutgers her top pick. Nevertheless, she still chose to apply to a variety of schools, including a couple of her *dream* schools, just to see if she would get in.

As Fatima began filling out applications and submersing herself in writing all the essays the applications required, the atmosphere at home grew increasingly tense. Qudsia Aunty had called twice and was trying to set up a meeting between her son and Fatima. All this time Fatima had been dodging the situation by citing her need to prepare for the SATs. Now her parents felt it was time she should meet with this young man

"The exam is behind you, so we can not push this off longer, Fatima," her mother stated. "We need to set some time to meet this boy."

"I know I know," Fatima mumbled, trying to avoid the subject. "Maybe during the summer we can work something out," she said cringingly.

"Are you okay? The summer?" Mummy slammed down the knife with which she was chopping onions. Her hands flew up in the air, "The mother has already called two times; I can not delay this any further. It would be utterly rude on our part."

She angrily picked up the knife once again to finish her chopping. Fatima just shook her head and rolled her eyes.

"Okay, okay. Do whatever you want," she rolled her eyes.

The details of the meeting were finalized by the mothers through phone calls which were awkward to say the least. Fatima made it a point to be around her mother when these calls were taking place, so that she could try to make out what was being said. Although she did not hear what Qudsia Aunty was saying, she could hear the uneasiness in her mother's voice. It wasn't the calm and confident tone that she usually spoke with. Instead there was a hint of anxiety, and a strong sense of formality in the dialogue between the two women. Fatima could tell that that this formality was not going to be easy to handle.

When all was said and done, the mothers had agreed on a manner of meeting that was commonly referred to as the "walk-by," which basically meant that the two families would just *walk by* each other (hence the name) at a "neutral" location, and carry on some small talk so that they got a better sense of who they were going to be dealing with. In this particular case, the families agreed to meet at the mall, so that the meeting would occur in an informal setting.

'Yeah right,' Fatima thought to herself.

"I am sure that will be *really* casual Mummy," she sarcastically said to her Mother.

"Yes it will be," her mother responded calmly after explaining to Fatima how the meeting would occur.

"So you are telling that we will *just happen* to run into each other at the food court. Where we *just happen* to start up a conversation?"

"Yes. What's wrong with that? This will allow you and the boy to take a look at each other. Then, if you think you want to pursue it or vice versa we can move ahead."

"So basically, we will go to check each other out?" Fatima interjected rudely.

"Tauba! Why do you talk this rubbish? In such third class terminology..."

"And this is soooo *not* superficial either Mummy," she said condescendingly.

"God knows what will become of you Fatima. You have a comment about everything," her mother said exasperatedly.

Fatima winced her eyes, scathing at the fact that she would have to go through something which she thought was so silly. 'Why make it all weird like this?' she thought to herself. 'If we are just going to take a look, why not exchange pictures or point each other out at a party? Why a *walk-by*? Ugghh...' she thought

Despite Fatima's aversion to this situation, she agreed to go through with it. But then again, there really wasn't much of a choice; certain things had to be done to maintain the family honor. NO family wants to be known as super picky or arrogant since this would ward off any good proposals that the future may hold.

When the day of the meeting arrived, Fatima's mother fussed over what Fatima was planning on wearing.

"What is this ugly outfit you have chosen," she remarked while holding up the black *shalwar khameez* that Fatima had placed on her bed.

"It looks like something you wear to a funeral. Wear something a little more colorful, something that suits you," she sifted through Fatima's closet.

"Mummy, please...!" Fatima replied frustratingly, "This is fine!"

"Fatima, must you always dismiss my advice? I am your mother, I know better," her mother insisted as she took out a dusty rose colored outfit.

"How about this? It's very decent and attractive. It will look very nice," she held it up to Fatima's silhouette.

"Yeah yeah..." Fatima shook her head despairingly.

"What's this yeah yeah, *bathamees*?" her mother prodded her.

"Okay Mummy, okay. The pink one is fine," Fatima grudgingly answered. She hung the black outfit back in her closet and pressed the dusty rose one that her mother laid on her bed.

'I can't believe this nonsense,' Fatima thought. 'Watch this guy turn out to be some oily haired, big mustached freak.' As much as she wished to avoid this, it was now too late; she had to go along with it.

They arrived at the mall after an unusually quiet ride. They quietly made their way through the mall. Fatima could feel her hands getting clammy and her ears turning red.

As they walked into the food court, Fatima saw a *Desi* looking family sitting in the center of the court. 'Damn that's them,' she thought. And of course, it was. Her head shot down, and she couldn't get herself to look up after that. Even as the elders greeted each other, Fatima struggled to look up. She smiled and nodded and that was about it.

The elders made polite conversation while Fatima and Saleem, the guy, sat quietly at opposite ends of the table. The fact that the guy was Saleem was not made clear, as there were no formal introductions. But Fatima figured that that had to be him because his head couldn't have been the gray haired one. So it was more a process of elimination.

Eventually, Saleem was dragged into the conversation by the two men, and it was Fatima who was left sitting quietly with no idea what to do. Fatima thought to herself, 'I better get a good look at this guy; it may be my only chance.' So Fatima began to twist and turn. She shifted to her left and then to the right. She moved her hand in front of her face and on to her *hijaab*, so that she could fake an adjustment and possibly catch an inconspicuous glimpse of Saleem. And that is exactly what she got. A glimpse. A not so impressive glimpse. But that glance was enough to let her know that, at least physically, he was *not* what she was looking for.

The bright Tommy shirt he was sporting made him look like a crossing guard. There was so much hairspray in his hair that if you lit a match next to his head, it could have caught on fire. And the fuzzy moustache looked like fungus growing under his nose. 'Holy crap,' she thought to herself. She looked away in disbelief. As the adults went on with their conversations Fatima's thoughts drifted further away. She lost all interest in the meeting and knew that it was going to be a big fat NO on her part.

Basically, it was all over. The meeting hadn't even ended, but Fatima had shut the door on this prospect. Fatima was actually relieved. Very relieved. It was a blessing that this fellow showed up the way he did. Fatima knew that her father would not take a liking to him nor would her mother. So she may be able to wiggle out of this whole situation simply through her parents' disapproval. But if that didn't work, it still wouldn't be an issue. Her 'no' was all it would take. 'This isn't so bad after all,' she precluded.

On the ride home, there was an awkward silence in the car. Not the tense quiet that engulfed them on their way to the mall, but a strange, uncomfortable silence. Fatima was waiting for her parents to ask her what she thought of Saleem. She had her reply meticulously planned out.

First she would respectfully respond, "Since both of you are a lot wiser than I am, I want to know what you both thought of him first."

This sly answer was devised knowing full well that no boy dressed like that would receive rave reviews from her folks. Once her parents would bash him, Fatima would respectfully declare, "I can not go through with this if you are not 110% happy with Saleem. So let's end it right here." Then she would sit back and bask in her 'dutiful daughter' glory. Aaaaaaaaaah. What a nice feeling that would be.

Fatima twiddled her thumbs and looked out her window waiting for the chance to reply to any questions in regards to the meeting. But there was nothing. No interrogation, no conversation, no looks, no weird body movements. Nothing at all. The silence was now perturbing Fatima. She thought and she thought and she thought some more. Should she start the conversation, or would that be totally unacceptable? Or should she lay low and let the whole thing fly over, since he was obviously not what anyone in her family would consider seriously. Or was this a trick that her parents were playing? Fatima's parents knew that she couldn't bear to be silent about any subject, especially one such as this. This would surely evoke a response from her. Were they just waiting to see how Fatima would react? Or were they avoiding the subject altogether? As these thoughts raced back and forth in her head, Fatima was about to explode. She opened her mouth to speak, "So Fatima what do you say?" her father calmly asked.

Caught off guard, Fatima had to stop, sit back, and take a breath. She opened her mouth...

"I don't think it is a suitable match," Mummy added.

Surprised yet again, Fatima's pupils raced to their right and left and then back again to their right, as if she were watching a tennis match. She sat back quietly; the cat had gotten her tongue.

"I didn't think so either but if Fatima says he is fine, we owe it to her to look further into the matter," Father said to her mother.

"So Fatima, any opinions?" momentarily turning towards Fatima.

Fatima waited a second before she began, just in case she would be cut off yet again. After a brief silence, she realized that she could finally speak. Knowing that she was exactly where she wanted to be, Fatima calmly replied, "I will agree with whatever you both have to say."

Her father and her mother turned towards each other in a knee jerk fashion. Both burst out laughing. Confused at this reaction, Fatima asked, "What's so funny?"

"Seriously Fatima…" her father couldn't stop laughing.

"Umm... I don't know why you two are laughing?" an annoyed Fatima said.

"*Beta*, we know you are an *American* girl, so we want to hear your opinion. All American girls have something to say. It is in their nature," Mummy said as she tried to stop giggling.

"What..." Fatima was irritated.

"Don't act like you don't have an opinion. We know you will not blindly follow our wishes. Just tell us what you think of Saleem."

Fatima didn't know whether she should feel insulted or if she should feel liberated. Here she was trying so hard to show respect to her parents in accordance with her *Desi* culture, but it was not okay with them. But at the same time she knew in her heart that this would not have been the case had she liked Saleem and her parents had disapproved of him. Then her liberated American side would have emerged which would have driven her to pursue what she felt may have been a potential match. Finally she thought, 'Screw it. I am not going to be a *Desi* or an American. So let me just exercise my Islamic right.'

"I am not interested in him," Fatima replied coldly.

And that was it. Saleem wasn't mentioned again. It was on to bachelor number two. And bachelor number three, then four, then five... All while still in high school.

Chapter 16

While most of her classmates were busy with their boyfriends and girlfriends in what appeared to be a race to lose their virginity, Fatima pondered over marriage proposals. Although she spent just as much time thinking about college plans, this marriage business was weighing heavily on her. Family was continuously bringing up new prospects and she was bombarded with lectures from her grandmothers about how "this was the age for good proposals."

"After all," she mimicked, "A woman after the age of twenty two is knocking on infertility's door."

At least this is what the elderly *Desi* women were convinced of.

Friends at school were horrified at the thought of marriage. They could not fathom that such a young woman would even consider marriage unless she was pregnant. Even then did she really have to be...ugh...gulp...*married?* What century was Fatima living in...???

"I can't imagine *marriage*...Why bother when you could have a boyfriend?" Joan snubbed.

"Maybe it's not all about getting laid Joan," Fatima slammed back.

"What would *you* know about ***that*** Fatima?" Joan laughed mockingly as she strode off with her over permed hair flying in Fatima's face.

"Uuugghhhhhh, I am gonna smack her upside her snotty little face," Fatima grunted.

Being a virgin was not an issue for Fatima. It never had been. But what Fatima could not understand was why did Joan, and so many of her other peers, act like it was the *only* issue?

Fatima was a firm believer in abstinence. In fact she was a master of abstinence in many fields. She had never touched any alcohol, any drugs, any pork, and never ever could she even imagine being with a boy without taking marital vows. This was probably true of ninety percent of her Muslim friends as well. So what's the deal with these other kids? Why were they hell-bent on screwing up their lives? It was a question that Fatima could easily pose, but never answer to her satisfaction.

Mrs. Sheehan, on the other hand, was Fatima's greatest crusader.

"Fatima you have your head on straight. Don't you let these silly teenagers mess with you. They are not thinking about what they are doing to their bodies and how they may suffer later on. They think they are immortal at this point...." she would kindly advise.

"I know Mrs. Sheehan, believe me I know..." Fatima agreed as if she had the years of experience that Mrs. Sheehan did. But then again, Fatima was always mentally well beyond her years. *"Buddi Nani", old grandmother*, her family had called her, on numerous occasions.

"Aren't they afraid of AIDS, and all those STDs? And why is getting drunk so cool? Why do people want to lose their sanity and act like total idiots – and then think that that is sooo cool??" she would ask Mrs. Sheehan, as they would converse endlessly about these topics, and all the other problems of the world.

The two spent many hours together, working on World Affairs Club projects and events, besides of course the classes that Fatima took which Mrs. Sheehan taught. Mrs. Sheehan wasn't just an academic mentor; she was also a revered advisor in issues of daily life, of theology and philosophy, of politics – both domestic and international, and of social issues. There was no subject that Fatima could not talk to Mrs. Sheehan about. Their respect for each other was constantly increasing.

Fatima's parents were interested in meeting the woman who their daughter was spending so much time with after school, and who she could not stop raving about.

They took the inconceivable step of inviting Mrs. Sheehan over for a traditional Hyderabadi dinner. Socially meeting people like Mrs. Sheehan was a first for Fatima's family. They had never ventured out of their *Desi* Muslim community. In fact they never thought that any Caucasian would even be interested in carrying on a friendship with someone who was not White; an idea that was stained in their memories from the times of British occupied India.

Fatima's parents were rather surprised that their daughter could carry on so well with someone who did not completely identify with their traditions and religion. For Fatima's parents the clash of cultures was socially very difficult to handle. It was something that they had avoided like the plague. Until now.

The Husains made every effort to ensure that Mrs. Sheehan would feel comfortable during her visit. Hospitality was of great importance within their religion; so much so that there were numerous traditions of the Prophet Muhammed on how to deal graciously with one's guests. Culturally, guests were treated like family. Thus, having Mrs. Sheehan over was not something that could be taken lightly.

The whole family had been prepped endlessly by Fatima on how to set up for the arrival of a non-Muslim and non-*Desi* guest. Her younger sisters were fully aware of how to deal with the situation since they too had their own American friends, not that that kept Fatima from putting in her two cents.

"Please light the scented candles after the cooking is done," Fatima requested of her mother. "The smell of our food could make her sick as soon as she walks in..." worried Fatima.

"Funny Fatima, I thought much of the world considers that *smell* a delectable aroma ..." her father remarked in annoyance.

Ignoring her father completely, Fatima started placing the candles all around the house.

"Daddy, are you really wearing those pants?" Fatima eyed her father's burgundy polyester slacks. He actually ordered polyester slacks from the Blair catalog. EEEW.

"You just worry about how you look Fatima. I am old and married; no one cares what I wear."

"Oh God...." Fatima groaned.

"Fatima, you really need to stop freaking out," snapped Ayesha. "You're acting like you're having a boyfriend over..."

"*Astagfirullah*!...God forgive us... What kind of nonsense spills out of your mouth!...*chi*.......boyfriend...You girls don't know when to keep your mouths shut," Fatima's mother cut in. She shook her head in disgust. 'How could the word 'boyfriend' even be uttered,' Mummy thought.

"And the silverware Mummy, is it all out?"

"Yes, Fatima. I took it all out of the hutch and cleaned it well," Mummy reassured her.

Desi cuisine is traditionally eaten with one's hands, as is the case with much of the food enjoyed all over the Muslim world. The Husains had also, like most Muslims and most *Desis*, enjoyed their food in that manner. They hardly used eating utensils. The few pieces of silverware that they did use were mismatched spoons and forks. The nicer coordinating silverware sat on display in the dining hutch, basically collecting dust. Now that someone who actually used silverware was coming to dinner, the cutlery was finally taken out of the china display.

That cutlery was set neatly on the table along with the prettier Corningware that Fatima's mother owned, the *old town blue* pattern, which she had reserved for special occasions. Mrs. Husain had owned another pattern of Corningware, the simpler *spring blossom green*, which was for daily use, but the blue pattern was reserved for special occasions.

For some odd, unexplainable reason, there was a deep fascination and love for Corningware amongst almost all of the *Desi* women that Fatima knew. In fact Fatima could swear that it was the *Desis* that kept the Corning Company in business. The craze amongst these women for this specific type of crockery was simply queer. The Corning outlet stores were scouted and hunted down by all of the NRIs, *non resident Indians*, and were infested with overflowing carts that were pushed by short *saree* clad Indian women. No other dinner service was even considered as a possibile purchase, and even the women back in the motherland had become hooked on this specific brand of dishes. How and why one will never know...

Never before had the table been set so formally. Most dinners at the Husain household were thirty people strong and required a buffet, where plates were simply stacked in a pile. But tonight the table was set *American* style. Fatima had to suddenly dust out her now cob-webbed knowledge, which she had originally deemed useless, from her Home Economics classes. The manner to set a table was forever engrained in her memory after having to take the test on a table's proper setting no less than four times. At last the dining room was prepared to host a dinner suitably enough for an *American* guest.

Just when everything was ready, Fatima looked down.

"Oh My God! Our feet! We can't walk around barefoot!" Fatima worried out loud.

"What? Something else is *wrong* with us?" her father condescendingly asked.

"Fatima, we are not *goras*. Deal with it! We always walk around barefoot in our homes. Heck if we could, we would walk around barefoot outside! That is the way it is, and we will not change every detail of our lives so we look more *refined* in front of your teacher!" shouted an exasperated Ayesha.

"Jeezus christ! I just don't want us to look like *jahils*! (ignorant folk) Is that too much to ask?" Fatima barked.

"You're asking for way more than that! You want us to change who we are!" Ayesha snapped back.

"Screw it! I am sorry that I asked."

"You damn well should be sorry"

"*Bathamees poti*?" (insolent street girl) Fatima grumbled.

"Mummyyyyyy....Fatima called me a *bathamees poti*!" Ayesha shouted running to her mother.

"And Ayesha said damn!" Fatima hollered in an even louder voice and rolled her eyes.

"Okay that is enough!" Mummy angrily stepped in. "All this chaos has to stop." She slammed the dish in her hand down on the stove. It was a miracle that it didn't break in to a million pieces. But then again it was Corningware. Maybe that's why all the *Desi* women loved it so....

"Fatima, you want to show that you are not *jahil*, well then stop using the language of the *jahil*. And stop demanding silly things. If what you say about Mrs. Sheehan is true, then she will appreciate our differences and not look down upon them. We are who we are, so let it be..."

Just then the door bell rang. Mummy turned and looked sharply at the girls.

"Now girls, we *will* maintain the family honor by behaving respectfully. No fighting and no arguing," she ordered in her most stern voice. Family honor. A concept of great importance for Muslims and *Desis* alike. It was everything to a person. Children who fight like cats and dogs would do nothing but bring disgrace to one's household. After all what kind of parents would tolerate such chaos in their home? A family with dignity would never conduct themselves in this manner, especially in public. If they did, they would shame themselves. And that's what it always came down to. Pride, and self respect. Family honor was everything. It would be maintained. At all costs.

Father was already at the door. He opened the door and smiled, "Hello, Mrs. Sheehan. I am Fatima's father. Welcome to our home!"

He swung his arm back and guided her inside; doing his best to forget all that had been carrying on in the house moments ago.

"Hi ya'll!!!!" a clearly excited Mrs. Sheehan said in her native Texan accent. "I am so thrilled to finally meet you all! I have heard so much about you from my friend here," she patted Fatima's shoulder.

"Very nice to meet you," Mummy replied demurely, forever playing the role of the perfect *Desi* homemaker.

After the family introductions played out, the family guided Mrs. Sheehan to the living room. Mrs. Sheehan noticing that no one was wearing shoes, asked, "Should I take off my shoes?"

"No, No Mrs. Sheehan. Please don't worry about that. Come join us," Fatima requested almost embarrassingly. She wanted to get off the topic of shoes ASAP.

"It smells divine in here..." Mrs. Sheehan remarked.

'She means it stinks in here' Fatima thought. 'I knew it would bother her.' Fatima's insecurity was getting the best of her.

"Indian food always has such a wonderful aroma..."she went on.

"Really? You think so?" Father asked, arching his eyebrow at Fatima. Fatima knew that response was meant specifically for her.

"Oh yes. Of course. Every type of cuisine has its own distinctive scent. Believe me I know. I love to dabble with international cooking..."

As the conversation took flight, Fatima's parents immediately took a liking towards this friendly lady. They were pleasantly surprised to find an individual who was so open towards cultural and religious diversity. Not only did she want to learn about the world's people and their traditions, she was also making an effort to understand why people thought as they did so that she could appreciate their diverse point of views. After that one meeting it became obvious why Fatima thought so highly of Mrs. Sheehan.

Dinner went well and everyone seemed to have thoroughly enjoyed themselves much to Fatima's delight. Pleased at the way things had progressed Fatima was very happy with the way that her family had worked to help her entertain her teacher. She understood that they didn't have to do all that they did. Their efforts were exceptional and she needed to be a lot more appreciative than she generally was towards them.

Fatima realized that she was blessed. Blessed with parents who cared deeply for her. Blessed with sisters who kept her grounded. Blessed with teachers and loyal friends who added depth to her life.

Chapter 17

Junior year had flown by. It had been a busy year, one filled with college entrance exams and intense courses that demanded excellent grades, that was if you were going to make something of yourself. Grades and exam scores were something that the youngsters avoided discussing, and wished their parents weren't always first to bring up. Whether it was with pride or inquisitiveness that would help them improve their own children's chances of success, SATs and ACTs were all the rave with the parents.

It didn't matter that many of these same parents had every intention of getting their daughters' married before the age of twenty two; she still would have to be a sparkling academic star. And their sons, well they had no choice but to be a success.

If their children weren't headed for medicine, law, or engineering, they just weren't up to par. Once the IT industry boomed, that too became an acceptable option. And of course there was the MBA, a naturally acquired inclination for many Indians and Pakistanis, one that seemed to transcend national boundaries as a top notch choice. Trade and commerce also seemed to be healthy alternatives for Muslims from all over the globe, especially in this land of milk and honey. Whether it was those who had verses of the Qur'an propped up on the walls of the liquor shops they operated, or English-encumbered immigrants who pumped gas and operated mini-marts, business was definitely an option. This was a nice out, especially for those who didn't fare that well academically, but had street smarts. Their bio-data would still read 'Occupation: businessman.'

For Fatima it was a 'none of the above' situation. Her heart still lay in the social sciences. Politics and religion were her passion, and she was sure that they were her calling. As college applications arrived in the mail, she knew that time was fast approaching to finalize her decision as to where to go. Rutgers University had clearly become her number one choice. But she chose to apply to other schools as backups, and of course there were the two or three schools that she applied to, just to see if she could get in.

"Daddy, I need checks for the application fees..." Fatima casually stated as she straightened out the large manila envelopes.

"How many checks do you need and for how much?" her father replied sipping his tea and without lifting his eyes off his newspaper.

"Well, each school charges a different amount. I think I need six checks in the amounts of 40, 45, 55, 85, 100, and 150."

"What? Are you crazy?" He threw the paper down with one hand and with the other he placed the tea cup on the coffee table before it spilled from his shaky hand.

"No Dad, see here are the fees," Fatima said pointing towards the fee amounts on each application packet.

"Why are you are sending out so many applications when you already know where you want to go?"

"I need some backups Daddy. And I would like to see if I could get into a few other places...you know just to find out if it could have been."

"Backups? Just to see... First of all you don't need backups, but I can still understand the desire to have a couple of those. But 'just to see'? What is that nonsense about? You're going to drive me crazy if you get into one of the big shot schools! You know you will not be allowed to go to that far off, so why are you setting us all up for *fitna*?"

"Daddy, be serious. I know all that. It's for my own ego. That's it. I know I am destined to stay no more than an arm's length from you all..." she rolled her eyes.

"Your ego is healthy enough. I don't think it needs any reinforcement," he replied in frustration. "I think this is more about 'oh Daddy I got into Yale but you wouldn't send me...'" he mimicked his daughter's talking patterns.

"Daddy, please stop. I promise that that won't happen. Could you please just give me the checks...?" Fatima whined.

Fatima's father continued grumbling even as he pulled out his checkbook and reluctantly wrote out six checks.

"I can guarantee that you will bite my head off if one of these hot shot schools accepts you..."

"Daddy you should be thrilled if I got into one of those schools. You could tell all of your friends about it for years to come..." Fatima sarcastically added.

"First of all, I don't brag about my children. Secondly, I don't need Yale University to tell me I have a smart daughter. What I need is a respectful daughter who will not cause problems for her father," he responded in an in-your-face manner.

When all was said and done, Fatima's applications were set to go. She added the signed checks to the envelopes feeling rather pleased with herself.

Senior year was supposed to be awesome, and Fatima had every intention of letting herself enjoy her last year of high school, within the limits of her religions and culture, of course.

This basically meant that Fatima's fun senior year was nothing like that of the average high schooler. Her idea of an enjoyable senior year, was slacking off to the point of earning a 'B' in her classes rather than her usual 'A.' And if things got real crazy on her part, maybe she would even go out to the movies with her friends to a PG-13 flick.

Obviously, this was not the senior year that many of her classmates had in mind. Many were planning keg parties and bar fests, all in addition to slacking off at school. But Fatima had no part of this, in fact she didn't even know what many of these gatherings entailed. After all, her exposure to adulthood was limited to sixth grade health class and a few teeny bopper movies.

Fatima wasn't the only exception to the partying seniors. Fareha and Mary had nothing to do with the party scene as well. These girls would have just as much "fun" as Fatima would in their last year at Pennsbury High School. The parents of these young women did have a tight grip on their lives, but even that could not entirely explain their extreme prudishness. Their conservativeness was no longer a result of the fear of upsetting their parents. The environment they were raised in had completely infiltrated into their personalities such that they themselves had come to feel very strongly against what was morally wrong. Pre marital sex was equated with lewdness and cardinal sin, and for Muslim girls, alcohol was a sure fire way to invoke the anger of their Lord. This was what they believed from the depth of their hearts. It was this devotion to their religion that kept them from losing control of their lives and sight of their goals, both spiritually and intellectually. Few shared their views on life.

"Did you know that Seth was arrested last weekend?" Mary asked Fatima, referring to a classmate.

Fatima's jaw dropped.

"What are you talking about?"

"Well, his parents were away in NYC when he decided to have all of his friends over. They got drunk and went for a drive. I guess they were driving like maniacs and hit another car. One of the passengers in the other car is in the ICU."

"Are you serious?"

"Their blood alcohol level was almost 1.0"

"No way!" Fatima gasped. "Who told you all this?"

"Seth's younger sister…" Mary laughed. "She sits with me on the bus and she can't stand her crazy brother. So she was airing out the family's dirty laundry this morning on our ride to school."

"That is just psycho…"

Seth's arrest became big news at Pennsbury. The entire school soon knew about what took place over the past weekend. An impromptu assembly was conducted regarding drinking and driving. Everyone knew precisely what had brought on the assembly. But the sad thing was that it seemed as if Seth wasn't affected by any of this. He sat in the assembly and laughed all through it. He was impervious. One hundred percent cold.

"Is it me or does it seem like Seth could care less about what happened?" a confused Fatima asked Mary over lunch.

"He's a jerk. Someone is fighting for his life because of his irresponsible behavior, and he is sitting there laughing. What an ass," Mary shook her head in disgust.

Fatima couldn't fathom the reality of that situation. How could one cause such havoc and act like nothing happened? How could anybody be so selfish and so stupid?

Fatima went home and shared the story with her parents.

"I don't know how he could be so cold about all that happened," she told her mother.

"*Beta*, the problem is not just his reaction; it is what caused all of this to occur. It's the drinking. Why was this boy drinking?" Mummy asked.

"I don't know Mummy. I never understood why it's so cool get drunk. Never. And now after this, I can't imagine why anyone else would even think of getting drunk. But I am sure they will…"

It is said that one will not miss what they never had. That was exactly the case with alcohol and Fatima. Never had it, never would. She couldn't imagine why anyone would drink or do drugs, knowing what comes as a result. But that was Fatima, a conservative Muslim teenager, mature well beyond her years.

And according to her family, she was now mature enough to consider marriage. Yep, now the marriage business seemed to have moved front and center in her life.

Proposals poured in. Traditionally, it was always the boy's family that would pursue the girl, so Fatima's parents had nothing to do but consider that bio-datas that were sent to them. But most never made it past this stage.

Occasionally a bio-data proved interesting, at which point, her parents would arrange yet another "walk-by." Having a semi-arranged marriage was hard enough, but this "walk-by" business was getting more and more difficult. The problem wasn't just the bachelors involved; many times it was the people that were involved in the matchmaking. There were pushy aunties who felt that they had found the "perfect" guy for Fatima, and would shove him down her throat even when he was not what Fatima had in mind. In fact it seemed none of the guys that were brought up to her were remotely what she was looking for, much to Dadima's dismay.

"These girls have too much of a say in marriage. In my time we obeyed our parents. They chose who they thought was best and that was it. And look at you," she pointed to Fatima. "Always finding some nitpicky point to reject decent proposals."

"Dadima, there hasn't been a decent proposal yet..."

"What do you mean? There have been one hundred good prospects. YOU are the picky one," she snapped at Fatima.

"What? What do you think I am looking for Dadima? I am not asking for much... "

"God knows what you are looking for," Dadima cut her off shaking her head, ever the drama queen. "You want an educated boy..."

"NO... that's my parents..."

"Okay *they* want an educated boy, but *you* want a tall boy who is good looking..."

"NO... that's what *you* want. My ideas of good looks aren't the same as yours Dadima...." Fatima giggled.

"Oh yes, now it is *our* fault that you don't like any of the guys..."

"Dadima, you guys have high standards too. You all want a guy of such and such profession, with such and such academic degree, and a Hyderabadi background, he must be this and he must be that..."

"No no... don't try to pin this on us. You have your own issues. Too many issues you have...." Dadima shook her hand up and down vigorously as is she was ready to karate chop a block of wood.

"Dadima, all I am looking at is the guy's personality and his perspective on things. Obviously FOBs will have different ideas and thoughts about marriage. So to avoid conflict I want the guy to be raised here, is that too much to ask...?"

"Even from the boys here, you say some are too liberal and some are too conservative..."

"Of course. You can't say yes to any American raised *Desi*. I won't jump on any Tom, Dick, or Harry..."

"That's exactly what we are all afraid of. That you will say yes to some Tom, Dick, or Harry. All the *goras* in this country running after innocent girls...*chi*... they will prey on our girls...."

"Oh God, Dadima. That's so crazy," Fatima replied, aggravated.

"Crazy? *You* are crazy! Seventeen and still sitting on my son's head. There are three more behind you. When will you move on and make way for them?"

Fatima walked out of the room in exasperation, yet again. Dadima didn't seem to realize that Fatima was *only* seventeen. And no matter how many times Fatima tried to talk to Dadima about marriage, they could never see eye to eye. There was no pleasing the elderly woman, unless it was an unconditional 'yes' to one of the many bachelors that she had introduced to the family. That's really all that Dadima wanted. Just a 'yes'.

Chapter 18

Yes!!!!! She'd been accepted at Rutgers University! Fatima jumped for joy reading the acceptance letter.

"Mummy, here it is!" she grinned proudly.

"Mashallah, I am very happy for you *beta*," Mummy stroked Fatima's back.

"You should first thank God for fulfilling your desire. Pray two *rakahs* in gratitude at once," she lovingly advised her daughter.

Fatima's father walked in on the conversation and was glowing when the letter was handed to him by his wife. Fatima's illuminated face said it all. He knew this was exactly what she had wanted.

"I am very happy for you. Everything you worked for will now pay off, *Inshallah*." He patted her head in his reserved fashion of showing affection.

"This is the reason we moved half way across the world. Accomplishments like this make our every sacrifice worthwhile."

"Thanks Daddy," Fatima said still fathoming the acceptance letter.

"But I am sure that you would have made it into any school..." he nudged his daughter proudly.

"Which leads me to ask.....have you heard from the *other* schools?"

"Not yet Daddy," Fatima replied nonchalantly.

"But, it doesn't matter any more. This is where I wanted to go."

She took back the acceptance letter and gazed at in awe. Fatima knew it wasn't a great feat to get into Rutgers, even though it was a decent school. What mesmerized her was the idea of getting into a school that she actually wanted to attend.

Asma had started there last year, and Fatima had recently met some Muslim girls who were also students there. These were no ordinary Muslim girls. These girls seemed to be much more sensible than most others their age. They were greatly inclined towards pursuing the understanding of their faith and learning how to incorporate it into their daily lives, so as to improve its quality. This really impressed Fatima. Meetings these girls was a huge motivation for Fatima to attend Rutgers. She knew that a Muslim population like that of these girls was essential to her happiness at a university. She desperately wanted to keep company with such balanced Muslims. She was tired of being one of only two Muslim girls in her entire school.

Fatima was sick of hearing about her peers, whose highlight of the week was sneaking into their parents' cupboards in order to get drunk. Or if they were really lucky they would have slept with more than one person by the time Monday morning approached. To Fatima this behavior seemed nothing better than animalistic.

The few college students that Fatima had met informed her that college would break all the social tiers that existed in high school. She wouldn't have to deal with people that she disliked. And that was exactly what Fatima sought. She wanted to get away from people who she thought were hell-bent on wasting their lives. She sought the company of people who had more to offer. More depth. More heart. And more of her faith.

Fatima's faith was an important part of her life, and she felt that surrounding herself with practicing Muslims would increase her spirituality. She was at a point in her life where she knew critical decisions would be made. And it was abundantly clear that peers carried an enormous influence upon these decisions.

Fatima was not going to dive into any social circle at college; she was determined to befriend those whom she respected and wished to learn from. She was no longer in search of being cool; she now wanted to be true to herself. Fatima was going to Rutgers seeking a lot more than just a degree. Fatima was searching for intellectual challenges, a new social environment, and a community that elevated her level of faith.

The pinnacle of all of her academic efforts over the past thirteen years had been reached. Her life would now be entering a new chapter, one that held endless possibilities. Fatima's countenance radiated positive energy. What could be better than this?

That weekend Fatima's family made their weekly trip to Somerville. Fatima knew that this visit would prove to be an interesting one, now that news of her acceptance to college would be made public.

"Mamma, your granddaughter will be starting at Rutgers University next year," her father informed Dadima with great pride.

Dadima blankly gazed at Fatima. She turned her head away and flapped her hand down from the armrest upon which she rested her elbow.

"Why? Get her married and into her real home," she matter-of-factly said to her son.

Fatima turned her head away and rolled her eyes. But before she could say a word, her father began, "Mamma, can't you be happy for her? She is not housewife material. She has quite a head on her shoulders, and can do a lot more than bear children and sit at home."

Shocked at the fact that her father actually responded to his mother's curtness, Fatima's eyes nearly popped out of her face. But Dadima reacted in no such way.

"No matter what you make of her, even a doctor, she will have to be a good wife and mother first. That is the destiny of all women..." Dadima calmly continued.

And yet again, the family tuned out Dadima's lecture on a woman's role in life. Fatima no longer cared. She'd lost interest in pursuing the approval of her grandmother. She knew that would only come with marriage. But the rest of the family was excited for her. She was the first member of their family in the United States who would start college. Her *chacha*s were thrilled at the prospect of the next generation of their family moving ahead in this new homeland of theirs.

"*Bhai*, this is great news. This is what we all are working towards. All our efforts and sacrifices are for what? For a day like this when our children come to us with such wonderful news," Saad *chacha* said to Fatima's father.

'Where have I heard that before?' Fatima thought.

Saad *chacha* lovingly patted Fatima's head.

"*Beta*, make us proud. We have a lot of faith in you and expect you to be the example for the rest of the family's children."

Fatima would never forget those words. She was to be the example. This was a responsibility that she took very seriously, since she had repeatedly heard it since the age of four. If she goofed up then who would her sisters and cousins emulate? Who would they learn from? There were no family members before her in America that could guide or offer advice to any of the younger ones on college and anything related to a higher education. All of the elders had been educated in India, and needless to say nothing was the same here.

Back at school, classes went on and Fatima's senior class was coasting along. Academics were there, but with most students already accepted into the college of their choice, the senior class was more occupied with planning the senior prank than maintaining their grades.

Fatima was keeping busy with the World Affairs Club to which she was elected President. She had ambitious goals for the club and was busy organizing events that would foster tolerance and understanding. Still under the guidance of its sponsor, Mrs. Sheehan, the WAC sponsored activities that attracted quite a following and were becoming the talk of Pennsbury High.

One such event was the after school *religious dialogue* series which invited leaders of various religious faiths/organizations to talk to high school students about a subject that few pondered over deeply. This opened up the door of dialogue between students of different faiths.

For the first time, it seemed that many of the Pennsbury High students were learning that Christianity, Judaism, and Islam actually had quite a bit in common. It felt as if these religions were not alien to one another, rather they simply were different branches that grew out of the same tree. Father Williams, Rabbi Steinberg, and Imam Bashir were leaders whom the students and teachers alike found to be very friendly and approachable. Each made their religion clearer to the audience and succeeded in fostering a sense of harmony amongst the three monotheistic doctrines.

Through these dialogues, a doctrine as alien as Islam had been, was suddenly a simple variation of a dogma that most students had felt was their own.

"Fatima, I never realized that we could all sit together and talk about our faiths without ripping each others heads off," joked Natalie, a Jewish classmate of Fatima's.

"Well, that's exactly what the WAC is trying to get across. We *can* sit together respectfully, and appreciate all that we have to offer one another," Fatima relayed. She was happy, almost proud, with the results of the series. And judging from the reactions of most of the students and teachers, so was everybody else.

"Miss Husain, a job well done," complemented Mr. Phillips, a sweet older man who taught American Government. Mr. Phillips was a devout Baptist, and for him to come and appreciate what this series had to offer was a measure of success for Fatima.

"Thanks for coming Mr. Phillips. It's great that you took time out of your day to share this event with us," Fatima politely replied.

"I had to. Mrs. Sheehan here would have had my head if I hadn't," he laughed as he jabbed Mrs. Sheehan's arm. She winked back at him.

"But seriously, this was a breath of fresh air for all of us. We need more activities that open our eyes to the rest of the world. This series has helped to begin spinning those wheels of change..."

With activities as successful as this series, the WAC quickly became the most active club in the school. Fatima became engrossed in organizing its events and planning activities that offered depth and insight. *Eid Ul Adha*, the Muslim holiday that coincides with the *Hajj* and marks the sacrifice Abraham was willing to make of his son, was rapidly approaching, and Fatima wanted to commemorate this Muslim holiday at Pennsbury in the same fashion that the WAC had marked the Christmas and Hanukkah holidays.

These after school events had been very successful in attracting many students and proved to be an arena for teaching the students the historical significance of the holiday that was being celebrated.

Fatima had an elaborate presentation prepared discussing the *Hajj* and the great sacrifice that Abraham was willing to make for God. She was excited at the prospect of relating this information to her peers in the hopes that this type of exposure to Islam and Muslims would allow them to see that Muslims were very normal, just like most everyone else on the planet.

The presentation was set to take place two days after the actual holiday, as the day of Eid fell on a weekend. That was perfect. It would allow Fatima ample time to enjoy *Eid ul Adha* with her family and friends; a holiday they'd celebrated together for as long as she could remember, and then explain its importance to her peers.

The day of *Eid* would always begin with an early morning prayer service. The entire Muslim community would come for the massive congregational prayer at which they would pray then listen to a brief sermon and pray the *salaat, or* prayer, which was designated for the day of celebration.

Fatima's family walked into the grand hall, decked out in the new outfits, which were bought specifically for this happy occasion. All of their friends' families had seemed to arrive, and they said some of their prayers before the service began. Oddly, a very close family of friends, the Faheems, was missing. It was strange that no one from that family had shown up, but considering that they were hosting the *Eid* dinner tonight for all of Fatima's family's friends, their absence was easily dismissed. Most figured that they were held up in preparations for that evening.

After the conclusion of the prayers, everyone stood up and greeted each other warmly with smiling faces and hearty hugs. It was a day of celebration and everyone seemed to be in the mood to do just that. Many left in a rush to offer their *qurbani*, to imitate the sacrifice of Abraham and his son, Ismaeel, while others relaxed as they had sent money abroad to carry out the sacrifice in a land where it may have been needed more desperately.

The Husains had their *qurbani* carried out in Hyderabad, so they were free from the obligation of the sacrifice right after the prayer. Instead, they headed off to Somerville, where they would have lunch with Fatima's father's family. Dinner was to be held at the Faheems, whose unexplained absence began to weigh upon the minds of Fatima's parents.

"They must be overwhelmed with all of tonight's preparations," Fatima's mother said to her husband.

"That can explain why the women didn't come, but what about the men? They should have been there," her father said in a concerned manner.

"True, but they also live at least an hour away. Maybe they are simply running late," Mummy said optimistically.

"I hope so......" Father replied, still disturbed.

They arrived in Somerville around noon and expected the traditional *Eid* hugs and kisses with their family. Lunch was served, and all of the cousins were standing by the meat-crammed table with mouths watering.

"Thank God we aren't vegetarians," Ayesha laughed.

"Yeah man, it's good to be a meat eater. We must be earning some major reward for eating all this meat..." Sana teased.

"For sure we are. I am sure that some of this meat has to be part of somebody's sacrifice..." Fatima added.

The cousins would all congregate and celebrate the day without any great hoopla. Ayesha was the joker who kept everyone laughing, Amina - now mature well beyond her years- was the wise soul of the group, and Malaika was still a youngling, busy in her world of dance and play. For the girls, it was simple - just family assembled together laughing and talking. At least that's how it was amongst the younger generation. The older folk would always engage in some political dialogue and wind up having some argument or another about some trivial subject. But for the girls it was a time to simply relax and enjoy the company of their cousins.

As lunch wrapped up, Fatima's parents received a phone call from Rizwan Uncle. 'Odd,' Fatima thought. 'Why would he call here?' Fatima's parents' friends never called her *chachas* in Somerville, what would make them call here now? Was it to wish everyone a happy Eid or was it something else? Fatima carefully watched her father as he talked on the phone.

His face was turning pale. His voice was trembling and he spoke very slowly. He grabbed a pen that was sitting by the phone and jotted down a number. That was it. He slowly put the phone down. After that, he was visibly shaken.

"What's the matter?" Fatima's mother asked.

"There's been an accident. We need to leave."

"What? Who was in the accident? How are they?" Mummy asked anxiously.

Struggling to compose his thoughts, her father took a few seconds to speak.

"It was the Faheems. They got into a car accident on the way to *Eid* prayers. They are at Dullestown Hospital..."

"Is everyone okay?" Mummy abruptly asked in a raised voice.

"We don't know…." father responded with his voice trailing off.

"What?" Mummy asked alarmingly. "How can we not know? Either they are okay or not? Let me call the hospital," she hastily took the phone and dialed the number her husband had scribbled down.

"Yes, this is a close family friend of the Faheems. We are trying to find out about our friends' condition…" she inquired. "Yes, I can wait."

As she was put on hold, Mummy became fidgety. Her legs were shaking, as were her hands. Father placed his head in the palms of his hands and everyone else looked on silently.

"What? Why can't you tell us over the phone?" Mummy started asking. She grew impatient with the nurse and began to raise her voice.

"Look , these are very good friends of ours, and we are worried about them. Please, tell us. What's going on?"

There was obviously no clear response from the nurse. Mummy angrily slammed the phone down.

"Something is very wrong," Father said to everyone in the room.

He then picked up the phone and called one of the older Faheem brothers. The calls were to no avail. Cell phones weren't around in those days, and it was impossible to get a hold of someone in this type of situation unless they contacted you.

Father stood up.

"Let's go."

He ordered his family into the car.

"We are going to Dullestown," he told his brothers and mother.

As Fatima and her sisters put on their shoes, the phone rang again. Once again it was Rizwan Uncle. Their father raced towards the phone.

"Yes I am here. How is everyone?" as he asked that question everyone's eyes were glued to his face.

He shut his eyes in anguish and softly spoke, "*Inna lillahi wa inaa ilayhi rajiyoon*" (the traditional Muslim prayer that is recited upon hearing of a death.) Everyone gasped. Fatima and Ayesha grabbed each other's hands, and their mother's face turned white. There was pin drop silence.

Father hung up the phone, and turned towards his wife. "There were some casualties…"

All of the women's hands covered their open mouths. The men grabbed a seat.

"What??? Some?? Who?? What??? How??" Mummy frantically questioned. Father placed his hands on her shoulders and calmed her.

"The Faheems were driving to the prayer with Ali Bhai's family. Both families were in their large van. Somehow the van spun out of control, went off the road, and slammed into a tree...."

He took a deep breath.

"Four have died," Father turned his face away.

"WHAT????"

Chaos ensued. Everyone was shocked and began to ask a thousand and one questions. The flurry of voices seemed deafening. But Fatima and her sisters sat in silence, in awe of what was being revealed to them.

Their father regained his composure. He asked everyone to calm down. He finally built up the courage to look at his wife. He turned to her and spoke in to her eyes, "Your friend, Sameena....."

Mummy began to quiver. "No, no... Don't say it..."

She shook her head violently and moaned in anguish.

"And her sister in law......."

"*Subhanallah!*" all the women simultaneously cried in disbelief.

"But that's not it....."

Father solemnly turned towards his daughters. He grabbed their hands. Fatima' heart began to beat thunderously. Faster and faster her heartbeat raced.

"*Beta*, your friends, Farhana and Mina have also ..." he briefly stumbled, "...passed away," completing his heartfelt statement.

And then everything went silent. It was as if sound was lost altogether. Fatima could hear no more. Her eyes gazed blankly as if she were frozen in time.

There was no fathoming such a loss. There was simply shock and disbelief. And for Fatima there was utter confusion.

In a state of numbness, the Husain family left their family Eid gathering. They stepped into the family car and drove for what seemed like an eternity to Dullesstown Hospital. No sense could be made of what was just told to them. Mummy couldn't stop sobbing, Father had a vacant look on his pale face, and the girls were all mutes staring vacantly out the back windows, almost as if they were searching for their friends in the sky above.

Upon arriving at the hospital, the family saw a mob of familiar faces weeping in the main lobby. Fatima's family joined the mourners, and were finally told the extent of the loss that the community had just suffered. Not only had four died, those that survived, were severely injured.

The children of the Faheem family were all under the age of twelve, and were suffering from cuts and bruises. They had not been told yet that their mother had died nor did they know that their father was in critical condition. The Khan family had lost everyone except Khan Uncle. In one horrible twist of fate that poor man lost his wife and two daughters. All this suffering on what was supposed to be one of the happiest days of the year.

The waiting area was flooded with family and friends who were in total shock and disbelief. There were moments when the crying of the women was uncontrollable, but for the most part it was a muffled whimpering that permeated through the lobby. The children were shaken up, Fatima's younger sisters included.

"Fatima *baji*, does this mean that we will never see Asiya Aunty again?" a confused Amina asked her older sister.

"Yes, Amina. That's what this means…"

"But what about Faseeh and Amaar? Won't they see their mommy again?" Amina asked timidly.

Fatima couldn't respond. Instead she began to cry.

"Fatima *baji*? What's wrong??" A nervous Amina shook Fatima's shoulders.

But Fatima couldn't stop. She tried to control her tears, but it was futile. Her emotions had overcome her.

How could such a horrible thing happen? How could so many people die so suddenly? That too from one family? Two aunties and two girls lost in one accident. And girls that were her age? How will the children that she had grown up with survive now that their mother was dead? What was going to happen to this family? Questions raced through Fatima's head and she began to feel nauseous. She quietly stood up, wiped away her tears and made it to the ladies room.

That night Fatima's mother stayed with the extended Faheem family, while her father drove the girls home. It was an eerie ride. All of a sudden, driving was a frightening experience. Fatima couldn't get the thought of losing control of one's car out of her mind. Every push on the brakes made her heart race and head spin. She constantly thought of Farhana, someone *her* age, who was no longer on this Earth. And Asiya Aunty, one of her favorite aunts, who was no different than family. She was one of her mother's best friends and a staple at every gathering of friends for as long as Fatima could remember. From the time they met nearly thirteen years before in Willingboro, Fatima enjoyed her fun loving nature. Both of these people, lost forever while simply driving in a car.

In bed, Fatima couldn't sleep. She tossed and turned, crinkling the sheets so tight that they no longer felt soft against her body. Images of Farhana's and Asiya Aunty's faces kept flashing before her eyes. Faces that she would see no more. She turned towards her nightstand. One o'clock read. It was the dead of the night and sleep was nowhere to be found. Fatima finally got out of bed and went downstairs. 'Maybe a little TV would get my mind off all this,' she thought to herself. As she made her way downstairs she peeked into her sisters' rooms. Ayesha was twisting and turning in the same way Fatima had just been doing, and Amina was not in her bed. She then peeked in her parents' room. There were Amina and Malikah sleeping with their father. 'They must have been too shaken up to sleep on their own,' Fatima thought, walking into Ayesha's bedroom.

"Ayesha, you up?" she whispered.

Ayesha's covers flew up in the air and she sat straight up.

"What? What happened?" she asked, obviously alarmed.

"Nothing. I just saw you rolling around in bed so I figured you couldn't sleep either."

Ayesha relaxed a little. Her hands flew up in the air. "I can't believe all this. I just can't believe it," Ayesha shook her head.

"How will those guys manage without Asiya Aunty?" she rhetorically asked.

"God knows. I am so nervous to see them. How will they react once they find out what happened to their mother?"

"And poor Khan Uncle," Ayesha added. "Losing his whole family in a minute.....Unbelievable....."

The girls, as tired as they were couldn't get their mind off all that had occurred over the last twenty four hours.

"Ayesha, let's sleep in Mummy and Dad's room. Amina and Malikah are already there. I think I would feel a lot better if we were all together. And maybe we can actually fall asleep in there."

Without wasting a moment, Ayesha grabbed her pillow and blanket.

"Let's go," she said.

Both girls placed a comforter and pillows on the floor, next to their parents' bed and lay down. With their blankets pulled over them and their family close by, somehow they managed to settle down a bit. In the midst of the comfort of loved ones, they slowly fell asleep.

The following day was just as morbid as the previous one. It was the day of the funerals of the four women who died. All of them. All at once. In accordance with Islamic tradition, the funerals were to be held as early as possible following the traditional bathing or *ghusl*, which is given to the deceased. But in this case there would be no *ghusl*. Everyone was informed that the bodies had been too mangled to tolerate a washing.

The Faheem children had finally been told of the loss of their mother. As scared and unsure as they appeared to be about the degree of their loss, they still insisted upon attending the funeral services. And so they came to the Masjid. As did hundreds of others. Never before had Fatima witnessed so many people packed in the large hall. They all stood and waited.

Four simple wooden caskets were carried into the Masjid. They were all laid in one straight line in the front of the mass of people. Closed. They were not to be opened. It was a striking scene.

The sight of those four caskets was daunting. Four people who everyone present knew, so lively and so vibrant, all laying lifeless inside those wooden boxes.

The Imam walked to the front of the hall and began the prayers. Everyone stood behind him in straight lines, shoulder to shoulder. The *janazah*, funeral prayer, was completed in less than five minutes. Brief. To the point. Muslim funerals are almost always conducted in this fashion. There are no drawn out eulogies or dramatic functions celebrating the life of the deceased. According to Muslim theology, the dead should be buried as soon as possible so that they can begin the life of the *Akhirah*. So that was it. Five minutes of prayer. A chilling five minutes. And then the caskets were prepared to be carried out of the main hall.

Traditionally family members vie for the honor to carry out their loved ones, and such was the case this time as well. However, the departure of the caskets at this funeral was particularly disturbing. Asiya Aunty's boys, Faseeh and Amaar, wished to carry out the casket of their mother. Yet, they were so badly injured that they could not do it alone. At that moment, Fatima witnessed a sight which she would never forget. A sight which no one who was there that day could possibly forget. The two boys, bruised and bandaged, were carried in the arms of their uncles. With their battered arms they symbolically hoisted their mother's casket and they carried her out to her final resting place.

Although four caskets left the Masjid, this was the one casket that Fatima couldn't take her eyes off of. Faseeh and Amaar, boys that she spent her childhood with, were sending off their mother. Despite their broken bones they honored her, and did their last service for her. It was a truly haunting scene.

The wailing women were unable to control their grief. Four of their own were gone. Never to be seen again. Even amongst the generally stoic men, tears ran freely. Fatima couldn't spot a dry eye in that entire hall. 'How odd,' Fatima thought. All that was important to them twenty four hours ago seemed so trivial at that moment. Nothing mattered but the ones you held dear. And the fear of death began to set in.

Fatima suddenly realized that death knew no age. It could come anytime, anywhere. She wasn't immortal nor was anyone she knew.

Despite all the teachings of her faith about death and the Afterlife, the whole concept never seemed so real than it was at that moment.

Fatima stood crying and holding on to her sisters' hands. She was filled with fear. Fear for what would happen to the families of those who had died. Fear of what would happen to the deceased after they were buried. And mostly fear of what would happen to her if death were to creep upon her as suddenly as it did upon these four.

Chapter 19

Sleep was hard to come by for days after the funeral. Fatima developed a fear of darkness and started to use a night light. Death became a word of greater importance. It became a reason to reflect upon one's purpose on this planet. Any mention of it stirred great anxiety within Fatima. Even jokes about it seemed distasteful and disrespectful as did anything that treated it lightly. She couldn't even flip through the paper, fearing that she would pass the obituaries section – a sight that would freak her out. Unnerved and on edge Fatima began to develop a much more spiritual side even as she became increasingly aloof.

Thoughts of death would cross her mind several times a day, and she began to distance herself from everything that seemed futile. Even school became a functional experience, one that would simply pass her time. Her thoughts were constantly on how to become a better Muslim, so that when death arrived, and it obviously could arrive at any moment as it did upon Farhana and Mina, she would be better prepared to meet her Creator.

For Muslims, she knew, this life is meant to be a test. A test of one's faith, love, and devotion to their Lord. God will test you as He pleases; it is how you react to these tests that will determine your status in the eternal life, the *Akhirah*, which commences after one's death. The consequences faced by those who are both doers of good and those who have sinned are outlined clearly in the Qur'an, she'd heard this regularly, over the years. And it was these consequences that instilled a fear like no other in Fatima's heart. Thoughts of the punishments outlined in the Qur'an haunted her day and night. She could not fathom suffering such punishments. Simply thinking about them robbed her of sleep.

It was this fear that drove her to elevate her level of practice and spirituality. She began to read more Qur'an and avoided what could lead her down the path of that which would displease God. She chose to shun listening to music and instead read more about her faith. She made it a point to not miss any of her five prayers, and she tried her best to avoid the company of those who did not take religion seriously.

The strange thing was that this did not mean that she simply desired to hang out with practicing Muslims. She actually enjoyed the company of devout Christians and Jews. They too enriched her life. They added depth and appreciation for what was generally taken for granted.

Anyone that had a higher level of faith in their life was not wasting their time on revelry or futile nonsense. They had an appreciation for what was blessed upon them. Their families, their health, their spirituality. All of this understanding and knowledge attained at such a young age. And Fatima was amazed by all of it.

Fatima began to take simple things much more seriously. Her parents for example. She could not appreciate enough what her mother and father did for her.

"I can't stop thinking about how life is for Asiya Aunty's kids now that she isn't around," she confided to her sisters.

"What would we do if Mummy wasn't here. How would life go on...?"

"And Daddy, God forbid if something happened to him what would we do?" Ayesha thought aloud.

"We can't thank God enough for all of His mercies. We need to stop and reflect on them more than what we do."

"So true...," added Ayesha. She too was distraught over the loss. As was Amina. Although they were all young, the girls knew what happened, and were trying to understand the scale of such a loss. It seemed that the whole family had a new found need and appreciation for their faith.

Religion was never on the sidelines for the Husain family. But after this tragedy it was more than just front and center. It was everything. Even Fatima's parents were terribly distressed. Not a day would go by without the mention of the death and how better to prepare for the arrival of their own.

"We all need to be aware that death is the only thing that we can guarantee will come to us. And we need to be prepared for it," their father told them.

"And if we are practicing Muslims, then we will not fear it. Better things await those who have pleased their Lord in this world."

"How do we know that we will be among those who enjoy *Jannah*, paradise?" Amina asked her father as she climbed into his lap.

"We don't know *beta*. It is our job to try to do our best so that we will *inshallah*, be of those who are admitted into *Jannah*."

"We have to help each other get to that point. We need to make sure that none of us miss our prayers. We need to work on doing more charitable deeds. There are a thousand things that we can do to improve our faith," Mummy added.

As a family they had all committed to becoming more devout in their faith and working towards higher spiritual goals. And Fatima had to return to school ready to share with the WAC what she knew about Eid Ul Adha. But in light of all that transpired, could she bring herself to do it?

"I don't think I can take this on right now Mrs. Sheehan," Fatima whimpered. Her very soul had been shaken and to discuss this holiday in light of such a tragedy was overwhelming.

"Honey, you don't need to dwell on this any further. You can do it later, or whenever you feel ready," Mrs. Sheehan comforted Fatima.

"I don't know what to make of this," Fatima shared with her teacher. "This loss is one for our whole community. This holiday will never be the same again for any of us. How can we celebrate the sacrifice of Abraham and the Hajj, when all that we can recall is the loss of our friends?"

"My dear, it's only natural that you feel this way. This is a real loss for every one of you. Something that you may never get over. But you will learn from this. You will grow from it. You will become a stronger person because of it," Mrs. Sheehan wrapped her arm around Fatima's drooped head. "You will realize that it's events like these that bring all of us closer to God."

Mrs. Sheehan was undeniably right. Fatima's relationship with God was rekindling as a result of this reminder of the temporal nature of this world. Not a day would go by when Fatima wouldn't think of the Almighty and the purpose of her life...

With her spirituality on the rise, Fatima took great comfort in the fact that she was headed off to college and out of Pennsbury. High school had been quite an experience, much like that of most American teenagers. But for Fatima it was one that clearly identified her as on a path that was quite different than many of her peers.

On this journey she had met some incredible people, like Mary, Tara, Vanessa, and Mrs. Sheehan. These were the people who created the fondest memories of her teenage years, and they were the ones that she would keep in touch with throughout her life. These were the faces of her adolescence. But now it had come time to move forward. Beyond Pennsbury and into a new frontier one could say.

On the day of her high school graduation Fatima performed an extra set of prayers before leaving for Commencement. She knelt on the ground. With her head down and her hands held up in supplication, she called upon her Lord.

"God, thank you for all that you have blessed me with. Thank you for allowing me to graduate with the grades that I have, and for making my family proud in the process. Thank you for helping me throughout these years. There were so many difficult times where I questioned so much about myself. But your guidance was always there. It kept me from falling in to the pitfalls that I watched so many of my peers fall into. I thank you for that dearly. I thank you for keeping my faith alive and constantly enriching it. I ask that you continue to guide me and my family upon the path of the righteous. I ask that you keep the love of our faith in our heart always and allow us to practice it in its purest form. Please help me on the path that I have chosen for myself as I am just beginning the long journey of adulthood. I am lost without you and seek your guidance and mercy at all times. Ameen."

Fatima stood up quietly and placed on her white cap and gown. She walked down to her family, who looked upon her with great happiness and pride. They all thanked their Lord for this day, and continued to ask for His direction and compassion in their lives.

As Fatima stepped outside, she noticed an unfamiliar car standing in the driveway. She turned to her mother, "Mummy, whose car is this?"

Her mother turned to her father.

"This is your graduation gift," he said as he handed her the keys to the Grand Am.

Fatima's jaw dropped.

"Are you serious?!?" she shouted excitedly.

"Yes we are. You are going to need a car when you go to college, especially since you will not be living on campus. So we thought we would get you this as a surprise…"

"It's unreal!!!!!" Fatima cried out. She threw her arms around her parents and jumped with joy. It may not have been a brand new car, but it was a very well kept Pontiac. It looked sharp and it drove well. What more could have Fatima asked for?

Chapter 20

Rutgers University's main campus was a fifty minute drive from Fatima's home. In the interest of avoiding a long commute, Fatima and her parents decided that it would be best for her to move in with Dadima and Nabeel *chacha*'s family, who lived fifteen minutes from New Brunswick. This way their daughter would not have to dorm on campus, and she would still be in the care of family.

Fatima happily agreed. She had known dorming was not an option her family would be comfortable with, and now that she had her own car it didn't really matter. Her independence was pretty much guaranteed.

Not everyone understood her excitement. Tara was surprised that Fatima was content with living at her uncle's rather than at school.

"I can't imagine giving up the chance to have your own place at school..." Tara said to Fatima over lunch.

"It's not a big deal Tara. I knew from the beginning that living at school wasn't an option. In fact that's what I had based my entire application process on – where I would be able to live. So I don't care much. It's that whole idea of 'you don't miss what you have never had'..."

"Still Fatima, you are really going to miss out on the college experience if you don't live at school," Tara added rather remorsefully." I beg to differ," Fatima said defensively. Then softening she added, "I wasn't going to do half the stuff that the students do outside of class anyway. And I don't need to hide anything from my parents. In fact I should be more concerned with fearing the consequences of God rather than those of my parents. So what's the big deal?"

"Fatima, I guess in *your* case it really isn't a big deal. But for most people it is rather strange, don't you think?"

"For most I guess it is. But I am not like *most* people. I have *never* been like most people. So it won't be that bad, believe me – I am looking forward to the whole experience."

"I guess so. After all, there were times I thought that you would not make it to college..." Tara chuckled.

"Huh?" Fatima wrinkled her brow.

"I mean... I thought... you might have gotten married off by now," she continued to giggle.

Fatima responded with a smile.

"Believe me, had my grandmother got her way that is exactly what would have happened."

Fatima was truly looking forward to the whole experience of college. Even living with her *chacha*'s family didn't seem to be so bad. She had always gotten along well with her *chacha* and *chachi*. As for Dadima, regardless of all her quirks, she was still Fatima's grandmother. And Dadima had always made it clear that Fatima was her favorite granddaughter.

Fatima moved into her *chacha*'s place a day before classes began. She spent the eve of her first day of college organizing books she had bought from the University bookstore on George Street earlier that day. She had taken five classes, so there had been a good amount of material to purchase. Her textbooks and notebooks were now neatly arranged, and all the materials that she would need for tomorrow's classes were put in her backpack

With all her preparations taken care of, Fatima had some time to relax before she hit the sack. She went into the kitchen and made some hot chocolate. As she was walking into what was now her room, blowing on the warm mug in her hands, she noticed that the light in Dadima's room was on. She peeked inside, and saw her grandmother sitting all alone, reading a magazine.

Dadima was beginning to look frail. She was no longer the vibrant and robust figure that dominated everyone's lives. Her age was slowly catching up with her. Mentally she was still sharp as a tack, but physically she was beginning to wear down. And at that particular instance she looked rather sad. A red haired old woman sitting alone in the dark, by her lamp, passing her time by reading silly Urdu magazines. Feeling sorry for her, Fatima decided to join Dadima. She knocked on the half open door and let herself in. Before Fatima could open her mouth Dadima put her magazine down and began, "*Beta*, college is going to be filled with temptations," she said in a sympathetic tone.

"It will not be easy to resist some of the stuff that happens out there."

"Don't worry Dadima. I know what goes on at college. I know how to handle it." Fatima sipped from her mug.

"That's what all young girls think," Dadima retorted.

"That's before they get caught in the tangled web of boys. So I want to tell you something up front. If you like any Muslim boy that you meet at college just let me know. Give me the sign, and I will take care of all of the details."

Fatima laughed. In her own strange way Dadima was looking out for her. She wanted to protect Fatima from heartbreak, and at the same time get her hitched. Two birds with one stone.

There was no point in saying anything to her. And besides, Fatima knew that the older woman's intentions were good.

"Okay Dadima, if I see anyone of interest, I will let you know..." she played along.

"Good. I am glad you agree. Now get to sleep, you want to be fresh on your first day..."

The next morning was bright and sunny. The weather was warm and so was the feeling Fatima had inside her. She was anxious to get to New Brunswick and start her classes.

Freshman orientation had prepared her well, showing her the location of her classrooms, student centers, computer labs, and the library. She knew exactly where to go for her first class – Calculus, a required course, all thanks to the thorough introduction.

She jumped into her Grand Am and drove down Highway 287. She thought excitedly about all that was waiting for her at this new school. She wasn't nervous like most freshmen are. In fact she was the complete opposite. She was confident that she was going to a better place than where she had been before, and that only good was awaiting her on the other side of River Road.

She was anxious to meet her new classmates, especially the Muslim ones. Although she knew that she could not live an isolated life solely within the walls of a Muslim community, she knew that this group of people would most likely be her comfort base. And friends outside of her religious community would surely come. After all she wasn't just a Muslim. She was also an American.

Fatima arrived on College Avenue vibrant and ready to celebrate each moment. She walked through the campus with a smile on her face with the sun shining down upon her, looking at everything through rose colored glasses. All that surrounded her seemed beautiful and positive.

The Georgian buildings appeared oh-so-academic. The students appeared to be so-very-collegiate. Even the infamous grease trucks were a novelty in her eyes. She felt kind of like Mary Tyler Moore in the intro of her show. All that was left to do was for her to throw her *hijaab* up in the air while a background singer sang "You're going to make it after all."

There was a new found independence to be enjoyed, and Fatima reveled in it. She was finally going to be able to conduct her studies at Rutgers without having to deal with the peer pressures that she encountered at Pennsbury. For Fatima this was an independence of spirit. And it was surreal.

She had seen people on this campus that looked and acted a lot like her, as an American Muslim that is. This in itself was an invaluable novelty. And the greater beauty of their presence was that they naturally flocked towards each other. It wasn't as if they sought out each other, it was more a case of their identity being the tie that binds.

Hijaab made it very easy to identify who the other Muslim women were. Of course there were many Muslims students who did not wear the *hijaab*, but they would be recognized as Muslim either by their names (Muslims generally have Arabic names regardless of their cultural background) or by their greeting the *muhajjaba* with the Islamic greetings. But there was something unique about that *muhajjaba* bond.

As for the practicing Muslim male students, the gender separation was well defined. Fatima knew that it would be improper to approach them in search of friendship; unacceptable to them, to herself, but most importantly in the eyes of her Creator. They were her brothers in the faith, even pleasant acquaintances, but they were never to become intimate friends. If there was a desire to further an interest in a member of the opposite sex, there were clearly defined avenues that would be taken. All en route to the only relationship, according to her, that was allowed to flourish between a man and woman outside of blood ties, the sacred bond of marriage.

This was an understanding that existed between faithful Muslim men and women, and those who adhered to their religious laws respected it.

Fatima thrived on meeting new Muslim women at Rutgers. Muslim women from all parts of the world. They were from India, Pakistan, Syria, Egypt, Palestine, Saudi Arabia, Jordan, Malaysia, and even good old fashioned Americans. Some were *muhajjabas* that wore simply a *jilbab* and *hijaab*, others dressed in regular American attire along with a *hijaab*. There were even those who did not cover at all. Just the fact that they had a common theology was reason enough to foster some sort of relationship. Even those whom Fatima did not know personally would flash a smile and make friendly eye contact. It was an affinity that developed effortlessly amongst them.

One didn't have to know the other Muslim(s) well. As long as they shared the fact that they were both practicing Muslims, they already had a ton in common.

Their experiences growing up in America would have many similarities, as would their rituals of practice. But above all else was the common fact they were not only Muslim, but they were all residing and learning in America. America was home.

But this commonality was only the basis for an initial understanding amongst the Muslim students. There was much more they all had in common. Being stressed about rigorous schedules and difficult subjects was a shared bond amongst all students and adjusting to college life was always a balancing act, socially and academically.

No matter how difficult Calculus was for Fatima in high school, at college it wasn't so bad. The comedic professor captivated his students and made the realm of Calculus -gulp– interesting. Fatima's good fortune did not end there. She was also amongst the lucky few that had a TA that was not only a Princeton grad, but also a real live local American math whiz, unlike most of her classmates who were struggling to decipher the thick accent coated English spoken by her TA's Asian counterparts.

In this class, Fatima established a rapport with a student named Angie, who turned out to despise Calculus as much as Fatima had.

"You know I wanted to shoot someone when I found out that we had to take Calc in our first semester," Angie frustratingly said as she flicked her manicured nails.

"Don't worry it's part of that whole freshman ritual," Fatima comforted her.

"At least we are all in the same boat…drowning together…" Fatima laughed.

"Misery loves company…" Angie quipped.

Gregarious Angie went on and on about everything under the sun. From the small size of her military-barracks-cum–dorm, to the horrible food that the campus cafeteria was trying to pass off as Italian.

"My grandmother would turn over in her grave if she had that pasta the cafeteria here called manicotti," Angie complained.

Angie also made it clear that she was having difficulty dealing with her roommate.

"I can't tell you how annoyed I am with this idiot," she said of her roommate.

"I have had enough of her and it has only been seventy two hours since I moved in..."

"Can't you switch rooms?" Fatima inquired.

"Not yet. It's too early. And since we're freshman there isn't much choice as where to go. I wish I would have just commuted." She chewed loudly on her gum.

"Where does your family live?" Fatima asked.

"Down the shore."

"You can't be serious; you could never have commuted from down the shore. You made the right decision," Fatima reassured her.

"Well, where do you live?"

"Actually my family lives in Pennsylvania, but I am living with my uncle and grandmother in Somerville while I am in school. I go home on the weekends."

"Sweet..." Angie hissed.

"Sweet?" a confused Fatima asked.

"Damn sweet. Get to live it up at Grandma's and go home to Mummy's cooking on the weekend, that's the life..."

"You don't know my Grandma..." Fatima laughed. "Actually she's not that bad, I shouldn't complain. It is a pretty nice set up, isn't it?"

"I'd say," Angie agreed. "I'll give you my number, you know in case we need to get notes from each other or something like that... But don't pass it around."

"Sure," Fatima took the post it from Angie's hand. "See you next Monday."

"Yeah see ya," Angie said as she walked off.

Fatima looked down at the yellow piece of paper. It read 'Angie Gotti 732 555 6549.' Fatima knit her brows. That name sounded familiar, but she just couldn't place it. She folded the post it, and slipped it into her Calculus folder for future use.

The second class of the day was Arabic. Fatima was really looking forward to this course. This was going to be the course where she would learn how to speak the language of the divine scripture. As if that wasn't reason enough for Fatima to take the course, this class had an additional fringe benefit. Many Muslim freshmen signed up for this course for the same reason that Fatima did. So it proved to be a haven for students who were just as eager as Fatima was to learn the language, and to meet fellow Muslims.

On her first day there, Fatima met three Muslim girls.

"*Assalamu Alaykum,*" was the greeting exchanged amongst the four girls who sat together in the back row of seats. They began chatting away about where each of them was from and what they expected from this course. To any bystander it would appear that the four had known each other for ages, but the reality was far from that. They'd simply aligned themselves with those who at the outset had one obvious shared trait – their faith. Like birds of feather they flocked together.

After the class ended Fatima left with the phone numbers of each of those girls as well. Feeling a strong sense of comfort, unlike any she had known before, Fatima was assured that her decision to attend Rutgers was the right one.

Later that week, Fatima made her daily call to her parents, and couldn't stop raving about her first week on campus.

"Mummy, the classes were actually interesting. I am really looking forward to going to the next class..."

"Good to hear...I hope you are eating properly?" Mummy asked. She worried about how and what her daughter ate now that she was not there to cook for her.

"Yeah Mummy, I ate well," Fatima answered quickly, and reverted back to the subject at hand.

"And you know Mummy, I met these girls in my Arabic class. They told me about the Islamic Society here and how it meets every Thursday night. They sponsor a lot of dinners and seminars that are supposed to be really good..."

"At night?" Mummy interjected.

"Yeah at night?"

"So you are going to be driving alone at night from school to Dadima's?"

"Yes..." Fatima mumbled. She knew that tone of her mother's voice was disapproving.

"I don't know *beta*. Is it a good idea for a young girl to be out alone at that hour, even if it is for an Islamic Society meeting?"

"Don't worry Mummy. It'll be fine. I am alone all day so what's a few hours at night?"

"*Beta*, the daytime is different. You being out alone at night worries me," her mother stated.

"Mummy, this is life at college. I am lucky that this semester I don't have classes in the evening. But there will come a time when I will have to take at least one class at night. What's going to happen then?"

"Fatima, I wish I could let you know how much we worry about you girls."

"I know Mummy, but you have to relax a little. How long can you keep us so tightly sheltered?"

"The sheltering has protected you from all the nonsense that goes on, hasn't it?" asked an obviously annoyed Mummy.

"Yes, Mummy, I see that. But you know that we can't go on like that forever. You have done your job, so just sit back and worry about the other three now."

"A mother can never stop worrying about her children. You will only learn that after you have kids of your own."

"I guess, but for now I need you to accept that I will be out alone at night. It won't be really late but I will have to stay on campus after *Maghrib*, the sunset prayers, at least a few times a week."

"Well, I have to go finish my work. I will talk to you tomorrow *Inshallah. Khuda Hafiz*," her mother said as she ended the conversation.

Her mother didn't sound thrilled with this new development in Fatima's life.

"*Inshallah. Khuda Hafiz*." Fatima hung up the phone.

She had just made great headway with her parents. Unbelievably, she had somehow managed to assure her mother that being out at night was a non-negotiable aspect of college. This would have been an unconceivable notion a few months back. But now here she was, a freshman in college, with a boatload of independence, like none that she known before. And this new-found independence now extended past sunset. One small step for the average freshman, one huge leap for Fatima Husain.

Although this was a remarkable turning point, the truth of the matter was that Fatima's parents didn't have much to fear. Fatima wasn't the type to run amuck, she had always been a responsible girl who had scruples. Most importantly her parents were aware that she was keeping company with other Muslim girls who seemed to be practicing their faith. What better environment could they ask for? They just had to accept the fact that their daughter was now going to make independent decisions without their shadow constantly lingering over her.

The next day Fatima had three classes, one of her longer days of the week. She started out the day with Biology, a class packed with *Desis* and Chinese, and a sprinkling of all other nationalities. Undoubtedly some of the many *Desis* in the auditorium were Muslim, but since none of the other girls there were *muhajjaba*, Fatima could not make out who was Muslim and who was not. And it really didn't matter if she could tell whether the guys were Muslim or not. For if she could tell a guy was Muslim, due to his long beard or mannerisms, he would surely avoid her as she was a Muslim woman. The gender boundary had to be respected by someone who chose to obviously identify themselves as Muslim. As strange as it sounded, Fatima realized that it would actually be easier to deal with men that were not Muslim, since they didn't have the laws to uphold that the Muslim men did. But knowing Fatima, she would just find a female classmate that she felt comfortable with to discuss this class or she would wait until lab period to further her acquaintances with her classmates. Biology was looking more and more like it was going to be strictly business. It was probably better this way, since the sciences would require her undivided attention.

After leaving the auditorium, Fatima walked through Busch campus, and waited for the bus to take her to where liberal arts classes were held, the College Ave campus. As she waited at the stop she couldn't help but notice how the Busch campus, home of the sciences at Rutgers University main campus, was overflowing with non-whites. Never before had she seen so many people of Asian descent in an educational setting. It was almost shocking to her. So many of obvious foreign ancestry walked by her, speaking in their native tongues, that Fatima was left speechless. It was almost as if English was a foreign language!

Fatima overheard an entire conversation being carried on in Urdu by two Pakistani guys standing behind her. She saw an Indian fellow walking with a *tiffin*, steel lunch box, in his hands, much like the one Nanima had in her home back in Hyderabad. And she watched as two demure Chinese girls giggled in Cantonese as they waited alongside of her. The feeling was surreal. It was as if she was transported into another civilization, yet she was still on American ground. This must be a tangible example of 'the American Salad Bowl' she thought to herself.

After getting off the bus at College Ave Fatima wanted to grab a bite to eat at the student center. She picked up a baked potato and frosty, one of her daily *healthy* meals, from Wendy's, and grabbed a seat at a small table. As she looked over her notes from Bio, she was joined by another *muhajjaba*.

"*Assalamu Alaykum*. My name is Haanya," she introduced herself with a huge smile and sat right down at Fatima's table.

Fatima, pleasantly surprised at Haanya's comfort with her, returned the greeting just as warmly.

"So what's your major?" Haanya inquired. "Can I guess...Bio or something science related..?" she laughed.

"No, I am the oddball. I am leaning towards the liberal arts…"

"*Masha Allah*, that's fantastic! So am I! All I meet are Muslims going into the sciences, especially from Egypt, that's where my family is from by the way. If the kids don't become a doctor or an engineer then *khalaas*…" she slid her hand across her throat.

Fatima laughed out loud, "That is exactly how it is with *Desis*! This must be more of a Muslim phenomenon rather than a cultural one," she hypothesized.

"Could be…" Haanya entertained the thought.

"Did you hear about the Islamic Society?"

"Yes, I did. It meets on Thursday right?"

"Yes at 8 pm, but at 5 pm the girls will get together for an hour of *tafseer*, study of the Qur'an, in the Student Lounge at BSC. So if you don't have class then, you really should come," Haanya insisted.

"Definitely," responded an enthusiastic Fatima. "That sounds fantastic!"

This was the religious direction that Fatima was in search of. It seemed as if opportunities such as these were inundating her, and Fatima was delighted at such prospects.

As happy as Fatima was with college, she had been struggling to sleep for the past few nights. She was having strange dreams about Farhana, Mina, and the horrible accident that took their lives. The nightmares would wake her at night and leave her restless and in greater fear of death than ever before. They had occurred randomly since the tragedy took place, but the fact the she was experiencing them more often now was making her very uneasy. This was another reason that she was desperately searching for Muslims that could help her find peace in her faith and spirituality.

Thursday night was the climax of Fatima's week. The Islamic Society functioned as an organization that provided a social network that tied the Muslims together as well as an educational forum that enlightened both its members and non-members about Islam. It hosted Ramadan gatherings that allowed the students to converge and break fast together at sunset. It invited scholars to speak about the philosophy of their faith and lead the way in hosting unity dinners and activities that were *dawah* (outreach) oriented. It also worked with the Student Centers to provide space for the Muslim students to pray their *salaat*, as they would undoubtedly be on campus when one of the five prayers' time came. Fatima was delighted at all the activities that she was able to participate in which were sponsored by this group.

"I am so thrilled to find people that think like I do. It's such a change from where I went to school," she related to her new friend, Maryam, over lunch at the packed Student Center.

"That's why I came here. The sense of community, the sense of actually belonging. I craved that," agreed Maryam.

"It's also nice to see the people you grew up with at the same college as you. It evolves into a deeper friendship when you spend more time with them," added Fadwa.

"Well, I didn't grow up with anyone that goes to school here except one friend that I hardly see because she is always on Busch while I am on

College Ave, so I can't say I relate much to that. But the strange thing is that I feel like I have known you all forever," Fatima remarked.

"Isn't that an amazing feeling?" agreed Maryam.

"We do have a lot in common. We are all Muslims living in America. But we also have this strong cultural identity that our parents have given us. So basically we are fusing these identities into one," said Fatima.

"Preferably one that identifies us most with our faith, since that is the greatest tie we have with one another," Fadwa added very matter-of-factly.

"Hey guys, what's for lunch?" asked Sarah, one of Fatima's classmates from her Arabic class, as she joined the trio on one of her rare visits to College Ave.

"What's the aeronautical engineer doing on College Ave?" Fatima teased Sarah.

"I just had to drop off some stuff at the library here, and I thought I would grab a quick bite," she said as she sat down with the girls. Sarah rarely had time to breathe. She was engulfed in her engineering studies and her active role in the Islamic Society. It was nice to see her off her feet for once.

"And it's time for the *Dhuhr*. I really need to pray before I head back to Busch?"

"Sure. I am almost done, so I'll join you," Fatima drank her last few sips of diet Pepsi and stood up.

The girls made their way up to the quiet lounge, where there was a sizeable niche in the far corner. A large enough place to allow four people to stand together for *salaat*. The girls prayed quietly, in a discreet manner, so as to not disturb any of the students that were studying in the large sitting room. 'Another beauty of my homeland,' Fatima thought to herself. 'Not many countries are as accepting and tolerant of displaying one's faith, as my country is,' she thought proudly. In fact Fatima knew of so-called Muslim countries where even the Muslims couldn't practice their faith as freely and openly as they did in America.

After *salaat*, each was on their way to class. While walking on College Avenue, Fatima bumped into yet another *muhajjaba*, Safia, who was headed in the same direction as she was. Fatima had seen Safia around campus, and at the Islamic Society in which she too was very active. They chatted amiably along the way to their classes.

"So how do you like it here so far?" Safia inquired of Fatima.

"I love it. I can't believe that I can actually get up and leave during lecture, without being asked any questions! That is such a big deal!" she laughed.

"Yeah, most freshmen are thrilled that they don't have to ask for a hall pass to run to the lav," Safia smiled.

"I am one of them," Fatima joked. "I am also really happy that I have met so many great people here. There's an awesome sense of community here, isn't there?"

"Yeah, *mashallah*, there is. Well, that's my class," she pointed towards Scott Hall. "I gotta run, *Inshallah* I will see you soon, maybe at *Jumma. Assalamu alaykum.*"

"*Walaikum Salam*," Fatima waved bye. Fatima bit her lip '*Jumma?* Where is *Jumma?*' Fatima thought to herself 'On campus?'

She didn't realize that the students were able to hold *Jumma*, Friday congregation, on campus. Now she was wondering where it was held, and how she could attend.

She walked into her class and took a seat in the middle of the room. As she thought about where *Jumma* could possibly be, an obviously Muslim student walked in. 'How many Muslims are there here?' thought an amazed Fatima. "I can't keep track of all the people I am meeting...'

This student's beard was well trimmed and he walked with his gaze lowered, trademarks of a traditional Muslim. He saw Fatima out of the corner of his eye, and walked on. No salaam no nothing. Fatima thought that maybe she should ask him about *Jumma*, but who knows how he would react. He knew that she was Muslim, the *hijaab* left no doubt about that. But even then he didn't bother to say salaam. Fatima figured that he may be a strict segregationist who doesn't talk to women unnecessarily.

She watched him discreetly. 'He was not *Desi*, too fair to be that,' Fatima thought. 'Or maybe he was from northern Pakistan where people were blonde haired and blue eyed. Or he could be a product of a mixed marriage. Or he could be Arab, probably from Syria or Palestine, since that's where it was said that most good looking Arabs come from.' Fatima found herself thinking about the nationality of this fellow in great detail until the Professor shattered her train of thought.

"Good afternoon class. Today's lecture..." began the Professor.

Fatima's attention diverted towards the Professor. Once lecture wrapped up, Fatima packed her books into her backpack and began to walk out. Then she heard it. The strongest, thickest, *Desi* accent that she had heard since Apu on The Simpsons. She instantly turned around to see who it was. Lo and behold, it was the fair Muslim boy.

"Oh my God!" Fatima said under her breath. No one could be trusted to be what they looked like. 'Who would have thunk it,' she thought as she almost laughed out loud.

Classes were in full swing and Fatima had quickly settled into her own routine at Rutgers. She was enjoying classes and all that the University offered to her. She had befriended more people in the past ten weeks than she had her whole lifetime, and her social circle grew exponentially. Before she knew it the end of the semester was only four weeks away. Fatima had no idea how the time had flown by. And in Dadima's eyes this meant trouble.

"*Dekho beta*, college is where it all happens. Don't you boys remember your college days?" she asked her sons, some of whom were listening to her, some who chose to pay her no heed. Their weekly gatherings at her house would always entail some negative reference to their past, and today was no different.

"It's high time you get Fatima engaged. Do you plan on keeping her until she is an old hag?"

"Mamma, please. When the right boy comes along we will work on it. For now let her be," Fatima's father responded.

"What's the right boy? Is there such a thing? Such good proposals are coming your way and you guys aren't even looking at them seriously. What is wrong with you all?" Dadima snapped.

"Like who Mamma? Like who? Please tell me who we haven't researched that was a suitable match?" Fatima's father asked.

"That Shamsi boy from Chicago! You know the one that Yasmeen recommended! He was a fine boy. Educated, Hyderabadi, from a respectable family. What happened to him?"

"For your information Mamma, we have not dismissed that boy. We are in the process of trying to find out some info in him…"

"Since when?" asked a shocked Dadima.

"Mamma, I have good friends who live in Chicago. I will call them and request that they find out more about this boy and his family," Fatima's mother stated calmly.

"Thank God that some sense has come to you two," Dadima said as she stared at Fatima's parents. She opened her purse and popped some betel nuts in her mouth.

"And when were you planning to let your family know that you were inquiring further into this boy? After the wedding? Huh?" Dadima went off on a whole different tangent.

Fatima overheard every word of the conversation from the kitchen. She just acted like she didn't. She sat quietly, sipping her diet Pepsi, reflecting on this Shamsi boy that her parents had mentioned to her a week back. His bio-data seemed worthy and his picture wasn't bad, but it wasn't great either. So Fatima remained impassive to the situation and let her parents follow the same old protocol, yet again. 'It would fall apart sooner or later as had happened with the fifty proposals that she or her family wound up considering and rejecting,' she thought still riding high on her new found freedom.

Chapter 21

Fatima went home that weekend. She thought she would just sit back and enjoy the company of her sisters, whom she was missing a lot more than she had imagined. As the girls sat in the family room drinking root beer floats and playing Taboo, Fatima noticed that their mother was on the phone in the dining room. Fatima knew that when the phone call wasn't being made from the family room, it was most likely an important call that needed to be discussed in a quiet space, i.e. the dining room. She slyly made her way over to the kitchen, so that she gave the impression of simply refilling her float. She began to eavesdrop on her mom, while putting together another drink. She worked slowly, taking her good old time, so that she wouldn't miss anything that was being said by her mother.

"We have heard good stuff about the family, but since you live in Chicago we felt that it would be best for you to find out more about what this family is really like and whether or not this boy is actually a good match for Fatima…."

Fatima rolled her eyes. 'Here we go again,' she thought. Yet another background check. This time her mother had called her childhood friend, Nyla, in Chicago to investigate the Shamsi lad. This friend had lived there for over twenty years, and was willing to do the research needed on this prospect.

"Mummy, is this all really necessary? I mean really – marriage at nineteen?" Fatima asked her mother after she hung up the phone.

"We aren't saying marriage today. We are just started to think seriously about it."

"Mom, I don't get this at all. You guys don't talk to me about anything that entails growing up – no talk about my cycle, no talk about growing all physically awkward, and God forbid – *no* talk about the birds and the bees. But when it comes to marriage – everyone is ready to get serious about it. What's that all about?"

"What? What birds? What bees? Are you okay? Talking about your cycle then insects? You are not making any sense..." her mother replied in utter confusion.

"Nothing Mom, Nothing. Forget I ever brought it up..."Fatima mumbled distraughtly.

"Don't worry about it Fatima. We have to do what we have to do. Anyway, why were you listening in on my conversation? Don't you have anything better to do?"

"Whatever..." Fatima replied disdainfully.

Fatima, although irritated, had other things on her mind. She had volunteered to help with Ramadan night at Rutgers and was busy organizing the event with her peers. Flyers had to be made, food had to be ordered, and many other details had to be ironed out; there was a lot to get done. Long shot proposals were not top priority.

Fatima was also busy with finals that were just around the corner. Papers and assignments were nearing their due dates and Fatima had much to complete. The most agonizing assignments came from her infamous Expository Writing class. This was a course that everyone dreaded taking, and now Fatima knew why.

"These stories are so boring," Fatima said to the student sitting next to her.

"I can hardly manage to stay awake when I am reading them."

Overhearing Fatima's comment, the student behind her, John, snapped, "That's why my papers are crap. This is such a stupid class."

John had not done well on any of his assignments and was at wit's end. The 'D' grade on the paper that was in his hands hadn't made things better.

"I was actually looking forward to this course," Fatima said as she reviewed the paper she had just received back.

"I thought I wrote pretty well, but this B- says otherwise..." she stared in disbelief.

If there was one thing that Fatima could have changed about her first semester at college it would have been Expos. Fatima couldn't stand the stories that they had to write about. They bored her out of her mind, yet she still felt that her assignments were well done. Obviously, the teacher did not agree. Leaving the class disappointed Fatima walked to the Student Center to grab a bite. Seated in a corner in the Atrium were Nelly and Saba.

"What did you guys think of Expos?" she asked the two seated girls.

"No comment," Saba laughed.

"Glad its over," said Nelly. "Don't worry, it's a part of being a freshman, you will get through it."

"I don't know guys. I am really annoyed with those stupid stories and my teacher...ughgh..." she shook her head in disgust.

"Don't worry about it, the semester is almost over."

"Alhamdulillah" Fatima sighed.

Saba stood up with her books, "Okay guys, I gotta run. See you tonight at the Islamic Society meeting."

"What about the *tafseer*? Aren't we meeting for that at 5?"

"Yes, Yes. I will *inshallah* see you there first! *Assalamu Alaykum.*" She waved bye and walked out of the Atrium.

"I can't remember what verse we left off on last week," Nelly said to Fatima.

"I have it written down with my notes. Hold on ..." Fatima scrambled through her backpack and removed a large green binder labeled '*Tafseer, Surah Nur.*' She flipped through the notes, "We ended on verse 39."

"Thanks, I'll try to refresh my memory before we start tonight. I have to run too. So see you at 5, *Inshallah. Assalamu Alaykum.*" Nelly gathered her things and left Fatima alone at the table.

Fatima opened up her Expos book and started to read for her next paper. Two minutes into the reading she was struggling to keep her eyes open. 'Forget this,' she thought. She put the book in her backpack and got up. It was time for *Asr* salaat. Fatima would pray upstairs before she took the bus to Busch.

Once at Busch, Fatima went to the quiet lounge and tried once again to do her reading. As difficult as it was, she managed to get half way through the short story when she felt a tug on the back of her *hijaab*. She turned around.

"*Assalamu alaykum* Fatima," smiled Sarah. "Now I should ask you, what is the liberal arts major doing on Busch?"

"*Walaykum Salam*. Yes, you caught me," Fatima laughed. "Actually I just got here a little early to read. Then I can join the *tafseer* at 5pm, *Inshallah.*"

"How is that going?"

"Really good, Sarah. I am really enjoying it. I have a whole new appreciation for reading the Qur'an after the *tafseer*. Usually I would just read the Arabic and skim over the English, but now I am actually taking the time to read the footnotes and look into the historical context of all the verses. It gives everything so much more depth."

"Alhamdulillah, I am so glad to hear that Fatima. I just wish that I could come more regularly. I can't always make it because of my classes."

"You can borrow my notes and read over what we have discussed," Fatima suggested.

"I might just do that," Sarah replied. "I gotta head to class now, but *Inshallah* I will be at the meeting tonight. See you there."

"*Inshallah*," responded Fatima.

After the *tafseer*, Fatima and her friends all had dinner together at the food court. There were about ten to fifteen of them, all laughing and chatting away. Coming from different cultures and backgrounds yet, they all sat together and conversed as if they were age old buddies. It was clear that these girls were American, their lingo and mannerisms left no doubt of that. But one couldn't deny or overlook their heritage. Some were of Indo-Pak origin, while others were originally from the Arab world, though others were local converts. The strongest tie that bound them all together, the tie that surpassed that of their cultural heritage, was that of their faith. Young Muslim women living in America. Muslim Americans. A new culture. A new identity. One that these young Muslims, being born and raised in America, were the pioneers of. After all, it was a new type of social and religious identity for most people to identify. But when one looked upon this table of young women there was no doubt that this was exactly who they were. American Muslims.

After dinner they made their way to the Islamic Society meeting. The meeting was about a controversy that was brewing between the Pakistani Student Association (PSA) and the Islamic Society(IS). The PSA was trying to work with the IS to sponsor an *Eid* celebration after the holy month of Ramadan. The IS had originally agreed, but then members of the IS found flyers that were being circulated by the PSA about this event. Their flyers informed, "Alcohol available for nominal charge." For any practicing Muslim this was a heinous statement. Alcohol was strictly forbidden under Muslim law and there was no way that alcohol could be served at an event that was celebrating a religious holiday. The IS was outraged that this event was being publicized under such pretenses.

"We have pulled back our sponsorship of this event, but it is now up to all of us to decide whether or not we should approach the PSA about linking alcohol to a religious celebration..." spoke Yunus, the president of the IS.

"It is incumbent upon you to do so!" shouted an angry Junaid.

"I can not believe that these fools have the nerve to promote drinking at an Islamic celebration!"

"We can't control everything that others do," opposed Anwar. "They will answer for their stupidity. Just let them do what they want."

"Are you crazy? It's people like them that ruin our name," responded a livid Jafar.

"No Jafar, there are many other idiots out there that are great at doing that. And we don't need to lose our tempers and come off as raging lunatics either. All we should do is avoid the event. End of story."

"Your passivity shocks me Anwar," said a disappointed Junaid. "We have to stop what is wrong with our hands first, if we don't do that then we should at least tell them what they are doing is unacceptable."

"I agree with telling them, but physically storming into their party is not the answer. If they want to get drunk, they will get drunk. Whether it's at this event or another, they will do what they want to do."

"I agree with Anwar," added Sarah. "We have to tell them this is wrong, but we can't physically stop them from doing something they are determined to do. This is America – they have their freedom."

"Freedom to screw up their lives…" mumbled a voice from the back of the room.

"What?" Saba blurted out as she turned towards the back. Unsure of who had just spoken, she turned towards the front again.

"*They* have to answer for what *they* do. This is not a military state where we are some sort of authority that will reprimand people for committing sin…" she went on.

The debate carried on for another hour. It was finally decided that the Islamic Society would openly denounce the PSA flyer and its President and VP would have a discussion with the PSA president and VP letting them know how the IS felt about this situation. The Islamic Society at large would receive an update at next week's meeting as to what was the status of the Eid event.

It was ironic that this was the major issue that these students were concerned with. Alcohol at a Muslim event. It wasn't international politics that they were obsessed with, or plots on how the West was evil, as much of the media would have liked to portray them. They had issues that arose within their own microcosmic world that needed to be addressed. How to remain a practicing Muslim in America was at the top of that list. Compromising their faith in order to socially fit in was not something these students wished to do. Although they lived in America they did not want to completely assimilate into mainstream society. Instead they wanted to be part of the larger montage of traditions that all came to America. The task was to become an integral part of that larger mosaic without losing their individual beauty.

Fatima and Fadwa left the meeting in disgust over what was taking place.

"I can't believe that there are Muslims out there that are doing something so clearly *haram* and then, as if that isn't bad enough, they are advertising it, like it's a good thing or something," Fatima said.

"Unbelievable," a sickened Fadwa replied.

"We just have to pray that God guides them. There is nothing more to it than that…" responded Fatima.

The week's events had been pretty dramatic, at least by Fatima's standards, and the weekend was a welcome break. Fatima went home to her parents' place and chilled with her sisters. It was after dinner and *Maghrib* that the girls decided that they wanted to rent a Bollywood movie. Before the girls were able drive to the Indian store, Fatima's parents called her into the dining room. 'Hmm this is rather strange,' Fatima thought as she left her sisters and walked towards her parents.

She found both of her parents sipping their tea seated on the dining table. It was obvious that they had something important to say.

"Have a seat," Fatima's father directed.

Fatima nervously sat down, unsure of what this was all about.

"Your mother's friend from Chicago called back…" he said slowly.

'Phhhew' Fatima breathed a sigh of relief. She had actually thought this was going to be a serious issue. But instead she figured that it was now somehow trivial. A little more relaxed she leaned back against her chair.

"That's nice," Fatima responded nonchalantly.

"Well, she said that the Shamsi boy is quite nice. He is from a good family, has a good job, and appears to be of good character…"

'But…' Fatima said to herself anticipating such a statement.

"But…"

'I knew there was a but! Yes! This is over…' Fatima excitedly thought to herself.

"But, there is a new development. After relating all the info we needed on the Shamsi boy, Nyla Apa asked your mother to consider her son for you as well."

"Ok…" Fatima suddenly sat up straight and arched her brows.

"Now from what we all have heard he is supposed to be a really good boy. And our family has known their family for the past thirty years. On top of all that, he is in med school and is not bad looking either..." Father tapered off as he slid over a picture that was under his hand. Fatima glanced at the picture placed before her.

"When did all this happen?" Fatima asked. All of this information was hard to process, and left her rather shocked and confused.

"What do you mean?" her mother replied.

"Well, first the call back with all the information that you wanted about the Shamsi boy, and then *this* picture getting here so quickly....All this happened since last weekend?" Fatima inquired.

"Nyla Apa works rather quickly I guess. She gathered the info on the Shamsi boy within two days. So when she called back, she shared the data on that boy, but at the same time asked us to consider her own son for you as well. As you can imagine, I was caught totally off guard. I wasn't sure how to respond. But then she herself suggested that a picture of her son should be sent to us along with the info that would have been on a bio-data. I agreed. So she followed up with this picture, which arrived yesterday," Mummy explained pointing to the picture.

"So which guy are we considering now?" asked a still perplexed Fatima.

"Which one do *you* want to consider?" asked her father.

Fatima was caught off guard by all this. She had just assumed that the Shamsi boy would fall through, so she didn't give any of it much thought. But now she felt blindsided by the rapidity of how quickly things had moved ahead. She couldn't fathom that she actually had to seriously consider these boys. This was all a bit overwhelming.

"I'm not sure Dad. This is just a little too fast for me."

"Take your time, *beta*. You can take as long as you want. I just don't want to string anyone along. That's why I want you to look at the pictures, review the bio-datas, and tell us who we should move ahead with; that's if you want to move forward at all."

He handed Fatima two sheets of paper with a lot of information on each. The pictures were already lying in front of her.

For a second Fatima didn't know what to think.

"Well, what do you guys think?" she asked her parents.

"We want what will make you happy," her father assured her. "Our research is done, and both appear to be fine boys. Now, you have to let us know which you want to pursue."

"Okay..." Fatima said, staring blankly at the bio-datas.

Slowly both of her parents left the room. Fatima was totally surprised by what had just happened. She was hoping to relax this weekend, nothing to stress about, all her papers done, and finals prep would begin only next week. But this turn of events changed everything.

Fatima told her sisters to go to the Indian store without her, and took the pictures and bio-datas upstairs to her room. She looked over both papers, as if they were applications for a job for which she was to select the better applicant. Of course, she could easily say no to both, but there was no sensible reason to do that. If they were decent boys, ones that her parents actually thought worthy of presenting to her, then there must be some hope for the two.

The first bachelor was Abbas Shamsi. He was an engineer, whose family immigrated to Chicago from Hyderabad, India in 1972. According to his bio-data he had two sisters and one younger brother. He currently resides with his parents and was working for Packer Engineering Corp. His picture showed him to be tall (6'2' his bio data read), with a five o' clock shadow, of darker complexion and a thick head of hair. His interests included football, squash, going to the movies (American, not Indian movies – this was clearly stated), and eating Indian food.

Bachelor number two was Talha Muhammed. Talha was a medical student at the University of Illinois. His family came to the United States in 1972 as well. He had one older brother, and was residing on campus in Chicago. His pictured presented him as a clean shaven young man, about 6' tall, and with very sharp features. His eyes were huge, and his hair was slightly curly. His interests included football, basketball, tennis, reading historical texts.

After carefully reviewing each, Fatima made a chart that said 'Pros and Cons.' After all, this was going to be a practical decision, so why not carry it out in a most practical manner? After filling in the chart it wound up looking like this:

Pros	**Cons**
Shamsi – Out of school	Talha – in school
Talha – likes to read	Shamsi – likes eating?
Talha – nice eyes	Shamsi – kinda chunky
Talha – lives at school	Shamsi – lives at home
Talha – know his family well	Shamsi – heard about family

After filling out the chart Fatima realized that something was missing. Something huge. Something that both candidates had neglected to address, but was of utmost importance to Fatima. Unfortunately, neither bio-data mentioned how important their faith and spirituality was to them. This was something that Fatima felt that she had to know before choosing one to move ahead with. In fact that alone could help change what she had figured to be most practical in a heartbeat.

However, what she had to take into consideration was that these fact sheets were most likely prepared by the parents of both these guys, so they must be taken with a grain of salt.

Fatima was itching to call one of her friend's about this situation. She really wanted to consult someone about all that was just thrown her way. But she knew she could not. Her parents would be very disappointed in her if she did. They did not want her to discuss this topic with anyone but them, simply as a protective measure. Proposals and situations of this nature were an extremely delicate subject to discuss, especially in respect to girls, within the *Desi* Muslim community. Rarely was anything mentioned about any girl, until everything was finalized by both parties involved. It was a matter of respect, dignity, and pride. So Fatima lulled over the two prospects until the next day. She had prayed extra *salaat* called, *isthikhaarah*, which asked God to guide her to what was in her best interest.

Although she was stressed about the issue, she kept telling herself that she wasn't agreeing to marry the guy; she was simply agreeing to pursue the matter further. That was all. If it fell apart - it fell apart. No loss to anyone. Which was very true.

After two days of thinking it over, Fatima sat down with her parents while her sisters were outside playing badminton. She placed the pictures and bio-datas of the two boys in front of them.

"Daddy, I looked at the bio-datas carefully, and I think that you should look into this one," she pointed to the picture of Talha. "But we need to find out what exactly he is looking for too, don't we?"

"Yes we do," he replied, "If you give the green light then we will move ahead and arrange for you both to meet so that we can all sit down face to face. Then I am sure you guys can discuss what it is that you both are looking for in a spouse."

'God,' Fatima thought to herself. 'I actually have to go through with another meeting?'

"But this one will be rather tricky to arrange, since he lives in Chicago. We may not be able to do our usual 'walk-by.' We may actually have to invite him to our home."

"What? Why?" asked a stunned Fatima. "We never did it before, so why would we have to do it now?"

"Two reasons," her mother relayed. "Firstly, he is the son of a very good friend of mine, so if he was in town I would have invited him over for dinner anyway. Secondly, if he comes here to meet you, then that's your chance to sit down and get all the info you need out of each other.

It's not easy to keep flying back and forth to Chicago, you know. So you have to make the most of that trip."

'Holy shit' Fatima thought to herself. What was she getting herself into? She realized that this would happen sooner or later but she was hoping it would be later on. Things of this nature could not be taken lightly, and now she had to worry about what this meeting would be like since it was like none other that occurred before – this one was going to take place at home!

Chapter 22

'First things first,' Fatima kept telling herself. She had to focus on her final exams, which were next week! She needed to forget about the Talha situation for the time being, and leave the arrangement of the meeting up to her parents. She could not stress about that – not just yet. There was tons of studying that had to get done.

For the first time in her life, Fatima realized the benefits of study groups. She had never before prepared for exams in this type of setting, but at college this seemed to be a very common form of exam prep. Being the outgoing person that she was, this method of preparation proved to be most fruitful for Fatima. She whizzed through the exams for which this type of study was suitable.

Unfortunately, this was not the case for all of her classes. Calculus, for example, had no study groups. Instead Fatima found herself staying late with the TA, struggling to grasp numerous new concepts that were just not sinking in. It was deja'vouz. She felt like she was back in high school calc class. After hours and hours of struggling in a field that was definitely not her forte, Fatima took the Calculus exam. Upon handing the completed exam to her professor, she squirmingly said, "Professor, I have just been to hell and back."

The Professor responded spiritedly, "Welcome back dear," with a huge grin.

Fatima couldn't help but smile. There was nothing else to do. The worst part was over, and now she had to move on.

After all of her exams were over, Fatima packed up her stuff at her *chacha*'s place and headed home. She knew that a huge quandary was awaiting her, a mountain of a hurdle named Talha Muhammed.

Fatima's mother was anxiously awaiting her arrival. After putting her things away in her bedroom, Fatima came down in to the family room and plopped herself down next to her mother.

234 Neither This Nor That

"So Mummy what's up?" she asked, unsure of what to expect.

"We have a guest coming next week..." Mummy's voice trailed off.

"Are you serious?" Fatima jerked back and sat straight up.

"Very serious," Mummy replied with a mischievous look.

"God, Mummy…I am so not ready for this…." Fatima grabbed her head.

"What? You knew this was going to happen."

"I know Mummy, but right after exams?" Fatima asked despairingly.

"Well, firstly, he isn't coming just to meet you."

"Wonderful…" Fatima rolled her eyes.

"Keep quiet and listen for a change will you?" Mummy snapped. "He is coming to visit his uncle and aunt, who live in Plainsboro. So while he is in the area, he'll swing by our place for dinner."

"Great…" Fatima moaned. She was definitely not sharing her mother's excitement.

"Why the attitude?" Mummy asked.

"There's no attitude Mummy. I just wanted to relax for a while, but instead you lay all this on me."

"You knew it was coming Fatima. We didn't hide anything from you."

"I know Mummy. It's just that…this…is…stressful."

"Why are you thinking of it as stressful? No one is pressuring you into saying yes. We just want you to meet him, and that too because you told us to pursue him."

"I know, I know…" Fatima shook her head. "I just need to sleep. I am sure that's it."

Fatima went into her room and tried to take a nap. But she couldn't get herself to relax enough to doze off. 'How was this guy going to be? How weird is it that he is coming to our home? What if it does work out? Then, am I ready to move to Chicago?' All these thoughts kept racing through her head, making it impossible for her to rest.

Instead she chose to pick up the phone and call her school friend, Mary. She figured that Mary wasn't really a part of her family's social circle, so it wouldn't upset her parents if she found it. At the same time, Mary would know exactly how to react to all that was transpiring.

Upon hearing Fatima's voice, Mary reacted, "Long time no talk! How was your first semester?"

"Great, I loved it, but I came home to a ton of issues."

"Meaning…"

"Meaning that my folks have this guy coming over next week and it's looking relatively serious…"

"Again? What's the big deal? You've met fifty guys already. Why are you freaking out about this one?"

"Mary, this is different. I can tell it is. Everything about the way this one is playing out is different. My mom, well, she actually seems excited about this one...."

"Hmm... Well what's wrong with him, on paper I mean, or even his picture? Anything stand out as weird?"

"Nothing! That's the thing! I can't find anything to say about him that is negative, at least not yet. Maybe when I meet him something will stand out, but right now, there is nothing wrong with him..."

"And you are scared? Is that what you are saying?"

"Well, no. Scared isn't it. I think I am just really nervous."

"Fatima, you of all people shouldn't be nervous! You're an expert at this by now! Just meet the guy and see if you click. How hard could that be?"

"I know, but I am just getting a weird feeling..."

"Weird in a positive way or weird in a negative way?" Mary pressed on.

"I can't say – I don't know what I am thinking anymore. This is just bizarre..."

Fatima never felt this way before, but for some odd reason she sensed that too much was right already to make this go wrong. But what to come of school? Her thoughts raced to Rutgers. Fatima loved school; she reveled in the environment of intellectualism. She couldn't imagine not tasting the pleasure of learning at Rutgers. Would she have to transfer if this worked out?? 'Damn,' Fatima thought. 'I don't even want to think of what school I would have to transfer to..."

The following weekend arrive a lot faster than what Fatima had anticipated. The week flew by and Fatima was feeling nauseous with nervousness. Talha was supposed to come for dinner in less than twenty four hours and Fatima couldn't stop feeling queasy. She had taken the practical step of writing down all that she wanted to know about him, but for some odd reason, she sensed that she would not be able to ask him much. She felt that this was going to be a strange set up. Much of that was because this was not taking place in 'neutral' territory; instead this was in *her* home. This would have made many girls more comfortable with the situation, but for Fatima it had the total opposite effect. For her, it was a matter of opening up her own personal comfort zone to someone who she hardly knew. She didn't like that. She didn't want to feel uneasy in her own home, but she knew that that was exactly what was going to happen.

As the evening approached, Mummy was scurrying around in the kitchen, putting the final touches on the feast that she had prepared. The *kabab* were baking, the meat for the *biryani* lay marinated in a large bowl next to the stove. The *chutney* was already prepared and cooling in the fridge along side of the *kheer*. The aroma was a delight to any *Desi's* senses. Fatima silently observed all the extra effort, and knew that her mother must be hoping for the best with this one. 'As if she would do all this, for a friend's son,' Fatima thought to herself. Fatima's self-imposed pressure was mounting exponentially.

Nevertheless she couldn't just watch as her mother worked like a horse. Fatima decided that she would start cleaning up before her mother would even have to ask. She took out the Hoover. As she vacuumed the house she noticed that her sisters were already busy cleaning the bathrooms and sweeping the floor. They obviously realized their mother's predicament well before she had. But then again Fatima had a lot more on her mind. She quietly went up to her room once her minimal work was completed.

Fatima sorted through her closet to pick out an appropriate outfit for this evening. She thought it would be in her best interest to select an outfit quickly, before her mom would have an opportunity to inspect what she chose.

As she looked at each hanger, Fatima realized that she didn't feel like dressing up. She was at home, 'why should I be decked out?' she began to think. But she knew that that line of questioning was unacceptable. She continued sifting through her stuff.

Finally, she settled upon the one outfit in her closet that she liked least. A silent protest to all that was going on around her. It was all getting to be a bit much, and Fatima was not sure she was ready to handle all that was unfolding.

While everybody else continued to prepare for this evening's dinner, Fatima stayed in her room. The inevitability of the meeting finally sunk into her head and her nervousness increased to unheard of proportions. 'Why is this so weird? Why is *this one* so different?' she kept asking herself. 'I've never been so nervous? Why am I such a wreck today? I can't be like this. I need to stay focused and confident. There isn't much time and I have a lot to ask and learn in this meeting so I have to relax. Deep breath now. Aaaaaaaaaah. Feels better. One more time….Deep breath …'

Once she decreased her heart rate and regained some composure, Fatima reviewed her note cards and tried to memorize the questions that she had written down to ask him. She planned out how she would ask what needed to be asked and how she would respond to a number of potential questions that Talha may pose. As she continued to reflect on potential inquiries the door bell rang.

Chapter 23

Fatima felt both light headed and sick to her stomach. She took some more deep breaths and struggled to walk down the stairs to greet the guests. Luckily by the time she made it down, the men were already in the living room, and the women had made their way into the family room. Never before did she feel as grateful as she did at that moment for the fact that men and women sat separately in her home. Now she could sneak into the family room from the stairwell without being noticed. She quietly tiptoed down the stairs and quickly made her way into the family room where her parents were already seated with Talha's aunt.

Fatima extended her hand and politely greeted Talha's aunt. Meeting this aunt was the easy part, Fatima had determined, so her nervousness began to lessen as they exchanged simple formalities.

"I hear you are at Rutgers... How do you like it?" Aunty asked Fatima.

"I love it. I never thought I would enjoy being in school so much," Fatima laughed. "I have discovered my calling at Rutgers"

"Really?" asked Aunty. "What does that mean?"

"It means I am committed to finishing what I started. In fact I am really hoping to go on to grad school," Fatima replied sincerely.

"That's wonderful," Aunty smiled. "I am glad to hear that you have high hopes and aspirations."

"How can I not?" asked Fatima. "Every *Desi* is taught that education is everything, I am not going to go against all that I have been taught from the time I was two…"

Fatima's mother beamed. She had done her job well.

Aunty reached over and gently patted Fatima's head, "Never let anyone tell you can't achieve your dreams dear. Reach high, aim for the stars. In this country you can have it all."

Fatima smiled and humbly looked down. The truth of this statement resonated through and through. '*My dreams, My hopes, My country…*'her thoughts wandered off into la-la land. A sudden realization crashed her dainty little daydream.. '*and my marriage*???' Suddenly she jerked her head up and flashed back to reality.

'Why are we here again?' she thought. And then her senses came back to her.

Fatima's mother left for the kitchen in preparation to serve dinner, and Fatima's anxiety increased. She knew once dinner was out, she would come face to face with someone who could be '*it.*' Twiddling her thumbs and looking down apprehensively, Fatima was unsure of what to do or say next. 'I knew having this guy come to our house was a bad idea,' she thought as she sat restlessly.

Even her sisters were staring at her, giggling at her state of nervousness. Their ever confident sister acting like such a chicken. Who ever thought…

"Let's eat," Mummy called out from the kitchen, inviting everyone to the dining room. Everyone meaning Fatima and Aunty from the family room, and the men from the living room. Ayesha, Amina, and Malikah had been instructed to make themselves scarce when dinner was served.

Fatima and Aunty stood up, followed by a curious Malikah. Without warning, Malikah let out a thunderous, uncontrollable belch. A vulgar disgusting one at that. 'No she didn't,' Fatima thought as she stared down her baby sister. Malikah had a sick look on her face.

"Mummy…" she said loudly."I am having these sour smelling burps and they smell really bad…" she whined while rubbing her belly.

Fatima's face turned beet red. 'Annoying little brat!' she thought. 'As if this isn't embarrassing enough I have a little twit sister belching up a smelly storm.' Seeing Fatima's discomfiture, Ayesha and Amina could not control their laughter. They cackled loudly, almost to a point of obnoxiousness, in Fatima's opinion. But the twosome just couldn't stop themselves. The humor of this situation was too much for them to keep inside. In their opinion, how much funnier could this get?

Aunty, on the other hand, walked into the dining room as if she heard nothing that was going on in the other room, and Fatima followed quickly trying to leave behind her rowdy siblings.

Already seated at the table were Fatima's father, the Uncle, and of course….Mr. Talha. Fatima said her salaams to everyone upon their introductions, but she chose to avoid eye contact with any man in that room. Even her father. She simply nodded her head and continued to

look down, feeling very awkward. She played with her utensils and
fidgeted, waiting for Mummy to join them, but Mummy was busy
garnishing the last dish that was to be brought onto the dining table.

'So.....' Fatima thought. 'I guess I better take a look at the dude,
because all I saw up to this point was a tan blur and I am not going to
move ahead with anything that I saw as a blur ....'

So she began to look around as if she was taking in the room for
the first time. Her eyes wandered from the drapes to the colonial trim at
the edge of the walls. They slowly moved along the trim to the clock that
hung in the center of the wall, which was hanging directly above Talha.

Now she just had to discreetly bring her sight down about thirty
degrees so that she could get a fair look at Talha without seeming to
forward. Her eyes strayed down and voila! Success. She had managed to
get a good look at him without staring or without looking him straight in
the eye. 'Well, he is no Brad Pitt, Fatima thought, 'but he isn't bad
looking either. But he's got really curly hair and no beard. Hmm no
beard...Maybe he isn't that religious? But then again guys who are
religious don't always have beards. And those eyes ...they are bigger than
they looked in the picture...or are they?'

She looked up to try to steal another look. 'Oh crap!' her head shot
down. 'Damn he saw me! He saw me looking at him. Damn, he wasn't
supposed to see that!' Fatima was so embarrassed. That's just not the way
things typically worked. The girl wasn't supposed to do the checking out,
even though it was only natural. She had to act prudishly, as if she had no
feelings whatsoever, that way her dignity was maintained, or so her
traditions taught her. Coming from this type of cultural brainwashing,
Fatima felt rather embarrassed that Talha and she had made eye contact.

'Aah, what the hell,' she shook her head. 'If we don't check each
other out now, when will we?' she thought as she looked up, but not at
Talha. Her *Desi*ness told her to keep her head down, while her
Americanness pushed her to take a good look at what she was getting
into. It was hard to maintain a balance of these two, and Fatima began to
feel like this situation was hopeless. But she was already there, and she
would somehow have to get through it.

She continued to look around the room aimlessly until she too caught
Talha looking at her. And just like her, his head shot down when she found
him out. This game of cat and mouse was really getting uncomfortable.
'Okay, this is just lame,' she thought. Right then she decided, 'When my kids
get married, this is not how things are going to be...'

Mummy finally entered the room with the final dish, and dinner
commenced. Everyone was having a good time, enjoying the feast and

pleasant conversation, except for the two parties for whom this evening had taken place. They were the most uncomfortable. Neither had spoken much. Neither appeared to be at ease.

Realizing the need for some exchange of information, Fatima's father addressed Talha, "So what do you like to do outside of med school?" while passing the rice dish in his direction.

"I like to watch Baywatch," Talha replied with a straight face.

Fatima went pale. Her father looked confused. Aunty looked horrified.

"What?" Fatima's father asked.

"Just kidding," Talha laughed, except that the elders didn't seem to get the joke.

"Actually, I enjoy playing basketball and football and I am a huge fan of Star Wars," Talha went on. Somehow, although bold and daring in the method that he had just employed, Talha had managed to break the ice with Fatima. There was no better way to win some points like showing a good sense of humor. At that moment Fatima was thrilled that her parents had no clue what 'Baywatch' was.

"And what do you plan on doing as a specialty?" her father continued.

"I can't say that I have made my decision yet. I am leaning towards Anesthesiology, but I also like Surgery. It will take a few more rotations for me to make my final decision," Talha stated.

"Anesthesiology? Isn't it boring to just put a patient to sleep?" her father asked.

Fatima let out a laugh. She tried to control herself, but she couldn't manage to hold her amusement back. Talha, noticing Fatima's laugh, smirked at her, and made eye contact once more. Down shot Fatima's gaze, once again.

He then turned to her father and coolly replied, "Actually, there is a lot more that comes with the Anesthesia turf. It's pretty intense. It also offers a good lifestyle, and the hours are conducive to people who are family oriented. I don't intend on sacrificing my family for the sake of my career. But most importantly, for me at least, it doesn't involve too much interaction with the patient," Talha laughed again at himself.

Unfortunately no one else joined in. Now Talha looked nervous.

'He is shooting himself in the foot over and over again,' Fatima thought. It dawned upon her just then, that he too must be just as uneasy as she was. These circumstances must be as difficult for him as they were for her. How could he not be nervous? Maybe that's why he was trying to be funny. Fatima began to pity him. Or was it more? She wasn't quite sure.

Her father continued asking Talha questions about his field of study along with general questions that would allow him to gauge how strong his family and religious values were. Talha seemed to answer most of these questions rather eloquently. By this time even Fatima seemed intrigued by the potential of this situation.

Once dinner wrapped up, Fatima went into the kitchen with her mother to help bring out dessert. Her father soon followed the two, leaving the guests seated in the dining room.

"I think there may be something worthwhile here. You can talk to him on your own if you wish," Daddy whispered to Fatima.

"Not alone," Fatima's mother stated firmly yet quietly. "She can talk if someone else is sitting with them. Ask the aunt to sit with them if need be, but I won't let her talk to him without any supervision."

"Is that okay Fatima?" her father asked.

"Yeah, sure," Fatima replied. There was something about this guy that didn't seem so bad. It was worth giving it a shot.

Her father went back in to the dining room and the two ladies followed him with the dessert. They all ate the dessert, when Fatima's father stood up and announced, "We will leave you two to talk," looking at Fatima and then Talha.

"This is probably the only opportunity you will have to speak in person, so take advantage of it."

He then turned towards Talha's aunt.

"Would you like to stay here with them?" he asked Aunty. She gladly obliged. Fatima's parents left the room.

Suddenly, the awkwardness of the entire situation reached a whole new level. Fatima squirmed in her seat.

"Well, I'm sure that was difficult for both of you," Aunty said.

"You think?" Talha laughed, looking at lot more relaxed. He finally looked at Fatima dead on, no longer feeling the need to look down. She however, couldn't manage to do the same. Not just yet.

"So now that you know all about my interests, I'd like to know something about you..." he asked.

"Well.... I am at Rutgers University, and I haven't decided what to major in yet.... I know it will *not* be a science related field since I have no interest in the sciences... But I haven't made up my mind as to which field I would like to pursue," she replied nervously, still unable to look him in the eye.

"What do you enjoy outside of college?" he asked.

"Not basketball and football," Fatima laughed.

"What else is there then?" he joked.

Ignoring his last remark, Fatima stated, "I enjoy reading. I enjoy movies. I enjoy politics. I love to travel. I like Seinfeld, but NOT Baywatch," she joked.

"And I really enjoy learning about our faith. I need to know that whoever I choose to spend my life with holds the highest regard for our faith and is committed to practicing it to their best ability."

"I'm glad to hear that," Talha said sounding genuinely content with that answer. With that Fatima began to relax – a little.

"I'm not as traditional as many girls from India are, but then again I am not as modern as others are either. I can enjoy a trip to India, but it will never be home. This is home. (Referring to the USA) So I guess I am an ABCD (American born confused *Desi*) in all respects..." she smiled anxiously.

"That's not a bad thing," Talha reassured her. "I can't imagine living anywhere else either. So I totally understand what you are saying."

Fatima was pleased with his response. She had to make clear that this was home. Fleeing the coop back to the Motherland was not an option.

Talha went on, "What are your thoughts on family?"

"Family is everything. It is my soul. My family gives me strength and confidence. My parents have always made it their number one priority and I intend on doing the same. But that doesn't mean I am going to sit at home. I have dreams and aspirations of my own. I want a balance of the two worlds," Fatima stated, regaining the composure that she usually spoke with.

Now she finally had the courage and confidence to make direct eye contact with Talha.

"I also value family," Talha said. "That's actually why my folks sent me here. They said that your family shares many of the same values that we do. And you've just confirmed that, so we are on the same page in that respect. But I would also like to know how would you feel about moving to Chicago?"

"Well......" Fatima was caught off guard. "I hadn't thought much about that. I have never been out there. I hear it is cold..."

"It's not the North Pole. There are warm months," he replied.

"That's nice. I just didn't put much thought into that at this point. In fact, don't take this the wrong way, but I didn't expect this to get as far as it had already..."

"Really? Why do you say that?"

"Because, it just never got this far before with any of the proposals that had come."

"How many did you consider so far?" asked an intrigued Talha.

"I don't know. Maybe twenty... I am sure you have done the same..."

"NO! This is the first time I am doing all this," Talha replied surprisingly. "So now I get to be compared to all of those guys?" he quipped.

Fatima laughed.

"No, I never had a conversation with anyone like this before. Usually the picture and bio-data were just sent back. I would never talk to the guy. This is the first time I am going through all this. And I must admit this is very nerve racking."

"So I guess I should feel special?" Talha asked smugly.

"Ha ha," she replied. "Your case was different because my mom knows your mom, and you were coming from out of town."

"I see," he paused for a second.

"So can you cook?" he then asked mischievously.

"Can *you*?" she retorted.

"I can fry an egg," he responded proudly.

"I can defrost a frozen dinner," Fatima said sarcastically.

Talha took a liking to the game Fatima was playing and went along with it.

"I like *Desi* food. I need my rice and *daal*."

"Well if you can turn on a rice cooker and boil some *daal*, you're good to go, huh?" Fatima felt like she was on a roll.

"No *seriously*, I *like Desi* food," Talha pressed on.

"Don't get me wrong, I love *Desi* food too, but I don't intend to spend my life in the kitchen."

Talha grinned. "I wouldn't have it any other way."

"I am glad to hear that. Now that you have made that clear, here is an FYI - I *can* cook. My mom has taught me a lot already, but there is always room for improvement. However, cooking is not my forte, nor do I think it will ever be."

Talha over-exaggeratingly wiped his brow.

"Thank God. You had me scared. I don't know if I could spend my life eating *gora* food."

'Spend his life?' Fatima knew right then he was open to making long term plans with her. But did she feel the same? What more could she learn about him to help her make such a decision? An awkward silence followed.

"Do you want to ask me anything else?" Talha asked sensing that she may want some more info about him.

"Would it be a problem for you if your wife visited her family regularly if she were from some place other than Chicago?"

"No, why should it be?" he replied assertively.

"And what about college? I would like to go on to a graduate level degree."

"You are entitled to study whatever you want for as long as you want. I am all for higher education, for *every* member of the family," Talha answered.

Fatima nodded, absorbing all his responses.

"How important is the *deen* to you?" she prodded on.

"It's the reason we are here, living and breathing. I hope to continue to learn more about it and to consistently improve my practice of it."

Fatima was pleased with that response. She needed to hear something along those lines to seriously consider a guy. And Talha had just hit the mark.

At that moment Fatima's parents walked back into the room, with hot tea for everyone. They all sat together once more making small talk, allowing another opportunity to share ideas and philosophies that they all had in regards to a myriad of subjects. And although Talha and Fatima did not speak directly to each other again, they were a lot more relaxed than what they had been when her parents had first left the room. They exchanged a few smiles throughout the rest of the evening and everything wrapped up rather smoothly. The guests left, faces beaming, and from their demeanor Fatima's parents anticipated that Talha's parents would be calling soon – with a formal proposal.

Ayesha, Amina, and Malikah were already in bed, while Fatima and her mother put away the dishes. Fatima's father sat at the breakfast table drinking some more tea.

"He didn't seem bad to me. I see potential in him," Daddy stated nodding his head.

Fatima listened quietly. She wasn't ready to express her opinion yet. She wanted to hear what her mother thought as well.

"What did you think?" he asked his wife.

"I liked him. We know his family and we know that he is a respectable young man. Everyone I asked about him had only good things to say," Mummy replied.

"Well then, now the most important opinion," he turned to Fatima. "*Beta*, what did *you* think?"

"I don't want to say anything. Who knows if his family will even call back…" she said yet thought otherwise.

"Well, we won't know that until it happens, but we need to have an idea of what you think at this point. You must have some opinion?" Father asked.

"He is not bad," Fatima responded.

"That's it?" Mummy inquired.

"I mean he is fine."

"Is that a yes?" Father questioned.

"Well, he fits the bill in all the logical respects. So I guess if you guys think he is a good match, then I am fine with him."

Fatima's parents exchanged pleased looks.

"Well then, if they call we know what to say," Father said as he stood up and put his teacup in the sink, by which Fatima was standing. He gently patted his daughter's head.

"Do the *isthikhara* prayers. Then only what is good will come," he said to Fatima.

"*Inshallah*," Fatima replied softly. She was done with the dishes and quietly went upstairs.

Lying in bed she thought about the evening. She had just done her *isthikhara* prayers, so she was confident that if this was meant to be it would work out. But she couldn't help but dwell on every sentence that was said, by her and by Talha. She thought about how he had answered all her questions, just as she would have wanted them to be answered. She thought of the smiles and looks that were so quickly exchanged. She couldn't say that she felt any physical attraction to him; it was too soon for that. He was good-looking, but not gorgeous, so it wasn't as if she was blown away by how hot he was. Which she thought was actually a blessing, because it allowed her to see his personality; one that she had taken a liking too. She thought of all that would change if he became part of her life. She worried about leaving her family and Rutgers. Would she be able to see her family as often as she would like? Would she enjoy college there as she did here? Would she be able to make friends like those that she had here? Countless concerns flooded her thoughts. But for some odd and indecipherable reason, there was an underlying peace associated with Talha. And everything just seemed like it would be alright.

The following morning Fatima was still thinking about Talha, and if this situation was practical. Logically it all made sense, but was her decision to be made on logic alone? Shouldn't she fall head over heels in love before agreeing to marry someone? She began to think a lot about this particular thought and it weighed heavily upon her. She liked Talha, but she wasn't in love with him. The American society that she lived in clearly accepted love as a pretext of marriage, not something that blossomed afterwards. But her *Desi* heritage, much like her Islamic values, acknowledged that true love could just as easily develop between two individuals who lived together as man and wife, and devoted their lives to each other and their family.

Fatima knew this to be true. Her entire family, near and extended, had been married under these mores, and not one divorce had occurred as a result of that route to marriage. Reflecting upon all this, she realized that she would never fall in love *traditional American style*. In fact she began to think, 'what is *traditional American style?*' Fatima was American. She firmly believed that she was just as much a Yankee as anyone else, so why should she define her Americanness and American culture as something that was different from what she personally knew it to be?

Fatima knew she liked Talha. There definitely was a spark between them. And then there were all those commonsensical things that made him a great candidate. So why not? Why second guess her gut instincts?

The day continued very normally. No one talked about the previous night, although it was clear that Fatima's parents were preoccupied, most surely with thoughts of the possible match of their daughter and their guest from last night. Fatima too, was reserved and her sisters remained unaffected by it all. Malikah, however, was still complaining of a sour stomach. Fatima was reaching into the medicine cabinet to get her some Children's Mylanta when the phone rang. She heard her mother pick up.

"*Waalaikum salam* Nyla Apa," she heard her say. Fatima's heart stopped. It was Talha's mother. 'This must be it – *the* phone call,' she thought. 'If it's coming the day after he visited, it *has* to be a proposal.'

She quickly gave Malikah a spoonful of the medicine and shooed her away, hoping to eavesdrop on her mother's conversation.

"Yes, it was very nice seeing them after such a long time. The last time we met they were in elementary school," her mother laughed.

Fatima crept up closer behind her mother so that she could better hear.

"Yes. Yes. I see," her mother answered.

'Come on Mummy. Say something besides yes...' Fatima thought. She desperately wanted to make out what was being said.

"Umm hmm. I see..." she continued.

Fatima rolled her eyes. The vague answers were killing her.

"Well, things look good from our end as well," her mother responded. At last. Some detail.

"We will have to talk it over with Fatima and give you an answer within the next day or two," Mummy stated.

Fatima knew that was it. Talha's mother had just popped the question. Butterflies scurried in Fatima's stomach.

It was understood that her mother couldn't agree right away. There had to be some further discussion between Fatima's parents and herself before they formally accepted the proposal. But all that aside, Fatima now knew that Talha was interested in marrying her, as was his family in extending the proposal.

Fatima's mother hung up the phone and called out to her husband. Once her husband joined her in the dining room, she let him know that *the* phone call had just come. Fatima's father said, "Well, both you and I are fine with it. The *isthakhara* prayer is done. So now all we need is Fatima's approval. Call her," he told his wife.

"Fatima…can you come here?" Mummy cried out.

Fatima made her way into the dining room, pretending not to have a clue as to what was going on.

"Yes?" she walked in angelically.

"*Beta* that was Talha's mother who just called. The formal proposal has come," he took a deep breath and folded his arms across his chest.

"Now, I know that you said you were fine with Talha, but I want to make sure that *you* are agreeing to this. Understand that there is *no* pressure from us, and that *you* are the one who must be happy and comfortable with this young man. Take as much time as you want to think all of this over and give me your final answer whenever *you* are ready," Father advised.

Fatima sat down, and then looked at both her mother and father.

"Daddy, I *am* fine with Talha. He seems to be a nice guy, and he fits all the criteria that I was looking for in a guy. And I think he is someone that you are happy with as well," she calmly stated.

"But this is not about us," Mummy stated. "It is about *you*. Make sure *you* are agreeing with this because *you* are happy and *you* want to marry him."

"I am fine, Mummy." She placed her hand on her mother's shoulder. "But I don't want the marriage to occur for at least another year or two," Fatima went on. "It gives me more time to adjust to all this, and get to know him better. And it gives me time to research universities in Chicago."

"That can be arranged. If I remember correctly his family wants to wait at least that long. Is there anything else that we need to address?" Mummy asked.

"College, Mummy. I know he told me that he was all for education, but you have to make clear to his family that I have ambition and drive. I am not the happy homemaker type and his family has to accept that."

"Of course. *I* will make sure they know and understand that," her father said. "That is something that I'll bring up when all of my daughters get married."

"Anything else?" Mummy asked.

"No, I am fine for now. But if anything else comes up I'll let you know," Fatima said with confidence.

And she truly did feel confident. She felt at peace with this decision and for some reason she knew that this was going to work out from the beginning. There was just too much that was right.

Her parents looked happy, yet sad. Their baby was now a young woman. One that was about to be engaged. Mummy looked down, tears swelling in her eyes. Father stood stoically, but obviously affected by all that was transpiring. Seeing their emotional state, Fatima stood up and went to them. She hugged them both tightly. Ayesha, Amina, and Malikah, walked in on the Kodak moment and were told of what the family had just decided. The three girls let out wild cheers and embraced warmly.

"Let's call and share the news with Dadima!" Ayesha shouted, winking at Fatima.

Everyone let out a roar of laughter.

Fatima just then began to fathom what her family meant to her. Their unconditional love, warmth and support were priceless. And now there was a new member that would be a part of this unit.

She couldn't contain her excitement and happiness. Everyone dreams of the day they will find Mr. Right or vice versa. For Fatima the day had come; she truly believed this. She couldn't believe that she had just agreed to marry a Muslim ABCD- American Born Confused *Desi*, one that fit the mold that both she and her parents were looking for. All the joy and contentment of the world was at her fingertips. And now the preparation had to begin. The planning of a monstrously large *Muslim* wedding, with all the *Desi* trimmings, organized by a young *American* woman......

Glossary:

Adab – etiquette

Adhan – call to prayer

Amreekan – American

Aray Wah – How wonderful

Assalamu Alaykum – Peach be with you -

Baji – a term of respect used to address an older sister

Bathamees – disrespectful

Bawarchi – chef

Begum – wife

Beta – child

Bhaabi – brother's wife

Bhai – brother

Bhen – sister

Biryani – an Indian rice and meat dish

Chacha – paternal uncle

Chachi- paternal aunt

Chai – tea

Chalo – let's go

Chapatti – flatbread

Churwa – a salty Indian snack

Daal – lentils

Dekho – look

Desi – a person of Indian or Pakistani origin

Dhuhr – the early afternoon prayer

Duaa – prayer

Dupatta – a long scarf that is worn with shalwar khameez

Firangi – foreigner

Fitna – division

FOB – fresh off the boat – new arrival from a different country

Gadha – an ass

Gora – Caucasian

Hajj – a holy pilgrimage to Mecca

Hajji – one who performs the Hajj

Halal – pure or in accordance with Islamic law

Haram – forbidden

Hijaab – head covering traditionally worn by Muslim women

Himmat – courage

Huffaz – people who have memorized the Holy Quran

Ihraam- the clothes worn by one who performs the Hajj

Inshallah – God Willing

Isthikhara – a prayer that seeks guidance

Jaldee – hurry

Jannah– heaven

Jilbab – long dress or long coat

Jumma – Friday prayers

Junglee – wild or unkept

Kaali poth – a necklace made of black beads that is the mark of a married woman in Indian culture

Khala – maternal aunt

Khalaas – finished

Kheer – rice pudding

Khuda hafiz – God protect you

Lengha – a fancy skirt

Maghrib– sunset prayers

Masala – spice

Masjid – mosque

Memsahib – Madam

Muhajjaba – women who cover

Nana – maternal grandfather

Nanima – maternal grandfather

NRI – non-resident Indian

Paan – an addictive leaf that people chew with tobacco

Pagal – crazy

Paratha – flatbread made with butter

Phuppu – father's sister

Qazi – Muslim priest

Qiraat – recitation of the Quran

Qismat – fate

Qurbani – the sacrifice of a lamb or goat

Ramadan – the month of fasting in the Islamic calendar

Sahib – Sir

Salam – literally it means peace. It's also a greeting.

Salaat – prayer

Shaami – minced meat

Shalwar khameez – clothes traditionally worn by Muslim women in the Indian subcontinent

Surah – a chapter of the Quran

Talbiyah - prayer invoked by the pilgrims as a conviction that they intend to perform the Hajj

Tafseer – exegesis or commentary of the Quran

Taraweeh- extra prayers that are made in Ramadan

Tiffin – Indian lunchbox made of steel

Yaar – friend